Books by P.J. Parrish

DARK OF THE MOON

DEAD OF WINTER

PAINT IT BLACK

THICKER THAN WATER

ISLAND OF BONES

Published by Pinnacle Books

# P.J. PARRISH

# ISLAND OF BONES

**PINNACLE BOOKS**
Kensington Publishing Corp.
http://www.kensingtonbooks.com

*For my daughter Renee,
and my cave-daughter Heather*

## ACKNOWLEDGMENTS

We would like to thank D.P. Lyle, MD, for his kind assistance on the medical aspects of this story. And we owe a debt of gratitude to Captain Dale K. Fewell, Ret., who patiently translated passages into Latin for us. *Experto Crede*. Also, thanks to Dave Jensen for his help with island geography; Linda Wigginton and Alina Lambiet for help with the Spanish; Marie-Pierre Carannante for help with the French. And a big hug to Val Viglione, who knows where the bones are buried.

"I believe that men are generally still a little afraid of the dark."
—Henry David Thoreau

# CHAPTER 1

Dark. It was so dark. She could see nothing.

But she could feel. She could feel the rain stinging her face, the trees tearing at her flesh. She could feel her heart hammering in her chest, feel the life beating inside her. She could still *feel* and that meant she was still alive.

She kept running.

The wind was blowing hard now, making the trees twist and groan above her. The wet leaves rained down, sticking black on her bare white arms. Her feet were slippery with mud and blood.

She kept running.

Something dark rose up in front of her. The fence . . . she had made it to the fence. She searched the dark wood, looking for a gate. Nothing, no way out. She had to climb over.

She jumped, grabbing the top of the fence. It was jagged, cutting into her fingers, but she held on. Bracing her feet on the fence, she strained to pull herself up. Her bare feet slipped on the wet wood but she was strong. She got an arm over the top and pulled herself up. The jagged wood cut into her as she jumped down, falling and rolling in the mud. There was a gash on her arm and something burned on her right foot, but she kept moving.

Mangroves . . . she had reached the mangroves. But where was the dock? She stopped, her eyes raking the darkness.

The light. Where was the light? There was a light on the dock. She had seen it before. She had seen the dinghy there, too.

She pushed her wet hair back off her face and tried to get her bearings. Had she gone the wrong way? Everything looked so different at night. The storm must have knocked out the power. *Where was the dock?*

A sudden gust of wind knocked her back against a tree. Her knees buckled and she grabbed the rough bark, pulling herself back up.

*A light. The dock light!* She could see it now, faintly through the trees.

With a cry, she pushed off the tree and stumbled toward the light.

She froze.

The light was moving. Jerking, swinging back and forth. It wasn't the dock light. It was a flashlight, coming toward her.

*God, not here! Don't let me die here!*

She pulled a ragged breath deep into her burning lungs, pushing down the fear that was rising in her throat. She sank back into the black mangroves, crouching in the rib cage of roots.

The beam of light grew larger and brighter. She bit down on her lip to keep from crying and tasted her own blood. A violent clap of thunder rose above the wind. She closed her eyes.

Then, suddenly, for just a moment, the wind died and it was quiet.

Her eyes shot open. A bump. In that one second of silence she had heard the bump of a boat against wood. Just a few feet away.

*Get up! Run . . . you can make it! Run!*

She could smell the water now and she moved toward it, feeling her way and stepping carefully over the high twisting mangrove roots. She could feel the cold mud covering her feet now and then the water rushing up over her ankles.

*Oh, God!* There it was! The dock!

And the boat was there. She could see it, a small slash of white bobbing in the churning black water.

She looked back. The flashlight was gone. Twenty feet, all she had to do was run twenty feet out in the open to the boat. Just twenty feet and she would be free.

She crept out of the mangrove cover and into the open. Her feet hit wood and she ran down the dock to the boat. She jumped inside, pulling off the lines. She pushed the boat away from the dock, grabbed the cord on the motor, and pulled hard. It jammed.

Her eyes shot to the dark shore. Through the slashing rain, she could see the flashlight. Faint but moving again, coming toward the dock.

With a cry, she yanked on the cord again. Something tore in her shoulder but she kept pulling. Finally, the motor sputtered to life, its whine rising above the roar of the storm.

She looked out at the water. Nothing. No lights, no land. Just the angry swirl of the night sky and the roiling black waves spitting out whitecaps.

She took one last look back. The flashlight was coming fast.

She hit the throttle and the little boat started away.

"Bitch! Where you think you're going, bitch!"

The rain was slicing into her like knives. A flash of lightning and for a second, she could see the huge waves, green and foaming.

Then a sharp crack of thunder so close she could feel it.

A sudden sting in her back.

A pain burning through her body like a hot sword.

She reached back to touch her back and felt something warm.

Another sharp, close crack of thunder.

She jerked as the second bullet pierced her neck.

Then it was quiet.

She couldn't see anything. She couldn't hear anything. She couldn't feel anything.

The motor sputtered out and the small white boat lurched sharply. A huge wave grabbed it, heaving it up on the foaming crest and then smashing it down into the trough.

When the boat bobbed upright, it was empty.

# CHAPTER 2

Her name was Alina. She was born during a sultry summer thunderstorm somewhere near Mali, a thing no one cared about in a place few had heard of. In Senegal, she inhaled the cool ocean breezes and in the Cape Verde Islands she found her fury.

By the time she reached Hispaniola she was a killer.

The first hurricane of the 1987 season turned out to be the most deadly in decades, ravaging the Caribbean, littering the beaches of Haiti with fishing boats and bodies. Then she sped through the Florida Straits, turned north and slammed into the southwest coast of Florida. Finally, Alina died, drifting away as a depression somewhere over Chesapeake Bay.

And now the shell seekers were out, celebrating her wake.

Louis watched them as they walked the beach. Every so often, someone would stoop, pick up a prize, and hold it up to the white morning sun before dropping it in a net bag. But mostly they walked, heads bowed, shoulders stooped, criss-crossing silently across the sand to the dirgelike drone of the waves.

The beach was a mess. The dunes had been eaten away almost up to his cottage, the sea oats beaten down, the sea grape trees snapped and stripped. About a hundred yards to the south, a sailboat lay heeled over in the sand, its mast bent like a straw, the halyards looped and tangled.

Louis looked back at his cottage. It was still standing, though last night he was sure it wasn't going to survive. Around midnight, the guy on the radio was trying to sound cool as he reported the wind was up to 110 miles an hour and that Alina was coming up out of the Florida Straits on a north-northeast course aiming right at Sanibel-Captiva. The cottage's roof was leaking, the old boards groaning. Finally, Louis put Issy in the cat carrier and ran down the street in the pelting rain to take cover in Timmy's Nook. He had sat out the storm in the restaurant drinking warm Heinekens in the dark with Bev and Carlo, listening to the *bam! pop! fizz!* of electrical transmitters blowing, watching the night sky turn acid green.

His first hurricane.

Bev, who had lived in Florida all her sixty-some years, called it a "pissy little blow job, nothing like Donna back in sixty." He didn't tell her it had scared the living shit out of him.

But he had survived. And now . . .

God, had the sky ever been bluer? Like it had been stripped clean and repainted. He drew in a deep breath of sea spray, looking again at the shell seekers. They always came after a big storm, Bev had told him, a horde descending on the beach to comb through the debris kicked up from the sea.

He wondered if anyone had died in the storm. The electric and phones were still out, so there was no way to tell yet. And the two-lane road that ran the length of Sanibel-Captiva was covered in sand and downed trees.

He glanced at his watch. Eight A.M. He had been awake all night, but he wasn't tired. There was still a charge in the air, the kind that came when something bad missed you and kept going, a bullet, a botched love affair, a speeding car.

His stomach rumbled. There was nothing to eat in the cottage and Bev had told him not to open his fridge because who knew how long the power would be out?

He decided to walk up the beach and see if anything was open.

Fish carcasses. Driftwood. Great green ropes of kelp.

Beer bottles, a broken lawn chair, rusted cans, a car tire.

A dead seagull. Milky-eyed fish. Blue-bubbled Portuguese man-of-war.

Chunks of Styrofoam, plastic flowers, a broken flip-flop.

Millions of shells. A mosaic of pink, yellow, purple, blue. All sizes and shapes. Geometric swirls, regal conchs, butterfly-winged coquinas. He had never seen so many different shells.

Louis stopped abruptly, his eyes on the wet sand.

It was big, much bigger than the other shells. That was what had made him stop. That and the color—a mottled rust that didn't quite look like any other shell.

He knelt and brushed away the seaweed. He drew back sharply.

It was a skull. Small, very small, maybe the size of a soft-ball. And human. He could see that now as he carefully lifted away the last of the seaweed.

It was wedged sideways, half buried in the sand. The waves crept up, sending a gentle stream of sea foam into the nasal cavity and out again.

Louis sat back on his legs, staring at the skull. He quickly scanned the surrounding debris but saw no other bones, no clothing, no evidence of a body. Just this tiny skull.

He squinted out at the gulf water, still churning green from the storm. Damn, where had it come from? A boat? A drowning?

He heard voices and looked up the beach. A couple was approaching, heads down, the man sweeping a metal detec-tor across the sand before him. The beach was already crowded and more people were coming. He was too far away from his cottage and couldn't call the cops anyway.

He looked back at the skull, then out over the gulf. He

couldn't leave the skull here for someone else to find. There was no choice. He quickly pulled off his T-shirt and spread it on the sand. Picking up a stick, he wedged it carefully in the eye socket. He extracted the skull from the sand and placed it on the shirt. Wrapping it up, he stood and hurried back to the cottage.

He set the bundled shirt on the chair near the door and picked up the phone. Still dead.

He walked back to the chair and unwrapped the shirt, staring at the skull. Damn . . . there were two holes in it that he hadn't noticed back on the beach. He squatted down to get a better look.

One hole right on the top about the size of a quarter and a second smaller one farther back. The holes were shaped like diamonds, and both were too perfectly formed to look like they had been made by accident. They reminded him of a wound profile he had seen in his police academy textbook. The wound had been made by a pickax.

With a sigh, he rose. Who would hit a baby hard enough to drive an ax through its skull? And where the hell had the skull come from?

He thought of Bev and her stories about Hurricane Donna. The storm had been so fierce, she said, that boats harbored in Pine Island Sound had been found ten miles inland, wrecked along the banks of the Caloosahatchee River. Someone had found a roulette wheel on Fort Myers Beach that was eventually traced to a casino in the Bahamas.

The skull could have come from anywhere. Louis knelt down again to stare at it. It was so small. So sad. And probably so far from home, wherever that was.

# CHAPTER 3

Louis set out a bowl of water and Tender Vittles for Issy and left the cottage, heading up the sand path that wound through the other cottages. Maybe Pierre had a radio he could use to call the sheriff. Up near the office, he saw Pierre standing out in the road, staring at the Branson's on the Beach sign. A slash pine had fallen across it, knocking it down.

Pierre saw him coming and pointed at the sign. "Look! *C'est foutue!*" He gestured wildly at the tree limbs and debris littering the grounds. *"Un vrai foutoir!"*

"I can't understand you, Pierre."

"You can fix, no?" Pierre asked, nodding at the sign.

"No," Louis said, bracing for the usual fight. He got a break in his rent for serving as Branson's "security chief" but it meant putting up with his surly landlord's attempts to turn him into his personal serf.

"No? No? *J'ai du pain sur la planche! J'ai d'autres chats a fouetter!* You can fix!"

"No," Louis said more firmly.

Pierre launched into a tirade of French as he began to tug on the tree limb.

"Pierre," Louis said, "do you have a CB radio or something?"

*"Quoi?"*

"A radio. The phones are out and I have to call the sheriff's department."

"The sheriff? *Je l'emmerde!* Forget that! I need help here!"

"I'll help later. I have something important to take care of first."

Louis turned and walked off, leaving Pierre yelling after him. He paused, looking at all the gawkers on the beach, then decided to walk down to the Island Store. He went the beach route, walking slowly along the shoreline, scanning the sand and hoping that if there were more bones, the shell scavengers would not know what they were seeing and leave them alone. But he saw nothing in the trash-clogged kelp.

The store was open. A small crowd milled outside, locals jawing about the storm and a few dazed-looking tourists. It was hot and stuffy inside, the AC above the door silent. The shelves were stripped clean. Batteries, toilet paper, bottled water, and anything worth eating had been snatched up the day the hurricane warning went out. Louis suspected that Roberta Tatum had made a small fortune selling everything she had in her store, right down to the last bottle of Perrier.

Louis was eyeing a lone can of pinto beans when she came up to his side.

"Well, I see you survived," she said. Her dark face was shiny with sweat, her hair hidden beneath a pink bandana.

"Yeah, I guess."

"Could have been a lot worse."

Louis nodded. "You don't have a CB radio or something, do you, Roberta?"

"Nope. Why?"

Louis hesitated but decided not to bring up the skull. "Got to get a hold of someone, that's all." He nodded to the can of beans on the shelf. "This all you got left?"

"I warned you to stock up. But you weren't hearing me, were you?"

"I guess not." Louis's eyes went to the coolers along the back wall. They looked empty. He sighed and picked up the can of beans.

"Jesus, you're pathetic," Roberta said. "Come with me."

He followed her up to the front counter. She reached beneath and tossed a loaf of wheat bread, a jar of Jif, and a package of Ho-hos on the counter.

She stood looking at him, hands on hips, a frown creasing her face."Go on, take it."

Louis grinned. "Thanks."

"Next time, listen to what I tell you. You don't screw around with a hurricane, even a small one. You hear me?"

"I hear you. You got anything to drink left?" Louis asked.

"Yeah, I got twelve cases of Coors back there that's hotter than dog piss."

"I'll pass. How about a bottle of brandy?"

Roberta moved away and returned with a bottle of Remy Martin.

Louis shook his head. "I can't afford that."

Roberta rolled her eyes. "Take it, damn it. I saw an ad for booze the other day and I thought of you. Went something like—claret's for boys and wine's for men. But brandy is for heros."

"I'm no hero," Louis said.

"Don't I know it."

Roberta leaned against the counter, fanning herself with a copy of the *Island Reporter*. He came in the store at least once a week but he hadn't noticed until now that she looked thinner. Two years had passed since her husband, Walter, had been murdered, and he wondered how she was doing. Not that he would ask. Even though he had played the main role in finding Walter Tatum's killer.

A man and woman came in, their sunburned faces animated. The woman was carrying a handful of shells.

"Could we bother you for a bag?" she asked Roberta.

Roberta gave her a cold stare, then snapped a plastic bag off the rack and thrust it at the woman. The couple left.

"Damn tourists, like buzzards picking through the garbage," Roberta muttered, fanning herself again. "What the hell do they think they're going to find out there anyways?"

Louis paused just a beat. "I found a skull."

Roberta threw him a look. "Yeah, right."

"I'm not kidding. I found a skull on the beach."

Roberta stopped fanning herself. "What? You mean a head?"

"No, it's a clean skull. It looks like a baby skull, but it looks old," he added, as if that made it easier to accept.

Roberta came closer. "A baby? What did you do with it?"

"It's back at my place."

"It's in your house? Where at?"

Louis shrugged. "In a chair wrapped in a shirt."

"You just left a baby's skull in your chair?"

"Well, it's a comfortable chair."

"That's not funny."

"C'mon, Roberta. It's not like it's . . ."—he paused, watching her—". . . a fresh victim."

Her black eyes pierced him. "You ever had a baby?"

"No."

"Ever even been around one?"

Louis shook his head, but he was remembering a moment long ago. He'd almost had one.

Roberta let out a huff. "Didn't think so."

"Christ, Roberta," he said, "I've seen bones, skeletons before. It's no big deal. It's just a skull."

She began to stuff his groceries into a bag. "Yeah, just a skull you leave in your chair and make jokes about. It's no joke. It's what's left of a baby. You hearing me?"

Louis felt his neck muscles tighten. "I'm hearing you."

She thrust the bag at him. "I doubt it."

Louis reached into his pocket for some money. Roberta shook her head when he held out the bills.

"Pay me later. The register ain't working anyway."

Louis hesitated, wanting to make things right but not understanding why Roberta was so bent out of shape in the first place. "I have to report it. You know anybody with a radio?"

"Nope." She turned away, fanning herself with the newspaper again.

Louis sighed, picked up the bag, and started out the door.

"Talk to Jay Strickland."

Louis stopped. "He's got a radio?"

"Should have. He's a cop."

"Where do I find him?"

"Last time I looked, he was out front. Can't miss him. Red hair, like Woody Woodpecker."

Louis stepped out into the sun. He spotted Strickland's spiky red hair immediately in the knot of men in the parking lot. Strickland was wearing cutoff jeans and a faded Hawaiian shirt, but Louis could see the police radio sticking out of his back pocket. He approached and introduced himself.

Strickland gave him a handshake and an easy smile. "Kincaid, yeah. I've heard the other guys talk about you. I was hoping we'd get to meet sometime."

Louis eyed the other men. "Could we talk in private, Officer?"

"Sure." They moved away. Louis studied the deputy. He didn't seem to be much older than his own twenty-seven years. Probably younger. Louis filled him in, and Strickland's expression turned somber as he put on his cop face.

"Can you call it in?" Louis asked.

"Sure. But I can tell you no one can get out here for hours, because the causeway road is out. I'm only here 'cause I live over in Sanibel." He nodded to an old green Vespa and grinned. "Rode over on my hog."

Louis saw Roberta standing in the door, watching them.

He waited, listening while Strickland called in to his station and reported the skull. He heard the harried dispatcher say that no one could respond. Strickland clicked off and turned to Louis.

"Looks like I'm it," he said.

They walked back to Louis's cottage, Strickland wheeling the Vespa. Inside, Louis started to the kitchen to dump the groceries.

"It's over there, in the chair."

"Wow . . ."

When Louis turned, Strickland was holding the skull.

"Hey, don't pick it up, man."

Strickland set it down quickly. "Why not? Not likely to get prints off a skull that's been in the water for so long."

"You don't know how long it's been in the water. You should treat it like evidence anyway."

"Yeah, okay. You didn't find anything else with it?"

"Not a thing."

Strickland knelt next to the chair. "It's probably a newborn," he said softly.

Louis came forward. "What makes you say that?"

Strickland pointed. "See the little holes on top?"

"Pickax," Louis said.

Strickland turned to look at him. "Pickax? No way, man. Those are fontenelles."

"What?"

"Fontenelles," Strickland said, standing. "Soft spots. Babies got 'em so their skull plates can compress while the baby travels down the birth canal." He used his cupped hands to demonstrate, drawing one set over the knuckles of the other. "They don't close up for months afterward, sometimes as late as two years."

Strickland saw the incredulous look on Louis's face and smiled. "My wife just had a baby."

Strickland bent down, hands on knees, to look at the skull

again. "Babies are so cool, man," he said. "Jenny made me read this book on how it all happens, and it talks about fontenelles and stuff. Sometimes, the skull comes out kinda mushed up from the baby going down the birth canal."

Louis suppressed a sigh. It was more than he needed to know.

"My daughter's head looked like an upside-down Dixie cup," Strickland went on, "so I made them wait a day to take the hospital photos. Ashley looked great then. Want to see her picture?"

Strickland had already gone for the wallet.

"Pretty," Louis muttered when Strickland thrust out the picture. He didn't add that he thought all babies looked like Karl Malden.

"Babies are so cool," Strickland said again, more softly now. "It's like when they're lying there looking up at you, it's like suddenly you get that you're it. You're life and death to them, man. You're everything."

Louis nodded like he understood. Strickland carefully put the picture back in his wallet.

"So," Strickland said, "where exactly did you find the skull?"

"C'mon, I'll show you."

He took Strickland to the place on the beach where he had picked up the skull. The beach was crowded, the shell seekers now joined by the curious who had just come down to see what havoc nature had wrought. Offshore, three surfers were bobbing on their boards, hoping the choppy water would yield a ride or two.

Strickland looked at Louis. "Think we should secure the scene?"

Louis nodded. "That would be a good start."

"How far you think we should go?"

"You're the responding officer. You decide."

"You got any tape?"

"No. Don't you?"

"In my cruiser, but it's sitting in my driveway with a tree on the hood."

Louis turned and looked out across the beach.

Strickland drew in a breath Louis could hear. "Look, I'm sorry," he said. "This is my sixth day on the job. Everyone else is tied up with other shit." Strickland ran a hand over his stubbly hair. "I'd appreciate any help."

Louis hesitated. He knew that in different circumstances, the whole beach would be roped off and a team of cops and techs would do a methodical search. But that wasn't going to happen right now. Every cop in the county was probably tied up with storm duty.

"What are we going to do?" Strickland asked.

Louis nodded toward an elderly couple coming toward them, the man sweeping a metal detector over the sand. "Get them to help."

"What?"

"People like to help."

"What do we tell them?" Strickland said, hurrying beside him.

"Tell them we found an old mysterious skull and we're looking for other bones."

"That'll gross them out."

"No, it won't. Trust me."

Strickland went up to the couple and showed his badge. He watched their faces go from surprise to horror, then to interest. They started nodding, and moved away, gently kicking at the sand, and whispering to each other.

Moved by his success, Strickland hurried on to another couple, then another, quickly building his team of curious volunteers.

Louis turned away and walked the beach, angling down toward the water, using a stick to search the debris. It occurred to him how strange it was that he had assumed the holes in the skull were the result of a pickax. That was the cop in him. A father had seen it differently.

He walked along, head down, stick poking the kelp. He was thinking of Roberta now and wondering why she had been so quick to take his dispassion for disrespect.

Like he had told her, he had seen bones before. He had seen the skeleton of a lynching victim lying in a shallow grave back in Mississippi. He had seen the bones of a murdered teenage girl laid out on an autopsy table.

*It's what's left of a baby . . .*

He had never seen a bone so small though. Maybe that's why he had no answer for Roberta's comment.

He looked down the beach toward Jay Strickland.

"Strickland! You find anything yet?" he called out.

"Nope," the deputy yelled back.

"Keep looking."

"I don't think there's—"

"Keep looking." Louis squinted out at the water. "Just keep looking, man."

# CHAPTER 4

The royal palms were still there. Seeing the towering trees lining McGregor Boulevard made him feel better somehow, as though the hurricane hadn't really touched anything or anyone.

But he knew that wasn't true. He could see that clearly now as he drove slowly down the boulevard toward downtown Fort Myers.

Louis had borrowed Strickland's scooter and he kept it at a careful crawl, going up on swales and lawns to avoid the flooded street and fallen tree limbs. It was oddly quiet, none of the usual traffic buzz, just the distant whine of chain saws or the chug-chug of generators.

Cars still sat abandoned in the street, and many trees were stripped or snapped, leaving homes baking in the hot sun, their windows blanked by big Xs of masking tape. The Buddha Bar and Grill, Giovanni's Deli, the Market Café, they all still had their plywood up. Two days after Alina and Fort Myers still had a forlorn aura, like one of those whitewashed, fading rust-belt downtowns.

It was so hot it hurt to take a breath and the sky was a cruel bright blue. Power was still out in most neighborhoods, so people were outside, looking up at their battered roofs, dragging palm fronds to the curbs. Everyone was moving slowly. Except the kids. They were laughing, the big ones paddling canoes down McGregor, the little ones splashing in the water in defiance of mothers and health department warnings about snakes, rats, and microbes.

At the police station, Louis left the Vespa in a bike rack up near the door. He took a moment to run a hand over his sweating neck, looking at the empty parking lot. Normally, it was filled with green-and-whites, but every cop in the county was out on cleanup duty today. Even Strickland had been called in, but not before coming over to Louis's cottage to tell him that Chief Horton wanted to see him.

They had news on the baby skull.

Louis was about to go in when the glass door opened and Al Horton came out, followed by a tall bald man in a suit.

"Kincaid!" Horton said, pulling up short. "Shit, I forgot you were coming in."

"I got here as soon as I could. The roads—"

"Yeah, yeah, I know." Horton ran a hand over his unshaven jaw. He looked harried and tired. "Listen, it'll have to wait. Mel and I gotta get going."

Louis looked to the man in the yellow-tinted sunglasses and black suit, the name Mel itching his brain. He had heard through the grapevine that Horton had hired a new chief of detectives, some guy from Miami. He had also heard that bringing in an outsider had caused grumbling in the department.

"What about the skull?" Louis asked Horton.

"Later. I got a body washed up in some mangroves out in the sound," Horton said, easing by.

"A body? Can I ride along?" Louis asked.

Horton stopped, running a hand roughly over his brush cut as if that might keep the brain neurons from shorting out. "Yeah, come on. We'll talk on the way," he said. "Meet you there, Mel."

The detective glanced at Louis through his yellow lenses and turned away. He headed toward his car, a patrolman hustling after him. Louis noticed the detective catch the uniform by the shoulder and order him to drive.

Louis followed Horton to a white Crown-Victoria. "That your new guy?" he asked, nodding toward the other car.

"Huh? Oh, yeah, that's Mel Landeta. Sorry I didn't introduce you. Got a few other things on my mind," Horton said as he slid into the car.

"Not very friendly, is he?"

Horton started the car. "What, you been listening to those baboons down at O'Sullivans? Landeta's a good man. He's not some old burnout."

"That's not what they're saying, Chief," Louis said. Even though he knew they were.

Horton looked at him.

"They just resent you going outside, that's all," Louis said.

"Landeta's just had a few rough years." Horton thrust the shift into reverse. "And I don't think we got enough chips in for you to be questioning my hires, Kincaid."

Louis sat back in the seat without responding. No chips in? That's how Horton saw it? They had worked Walter Tatum's murder together. But that was as far as it had gone. And as far as it would always go, given the line that separated cops from PIs.

They were back onto McGregor before Horton spoke again.

"Look, I'm sorry, Louis," he muttered. "I didn't mean anything by that. You know I've got a lot of respect for you. It's just that I haven't been home since they issued the warning, I'm stretched too thin and I'm running on empty."

"Apology accepted, Chief," Louis said. "Anything I can do to help out maybe?"

Horton shook his head. They slowed to go through a flooded area, the Crown-Vic's wake washing up into someone's driveway.

"How come you didn't apply for the opening?" Horton asked.

It was Louis's turn for silence. He had known about the opening for a patrolman. Once, he had come close to calling Horton. But he hadn't, and he knew he never would. He did owe Horton an answer though.

"I've kind of gotten used to working freelance, Chief," Louis said.

Horton glanced over at him. "You get that PI license yet?"

Louis nodded slowly without looking at Horton.

"Gun?"

"Yeah, a Glock."

Horton raised a brow. "Well, I guess that makes it official."

They followed the other car as it made the turn onto Fowler heading toward the river.

"So what are they saying about Landeta?" Horton asked. Louis hesitated and Horton saw it. "Come on, I need to know."

"That something happened and he's lost it."

Horton let out a sigh. "A few years back Mel had an accident. He was in a pursuit and some kid ran a light. He hit Mel broadside. Mel came out okay but the kid ended up a paraplegic and his family sued. The kid was at fault but the city didn't care. They settled the suit and got Mel on breaching departmental policies. He said he was forced to resign."

"Tough break," Louis said.

He was thinking that Landeta didn't look old enough to be near pension age. He had the lean body of a basketball player. The bald head, he guessed now, wasn't bad genes but probably a style choice to go with the black suit, white dress shirt, black tie, and yellow aviator shades.

"How old is he?" Louis asked.

"Forty-five. Been a cop since he was twenty." Horton was quiet for a moment. "Mel's a good man," he said again.

There was something final in Horton's tone that let Louis know the subject of Mel Landeta was closed. At the docks, the three of them boarded the patrol boat. Landeta took a spot standing by the officer who was driving, his eyes trained straight ahead as they motored down the river toward the open waters of Pine Island Sound.

Louis's eyes scanned the riverbanks. Many of the homes had missing shingles and tiles, and one old bungalow had a bright blue plastic tarp covering a large hole on the roof. Splintered docks floated near battered seawalls, giant twists of metal and gray screening hung over pools like shrouds.

Louis took a seat nex t to Horton. "Where we going?" he asked.

"Monkey Island, up near Useppa. Uninhabited, just a bunch of mangroves."

Louis had heard of Useppa. It was an exclusive private island club of homes. You had to have a boat—and big bucks—to get there. Monkey Island on the other hand was probably just one of the hundreds of little scrub keys that pockmarked the sound.

"So, what about the skull?" Louis asked.

"Oh, yeah. I overnighted it to the State Bureau of Archeological Research," Horton said.

"Archeologists?"

"Yeah, it's standard procedure when we're not sure what we're looking at," Horton said. "The skull could've floated out of a cemetery or some damn Indian burial ground or something."

He saw Louis staring at him.

"Calusa Indians. We got a mess of their burial places around here. So every time we find a bone we gotta call the eggheads in Tallahassee."

"And?" Louis asked.

"They check their files to see if the place where it was found matches somewhere in their computers, like a historical or aboriginal type of place. Your find didn't match anything. They don't believe the skull is an Indian bone or anything weird like that."

"So what do they think it is?"

Horton shrugged. "They don't know and they don't care. So they're sending it back to me."

"Were they able to tell you anything about it?"

"They said it probably got dredged up during the storm, maybe from an abandoned waterlogged cemetery or the bottom of the gulf. Plus, they said it was at least fifty years old. No rush on solving that one."

"I guess not," Louis said.

"Just as well," Horton said. "Last thing I need right now is an infant homicide."

They were out in the sound now. It was coming up on eleven A.M. but there were no other boats out and the water was as flat and silver as a mirror. The driver throttled up and the boat cut across the water, heading north.

The motor's noise made talk impossible, so Louis sat back in the seat. He was disappointed about the skull. Then it occurred to him how sick it was for him to be disappointed that it was not a homicide but probably a natural death that happened half a century ago.

That was the cop in him, the part that felt a rush every time a body washed up or a question mark came up. It was the part of him that would never go away. It was why he was tagging along with Horton now, like some voyeur, hoping for a vicarious cop fix.

After about a half hour, the boat slowed. They were approaching a small thatch of dark green that looked more like a discarded clump of sod than an island. Horton stood up, his eyes scanning the greenery.

"So what are you going to do with it?" Louis asked.

"With what?" Horton asked.

"The skull."

Louis saw Landeta glance back at them.

Horton shrugged. "Hell, I dunno, Louis. Stick it in the evidence room, I guess. Maybe I'll give it to Vince."

"Vince? Why?"

"He has a skull collection in his office. Has them lined up on his bookcases like bowling trophies."

Louis looked down at his hand, seeing the small skull in his palm. Man, he just couldn't see it sitting on some dusty old shelf in the evidence room next to rusting guns and rape slide smears. And he sure couldn't see it ending up being just a macabre souvenir on the medical examiner's shelf.

He thought of Roberta Tatum again. *It's what's left of a baby.*

They were slowing, coming up alongside an old skiff bobbing empty. Then he saw a man in a wide-brimmed hat waving at them from the mangroves.

"Can I have it?" he asked Horton.

"The skull? Why?"

"I don't know. Maybe because I found it."

"Hell, I don't care. I'll give you a call when I get it back."

The officer looked back at Horton. "Low tide. This is as far as I can go without grounding her, Chief," he said.

Horton surveyed the island still a good twenty-five yards away. Between them was shallow water and then a stretch of black mud leading into the dense, twisting roots of the mangroves.

"Shit," Horton muttered.

With a grunt he hoisted himself over the side and landed with a splash in the knee-high water. He started slogging toward the man in the straw hat.

Louis watched as Landeta calmly took off his suit jacket, folded it, and laid it on a seat. Then he carefully climbed out and eased himself down into the water. He started slowly after Horton, his arms held up, a gold watch glinting in the sun.

The driver was looking at Louis. Louis glanced at the mangroves, then back at the patrolman.

"I guess I should leave my shoes on," Louis said.

"I would, sir. Don't want to cut yourself on those oyster shells or kick up a stingray."

Louis got in the water. It felt good, cool after the hot sun. But the feeling vanished as he reached the mud flats. The low-tide stench was overwhelming and the black mud sucked him ankle-deep as he trudged toward the mangroves. When he pulled up next to Horton and Landeta, he was breathing heavy and sweating.

The man who had been waiting for them was wearing tattered shorts and a shirt, a grimy straw hat covering his hair. "I've been keeping an eye on her," he said. "I had to leave to call the cops but I came right back. She ain't moved. You can see her good now that the tide's out."

"How'd you find her?" Horton asked.

"I fish for mullet every night around here," the man said. "At dawn, I went in to pull my nets. That's when I saw the white thing in the water by the roots. I thought it was just a trash bag but when I went close I saw that it weren't. So I got out of here and called you guys."

"Where's the body, Mr. Peg?"

Louis turned at the sound of the deep soft voice. It was the first thing Landeta had said all morning.

"Peg, it's just Peg." The old man pointed into the gloom of the mangroves. "Over theres. You don't mind if I stay here, do you?"

Landeta didn't answer. He headed straight into the dense trees, picking his way carefully across the exposed mangrove roots. Horton stayed to question the old man. Louis decided to follow Landeta.

He entered a cave of branches, the sun suddenly gone. The stink was incredible. A suffocating brew of rot, fetid water, dank dirt, and bird droppings. Louis started to gag and had to stop. The moment he did, the mosquitoes closed in.

He pulled a deep breath and trudged on, grabbing the mangrove branches to keep moving through the gloom. Landeta was a patch of white ahead, his dress shirt sweat-plastered to his back. Finally, Landeta stopped.

Louis struggled to his side and looked down.

For a second, he thought she was just a girl. But then he realized it was only because of the way the body was compressed into the tangled mangrove roots.

He guessed the force of the water had done it somehow, but it was still grotesque. The torso was facing outward, but was bent forward at the waist around a large root. The right arm was twisted back over the shoulder, the left arm hanging limp in front. The head hung oddly low on the chest, like the neck was broken.

Her face was hidden by her jaw-length hair, which hung lank and mud-caked, looking almost exotic, like dreadlocks.

Louis heard the snap of latex gloves and looked up at Landeta.

"Want to take a closer look?" Landeta asked.

Louis could see Landeta's eyes through the yellow lenses but couldn't read the expression. Was this some kind of challenge?

Louis crouched in the muck. The sickly sweet smell of death rose up to him over the tidal stench but he didn't move back.

He felt a slap on his shoulder and looked back to see a pair of latex gloves hanging from Landeta's hand. He took them and put them on.

"What condition is the skin in?" Landeta asked.

"No separation or swelling."

"Can you reach the head?" Landeta said.

"Yeah."

"Pull it up."

"I think her neck is broken."

"Use the hair."

Louis swallowed dryly and grabbed a hank of hair. He carefully pulled up the head. Her mouth was open. So were her eyes. Blue . . .

"Do you see any wounds? Signs of trauma?" Landeta asked.

"No."

Louis looked at her twisted body, thinking about what Bev had told him about hurricanes smashing boats to bits.

"Can you move it?"

Louis looked back at Landeta. "What?"

"Can you move it? We need to see the back."

She was wearing jeans, ripped at the knee, and a sleeveless white blouse. Louis grabbed the blouse and gave a pull but the body was held tight against its cage of roots. "The roots are holding her," he said.

"What?"

"The damn roots. Maybe we should wait for the medical examiner."

"Maybe you should find another profession," Landeta said.

Louis's eyes shot back to Landeta. He was just staring back calmly.

*Fuck you, burnout. . . .*

"Try," Landeta said.

Louis inched closer, grabbed the blouse with both hands, and gave the torso a hard tug. It took two more tries before the body slumped forward. There was a hole high on the back of the blouse.

"What do you see?" Landeta asked.

Louis leaned closer. "A bullet hole."

"How big?"

"Big."

"Gunshot residue?"

"She had to have floated here from somewhere else. Wouldn't the water wash it away?"

"What do you think?"

"Hell, I don't know. Probably."

"Not if it was a contact wound. It would've burned the blouse. Do you see any?"

Louis shook his head, wiping away more sweat.

"Lift the blouse and look," Landeta said.

It was hot and the whine of the mosquitoes and the smell

was making him sick. *Why don't you come down here and lift it, motherfucker?*

Louis stretched lower, lifting the blouse, trying not to touch the flesh. There was a quarter-sized hole in her back, just under the bra. The tissue around the hole was bubbled and flaking. But no evidence of burning. He saw something on her neck and carefully moved her head.

"What is it?" Landeta asked.

"Another bullet hole. In her neck, left side."

Louis closed his eyes briefly, fighting nausea. "I'd bet it's the same caliber as the one in her back."

"Anything else?" Landeta asked.

Louis wiped his sweaty face and looked back at Landeta's mud-caked trousers. "What?"

"Do you see anything else?"

Landeta seemed to be waiting for him to reveal some miraculous observation that only Landeta knew existed. If this was a test, he was getting damn tired of it. Where the hell was Horton anyway?

Louis leaned back to the body and let his eyes wander its length. He focused on her bare feet. They were badly cut up, especially the soles.

"She didn't lose her shoes in the storm. She was barefoot," Louis said.

"Why do you say that?"

"Look at her feet. They're all cut up."

Landeta didn't move.

Louis was about to stand up, move away, and leave Landeta to his little games when he had a sudden memory. A night a long time ago when he had stood over his bathroom sink trying to wash blood from a blue uniform shirt. He had ended up letting it soak for two days and still the blood did not come out.

"What is it?" Landeta asked.

"There's no blood," Louis said quietly.

Landeta was silent.

Louis stood up, steadied himself, and looked at Landeta. His shirt clung to his body and he could feel the sweat dripping in his eyes.

"There's no blood or stains on her clothes," Louis said. "She was in the water when she was shot or went in right after."

Horton came breaking through the trees at that moment, panting and sweating. He stopped abruptly when he saw the body.

"Jesus H Christ," he whispered. He put a hand to his mouth.

Louis looked at Landeta, holding his gaze for a moment before turning to Horton.

"Two shots, Chief, in the back and neck," Louis said, yanking off the gloves. "And it had to have happened in the last two days, probably around the time the storm hit."

Horton looked quickly at Landeta, but the detective said nothing.

"I'm guessing she was trying to get away from someone," Louis said. He looked around the mangroves. "In a place that tore up her feet. She ran into the water and someone shot her."

Horton was staring at the body. Landeta was looking at Louis. Louis looked back at the body.

He was noticing the style of the jeans and blouse. She was young, he guessed.

His eyes went up to her face, to the open eyes and mouth frozen in a grimace of fear. What had terrified a girl so much that she would run into the face of a hurricane?

Louis heard Horton cue his radio. But he wasn't listening. He was staring at the woman's hand. It was lying across her chest, almost as if she were proudly displaying something.

A ring. On the fourth finger of the left hand. A white band.

He heard Horton come up to his side. "CSI and medical examiner are on their way. We gotta get her out of here before the tide comes back in." Horton paused, looking at the body. "Can't believe it. Still no one reported missing from the storm."

"Someone is missing her," Louis said, nodding to the ring. "Probably her husband."

# CHAPTER 5

Louis dragged a palm frond out to the road and tossed it on the ten-foot pile of debris. He paused to wipe the sweat from his eyes and watch the slow line of cars creep along the beach road. The causeway was open again. Things were getting back to normal.

Everything except his own cottage. The hurricane had torn away a section of his roof, right over his bed. Pierre had promised to fix it three days ago. But the roof was still covered with a tarp and he was still sleeping on the sofa.

A car slowed, and a woman leaned out the window. "Excuse me, is this Branson's on the Beach?" she yelled out to Louis.

"Yeah, the sign's down," he said, pointing. He stepped aside and she pulled her Honda in, parking near the office. He was throwing another frond on the pile when the woman came up to him.

"Can you tell me where I can find Louis Kincaid?" she asked.

"You found him," Louis said.

Her eyes quickly took in his dirty jeans and bare sweaty chest. "Oh, I thought—" She held out her hand. "I'm Diane Woods."

Louis pulled off his work gloves and shook her limp hand as he sized her up. Short dark hair, tall, in her mid-thirties. Conservative blue suit, sensible heels, nice but not expensive—and panty hose, even though the temperature was ninety-five. A secretary, he guessed, and from the pinched, tired look on her face, another mother looking for help in getting a kid back from an AWOL ex.

He suppressed a sigh. Man, he hated child custody cases. Too much work for too little money, with the great payoff of watching a social worker stuff a crying kid into a car.

"I don't know how this is done," Diane Woods began.

"You want to hire me to investigate something, right?" Louis asked.

She gave a small nod, like she wasn't sure.

"Why don't you come inside and we can talk?" Louis said.

He led her into his cottage, setting aside the pile of laundry he had dumped on the sofa. She perched on the edge, clutching her big tote bag.

"Can I get you something, a soda?" he asked.

"Water?"

Louis brought her a glass of water, then excused himself, going into the bedroom to throw on a T-shirt. When he returned, she was just sitting there, the water untouched, eyes downcast.

He flipped on the AC and the ancient wall unit gave a cough and began to spit out a thin stream of air that did little to dissipate the heat.

"So, what do you want me to investigate?" Louis asked gently, sitting in a chair across from her. Something about this woman told him to take it slow and easy.

"I read—" She paused. Then she reached in her tote bag and pulled out a newspaper. With a shaky hand, she unfolded it and held out the section to Louis.

Louis took the paper. It was yesterday's *News-Press,* the front page still filled with storm cleanup news. Louis looked up at the woman expectantly.

"The story on the bottom," she said, nodding.

Louis looked back at the newspaper. There was a story about the body they had pulled out of the mangroves on Monkey Island. She was still unidentified but there was a closeup photograph of the ring with a caption saying police were hoping someone would recognize it.

"What about it?" he asked.

"I think I might know something about her," she said softly.

Louis waited, but when she said nothing, he leaned forward. "Do you know who she is?" he asked.

She shook her head.

"Do you know who killed her?"

Diane Woods looked at her shoes. Louis held the newspaper out to her. "I think you should go to the police," he said.

She looked up quickly. "No."

"If you know something, you need to go to the police."

She was silent.

"Why did you come to see me?" Louis asked.

She didn't answer. She was just sitting there, head bowed, tote bag clutched to her chest.

Louis ran a hand over his sweaty face. "I can't help you if you won't talk to me," he said. He started to rise.

"No, please." She looked up at him. "I found that same article in my father's desk drawer yesterday. He had clipped it out."

"So what?"

Diane Woods's brown eyes were scanning his face, like she was looking for something there. He had seen it before in people looking to hire him—hope that he could put something right, something that had gone horribly wrong in their lives.

He sat back down. "Why are you here, Miss Woods?"

She hesitated, then reached into her tote bag again. She handed him a folded paper.

He opened it. It was a Xerox of another newspaper article. The headline said NO CLUES IN GIRL'S DISAPPEARANCE.
There was a small photograph of a teenager with the name
Emma Fielding under it. The girl was thin-faced, with limp
blond hair and a curiously flat gaze—and looked nothing
like the young woman he had seen in the mangroves.

Then he noticed the date on the article: June 18, 1953.

He looked up at Diane Woods.

"Why are you showing me this?" he asked.

"I found it in my father's desk . . . with the other article. I
think he killed her."

Louis's eyes went from the copy to the current *News-
Press*. "Which one?" he asked.

"Both," she said.

Louis took a breath, sitting back in the chair. The articles
were thirty-four years apart. "Do you know *this* woman?" he
asked, holding out the 1953 article.

"No."

"Then what's the connection?"

"I don't know. All I know is I found both these articles
paper-clipped together and hidden in my father's desk."

"Maybe he knew her. Maybe he's got some fascination
with missing people or homicides."

Diane shook her head slowly. "He doesn't."

Louis stood up, turning his back to her. He glanced again
at the old clipping, then turned back to her. He was going to
tell her he didn't want the case, and that anything she knew,
no matter how insignificant, needed to be told to the cops,
but she spoke first.

"He has a rifle," Diane said. "The newspaper said the
woman in the water was shot with a rifle. He has one."

"Anything else?"

"He's acting strangely. We always go out to dinner on
Saturday. He's missed dinners. And he seems . . . depressed."

Louis glanced back at the newspaper, then shook his head.
"That's it? There's nothing else?"

"No," Diane whispered. "Nothing else."

Louis let out a sigh.

*"Please,"* she said quickly. "Just check into it. Just watch him and follow him. Let me know if he does anything strange. Can't you do that?"

Louis shook his head. "I have to go to the cops if I have a suspect."

Her eyes teared. "No, no. If you do that, he won't have a chance. The newspapers, TV . . . they will say he did it even if he didn't. His life will be ruined. He couldn't take that, he just couldn't take that."

"That's not the way—"

"Yes, it is. You know it is. You know how they treat suspects. He'd lose his job, he'd be ruined . . . it would kill him, Mr. Kincaid."

Louis stared at her.

"I just want you to watch him." She wiped at her eyes. "Can't you just do that?"

Louis shook his head slowly.

"Can't you talk to him, maybe, without letting him know who you are? Can't you just tell me if . . ."

Her voice caught and she dropped her eyes to her lap.

"What if I find out he did it?" Louis asked gently.

Diane's shoulders dropped and she let out a long sigh.

"I would have to go the cops," Louis said. "You understand that, right?"

She nodded, her eyes still downcast.

"You understand that you're hiring me to investigate your father and that you might not like the result?"

She looked up at him. Her eyes still held that desperate look of hope. "I have to know," she said.

# CHAPTER 6

Louis stood at the magazine rack in the Lee County Library, a copy of *Field and Stream* open in his hands. But his gaze was on Frank Woods.

If ever there was a man who defined "average," Woods was it. He was in his late fifties, about five-nine, maybe a little overweight. His complexion was not especially light or dark and he had a sort of gray cast, like he spent too much time indoors. His hair was dark but heavily peppered with gray, and he kept it trimmed short, like it was more a time consideration than style. His clothes were as innocuous as the rest of him. Long-sleeved white cotton shirt, buttoned at the collar and set off by a dark tie, wide enough to look like it came from the sixties. His plain brown trousers were clean but didn't have any crease. It was clear he didn't care about any notions of fashion. The only thing about him that could make him stand out at all was his short salt-and-pepper beard. Other than that, Frank Woods looked exactly like what he was—everyone's clichéd idea of a librarian.

Louis flipped through the magazine.

Diane Woods, Louis had discovered, was a high school principal, an only child whose mother had died when she was young. Diane was obviously a smart woman who was close enough to her father to have regular dinners. If anyone could judge whether Frank Woods was capable of murder, you would think it would be his daughter.

Louis watched Frank Woods as he wheeled a cart of books away from the desk.

He didn't believe families never saw it coming. They knew. They might be in denial, but they knew. And Diane Woods knew something, too. More than she had let on.

Louis set the magazine back and wandered toward the front of library, making his way closer to Frank Woods.

Woods was filing books from a cart and every once in a while, he would look up and Louis could see his eyes—brown, alert, intelligent—sweep the library. Then he would pick up the next book and silently slide it into place.

Louis eased closer, pretending to look at books. Suddenly, Frank disappeared around a shelf. Louis sighed. He had wanted to use this first visit to size Woods up, to get a sense of what kind of guy he was, maybe even find a reason to talk to him. But the library was nearly empty and he suddenly felt very conspicuous.

"Can I help you?"

Louis turned, feeling himself jump.

Frank Woods was right next to him, his brown eyes intense.

"I was looking for something," Louis said. He looked at the shelf in front of him. South American poetry . . .

"What's the title? Maybe I can help you find it," Woods said. His voice was soft, parental, as if he were gathering children for Saturday morning story time.

"Uh . . . local history," Louis said finally. "I guess this isn't it."

Woods's lips pressed together, and for a moment Louis felt he was caught, even though he knew Woods had absolutely no reason to suspect anyone was spying on him.

"This way, please," Woods said.

Woods had an erect posture and an oddly light way of walking, as if he were afraid of waking someone up. Louis tried to imagine him chasing the Monkey Island woman across God-knows-what kind of terrain and it wasn't coming. But then he remembered Frank Woods owned a rifle and thought of hunters stalking prey.

"What exactly is it you need?" Woods asked, his eyes scanning the books as he walked slowly down the aisle.

"I'm not sure."

Woods looked back at him. "You're not sure?"

Louis paused just a beat. "College. I'm doing a paper." Another beat. "On Captiva Island, history, that sort of thing."

"It's your term paper?" Woods said.

"Yeah."

Woods was staring at him. "Where do you go to school?"

"Community college." Louis shrugged. "I got a late start."

"So you're over at Edison Community College then," Woods said, running a finger around the book spines.

"Yup. Maybe I should start with newspapers," Louis said.

Woods turned. "We have the *News-Press* in binders going back to 1970. Anything older than that is on microfiche, over there." He nodded toward the back of the library. "However, I think you would have more luck with books. Local history is in the 917 section." He started away.

"Maybe you would recommend some books?" Louis asked.

Woods hesitated. "All right. Follow me, please."

Louis followed him to another shelf and watched as Woods pulled down three books. He held out the first to Louis.

"This is about Captiva Island, its local color, history, and people, from 1900 until about 1976," Woods said. "This one is a pictorial of Fort Myers, and this last one deals with the 1800s and the settlement of the outlying islands."

Frank dumped the books in Louis's arms and started off.

Louis glanced at them, then back at Woods. Either he knew or he didn't. His next question wouldn't matter.

"What do you have on runaways?"

Woods stopped, took a breath that expanded his round shoulders, and turned.

"You're writing a paper on that, too?"

Louis forced a smile. "Heavy class load."

Woods's lips tipped a small smile. "Odd time of year to be writing term papers, August."

"Summer school. Like I said, I got a late start."

Woods stared at him, his eyes growing distant. Then he turned quickly and moved away. He returned a minute later with two more books on the psychology of teenage girls.

"This should get you started," he said. He left, without saying another word.

Louis watched him go back to the front desk. He set the books on a table and headed toward the archive department. It was in the back, shielded from the front desk by shelves. With the microfiche reel for 1953, it took Louis a half hour to find another reference to Emma Fielding. It was only one short article, saying Emma Fielding had never been found. He printed out a copy, picked up his books, and started to the front desk.

Woods looked up.

"I'd like to check these out," Louis said.

"Your card, please."

"Ah . . . I don't have one."

Woods stared at him. "Do you have a driver's license?"

Louis pulled his wallet from his jeans and slipped out his license. Woods took it and started filling out a form. Halfway through it, the pencil paused.

"Is there something wrong?" Louis asked.

Woods didn't look up, but shook his head. He finished completing the form and pulled a small blue library card from a drawer. In cramped, small handwriting, he filled in Louis's name and address.

After running the books through the scanner and slipping the cards in the back, Woods stacked them and slid them across the desk to Louis.

"Thanks," Louis said. He hefted the books and started away.

"Mr. Kincaid?"

Louis turned.

"Your library card," Woods said, holding out the blue card.

Louis came back and took the card. "Thanks." Louis slipped the card inside one of the books and started away.

"Have a nice day, Detective," Woods said.

Louis hesitated, debating whether to turn back, but decided to keep going.

Detective? How the hell did he know? Did he recognize the name from the newspapers? Or was he expecting someone to come looking for him?

As Louis got to the front glass doors, he paused just long enough to glance back at the desk. Frank Woods had disappeared.

# CHAPTER 7

The phone was ringing when Louis got back to the cottage around five. It was Horton's secretary.

"The chief just wanted to let you know that the baby skull came back from Tallahassee." She paused and Louis could almost hear her thinking that he was some kind of ghoul or something. He didn't care.

"Do you want it?" she asked.

"Yes. I'll come over now."

Louis hung up and stood there for a moment, listening to the whisper of the surf. The sun was starting its descent into the gulf and it was filling the cottage with liquid gold light. His eyes wandered to the shelf near the sofa.

A couple of months ago, he had finally unpacked the last of his boxes, conceding he was staying if not really putting down roots. His books now were lined up next to his fast-growing collection of blues and rock CDs and tapes. But the top shelf he had left empty—except for four items.

He had never thought of himself as a sentimental man. The closest thing he ever had to souvenirs were the Tiger pennants back on the bedroom walls of his foster parents' house.

But for some reason, he had felt the need to put these four things out where he could see them.

Louis went to the shelf. There was the snowflake obsidian that his partner in Michigan, Ollie Wickshaw, had given him. Next to it lay a puka bead necklace. There were two picture frames. The smaller one held a sepia-toned portrait of his mother, Lila. The other was a letter with a quote from Winston Churchill: "The only guide to a man is his conscience . . . with this shield, however fates may play, we march always in the ranks of honor."

Louis picked up the obsidian, rolling the smooth black stone between his fingers. *It is a stone of purity, Louis, that balances the mind and the spirit.*

He was thinking about the baby skull, trying to figure out why he wanted it. He shook his head. Maybe the thing just needed a home.

The light was fading. He glanced at his watch. He had to get to the station.

It was after six by the time he got there and he realized Horton had probably already left. As he climbed the stairs, his thoughts turned to Frank Woods again. He would have to tail him, see what kind of life he led outside the library. But he had the feeling Frank Woods was one of those guys leading a life of quiet desperation, as the saying went. And that this case was going to be even more boring than usual.

At Horton's door, he stopped to knock.

"He's left for the day."

Louis turned to see Mel Landeta standing in the doorway of another office, a file folder in his hand. His tie hung loose and his black suit looked like he had slept in it.

"Figured as much," Louis said. "You know if he left anything for me, a Federal Express box?"

"You mean the skull," Landeta said, taking off his yellow-tinted glasses.

"Yeah. He said I could have it."

Louis waited for a reaction from Landeta, but the detective just rubbed the bridge of his nose.

"It's in here," he said, nodding to his office.

Louis followed him in. Landeta's office was small and furnished with only a desk, two chairs, and some black file cabinets. The blinds to the street were rolled shut, and there was not one certificate, plaque, or picture on the walls. The place was lit up like a hospital operating room.

Landeta set the folder down, then reached down beneath his desk. He set the Federal Express box on the desk.

The top was open and Louis looked inside. The skull was nestled in a bed of Styrofoam peanuts. Louis carefully lifted it out.

Louis felt Landeta's eyes on him and turned. Landeta was sitting at his desk, still holding the file folder.

"So what are you going to do with it?" he asked finally.

"I don't know. Try to trace it, maybe."

"Why?" Landeta said.

Louis shrugged. He carefully set the skull back in the box. Landeta was whistling softly, a low sad-tinged sound with no particular melody.

"Well, I gotta get going," Louis said, picking up the box and starting to the door.

"You want to hear about Jane Doe?" Landeta asked.

Louis hesitated. "You got an ID yet?

Landeta shook his head. "Not yet and she has no prints in the system. We put out a statewide BOLO and sent out a sketch of her face and a photo of the ring to the papers. Nothing. *Nada. Rien.* Zero."

Louis came back in, setting the box on the desk. "Is there any way to tell where she went into the water? You know, currents and stuff?"

"Normally, maybe. But not with the storm."

"Maybe the ring can be traced. What's it made out of?"

"Coral."

"Seems someone would know."

"Someone does know. They just aren't talking."

"Nothing in her jeans? Wallet? Papers?"

"Not a thing," Landeta said. He picked up a folder. "This just came in a few minutes ago. It's the autopsy report. Haven't even had a chance to read it yet."

He held it out to Louis. "Go ahead, take a look. You can read it to me while I clean up," he said, going behind his desk.

Landeta didn't offer a chair but Louis sat down anyway. He opened the folder. "No skin separation or swelling. So estimate is, she went in the water the night of the storm," he began.

"That's what I thought," Landeta said, moving folders and boxes. "Go on."

"She was shot from a distance of about fifty yards. The bullet was a .250-3000 Savage." Louis looked up at Landeta. "Probably from a Savage model 1899 rifle."

Landeta paused, a box in his hand. "They shoot small and medium game with those," he said quietly. "I think they stopped making them some years ago."

Louis went on. "She had salt water in her lungs, but probably not enough to drown her. The ME says she died of the gunshot wound first."

Landeta nodded thoughtfully. "Any blood, hair, skin found under her nails?"

"Just dirt," Louis said. "Soil consistent with local mangrove habitats."

"Well, that narrows it down," Landeta said. "Any indication of trauma, defense wounds?"

"Vince added a note about that," Louis said. "Says she had lots of fresh cuts and abrasions on her body, but he can't say they didn't come from getting tossed against rocks, coral, or something in the storm. In fact, he found particles of oyster shell in her skin."

Landeta finally settled in his chair. "That makes sense. Oysters attach themselves to mangrove roots. We found her in mangroves. Anything else?"

"No drugs or alcohol. No food at all in her. No stomach contents."

Louis went on reading. Landeta swung back and forth in his chair, his gaze fixed on the blank wall. Louis continued to read. The room was quiet except for the squeaking of Landeta's chair.

Louis let out a breath.

"What did you find?" Landeta asked.

"A recent history of abuse that Vince says definitely predates the storm," Louis said. "Older bruising on upper arms and face. Ligature marks on wrists, ankles, and neck. Anal and vaginal abrasions."

The squeaking stopped.

"Holy shit," Louis said softly.

"What?"

"She was pregnant," Louis said. "Twelve weeks."

Louis looked up at Landeta but his face showed nothing.

"We have to consider a boyfriend or married lover," Landeta said.

Louis was thinking of Frank Woods and just couldn't see the guy involved with a young woman. But he knew that people had shadows and secrets in their private lives and that even the most normal man had things to hide.

Landeta pushed himself out of the chair. "It's been a long day," he said. "I'm out of here."

"Is there anything I can do?" Louis asked.

"About what?"

"I mean, could you use any help on this?"

Landeta cocked his head, looking at him. "I heard you used to be a cop," he said.

"Yeah. Used to be."

"You know, you've got quite a rep down at O'Sullivan's," Landeta said.

"I've caught a couple of big cases," Louis said. "No big deal."

"So why'd you quit?"

There was a bite to the word *quit,* like it was a taunt. Louis had a feeling Mel Landeta already knew the answer, knew his whole history as a cop, in fact, but that he wanted Louis to tell the story for his entertainment. Well, he wasn't going to give the sonofabitch the satisfaction.

Louis rose, tossing the autopsy file on the desk. "Tell the chief I was here," he said.

"Don't forget your head," Landeta said.

Louis picked up the Federal Express box and started to the door.

"Hey," Landeta called out.

Louis turned.

"So how long did it take before you didn't miss it anymore?"

*Try a lifetime. . . .*

Louis knew what he meant. How long before you missed being a cop, but he had the feeling Landeta was baiting him.

"You get used to it," Louis said. He hesitated, then nodded to the Jane Doe file. "Let me know if you need help."

Landeta stared at him, his eyes looking jaundiced behind the glasses. "I can handle it from here on out," he said.

He tossed the file to the box on the corner of his desk. It missed and fell to the floor. Landeta ignored it.

Louis left the office. He was about to turn back and say good night, but the door swung shut. He could hear Landeta whistling the same melancholy tune again.

# CHAPTER 8

It was dark by the time he swung the Mustang into Branson's on the Beach and parked by his cottage. He popped open the glove box and took out the Glock. Getting out of the car, he clipped the holstered gun at his hip and picked up the Federal Express box. Closing the door with his foot, he started toward the cottage. He drew up short when he saw his front door wide open. The living room was dark but he could see a light on, back in the bedroom.

Silently, he set the box on the porch step and crept up to the door. He could see through the cottage to the open bedroom door and to the nightstand with its small bedside lamp. The shade had been knocked off and in the bare-bulb light, he could see a shadow moving along the wall. He pulled out his gun and crept forward.

Banging and scraping sounds, like someone searching through the dresser drawers. A shadow against the wall. He spun into the doorway, gun raised.

"Don't move!"

The man crouched in the corner jumped, dropping something to the floor as his head snapped to Louis.

*"Putain de merde!"* he screamed.

Louis lowered the gun, letting out his breath. "Jesus, Pierre. What the fuck—?"

Pierre was cowering, one hand outstretched, the other to his bare chest. "Louis! You scared the shits from me!"

Louis came into the bedroom, his eyes going up to the plastic drop cloth covering his bed, the ladder, and finally up to the ceiling with its fresh coat of plaster. He let out a sigh and looked back at Pierre.

Pierre shrugged. "You said to fix the leak. I did."

Louis lowered the gun. Pierre was wearing only his underwear—old shorts that hung low under his belly. He was streaked with sweat and white plaster.

"Jesus, Pierre, why didn't you turn on the AC?" Louis said, moving to the wall unit.

"It is dead."

Louis stopped and looked back at Pierre, who shrugged again.

"I don't suppose you can fix it," Louis said.

Pierre shook his head. "Too old. It was its time."

"How am I supposed to sleep?"

Pierre shrugged again.

"What about a new one?" Louis asked. Sweat was already starting to drip down his back.

Pierre shook his head slowly, but then he smiled. "I bring you a fan," he said, bending to pick up the trowel he had dropped.

"Come on, man, it's like a hundred degrees tonight," Louis said.

"It's a good fan," Pierre shot over his shoulder.

Louis heard the screen door slapping shut behind him.

"Shit," he muttered, staring at the air conditioner.

He stood looking at the mess for a moment, then unsnapped the holster. He slid the Glock in it and then placed it in its usual spot in the nightstand drawer.

He peeled off his sweaty shirt, throwing it at the pile of

dirty clothes in the corner. Pulling on a clean T-shirt, he went out to the living room and switched on a lamp.

He glanced at the living room AC unit, but he knew it was on its last legs, too. He went to the jalousie windows and cranked them wide open. Nearly eight at night and the temperature was still in the eighties, typical mean August weather. But at least there was a breeze blowing in from the gulf tonight. He could feel it, warm and moist on his sweaty skin. He could hear it, whipping through the palms and rattling the auger shell chimes out on the porch.

The porch . . . he had left the Federal Express box out there.

He went out, retrieved the box, and came back in, setting it on the kitchen table. His rumbling stomach made him realize he hadn't eaten so he pulled out a jar of Jif, some jelly, and a loaf of bread and sat down at the table.

As he slapped together two sandwiches, his thoughts went back to the autopsy report. Abused . . . and twelve weeks pregnant.

And that coral ring. She wore it on her left hand but it didn't look like any wedding ring he had ever seen. And if she was married, why hadn't the husband come forward? Men who abused women were usually hyperpossessive. Maybe she had been trying to leave him and he snapped and shot her.

Louis stood up and got a Heineken, coming back to finish his second sandwich.

He thought about what Landeta had said, that they had to consider a possible lover. Maybe the abusive husband shot her in a jealous rage and the pregnancy was just an odd coincidence.

Coincidence . . . like Diane Woods showing up at his door and telling him her father had a rifle and a collection of articles about missing women?

Louis took another swig of beer. He was thinking of Frank Woods now. He was trying to see Woods as Jane Doe's secret lover. He was trying to see Frank Woods as the kind of man who could shoot a woman.

Neither image was gelling. Frank Woods seemed to be an ordinary middle-aged guy, with an ordinary job and an ordinary life. But then why had he kept an article about a missing girl for thirty-four years?

Louis rose and went to the bedroom. He rummaged through some papers on the dresser until he found the copies of the articles Diane Woods had given him. Taking them back to the table, he read the one from 1953 about the missing Fort Myers woman, Emma Fielding. No mention of her being pregnant. But then again, there was no mention of her even being dead.

Louis set the article aside. Now he was trying to picture Frank Woods in 1953. He would have been what, about twenty-five? He was trying to picture him with a wife and a baby daughter—and a girlfriend on the side.

But to do it twice? It was one thing for Frank Woods to get involved with Emma Fielding when he was a young man. But did he make the same mistake thirty-four years later? Did a fifty-something widower librarian have an affair with a young woman, get her pregnant, and then shoot her, just so he could keep his life nice and neat?

Louis took another long swig of beer.

Okay, to all appearances, Frank Woods was ordinary. But sometimes ordinary people did extraordinary things. Like have affairs. And then they often did something stupid when things went wrong. Like getting a young woman pregnant.

He rose and went to stand at the open screen door. It was pitch-black out in the yard but he could hear the soft hiss of the waves breaking on the beach.

*Roberta asking him: You ever had a baby?*

*Almost . . .*

When he turned back, his eyes fell on the Federal Express box sitting on the table. He went to it and opened the cardboard flaps. He carefully lifted the skull out of the Styrofoam peanuts and held it up to the light, turning it over, looking at the holes on the top.

It was so light, and the whole thing fit neatly into his hand. He stared into the empty sockets, little holes no bigger than pennies.

What color had its eyes been?

*Brown, like hers? Or gray, like mine?*

What had its hair been like?

*Coarse, like hers? Or soft, like mine?*

What color was its skin?

*Black, like hers? Or . . . like mine?*

Louis set the skull down on the table and took a step away from it. He could see her in his mind, see her face the way it had looked that last day he saw her. Jaw clenched, tear-filled eyes that snapped with anger, love, and new hate.

*It's yours, Louis, you know it is.*

*Shit, Kyla, what do you want from me? I'm twenty years old and I don't want my life to be over!*

*Your life! What about mine! I'm getting rid of it!*

*Go, then. Just go. . . .*

Louis reached up to wipe the sweat off the back of his neck. The room was stifling, like the night breeze had suddenly died.

He heard a noise out in the dark and a moment later, he saw Pierre coming up the steps. He was lugging a large fan.

Pierre pushed open the screen and came in, setting the fan down with a huge exhalation.

*"Voila!"* he said.

"I still want a new air conditioner," Louis said.

"Yes, yes," Pierre said, flapping a hand. His eyes went to the skull on the table. He stared at it for a long time, then turned to look at Louis.

"What is that?" he asked.

"A baby," Louis said.

*"Mon Dieu.* Where did you get it?"

"I found it on the beach."

Pierre's tan face went a little chalky. "Dead babies on my beach?"

"No, no . . . it's old."

"Who is it?"

Louis shrugged.

Pierre started to pick it up.

"Don't touch it, please."

Pierre backed up, looking at Louis oddly. "You are not going to find out who it is?"

"It could have come from an abandoned cemetery. There's no way to know."

"You should ask Bessie," Pierre said.

"Who?"

"Bessie Levy. She knows about old things."

"Is she a historian or something?"

Pierre frowned. *"Historienne?* Oh, no. Bessie is *une vieille femme.* She has been here forever, up in Bokeelia. She is old, very old, that is all. And maybe a little gaga."

Pierre wagged a finger at his temple.

Louis sighed. He had been thinking about trying to trace the skull ever since Landeta had asked him what he was going to do with it. But he knew he needed to spend his time on Frank Woods. Diane Woods had already paid him five hundred dollars. And he hadn't done much yet to earn it.

Louis picked up the skull and carefully laid it back in its box. He heard a whirring sound and turned to see Pierre positioning the fan near the sofa.

Pierre spread an arm out to the fan. "You will sleep good now."

"I doubt it," Louis said.

# CHAPTER 9

It took an hour to get through the traffic jams in Cape Coral and another half hour before he was past the new subdivisions that were sprouting like mushrooms after a heavy rain. By the time Louis touched on to Pine Island, he knew he was going to be a good forty minutes late.

"Be on time. I got a hot date at four," Bessie Levy had told him on the phone. She had hung up without another word.

Louis turned north on Stringfellow Road. The Federal Express box on the passenger seat slid and he grabbed it before it fell. He glanced down at the skull, but it was snug in its bed of Styrofoam peanuts.

Chances were slim to none that the woman could tell him anything about the skull. Even if she could pinpoint where it might have come from, there was no way he could ever find out its identity.

Still, it was like starting to read a book and leaving it unfinished. And searching for a nameless baby was a helluva lot more interesting than tailing a boring middle-aged librarian.

He had been wrong about Frank Woods. He wasn't ordinary. He was dull—depressingly, desperately dull.

Three days and nights spent watching him had been like watching paint dry. Watching the guy get in his old Honda Civic at seven forty-five every morning. Following him to the library. Trailing him to the Denny's down the block at noon. Waiting for him outside the library and tailing him home again. Sitting in the Mustang, watching the blue light of the television play against the drapes until Woods turned it off at eleven-thirty and went to bed.

Three days and three nights and the guy hadn't changed his routine. Right down to sitting in the same seat at the Denny's counter and ordering the same patty melt with fries. No one came to visit him and Woods never went out. The only change in the man's stupefying routine came on Saturday, when Diane came over to pick him up and they went to Shoney's for dinner. They returned ninety minutes later and Diane dropped him off, barely stopping long enough to let the guy out at the curb before she sped off. Louis noted that she looked upset, but Frank seemed his usual mundane self. He went inside and a moment later, the blue light of the TV came on.

That night, Louis had stayed outside, just to make sure Frank wasn't slipping out after the TV went off. But he never left. Finally at three A.M., Louis had gone home, lying awake on the sofa while Pierre's fan cooled the sweat on his body.

This morning he had called Diane Woods. He heard relief in her voice when he told her he had found out nothing.

"So what now?" she asked.

"Your father is as normal as the sun coming up every day," he told her. "I can't go on taking your money."

"Please, just a few more days," she said. "I want to be sure."

Louis reluctantly agreed to stay with it for one more week. He needed the work, but he knew it wasn't right to take Diane Woods's money. Especially since he was taking the day off today to see Bessie Levy about the baby skull.

A green road sign announced he was coming into Bokeelia.

Bessie Levy had said to go to the marina across from Cap'n Con's Fishhouse and ask for directions from there.

Louis pulled up to the white clapboard restaurant and got out. The bright orange sign in the window said CLOSED. The marina across the street was nothing more than a dock with about ten slips. He spotted a man on one of the boats and went out to him.

"Excuse me, can you tell me where Bessie Levy lives?" Louis asked.

The man's eyes disappeared into his catcher's mitt of a face as he squinted at Louis.

"There," he said, flicking a hand over his shoulder before turning back to his lines.

Louis looked out over the blue waters of Charlotte Harbor and saw a ramshackle wood house built up on stilts about five hundred yards offshore. He let out a tired sigh.

"How do I get—" he began.

"Well, you can swim. Or I'll take you out for ten bucks," the man said without looking up.

Louis hesitated. "Okay, I'll be right back."

The man had the boat's motor running when Louis came back carrying the box and they motored out to the stilt house. Louis handed over a ten and climbed up the wood ladder, the box tucked under his arm.

Bessie Levy was waiting at the open front door. She was tiny, not even five feet, dressed in a faded denim shirt, old khakis, and green rubber waders. Her hair was a thin fuzz of brightly dyed red around a face deeply creased by age and spotted by the sun.

Her buckshot eyes immediately silenced him.

"You're late," she barked.

She stood there, arms akimbo, legs planted on the warped wood deck, her chin scored by frown lines. With the red fuzz of hair and little puppet chin, she reminded Louis of Howdy Doody.

"I know, I know," Louis said quickly.

She started gathering up a pail and shovel by the door. "I told you, I got—"

"A hot date, yeah, I know." Louis shifted the box to his other arm. "Look, Miss Levy, I need—"

"Too late. I gotta get going, 'cuz if I'm not in that bed by four, I don't get any."

"Please, Miss Levy, I just want you to take a look at my skull—"

Her black eyes shot up. "Your skull?"

Louis held up a hand. He set the box down and opened the flaps. Bessie Levy came forward and looked in. Her eyebrows twitched.

"Where you find that?"

"Captiva. On the beach after the hurricane."

She looked up at Louis. "That's a baby skull."

"I know."

"It's old."

"I know that, too. But that's all I know. I was hoping you could tell me more."

Her eyes went out over the waters, now tipped with silver from the slanting sun.

She looked at Louis. "You like oysters?"

"Yeah, I do."

"Well, too bad. You ain't getting any tonight and neither am I."

She set the pail down with a clang and nodded to the door.

"Come on in then. Let's go have a look at your baby here."

# CHAPTER 10

Louis paused in the doorway, blinking to adjust his eyes to the dark after the sunlight outside. It took him a moment to make out Bessie's form over in the corner. She was pulling off her rubber boots. They landed in a corner with a thud and she turned to face him.

"Let's take a look then."

He came forward and put the box on a table in the center of the room. While Bessie busied herself trying to find her glasses, he looked around the room.

The windows were shuttered, with only slits of sunlight seeping in. From what he could see, the walls were covered with shelves, all filled to bursting but with what he couldn't tell. It was one big room with a kitchenette off in one corner. There was little furniture—a couple of old stuffed chairs, a worn sofa, a bed tucked behind a wicker screen, and the large wooden table in the center.

"Where the hell are my specs?"

Bessie switched on a gooseneck lamp and the room came to life. The walls were festooned with fishing paraphernalia, blue-bubbled glass buoys, old life preserver rings, a tattered black-and-red hurricane warning flag. Old netting hung from the rafters like spiderwebs, skeins of boat line were looped between the beams. Every surface was covered with shells and pieces of coral. Pink conchs as sensuous as a woman's lips, sea fans that looked like delicate bonsai, and countless chunks of branch coral, each as infinite in its design as snow-flakes.

A four-foot stuffed alligator was sprawled atop the sofa, and six sets of shark jaws were lined up on a spice shelf above the small stove—arranged from the smallest to the largest, a gruesome bone maw with two-inch teeth.

Louis spotted an odd iron contraption on a shelf and went to it. It was rusty and crusted with tiny shells. Bessie saw him looking at it.

"Go ahead. You can pick it up," she said.

Louis hoisted up the two U-shaped loops on an iron rod. It was heavy.

"That's from the *Henrietta Marie*," Bessie said over her shoulder. "She went down in a storm off Key West in 1701. But the cargo had already been safely delivered to Jamaica."

Louis hesitated, then held one of the loops near his wrist.

"Slaves?" he asked.

Bessie nodded toward the irons. "That one's probably from a child."

Louis carefully set the manacles back on the shelf.

"Was this was all you found? No other bones?" Bessie asked.

"No, nothing else."

Bessie went to a crowded desk, pulled something out of a drawer, and came back. Louis was surprised to see her snap on a pair of latex gloves.

"You didn't handle it, did you?" she asked.

"Not any more than I had to," Louis said, slightly an-noyed.

She gave a grunt and bent the gooseneck lamp closer. She carefully lifted the skull out and set it on the table.

"What made you think it's newborn?" she said.

"The fontenelles."

"Was the skull in pieces when you found it?"

"No, it was whole. Why?"

"Come over here," Bessie said. When Louis came closer, she pointed to what looked like four cracks in the skull. "These things are sutures, where the skull has come together. It takes at least three months for the skull to fuse, more like six."

She looked up at him. "No way this came from a newborn baby. A newborn's skull would have been in pieces. Like a broken egg."

"So it couldn't have survived being tossed around in a hurricane," Louis said.

"Nope. My guess it was kicked up from the gulf bottom. Could have been lying down there, snug in the sand, before the storm currents woke it up."

Bessie picked up the skull and peered into the tiny sockets. "How old they tell you it was?"

"Fifty years."

"Who told you that?"

"State archeology lab."

"Bureaucrats," Bessie mumbled. "They didn't bother to carbon-date it, did they?"

Louis shook his head. "Police didn't want to pay for it."

"I'd guess it's a lot older 'cuz of the color. But you're never gonna know for sure unless you carbon it."

Bessie was using a magnifying glass now to examine the skull. It was quiet except for the groan of the pilings and the lapping of water.

"Pierre said you were an expert on Indians and local history," Louis said.

"Pierre? Pierre Toussaint?" She glanced up at him. "That old frog still croaking? Tell him he owes me twenty bucks from when I beat him at pool."

She set down the skull and went to a shelf. She stood on her tiptoes, running a finger along the books.

"My husband and me ran a ship salvage operation for

thirty years before he died," she said. "I can't dive anymore 'cuz of my blood pressure. But my memory's still good. Folks pay me good money for what I can remember."

Cursing softly, she hauled a stool over, got up on it, and pulled a huge dusty book off the top. Louis was about to run over and help her down when she jumped lightly to the floor.

"I don't think this skull is from an Indian burial ground," she said, lugging the book back to the table. "The Calusas weren't above sacrificing their firstborn to the gods, but they were careful about where they put their dead. And we've found most of their burial mounds."

Louis's eyes went to the skull and back to Bessie.

"I'm guessing your skull here came from a shipwreck," she said. "And it being a child, I'm thinking it came from Emanuel Point."

"That's a ship?" Louis asked.

"Nope. A place. In 1559, eleven Spanish ships sailed into Pensacola Bay to start a colony under a captain named Don Tristan de Luna. Think of it—a thousand people, leaving their homes, risking their lives, bringing everything they needed to survive in the wilderness, sixty-one years before the Pilgrims set foot on Plymouth Rock."

Bessie was still bent over the book. "They brought everything—slaves, priests, wine, horses. And their children." She paused. "The colony was wiped out by a hurricane before they even finished unloading the ships."

Louis shook his head. "Pensacola is way up in the panhandle. That skull couldn't have come from there."

"Didn't say it did. I'm thinking this could be a baby that died at sea." She turned a page slowly. "My husband, Bill, and me worked the wreck so I got pretty familiar with it. I remember reading about a baby's funeral held on board before they got to Emanuel Point."

She pointed to a paragraph. "Yup. I knew it. Right here in the Luna translation, from the manifest. 'August ten, 1559.

Infante Isabella Maria Carreira de los Reyes. *Mortis A Seis Mes. Vios Con Dios Preciosa Angelita.'* "

Louis bent to look at the line in the book under Bessie's finger. Then he looked at the skull. He had been right. It was very old and very far from its home.

"Isabella," he said softly.

He felt Bessie's eye on him and looked down at her. He could see there were questions in her eyes, things she wanted to ask him. Like why he cared so much about a baby who had died hundreds of years ago. He looked away.

"Well, I don't know if that helps you," she said, giving a little shrug. "What you going to do with the skull? I mean, if you don't want it, I'd love to—"

"No, I'm going to keep it," Louis said quickly.

She nodded, her eyes locked on his.

Louis picked up the little skull and carefully put it back in its box. He closed the flaps.

"Thanks for your help, Mrs. Levy," he said, holding out a hand.

She gave him a smile and her hand. It was calloused with a firm grip. "I could be wrong, you know. I'm not usually. But this might not be who I say it is."

But he wanted it to be somebody. "How many old baby skulls could there be out there?" he said with a smile.

Bessie shook her head. "This place is built on skeletons, young man. Millions of humans, millions of sea animals, dead and gone. Florida is just one big long island of bones."

She switched off the light and for a second, the water lapping on the pilings below his feet made Louis think of someone sighing.

"Come on," Bessie said. "I'll motor you back to land."

# CHAPTER 11

Louis sat up in the Mustang's seat and rubbed his neck. He checked his watch. After seven. Five hours of sitting down the block from Frank Wood's house, another wasted day. The only thing the guy had done all day was take out his trash.

*Enough of this shit.* He turned the ignition, but saw a blue Honda pull into Frank's drive. Diane got out and went to the front door.

Saturday . . . another one of their weekly dinners together. He shut off the motor and waited. Five minutes later, they came out and left in Diane's car. He followed them to the Shoney's restaurant on Cleveland Avenue and waited until they got inside. This time, he decided to go in and watch them.

He wasn't sure why. Maybe just to see if Frank was acting squirrely or to get some sense of their relationship. Diane had clearly been upset after their dinner last week. Maybe it had finally dawned on her what might happen if her father did turn out to be a killer, and she regretted having him watched. People who hired Louis often came to regret it. He had discovered that relatives really didn't want to know the truth—whether it was about a cheating spouse or a violent weirdo hanging out in the far branches of the family tree. If Frank Woods turned out to be a killer, it was a sure bet that his daughter wasn't going to be happy knowing that the same bad blood ran through her own veins.

He spotted them in the smoking section in a booth. Diane looked tired and distracted. Frank was hunched over, staring vacantly out the window. Louis slipped into a booth nearby, out of their sight lines. He ordered a cup of coffee and sat back to watch.

Frank lit a cigarette. Diane made a face and said something. Frank turned his face to blow the smoke away from her. They both hid behind their menus.

They spoke and Louis strained to hear. Diane was asking her father how his job was. He shrugged and muttered something, tapping the cigarette in the ashtray. Diane folded her hands in front of her face and looked at her father. She was facing Louis and he could see her expression. Exasperation? Or worse, contempt?

There were more attempts at talk, but they always trailed off into silences. The waitress brought their meals. Fish and salad for Diane. A big cheeseburger and fries for Frank. They began to eat, seemingly grateful for something to do.

Diane said something and Frank shook his head slowly. She leaned forward, still talking. Frank kept his eyes on his plate.

Her words rose over the clatter of dishes. "I'm worried about you."

"Don't be," he said.

"But you're—"

"Let it be, Diane. Just let it be."

Frank pushed his plate away and leaned back in the booth, lighting a fresh cigarette. Diane went back to pushing the food around on her plate, her eyes downcast.

The waitress came up to Louis's table with the coffeepot. He shook his head. He had drunk five cups already and had nothing to show for this night but a bursting bladder.

Frank got up. Diane did, too, picking up the bill.
*Thank God . . .*

Louis waited until they were outside, then left. They were
standing by Diane's Honda, talking, this time with more ani-
mation. Louis had no way of getting closer to hear without
showing himself, so he stayed behind the bushes.

Suddenly, he saw Diane put her hands to her eyes. She
turned abruptly and got behind the wheel of her car. Frank
stood there for a moment, eyes on the ground, cigarette in
hand. Then he crushed the glowing butt between his thumb
and index finger and put it in his pocket. He got in the car.
Diane pulled out, heading fast down Cleveland Avenue.

Louis followed them back to Frank's house. Diane didn't
even wait until Frank was in the door before she backed out
of the driveway and raced off. Louis watched the lights come
on behind the drapes of Frank's house, and then he followed
the red taillights of Diane's fast-disappearing car.

She kept going up Cleveland, heading for the Caloosahatchee Bridge. She was obviously headed back home to her
apartment over in Cape Coral. Good. He could call it a night.
Louis slowed, starting over to the left lane so he could head
over to McGregor and get back out to Captiva.

Suddenly, the Honda braked and did a hard right onto
Martin Luther King Boulevard. Louis cursed and swung the
wheel, getting a horn from the truck behind him. He sped to
catch up to Diane.

She braked hard again and swung left. Louis pulled up
just in time to see her go into Boopie's Beer & Wine.

"Well, well, well," he murmured.

She came out a couple of minutes later, clutching a small
paper bag. Two black men in the parking lot stared at her as
she got in her car.

Louis put his car in reverse, ready to take flight again.
Diane's Honda didn't move. Louis waited. But Diane hadn't
even started the engine. He couldn't see her from where he
was, so he put the car in gear and inched forward. Now he

could see her profile. She was just sitting there behind the wheel, her face painted pink from the neon of the liquor store's sign.

Diane brought the paper bag to her lips and took a drink. She closed her eyes, leaning her head back against the headrest. Then she took another drink.

The two black men were watching her. She didn't even see them. She took a third long drink.

"Christ," Louis whispered. He was thinking about getting out and going over to her car, but she suddenly started the motor. A moment later, she pulled out.

Damn, he had to follow her. If nothing else to make sure she got home okay.

She drove more slowly now, getting across the river and into the parking lot of her apartment complex without mishap. She walked slowly up the stairs to her door, her purse and the paper bag in hand, and went inside.

Louis let out a tired sigh. This was nuts. He couldn't afford to keep wasting time on this, and Diane Woods certainly couldn't afford to keep paying him for it. Frank Woods had not done a thing that could possibly connect him to Jane Doe's murder, and the more Louis saw of Diane, the more convinced he was that she was just paranoid and maybe just a little embarrassed by her odd—but normal—parent.

He was quitting.

Louis pulled himself from the Mustang and went up to Diane's door. He rang the bell.

The outside light went on and the door jerked open. Diane stood there, still wearing her dress, but with her shoes off and her collar open. Her face was flushed. She was holding a crystal goblet of clear liquid. Louis could smell the gin. And he could see she was trying hard not to sway.

"What are you doing here?" she asked.

"We need to talk."

She walked away, leaving the door open. Louis came in and watched her as she went into the kitchen, put the gin bottle in the cabinet, and closed the door. Every move she made was with the careful effort of a drunk trying not to look like one.

The apartment was quiet except for the hum of a refrigerator somewhere. Louis looked around, taking in the neat rows of best-sellers on the bookshelves, the mauve and gray furnishings, the careful fan of *Gourmet* and *House Beautiful* magazines on the coffee table, the perfect arrangement of Lladro porcelains on an elegant étagère. Not a fingerprint on glass, not a book jacket frayed, not a speck of dust anywhere. The place screamed taste and order.

She came back to the living room, smoothing back her hair with one hand and holding the gin in the other.

"Okay," she said, dropping into a chair. "So talk."

"I don't think this is working for either of us," Louis said.

"You promised me one more week."

Louis shook his head. "There's no point. I've followed your father everywhere he goes, which isn't too many places. He does nothing, and I mean nothing, suspicious."

"But he had the newspaper clippings."

"So what? Why don't you just ask him why he cut them out? Jesus Christ, Diane, he's your father."

She looked away, her eyes falling on the glass of gin. He knew she wanted to take a drink, but something was stopping her. Could she possibly think he didn't know she was drunk?

She lowered her head into her hand, her fingers splayed across her forehead. "I can't talk to him."

"But you can think him capable of murder."

She closed her eyes, her chest rising with a deep breath. "Get out. Quit if you want."

Louis sighed, and turned toward the door. He heard her slurp softly. When he looked back, her cheeks were flushed and the glass was empty.

"Okay," Louis said. "I'll finish out the week."

She looked up at him, her eyes trying to focus. "Do what you want."

Louis opened the door, and let himself out. He paused at her window, peering through the slats in the blinds.

Diane was wobbling back to the kitchen. Louis watched as she pulled open three different cabinets before finding the gin. She raised the bottle to her mouth and slugged down a shot.

He turned away and started down the steps. A car door slammed in the parking lot and a man got out.

Louis froze on the top step. Shit, it was Frank. And there was nowhere to go, no place to hide before Frank saw him.

Louis stopped on the top step as he watched Frank Woods lock his car. He turned and looked up at his daughter's apartment, his eyes settling on Louis, fully illuminated in the amber light.

Frank spun and hurried back to his car, jumping inside. Louis started to call to him, but stopped.

Hell, what could he say? I was just here telling your drunk daughter I wanted to quit spying on you?

Frank threw his car in reverse, then squealed out of the parking lot. For a second, Louis thought about following him. But he would never catch him. And what was the point anyway?

Louis rubbed his gritty eyes. The hell with it. He was tired and he was going home. There was one Heineken left in the fridge and it had his name on it.

# CHAPTER 12

One Heineken hadn't been enough. After a fitful night, he was awake but just lying there, sweaty and tired. The sheets were kicked to the floor and even Issy, who usually slept by his side, had retreated to the cool of the terrazzo floor.

The phone rang and he glanced at the clock. Eight-thirty A.M. He let it go ten times but it wouldn't stop. Finally, he rolled out of bed and picked it up.

"Mr. Kincaid? This is Diane Woods."

She was speaking carefully. He knew that meant hangover.

"He's disappeared," she said. Now he heard the catch in her voice, too.

"What do you mean?"

"My father. He's gone."

"How do you know?"

"I called him first thing this morning. He didn't answer and when I called the library, they said he hadn't come in. I am on my way over to his house now. Will you meet me there?"

Louis suppressed a sigh as he looked at the clock again.

"He might be inside," Diane said. "He might have done something to himself."

"Look, Miss Woods, you really should go—"

"Please. I don't want to go in there alone."

Louis had been leaning on his knees, head down. He sat up. "Where are you?"

"I'm at home."

"Okay, meet me at his house in a half hour."

Diana's Honda was in the drive of Frank's home, and she got out as he pulled up. As he walked toward her, Louis glimpsed her face in the morning sun. She was dressed in a dark skirt and red blouse, her hair neat around a made-up face. She was wearing sunglasses.

"Thank you," she said softly.

"Maybe we should call the police."

She shook her head. "Please, just come in with me."

He followed her to the porch. It was covered with leaves and there were a couple of plastic-bundled copies of the *News-Press*. A white plastic planter hung by the door but there was nothing in it but dirt. Diane reached up to the planter and dug out a key.

"You don't have your own key?" Louis asked.

She turned to look at him but he couldn't see her eyes through the dark glasses. "No. Why would I?"

*You're his daughter,* Louis thought, but he let it go.

"He leaves a key outside because he is always losing his own," Diane explained, unlocking the door.

Louis went in first and did a quick walk-through of all the rooms. He saw nothing; there was no one in the house. He came back to the front door, where Diane was waiting.

"He's not here," Louis said.

Diane shut her eyes in relief.

Louis turned and looked around the living room. It looked much like he had imagined from what he had been able to see during the long hours he had spent hidden in the shad-

ows of the bushes down the block. Plain, a little run-down,
like no one really had the time or energy to invest it with the
small things that made the difference between a house and a
home.

The living room was browns and tans, the furniture non-
descript and old. Cheap bookcases, filled to bursting. There
were a couple of generic framed landscapes on the walls but
there was nothing to really speak of the personality of whoever lived here. Nothing except a framed photograph on the
end table next to an ashtray overflowing with cigarette butts.
It was of Diane, her hair longer, her smile shy, her cheeks
and lips tinted pale pink in the style of old high school senior
portraits.

The room smelled. It smelled of cigarettes, must, and
something Louis recognized but could not name. He had
smelled it once before, in the closed-up cabin of an ex-cop
named Lovejoy. It was the lonely odor of one man alone, undi-
luted by fresh air, sunlight, or the perfume of other human
beings.

Louis heard the rasp of drapes and turned to see Diane
working at closing the gaps facing the street. Then she turned.
She had taken off the sunglasses and she was looking at the
room.

She looked at Louis. "I . . . I'm sorry, the place is a mess."
She went to the overflowing ashtray, picked it up, and looked
around the room, like she wanted to empty it. Then she just
set it down on the dusty table.

"My father is not the neatest man," she said. And then she
gave Louis an odd smile, like she was apologizing.

"Can I look around some more?" Louis asked.

She nodded and headed toward a back room. The bedroom drapes were drawn so she turned on the overhead light.
Louis paused by the door, looking at the room.

It was like the living room, the bed unmade, another overflowing ashtray, a jumble of clothes in a laundry basket in the
corner. In the open closet, Louis could see the white shirts,

brown slacks, and jackets that made up Frank's library uniform. On the nightstand, there was a plate with a half-eaten sandwich and a small stack of books with one volume spread open, facedown. A pair of half-lens reading glasses were lying on top of the book.

Louis picked up the book. The title was *Theory and Practice of Romance Etymology.* Louis set it back, putting the glasses on top exactly as he had found them.

"I don't think he's gone anywhere. At least not for good," he said. When Diane didn't answer he turned to her.

She was looking around the room, her mouth hanging slightly agape, her eyes not quite concealing her disgust. He knew now why she didn't have a key to her father's house. It gave her an easy reason to stay away.

She saw him staring at her and went slowly to the bathroom. "His toothbrush is gone," she called out.

"Maybe he's spending the night somewhere. Maybe he has a new girlfriend."

She came back into the bedroom. "You've been watching him. He doesn't have a girlfriend. He doesn't even have any friends. He barely has a life."

Louis watched her as she went to the bureau and slowly pulled out the top drawer.

"You sound like you're embarrassed by him," Louis said.

She spun around. "I'm *protective.* How can anyone be embarrassed by their parent? They are what they are."

She went back to searching through the drawers, but more slowly now, like she had no idea what she was looking for.

"What happened to your mother?" Louis asked.

"She died when I was seven," Diane said.

"How did she die?"

She shut the drawer, turning to face him. "He didn't kill her if that's what you're wondering. She died in a car accident. He was at work when it happened."

Louis didn't reply.

Diane took a deep breath. "My father raised me alone after that. It wasn't easy for him. He's kind of a closed man . . . didn't ever really understand me, I suppose."

Louis glanced around the room. More bookcases like the living room, the shelves all filled. There wasn't even room to slide in a pamphlet. Louis scanned the nearest shelf. The books all appeared to be scholarly stuff, many of the books about foreign languages. No novels or light reading.

Louis turned back to Diane. "Do you notice if anything else is missing?"

She looked around, shaking her head. But then she stopped, and moved to the closet. She pointed to the shelf.

"His rifle," she said. "He kept it in a case on that shelf."

"How long has he had it?"

Diane blinked. "Forever. I mean, it's old. I remember I used to watch him clean it when I was little. He would take it out of the case, lay it out on a towel on the kitchen table, and spend hours cleaning all the parts and then put it all back together again. He never took it out except to clean it."

"He didn't hunt?"

She shook her head. "He wasn't interested in the outdoors. I never saw him use it. Not once. I always got the impression it was an heirloom or antique or something and that was the only reason he kept it. He never said."

"Do you know what kind it was?"

She shook her head.

"Think. Did he ever call it a Savage?"

"I don't remember. I don't care, I hate guns."

Louis's eyes scanned the bedroom once more. There was a desk crammed in one corner. "Is that where you found the articles?"

Diane nodded and went to the desk, pulling out the top drawer.

"They were in here," she said, handing him a leather binder. "I put them back after I made the copies I gave you."

Louis flipped through the book. It was an old date book

from 1983, but most of the pages were blank. There was an occasional reminder of an appointment, but nothing out of the ordinary.

He sifted through the stack of papers under the book. Utility bills, receipts from local stores, statements from the Lee County Library Credit Union, a dry cleaner's claim stub for three pairs of men's slacks.

He found a receipt dated yesterday. It was from Seven C's Bait and Tackle Shop in Fort Myers.

"Does your father fish?" he asked.

"No." Diane's brow furrowed. "He wouldn't even eat fish. He was allergic to it."

Louis glanced into the untidy bathroom and turned back to Diane. "Show me the rest of the house."

She led him to a small second bedroom that she said used to be hers as a child. The room was as neat and orderly as a lawyer's reception area. They ended up in the kitchen.

It was a mess. The Braun coffeemaker still had a cup or two left in it. There were dirty dishes in the sink and an egg-crusted pan on the stove. Louis glanced around, and seeing a door, walked to it. It opened into a small garage. Small slits of sunlight squared the garage door. He tried the light, but it was burned out. Stepping down into the shadows, he used the light from the kitchen to maneuver the two steps. He spotted a flashlight and turned it on, shining the beam over a cluttered tool bench, storage bins, and the garage walls. The light flashed on something metal in a corner and Louis went to it.

It was a fishing rod, hung on two brackets. It was an old rod, coated in dust. But from the little Louis had learned about fishing, he could tell the rod was expensive, not something your average pier-dangler would have in his garage.

There was a second set of identical brackets below the rod, empty.

Louis took a step and something crackled under his foot. He trained the light down and it picked up several large white plastic bags with the red letters TAL BRODY'S SPORTS CITY. He started going through the bags.

Diane came up behind him. "What are you looking for?"

Louis didn't answer. Finally he pulled out a small paper and trained the flashlight on it. It was a sales receipt. The first item was a Coleman Sundome tent.

"He's gone camping," Louis said.

"Camping?"

Louis held up the receipt. "In a brand-new tent. And with a new lantern, first-aid kit, water bottles, the works. Six hundred and eighty dollars' worth."

Diane took the receipt and shook her head slowly. "My father has never spent a night outdoors in his life."

"You said he doesn't fish either." Louis shined the beam up on the rod and empty brackets.

Diane was staring at the fishing rod. "That can't be. He didn't even like being near water." Her voice was soft, like things were just now coming back to her. "I remember once, when I was little—I must have been little, because it was just after my mother died—we were down by the pier and there were these boats. I asked him if we could go out on one. But he said we couldn't. He said he didn't like the water because he couldn't swim."

She turned abruptly, heading back to the kitchen.

Louis found her standing in the center of the living room, eyes vacant.

"I thought I knew him," she said softly.

Louis stopped a few feet from her. He felt like telling her the first thing that had popped into his head, that no one really knew their parents. You only knew the idealized version—dependable, desexed, and devoid of human failings. If you were lucky. If you weren't lucky, you saw your parents in all their ugliness. Like the sad woman he remembered, withered in her addiction. Or the faceless man in the faded photograph, the only image he had of his father.

He turned to Diane. "Look, Miss Woods, I think you are worried for no real reason."

"No reason! What about the articles?"

"By themselves, they mean nothing."

"Then why did he keep them?"

"Why don't you just ask him?" Louis said firmly.

"I can't," she said.

Louis shook his head. A voice inside was telling him to just leave, and not get pulled any further into some messy emotional drama with her and her old man. Besides, even if he were to go after Frank Woods, he didn't know where to begin. There were a million places he could hide in, not just the usual campgrounds and parks but dozens of forgotten little islands where a man could put in a boat and get lost forever.

"I'm leaving," he said. He went back into the kitchen. She followed and grabbed his arm.

"Wait. There's something else," she said. She let go of his arm. "Please, just wait."

She disappeared back into the bedroom. When she came back, she stood there for a moment, her eyes searching his face.

She held out her palm and he looked down.

In her hand was a white coral ring. It looked exactly like the ring Louis had seen on the finger of the dead woman on Monkey Island.

"You've had that the whole time?" he asked.

She nodded.

Louis looked away, his chest tight. "Where did you find it?"

"In a box in the bottom of one of his desk drawers."

"You never saw it before?" Louis asked.

Diane shook her head. "No, never."

"What about your mother? You're sure she never wore it?"

She shook her head again. "No, her wedding ring was a plain gold band. After she died, my father gave it to me." She held up her right hand. "I wear it now. It's the only thing I have to remember her by."

She looked like she was going to cry. It struck Louis that it was the first time he had seen her look genuinely upset.

"You should have given me that ring the first day," Louis said. "How the hell can you expect me to waste my time on something when I don't have all the evidence?"

"If I had given it to you, you would've turned it over to the police."

"Damn right. And that's still what I'm going to do," Louis said. "This is important. This is more than just suspicion. This is a link, Miss Woods. To a murder victim."

She closed her fist quickly over the ring and stepped back. Louis held out his hand. "Give it to me."

"No."

"Suit yourself. I'll just tell the cops what I know and what you have and you will be charged with obstruction. How's that?"

"You can't do this to me."

"You've done it to yourself," Louis said. "I'm leaving. Put your last check in the mail."

Louis started away but she grabbed him again. This time, he jerked away and spun to face her.

"Look, lady—"

"I'll give you five hundred dollars more to find him first. Just give him ten minutes . . . Talk to him . . . please."

Louis headed to the front door and pulled it open.

"A thousand!"

He turned. "You can't afford that. Look, just—"

Diane came to stand in front of him. "You said yourself he's an ordinary guy. You said he was *normal.*"

Louis rubbed his face. "I don't know what normal is any more than you do, Miss Woods."

"Please," she said. "I just want this to be quiet."

Louis just looked at her.

"The police," she said, "I don't want . . ."

Her voice trailed off and Louis knew what she wanted. Or rather didn't want. Diane Woods didn't want to see the spectacle of her father being hauled into the police station on the nightly news. For a moment, he was disgusted. But then, who in their right mind would want to be part of the circus?

He looked at her balled fist. And there was the ring. No way was she going to give up that ring without a fight, and he had no authority to take it from her. Hell, for all he knew, she was just going to go throw it in some canal as soon as he left.

"All right. If I don't find him by tonight, you give me the ring and I go to the cops."

She nodded. "Just find him. And make sure he doesn't get hurt . . . or try to hurt himself."

Louis looked back around the room, his eyes falling on the filled ashtray. There was a book of matches next to it. Louis picked it up. Sutter's Marina. He knew that place. It was down the street from Roberta Tatum's store. It was a popular place for fishermen or anyone looking to rent a boat or catch a ferry.

"Now what happens?" Diane asked.

Louis pocketed the Sutter's Marina matches. "We hope your father has just gone fishing," he said.

# CHAPTER 13

The leather-faced guy behind the counter at Sutter's Marina handed Louis the picture of Frank Woods and went back to picking his teeth.

"So have you seen him?" Louis asked.

"Not sure. Maybe."

"Think harder."

The guy tugged on his sweat-stained ball cap. It was embroidered with a blue Grateful Dead bear. "You a cop?"

Louis had a feeling the guy had spent some time in the backseat of a squad car. "No, I'm not."

The guy pursed his lips. "Yeah, I saw him. He was in here yesterday asking about ferry service."

"To where?"

The guy shrugged.

"Okay, so where do your ferries go?" Louis asked.

"Anywheres with a dock. Useppa, Cabbage Key, Cayo Costa, Bird Island, Safety Harbor." The man leaned over the counter. "And me personally, I got a skiff that can take you a few places without docks. If you know what I mean."

Louis knew exactly what the guy meant. His eyes drifted out the open door to the sun-silvered waters of Pine Island

Sound. Even from here he could see about a half dozen small green islands and he knew there were dozens more. Some owned by the state, some private, some inhabited, some nothing more than tidal flats colonized by mangroves. But dense and isolated enough for a man to get lost in, especially if he wanted to.

"So did he take a ferry or not?" Louis asked.

"Seems I remember him buying a ticket, yeah."

Louis was losing patience. "To where?"

The guy shrugged his bony shoulders again. "Cayo Costa. But I sure as hell wouldn't want to go camping out there, man."

"He had camping equipment with him?" Louis asked. When the guy nodded Louis went on, "Why do you say you wouldn't want to go there?"

The guy looked at him like he was crazy. "It's August, dude. The skeeters eat you alive unless you stay out near the gulf."

Louis glanced at his watch. Nearly four. "Give me a ticket to the island."

The guy eyed Louis's khakis and polo shirt. "Kinda late to be going out there. There's only one boat coming back at six."

"I'll take my chances," Louis said, slapping some bills on the counter.

He was the only passenger on the ferry. As it chugged out into the open waters of Pine Island Sound, his thoughts came back to something that had been bothering him from the day he looked down at Jane Doe's body lying twisted on that stinking little mangrove island. Water . . . it touched everything here. Literally, water surrounded the barrier islands and streamed up the river and estuaries of the Fort Myers mainland. Figuratively, water touched the lives of the people, from the shrimp fishermen to the girls who sold suntan lotion on the beach. Water was probably the most important part of his new home's makeup. Yet he knew almost nothing about it, or the whole outdoor thing really. Neither did Frank Woods, if Diane knew what she was talking about. But something told him she didn't.

The ferry let him off at a small dock on the east side of the island. He saw a sign with an arrow that said CAMP-GROUND. He followed the path through the mangroves and came to a large clearing sheltered by high-arching Australian pines. There were some tent sites, picnic tables, and a few primitive-looking cabins. But not one person.

Louis stood there, listening to the wind in the pines. *Shit, now what?* He thought about what the Deadhead had said about no one wanting to camp this time of year. Maybe Frank had camped somewhere over on the gulf side of the island. He glanced at his watch. He had more than an hour until the ferry came back.

With a look up at the sun low in the western sky, he started toward it, down a path leading into a tunnel of brush and trees. Soon he was dripping with sweat and the mosquitoes were starting to swarm in the heavy, motionless air. Sounds rose up around him in the gathering dusk. A strange cry of a bird somewhere above. A groan of some unknown creature below. He felt his heart quicken slightly and picked up his pace.

Bessie Levy came to his mind, something she had said as she motored him back to the Bokeelia dock.

A pelican had soared over the boat and she had pointed to it saying, "Look! Ain't that beautiful?"

"It's ugly, like one of those prehistoric birds," Louis had said.

She had laughed at him. "Well, that's what this place is. Pterodactyls on our docks, centrosauruses crawling out of the canals to eat little dogs. Florida is a prehistoric place, young man, where the sea is still close and the sky still burns at night. Here, in this place, we humans are still very close to the moment we crawled out of the slime."

He had looked at Bessie Levy, looked at her sitting there

holding the tiller of her boat, face lifted to the sun and salt spray. He looked at her and saw an old woman unafraid of the seething, sodden mysteries of the natural world.

He knew he could never be like her. He could face a psychopath waving a knife. But he could live a hundred years and still would always jump when he heard an animal cry in the dark.

Louis paused at a fork in the trail. He could just make out the small sign that read CEMETERY TRAIL. It seemed to go back inland. He could see the sky reddening above the tops of the trees. He decided to take the other path.

He walked more slowly now since the path was just a streak in the quickening dusk. The path narrowed into heavy brush and he had to push his way through. He brushed against something and jerked back, feeling a sharp sting.

"Shit," he muttered, grabbing his arm.

He had been pricked by something, and a small bubble of blood was already visible. He looked at the short palm he had brushed against. It had five-inch thorns on the fronds. He clamped a hand over his bleeding wrist and moved on.

He stopped abruptly. Something white loomed before him. *Jesus . . . bones?*

They looked like giant animal bones sticking up from the sand. He crept forward and let out a breath.

Trees . . . just dead trees. They looked like the sea grape trees in front of his cottage, but these were dead and bleached pure white, twisted and bent low by the wind and salt tides.

He stopped. The huge silence rushed in, and he heard water—the soft hiss of the tide on the beach. He was near the gulf. Then he saw something about a hundred yards ahead, beyond the naked white trees—a faint light, moving slightly.

A lantern. It had to be Frank.

Louis started across the grove of dead trees, picking his way carefully over the exposed roots, crouching to move beneath the giant rib cages the trees formed over him. Finally, he made it to the other side. He stood, dripping with sweat, his heart hammering. The lantern light had disappeared.

He felt a jab in the back and froze.

"Don't move," a voice said. "Put up your hands."

Louis drew in a breath. "Frank? Frank Woods?"

"What are you doing here?"

When Louis didn't answer, Frank jabbed him harder in the small of the back.

"Easy, man, put the rifle down," Louis said.

Frank was silent but he hadn't moved the barrel.

"I just want to talk, Frank, that's all."

It was quiet for a second.

"You're bleeding," Frank said.

Louis felt the gun barrel leave his back.

"Turn around," Frank said.

Louis turned slowly, lowering his hands. Frank was standing there in the deep shadows. In his hand was a stick. Louis let out a breath. He could feel his own gun on his waist and debated pulling it, but decided against it.

"How'd you know I was here?" Frank demanded. Then he shook his head. "Never mind, that's not important. Why are you following me?"

"Look, Woods—"

"You've been following me for days now. I want to know why. Who sent you?"

Louis couldn't make out Frank's face but he could hear the tension in his voice. The man was afraid of something.

"You got a camp somewhere?" Louis asked.

"Yeah, over on the beach."

"Let's go and talk."

Frank hesitated, then started away. Louis let him lead the way. They emerged from the brush onto a wide beach and Louis saw the lantern again. And then a small tent, sitting between two gnarled sculptures of dead mangrove trees.

"Wait here," Frank said at the tent. He dipped inside and emerged with a first-aid kit.

"You better clean that up," he said.

Louis had been holding his arm and now, when he let go, he was shocked to see a knot forming on his wrist.

"What happened to you?" Frank asked.

"A palm tree with thorns the size of stilettos," Louis said.

Frank made a wry face. "Probably a date palm. If any of it's still in your skin, it can get septic. It happened to me once."

He held out the kit. Louis took it and sat down on a piece of driftwood near the Coleman lantern. As Frank bent down to turn it up, Louis got his first good look at him. He was wearing old jeans and a worn denim shirt with an old fishing hat covering his hair. In the white glow of the Coleman lantern, Frank's eyes were underscored with bruises of exhaustion. He looked nothing like the benign librarian of a few weeks ago. Now he looked like a haunted—or hunted—man.

Frank moved away and Louis concentrated on the puncture on his arm. It had swelled up to the size of an egg and he could feel his wrist stiffening. Probing at the wound, he couldn't see any remnant of the thorn.

"Pour on some hydrogen peroxide," Frank said.

Louis found the small plastic bottle and poured it over his arm.

"Is it bubbling?"

"Yeah."

"You'll live then."

Frank came back toward the light, pulling off his fishing hat, letting loose a bush of gray hair, again far different from the trimmed look Louis had seen in the library. Frank crouched by the fire and added some new branches from the small pile nearby. Louis noticed the fire had been made in a pit scooped out of the sand and lined with shells.

"You've been watching me," Frank said. "Why?"

Louis looked up at Frank but said nothing.

"You are a private investigator, Mr. Kincaid," Frank said. "I knew that when you came in to get your library card. People hire private investigators to do things. Why did my family hire you?"

"Your daughter is worried about you," Louis said as he twisted the cap back on the bottle.

Frank's expression stiffened. "Diane hired you?"

Louis nodded.

Frank stood up and took a few steps toward the tent, then stared out at the gulf. The sun was gone, leaving only a bruise of purple on the horizon. Louis glanced around the campsite for Frank's rifle but didn't see it. He pressed his elbow against his Glock.

"She's concerned about you," Louis said.

"She worries too much."

"She's your daughter."

Frank glanced back at him, then looked back out at the water.

Louis heard a whine in his ear and then the sting of a mosquito at his neck. There wasn't a hint of a breeze coming off the gulf tonight, nothing to keep the mosquitoes from swarming out from the nearby mangroves. Louis turned his arm toward the lantern to get a look at his watch but could barely flex his wrist now. Almost seven. The last ferry had left. No way to get off this damn island tonight.

"Daughters," Frank said softly.

Louis looked up at Frank's back.

"Most men want sons. You know, someone who looks like them, acts like them. They want sons so they can see themselves young again and fool themselves into thinking they aren't going to die."

Frank turned but didn't look at Louis. "Daughters are different. They aren't you. They are what you could have maybe been."

He met Louis's eyes. "You got kids?"

Louis shook his head slowly.

"There's something about a daughter that makes a man do strange things," Frank said. He looked away again.

"I need to ask you some questions," Louis said.

"Does my daughter think I'm getting senile?"

"No."

"Then why did she hire you?"

"She found some newspaper clippings in your desk drawer. One is about the unidentified body found on Monkey Island last week and the other is about a missing girl, from 1953."

Louis could see a tension in Frank's jaw and a vein moving in his neck. He couldn't tell if Frank was upset about this revelation or just about the fact that his daughter had gone through his desk.

Frank reached to his pocket and Louis tensed. But Frank just withdrew a pack of cigarettes and some matches. He cupped a match to light the cigarette, took a long slow drag, and let it out in a tired sigh.

"I thought I recognized the dead woman, that's all," he said. "I was wrong. I forgot to throw it away."

"What about Emma Fielding, the missing woman from 1953? Why did you keep that article?"

"I knew her in high school."

"Do you know what happened to her?"

"No."

"Where was high school?"

"Sarasota."

Louis heard a noise in the brush and jumped. Frank saw him and smiled. "Don't worry, it's probably just a snake. Or maybe a boar. There's a bunch of them running around wild on this island."

Louis rubbed his burning arm, his eyes still on the brush.

"That can last for days," Frank said, nodding toward the puncture.

"There's one more thing, Woods," Louis said. "There's a ring at your house. A white coral ring, just like the one the dead woman was wearing."

Frank's eyes narrowed as he drew hard on the cigarette.

"Talk to me, Woods."

Frank's face grew slack as he took the cigarette out of his mouth. "My daughter thinks I killed those women, doesn't she?"

Louis drew out his Glock with his stiff right hand, shifting it to his left. He held it sideways, ready but relaxed.

"Yes, she does. She wants you to come with me to the police. That's why she hired me. She was afraid you would panic if you were just confronted."

Frank looked over at him and saw the gun. "You don't have the authority to arrest me, Mr. Kincaid."

"I don't want you to try anything stupid, either."

"I'm not a stupid man."

"I know that."

"I'm not a killing man, either."

"Then we can just go talk to the police and you can tell them what you know about the rings."

"I can't do that. You'll have to shoot me or drag me. And that won't be easy with that arm of yours. Besides, neither one of us is going anywhere tonight."

Frank knelt and prodded the fire. The fire spat out a stream of sparks. Frank's eyes followed them up into the black sky.

"When's the first ferry back?" Louis asked.

"Eight."

"We're going to be on it."

Frank's eyes went to the Glock, then up to Louis's face.

"All right," he said softly. "I'll do it for Diane's sake." He nodded toward the gun. "You can put that away. You won't need it."

Louis didn't move. It was quiet except for the snap of the fire and the waves on the beach.

"The mosquitoes are getting bad," Frank said. "I'm getting in the tent."

He rose slowly. "I'm not supposed to have a fire out here so if you keep it going, keep it low. And if you smoke, be careful with matches."

Frank took one last drag from his cigarette; then taking it from his lips, he calmly used his forefinger and thumb to snub out the glowing tip. He put the butt in his pocket.

"I'm sorry. It's a one-man tent," he said.

"I'll be fine right here," Louis said.

Frank hesitated, then nodded slowly. "I've got a blanket. I'll get it. And some Deets for the mosquitoes. You're going to need it."

He turned and crawled into his tent. Louis waited, listening to him rummaging through something. His gaze drifted to the fire, which was quickly dwindling. He rubbed his sore wrist, thinking again of what Diane had said about her father, that he had never spent a night outdoors in his life. But it was obvious Frank Woods was a man who was not only comfortable outdoors but knew something about it.

The mosquitoes were a steady whine in his ears. It took him a moment to realize it was the only sound he could hear.

He stood and walked to the tent. "Woods?"

No answer. Not a sound. "Frank?"

Louis flipped back the flap of the tent and peered inside. It was empty.

Louis scrambled inside and pressed a hand against the back of the tent. It gave way, sliced open down the middle of the nylon. Louis held it open and stared into the thick, black brush.

Frank Woods was gone.

Louis withdrew and stood up quickly, straining to see in the darkness. The fire was about gone. There was nothing left but the white-hot glow of the lantern.

Louis snatched up the lantern and trudged up to the mangroves, whirling it around toward the black trees. The mangroves came alive, their roots glowing eerily bright against the deep shadows.

"Goddamn it," he said.

There was no way he was going into that brush. There was

no way he was going anywhere until morning. He slowly backed up, until he was near the dying fire. His eyes swept over the dark brush. Every nerve in his body felt as if it were on fire. He turned up the lantern and sat down.

"Goddamn it to hell," he whispered.

# CHAPTER 14

It was only ten A.M. but Louis could feel the damp heat blanket his body as soon as he stepped out of the Mustang's air-conditioning. His own smell rose up to him, sweat from the night spent in the tent on Cayo Costa.

The longest night in his life. A night spent crouched in the tent, slapping at mosquitoes and jumping every time something moved outside. He was back at the dock by seven-thirty A.M. waiting for the ferry—and Frank Woods—to show up. But there was no sign of Frank and Louis had no choice but to board and go back without him.

Back at Sutter's Marina, he called the library to see if Woods had come to work. The woman who answered said he was scheduled to work but had not shown up yet. Louis had headed right over to Fort Myers. He wanted to get to Horton and get this over with.

As he started across the street to the station, Louis rubbed a hand over his stubbled jaw. Shit, it was probably just the stink of fear he was smelling. How the hell was he going to tell Horton he had let Frank Woods get away?

Louis slowed his pace near the entrance. There was a woman newscaster doing a live remote next to a WINK van, her blond hair-helmet glowing in the bright sun. Louis recognized her from the evening news and tried to place the name. Heather something . . .

Was there something new on the Monkey Island Jane Doe? Louis stopped close enough to eavesdrop.

"The police have identified the victim as Shelly Marie Umber, age twenty. The identification came after a family member called the police late last night and was confirmed this morning. Miss Umber is reportedly from Fort Lauderdale . . ."

Louis moved on, walking a wide circle around the reporter. He heard her sign off. Heather Fox. That was it.

"Mr. Kincaid? Louis Kincaid?"

He stopped, drawing in a breath. He heard footsteps behind him and turned just as she came up to him. He glanced at the camera. The red recording light was off.

"Are you involved in this case?" Heather Fox asked.

"No."

She swept back her hair with red-nailed fingers. "Then why are you here?"

"Donuts," Louis said.

She laughed, and he walked away.

Inside the door, he pulled off his sunglasses. The airconditioning felt good against his face and he took a second to let it soak in. He waved to the female uniform behind the glass and mouthed Horton's name. She smiled and buzzed him in.

Horton's door was open and he was standing behind his desk reading something. He looked up when Louis approached.

"Hey, Kincaid, good timing. Come on in. We ID'd the Jane Doe."

"I heard outside," Louis said. "How'd it happen?"

"Mel found a BOLO from Fort Lauderdale police. That's where she's from. The parents came in last night. Mel's questioning them right now."

Horton's eyes drifted to the door and Louis instinctively

knew the chief had been the one who had broken the news to the parents. Horton hadn't foisted the job off on some Fort Lauderdale cop. He had made the call himself.

"How'd they take it?" Louis asked.

Horton shook his head slowly. "I didn't really know until I saw them this morning. The mother's in shock, I guess. The father—" Horton let out a breath. "He started screaming at me about the cops and the judges letting animals run loose on the streets, that sort of shit." Horton sat down in his chair behind the desk. "Man, I want this guy caught, whoever it is."

Louis rubbed a hand over his face. "Chief, there's something—"

Landeta came in, moving right to Horton's desk. He didn't see Louis hanging back by the door.

"No way this girl was a runaway," Landeta said.

"How do you know?" Louis asked.

Mel spun to face Louis. He gave him a look of contempt and turned back to the chief.

"The parents spend the winter in Lauderdale, then go to their home in North Carolina for the summer," Landeta said. "They left Lauderdale on April second and the daughter stayed behind in the condo. She was a student at Nova University and was supposed to fly back north when she finished the spring semester."

"When did they last talk to her?" Horton said.

"A couple of weeks later," Landeta said. "The father took off to France on business in early May, and the mother joined him there a week later. They were going to be in Europe all summer on vacation. The mother said she talked to the daughter just before she left. The mother called a couple of times while they were in Europe but always got the answering machine. Said she didn't think it was strange."

"That explains why no one came forward," Horton said.

Mel nodded. "The mother finally got worried enough to call the condo and have somebody go up and check. Then they called the cops, who found out the girl hadn't been to classes in four weeks. They found her car in the campus lot. It was unlocked and there was some blood inside. That's when the BOLO went out."

"Did the parents know she was pregnant?" Horton asked.

Landeta shook his head. "The mother was pretty shocked when I told them. She told me the daughter had a fiancé up in North Carolina, a med student named Jeremy Maynard."

"Any chance this Maynard guy is the father?" Louis asked.

Landeta didn't even look back. "Maynard said the last time he saw Shelly Umber was at Christmas. I called up to Duke and talked to some doctor who said Maynard is doing his residency at the university hospital there. It keeps him too busy to take a shit let alone fly down to Lauderdale and shoot his girlfriend."

"How did he take it?" Louis asked.

Landeta turned. "Who?"

"Her boyfriend."

Landeta stared at him for a moment. "How do you think?"

"Hey, look, man—" Louis began.

Horton sat up in his chair. "Save it. What else, Mel?"

"The parents say she was a great kid, good student, homecoming queen, the whole shot. She was also an athlete who made all-state lacrosse team in high school and liked to ski and hike. All she wanted to do was finish college, become a pediatrician, marry Dr. Jeremy, and climb Mt. Everest someday."

"Family have any connections here?" Horton asked.

"No," Landeta said. "They've never set foot in Fort Myers before and I get the feeling they never want to come back."

"So we're looking at an abduction," Horton said. "We'd better get with Lauderdale and see if there's anything similar over there."

Louis took a step forward, but Landeta spoke first.

"The father said something strange," he said. "They said when they were taken in to ID the daughter, they weren't sure it was her at first."

"How come?" Horton asked.

"They said she had changed, said she was a lot thinner. And the mother was upset about the girl's hair being cut off. She said that her daughter had long hair, like down-to-the-waist long, and never wanted to get it cut. Always wore it in a braid."

"I remember her hair," Louis said. "I thought it looked weird, like someone had tried to cut it off with a knife or something."

Landeta back glanced at Louis. "Why didn't you say something at the scene?"

"It didn't seem important then," Louis said. "But this is a girl from a family with money, a girl who cared about her appearance and was probably strong enough to put up a fight. Whoever abducted her might have cut off her hair to humiliate her as a control thing."

"And kept her outside and starved her . . ." Horton said. His voice trailed off as images filled the silence.

Louis shook his head. He had to get this over with.

"Chief, can I say something?"

They both looked at Louis.

"I think I have a suspect."

Landeta stared at him through the yellow glasses. Louis couldn't tell if Landeta was annoyed or impressed.

"You been doing a little investigating on your own?" Horton asked.

"Sort of. Well, yeah. A woman came to me a day or two after the body was found and asked me to follow her father. She thought maybe he was involved."

Horton and Landeta exchanged glances but said nothing.

"The father had the *New-Press* article on Jane Doe. He also had an old article on another missing woman from 1953." Louis took a breath. "His name is Frank Woods. He works as a librarian here in town."

"A librarian?" Landeta said.

"So you *investigated* this man?" Horton asked, ignoring Landeta.

"I followed him. That's all I was asked to do."

"All you were *paid* to do, you mean," Landeta said.

Louis shot Landeta a look. "He did nothing," Louis said. "He's as ordinary as a Ritz cracker. I was about to tell the daughter I couldn't do any more when she dropped the ring on me."

Landeta took a step toward Louis. "Ring? A ring like the one we found on Shelly Umber?"

"Yeah. Just like it."

"You have this ring?" Horton asked.

Louis shook his head. "The daughter has it."

"When did she show it to you?" Landeta asked.

"Yesterday."

Horton stood up, his face flushed. *"Yesterday?"*

Louis tightened. He started to say something, make an excuse, but there was none. He had waited too long. He had been sucked into believing Frank Woods was harmless. Even believing he was suicidal. He'd been wrong to wait.

Landeta's face was suddenly in his, the yellow glasses an inch from his own eyes.

"You got that kind of lead in a fucking homicide and you sit on it? Jesus Christ—"

Louis braced himself.

"Mel, back off," Horton said. When Landeta didn't move, Horton pulled at his arm.

"Stupid sonofabitch," Landeta mumbled as he moved away.

Louis stared at the window behind Horton, his chest tight.

Horton slid a legal pad at Louis. "Okay, give me names, addresses, and anything else you can think of, you got that?"

Louis grabbed a pen and starting writing.

"Where is this Woods guy now?" Horton asked.

Louis drew in a deep breath before he looked up at Horton. "I don't know."

"You don't know?" Landeta asked from behind Louis. *"You don't know?"*

Louis slid the pad to Horton. "I think he's gone under. I'll let you know if he tries to contact me."

Horton rubbed his face, his eyes on Mel Landeta. Louis waited, knowing that Horton wanted to chew his head off but knowing that he wouldn't. Not in front of Landeta, at least.

"Mel, go see the PIO."

"What for?"

"To set up a press conference. I want to use the media to help us find this guy. And tell her to make it clear that Frank Woods is only a 'person of interest' at this point."

"Chief, what about—"

Horton held up a hand. "I'll take care of it."

Landeta gave Louis a final look of disgust and left. The office was quiet and it was a moment before Louis could look up at Horton.

"Okay, what the hell is going on here?" Horton asked.

"I told you, Al. I told you everything I know."

"Goddamn it, you're smarter than this, Louis."

"I know that."

Horton started to say something, then stopped. He ran a hand over his hair and waved at the chair. "Sit down."

Louis took the chair across from Horton. Horton went back behind his desk and sank into his chair.

"After Mr. Umber was done chewing my ass off, he started crying," Horton said. "I mean, like bawling, and the mother was just sitting there like a zombie, not even looking at him. Then suddenly she talks, like for the first time since they came in."

Horton shook his head. "She looks up at me and asks if I know who killed her daughter. I didn't have an answer for her." Horton looked at Louis. "You wanna go out there and try?"

Louis was silent.

Horton picked up a folder, pursed his lips, then dropped it.

"Look, I don't know what we're dealing with here," he said, his eyes still on the folder. He poked at it, like he didn't want to touch it.

"This guy, whoever he is, is a real sadist. I don't know if that old article about the other missing woman means anything. All I know is I have a real body over there in the morgue and real parents here in my station wanting to know who killed their kid."

"Al, you know as well as I do that if he took one, there could be others, and this thing from 1953 could be part of it," Louis said.

Horton was silent. "God, I don't want to go through this again," he murmured finally.

Neither did Louis. He had only dealt with one serial killer but he had learned that the wake they left behind was more than just a matter of body counts. It was the terror of having to descend into the blackest pit of human nature and hope you could climb back out when it was over.

Horton was staring at the file on his desk. He reached out and pushed it across the desk with his index finger.

"I'm going to do you a favor," he said, looking up at Louis. "I'm going to let you redeem yourself."

Louis could read the tag on the file. It said 87-23445 UMBER, S.

"I want you to work with Landeta on this," Horton said.

Louis sat back. "Shit, Al—"

"I've got no men free I can put on this case right now. You've got experience with this kind of case and you've got a relationship with this guy's daughter. If he makes contact, it'll be with her, right?"

Louis was silent, his eyes on the file. He could hear the phone ringing outside, hear the sharp laugh of two men out in the hall somewhere.

"I don't like the guy, Al," he said.

"I'm not asking you to. I'm asking you to help him find out who killed this girl."

"He knows I'm going to be working this?"

"Yeah, he was as excited about it as you."

Horton leaned forward and pushed the file across the desk. Louis didn't touch it.

Horton sat back in his chair, his tired brown eyes on Louis's face.

"Look, I already told Mel he had no choice in this. But you do," he said. "So you wanna play cop again or not?"

Louis hesitated.

"I'm not hiring you officially," Horton said. "I'm not going to pay you. But I want you to work with Mel on this." He paused, his eyes steady on Louis's. "Do you understand what I am saying?"

Louis understood exactly. Without a badge he had fewer legal restraints. He could go anywhere, talk to anyone, and get what he needed by whatever means it took. He could do everything Mel Landeta could not.

Louis picked up the Umber file. "Okay, now what?" he asked.

Horton rose and straightened his tie. "I'm going to talk to Mr. and Mrs. Umber again. And you're gonna go make nice with Mel."

# CHAPTER 15

Louis had been the one to suggest they go over to O'Sullivan's for a drink. Landeta had just stared at him, then started off in the direction of the bar. They had said nothing to each other on the short walk over. Inside, Landeta had taken a table near the door, slipping into the chair nearest the window. Louis was forced to sit facing into the glare, squinting into the sun at Landeta's backlit face. He was sure Landeta had done it on purpose, a power-trip thing, and it pissed him off.

"You're in the glare. You mind moving your chair?" Louis asked.

"In fact I do," Landeta said. He reached into his breast pocket for a handkerchief. He slowly and carefully began to clean the yellow aviator glasses.

Louis sat back as the waitress brought their drinks, a beer for Louis and a Diet Coke with lemon for Landeta. Shelly Umber's case file lay on the table between them.

Louis picked up his beer and took a quick drink. He spotted a couple of cops he knew sitting at the bar. They were staring at him and Landeta, whispering.

"I don't like fuckups, Kincaid," Landeta said quietly.

"I don't like assholes."

"*I* didn't lose a suspect."

"I haven't lost him."

"Do you know where he is?"

"No."

"Then you've lost him."

"Temporarily."

Landeta rubbed the bridge of his nose and slowly put his glasses on. "How in the hell did you convince the chief to let you in on this?"

Louis was silent. Part of the reason was that Horton was worried that all the talk about Landeta was right, that the guy was, in fact, a burnout who needed help on a high-profile case.

"Frank Woods needs to be brought in alive and the chief thinks he'll come with me," Louis said. "His daughter is afraid he'll cash it in if he's surrounded and pressured."

"Would save us a lot of paperwork, I say."

Louis took another drink of beer. Man, what was with this guy anyway? He was tempted to just get up and leave. But he owed it to Horton to try. And to himself, for that matter. How many chances was he going to get to work a real case?

"I don't want Frank Woods dead," Louis said.

"Why not?"

"I want to know."

"Know what?"

"The answer to the mystery."

Landeta picked the lemon off the rim of his glass and squeezed the juice into the Diet Coke. "Woods probably killed both those women because he's a sociopath with a twisted gene or two. No mystery there."

Louis didn't say what he was thinking, that the need to know *why* was what made any cop good. But then, Landeta didn't seem like the type who had read the Hardy Boys when he was a kid. The man probably didn't have an imaginative bone in his body.

Landeta was turning the lemon over in his long fingers, staring at it intently. He pushed the rind with his thumbs, exposing the pulp. He began to eat it. Louis drummed his fingers lightly against the beer glass, waiting. But it was clear Landeta wasn't going to say a thing.

"Al says you're the best detective he ever worked with," Louis said finally.

Landeta went on slowly eating the lemon.

"You need a good imagination to be a detective," Louis said.

"Who says?"

Louis let out a sigh. "Forget it, man."

Landeta tossed the rind down. "I suppose you thought you were Detective Rocky King or something when you were a kid."

"Who?"

Landeta waved a hand. "Never mind."

"Actually, I read books."

"You musta been a lonely kid."

"I read true crime," Louis said. "I always tried to find the holes in the case or in the investigation. When I finally got good at it, I knew what I wanted to do."

Landeta finished his Diet Coke in two long gulps and set the glass down hard. "Well, enjoy it while you can, Kincaid. Not a lot of opportunities in this life to do what you want to do."

"You make your own opportunities," Louis said.

"And fate takes them away."

Landeta rose suddenly and went to the bar. Louis watched him, trying to remember what Horton had told him about Landeta. Something about an accident and a lawsuit.

Landeta slid back into the booth with a fresh pack of cigarettes. He lit one quickly, without asking Louis if he cared.

"I heard you had a bad break," Louis said.

Landeta tapped the cigarette in the ashtray. "Yeah, I had a bad break."

"Everyone has them."

"Man, you don't *know* what a bad break is," Landeta said. "You're twenty-seven fucking years old with a college degree, and you live in a beachfront cottage on a goddamn island paradise. You're respected and you're healthy and you can do anything you want. Don't tell me about bad breaks, Rocky."

Louis sat back, as if he'd been hit. How in the hell had Landeta found out that much about him? Landeta took a hard draw on his cigarette, looking away.

*Make nice . . .*

"So talk," Landeta said, blowing a plume of smoke in Louis's direction.

"You talk."

Landeta chuckled and shook his head slowly. "How old are you?"

"You know damn well how old I am. Let's stick to the case," Louis said.

More silence.

"So what did the parents say about the ring?" Louis asked.

"They said they had never seen it before. It was not something she'd own. She was into silver. And Dr. Jeremy didn't give it to her either."

"Who saw her last?" Louis asked.

"According to the original missing person's report, Shelly went to a night class May second. That's what her professor told the Lauderdale cops. That was the last time we can confirm anyone seeing her alive."

"So this guy drove 130 miles across the state to abduct her, then drove back across Alligator Alley to kill and dump her?" Louis shook his head. "Not your classic profile."

Landeta's hand paused over the ashtray. "You know about profiling?"

Louis nodded as he sipped the beer. "I worked with a Miami FBI agent once who was into it. She taught me a lot."

"So tell me about this Woods guy," Landeta said.

"He's not your classic suspect," Louis said. "Older, intelligent, has a family, a steady job where he's respected. He's just not your standard loser."

"Neither was Ted Bundy."

"Woods has a whole library in his house."

"What kind of books?"

"Academic shit on language origins, Roman history . . ."

Landeta took a drag on the cigarette. "The guy do anything strange while you were following him?"

Louis shook his head.

"What about the daughter? Why would she have you tailing her old man?"

"I told you. She found the articles and the ring." But Louis knew that was not what Landeta meant. He was wondering what kind of daughter would suspect her own father. He had been wondering the same thing since the start of all this.

"You can do better than that," Landeta said.

Louis stared at him. "What?"

"I said you can do better than that. Come on, Rocky boy." Landeta smiled and started humming The Beatles' "Rocky Raccoon."

Louis raised his beer, finished it in one gulp, and slammed it down.

"Fuck this, man," he muttered, rising.

"You leaving?" Landeta asked.

Louis didn't answer. He pulled out his wallet. He only had a twenty. But he'd be damned if he was going to leave without paying for his beer. He went up to the bar and asked for change.

"Hey, hon, bring me a Jack Daniels on the rocks."

Louis glanced back at Landeta. He was waving to the waitress. He saw Louis staring at him.

"Thought you were leaving, Rocky," he called out. "Well, go on, get out of here. Just go."

The bartender set a stack of bills on the bar in front of Louis. The other cops were staring at Landeta and Louis.

*Go. Just go.*

*Don't make me part of this. I want to finish school. I want a degree. I want to be a cop. I don't want a kid, Kyla.*

*Go . . . just go, Louis.*

Louis looked back at Landeta. He was just sitting there, looking off into space. Then, in one sudden liquid movement of his long hand, Landeta raised the shot to his lips and sucked it down.

*Oh, man . . .*

Louis hesitated, hand on the glass door.

*No. I don't need to be dragged into his shit.*

He pushed open the door and went out into the sun.

# CHAPTER 16

Louis waited until eight P.M. before hitting the library. It was a Saturday and he figured the place would be fairly empty an hour before closing, giving him more privacy to search through Frank's work area.

Fort Myers uniforms had already been through the library earlier; Horton had dispatched his men there and to Frank's home but nothing had been found.

Including Diane Woods herself, Horton told him. She wasn't home and her car was gone. Horton said he was putting a cruiser out front to watch for her.

Louis paused just inside the library door. He knew this was a long shot. If there was anything worth confiscating here, Horton's men already had it.

Louis spotted a girl at the front desk. Still, sometimes a pointed but gentle probing of coworkers could get results.

The girl was checking out books for a teenage boy with a backpack. Louis walked up, standing a few feet away while she finished.

The girl's small brown eyes drifted to Louis's face. She was plump, maybe eighteen, her pretty round face set off with glossy brown hair. She was chewing gum, working it hard.

"Can I help you?" she asked. Her voice was small and childlike.

Louis gave her a smile. "I'm a private investigator working with the Fort Myers police." He was hoping she wasn't smart enough to ask for a badge or something. Horton had told him he wasn't even going to get a police ID.

"I don't know where Mr. Woods is," she whispered, glancing around, as if she were expecting Frank to appear out of the shelves.

"I know you don't, but I was hoping you could tell me about him. That might help us find him."

"Mr. Woods is my boss." She cocked her head, waiting.

"We just need to talk to him."

"Yeah, I know. It was on the news tonight." She made an odd face, as if she smelled something burning. "Did Mr. Woods kill that girl they found?"

"We don't know anything yet, Miss—" Louis tried a smile. "What's your name?"

"Holly. Holly Russell. Mr. Woods was the one who hired me."

"Will you talk to me about him?"

"I don't know. Is he gonna be like arrested or something?"

"I don't know. But I don't think it will hurt for you to talk to me."

She shrugged and snapped her gum. "Okay."

"So what can you tell me about him?"

"Well, he was always looking at my boobs."

Louis stared at her. "Why would you tell me that?"

She shrugged again. "Isn't he, you know, like a pervert or something?"

"Not exactly. Did you ever notice Mr. Woods doing anything strange while he worked here?"

"You mean besides looking at my boobs?"

"Yes."

She hesitated thoughtfully. "He read the newspapers a lot. I mean, like every day, every paper that came in here, page by page."

"Anything else? Phone calls that seemed odd. Visitors?"

She shook her head, like she was trying hard to remember.

"Did he seem . . ." Louis couldn't find the word. If Frank was a guilty man, he would have lived like he was expecting someone to come around the corner any minute. "Did he seem watchful?"

"What do you mean?"

"You know, like if someone came in the library, did he keep an eye on them?"

"Like if they were going to steal a book?"

Louis shook his head.

"Wait a minute," the girl said. "I remember he was nervous like once."

"When?"

"It was this charity thing we had, you know, Friends of the Library," she said. "Mr. Woods came with his daughter and he didn't seem . . . you know, very comfortable like."

"What about his daughter?" Louis asked. "How did she seem to you?"

The girl giggled. "Snotty. Like she had a stick up her butt. And like she didn't want to be there, you know, like at Christmas when you gotta be with all your creepy relatives and you don't want to be?"

Louis knew there was nothing else the girl could help him with. "Why don't you show me his office?" he said.

"No prob."

Holly got another girl to watch the front desk and she led Louis to the back. The sign on the closed door said F. WOODS, RESEARCH.

"Mr. Woods is the head of our research department here," Holly said, opening the door.

Louis glanced around. Standard-issue file cabinets and bookcases, a plain metal desk. The top of it was bare except for some cords, strewn like small snakes and attached to nothing.

"They took his computer," Holly said. "I told them the only thing on it was library business, databases and stuff, you know, but they didn't listen."

"What else did they take?"

"His personnel file and some stuff from the drawers."

Louis turned and gave Holly a smile. "You have been very helpful. May I look around in here?"

She smiled back, then nodded. "Sure. But we close at nine."

When she left, Louis pulled on a pair of latex gloves and sat down in the rolling chair. He started on the drawers, but there was nothing important, just routine papers, and in the bottom drawer, a messy assortment of personal items, the kind of stuff everyone kept at work: Wrigley's Spearmint gum, a bottle of Tylenol, a clean Tupperware container, a copy of Virgil's *Aeneid,* a beard trimmer.

He pushed the chair over to the file cabinet and opened the bottom drawer. The files in front appeared to be library business files, but Louis dug to the back, hoping something had fallen between and been overlooked.

Nothing.

He stood and scanned the small office. If Frank had hidden anything here, he certainly would not have put it in a drawer or cabinet. He would put it somewhere that felt safe to him.

He heard a tap on the door and turned. Holly poked her head in. "I'm sorry, but we're, like, closing now. . . ."

Louis sighed and looked around the office again. "Holly, does anything look odd to you in here?"

Her eyes widened. "Odd?"

"Weird," Louis corrected. "Like is there anything missing—"

"I told you, they took all—"

"I know that. But look around. Try hard."

Holly bit her lip, looking around. Suddenly her eyes stopped on a shelf of books. She pointed. "Well, there's a book missing."

Louis looked. It was a shelf of reference books, dictionaries, almanacs, atlases, the Columbia Encyclopedia. And there was one gap.

Something clicked. The book in the desk drawer. It was the only book in this office that wasn't for work purposes. He went to the desk and pulled open the drawer, taking out the copy of Virgil's *Aeneid*.

He began to flip through the pages. Finally, he just turned it upside down and shook it. Four white index cards fluttered to the floor.

He heard Holly let out a gasp. Louis quickly gathered up the index cards before she could see them.

"Holly, would you mind waiting outside, please?" he asked, turning.

She nodded quickly and left, but hovered outside the door, watching through the glass. Louis turned over the first card.

It was a small photograph of a young woman, cut out of yellowed newsprint and carefully pasted to the index card. Underneath it was printed: ANGELA. 1984.

The three others were the same. Other newsprint photographs, other girls' names, all written in Frank Woods's small, cramped handwriting. Louis sat down at Frank's desk and slowly arranged the cards in order of their dates.

The first was a young woman about sixteen, straight blond hair, wearing a dark sweater. Underneath, Frank had printed CINDY, 1964.

The next looked older, maybe eighteen. She was plump with long curly hair, wearing a white blouse and a pearl necklace. The writing underneath said PAULA, 1965.

Next was MARY, 1973, cute in an innocent sort of way with mousey brown hair, full lips, and large dreamy eyes.

The last was ANGELA, 1984. Wavy dark hair, slightly exotic looking, maybe Hispanic.

Louis sat back in the chair, staring at the women.

*Jesus Christ.* What was this?

All the photographs were on newsprint, that much was clear. Had they been cut out of newspapers, like the photos of Emma Fielding and Shelly Umber? And like them, had they gone missing, too? Was it possible this quiet old widower had been a serial killer for decades? And were there more they had yet to find?

"It's almost nine."

He looked up. Holly was standing at the door, but her eyes were on the index cards.

"What are those?" Holly asked, biting her lip.

"Nothing important." He gave Holly a smile and stood up. "Can I make some copies?"

Holly returned his smile and tilted her head. "Sure, follow me."

Louis followed her out to the main part of the library. Holly hovered nearby while Louis copied the cards. When he asked her for an envelope, she produced a manila envelope from under her desk and gave him a smile.

Louis slipped the cards in. "Thank you for your help, Miss Russell."

"So is Mr. Woods coming back?" she asked, twirling a strand of her long dark hair.

Louis hesitated. "Do you want him to?"

The girl's smile faded and the twirling stopped. "Well, I mean, I don't *really* think he killed anybody but . . ."

Louis waited.

Holly Russell shrugged. "But he was kinda, I don't know . . . weird like. I mean, you know?"

Louis nodded. "Yeah, I know."

# CHAPTER 17

Louis paused outside the library entrance, watching a Fort Myers police cruiser pass by.

*Damn.* Mel Landeta. He had almost forgotten that Landeta had called him earlier, asking him to come by the station after seven. He was two hours late.

He drove back to the station on the hunch that Landeta would still be there. The station seemed quiet. There were a few uniformed officers outside, talking. Louis gave them a nod as he walked in.

He took the steps two at a time, and stopped outside Landeta's office door. The door was closed, and he tapped on it lightly.

There was no answer. But the lights were on. The asshole was probably just ignoring him. Louis knocked harder.

The door swung open quickly. The bright fluorescent lights made Landeta's head gleam like a cue ball.

"You're late," Landeta said. "I have better things to do than sit here waiting for you."

"I was busy at the library, talking to one of Frank Woods's employees, a girl named Holly Russell."

"Our guys already talked to her and went through the whole place," Landeta said, turning away.

"Well, they missed these," Louis said, stepping in and holding out the envelope.

"What's that?"

"More missing girls, I think. From the sixties, seventies, and eighties. Frank cut their pictures out of newspapers and taped them to index cards."

Landeta faced him slowly. "How many?"

"Four."

Landeta held out his hand and Louis slapped the manila envelope into his open palm. Landeta dumped the cards on the desk. He picked up the one labeled CINDY, 1964. He set it back down with the rest.

"Where'd you find these?" he asked.

"In a copy of Virgil's *Aeneid*."

Landeta glanced up at him, then back at the cards. "So with the first clipping, the one of . . ."

"Emma Fielding," Louis said. "From 1953."

"That makes five girls in four decades," Landeta said.

"Right. Shelly Umber makes six."

Landeta began to carefully stack the index cards together.

"So did you get anything out of the girl you spoke to at the library? What was her name? Polly?"

"Holly," Louis said. "Yeah, she said Frank Woods was weird."

"Weird? Come on, you can do better than that."

"That's all she said."

Landeta turned away, going behind his desk. He opened a drawer and pulled out a small plastic evidence bag and put the index cards in. He sealed it with orange tape and then hesitated, looking up at Louis.

"I guess you should initial and date it," he said.

Louis stepped forward, snatched a pen out of the holder on Landeta's desk, and filled out the label.

Landeta picked up the evidence bag as soon as Louis finished.

"I'd like to follow up on those girls," Louis said.

"I'll do it."

"I'd really—"

"I said I'll do it. I make the assignments here. Not only am I point, I'm a cop. You're not."

Louis's jaw tightened. "Horton *asked* me to work this with you."

"Horton's letting you play Rocky King Detective, just like on TV, that's all."

"Playing?"

"And if you want to keep playing, you'll take the assignments I give you."

"I don't need your shit, Landeta," Louis said, turning to the door. "Work the case by yourself."

Louis started down the hall.

"Hey, Rocky!"

Louis kept walking, starting down the steps.

"Kincaid. Wait."

Louis turned. Landeta was at the top of the stairs.

"Okay," Landeta said. "You know where Naples is?"

Louis said nothing.

"That's where Emma Fielding's brother lives. Go down there and see what you can get out of him. Here's his address and a copy of the original police report." Landeta held out paper.

Louis stood there, hands on his hips. *You asshole. You know how much I want to be in on this.*

Louis walked slowly up, grabbed the paper, and went back down the stairs.

# CHAPTER 18

Louis stopped the Mustang and glanced down at the copy of the Emma Fielding police report lying open on the passenger seat. According to the 1953 report, Emma had run away from home when she was sixteen. Her stepfather, Cliff Parker, had reported her missing to the police, saying Emma might have run off to live with her older brother, Neil. But when police questioned Neil, a construction worker living in a trailer park in East Naples, he said he hadn't seen his sister in six months.

A year later, a drunken Cliff Parker drove his pickup into a canal along Alligator Alley, drowning himself and his wife. Emma was never heard from again and police shuffled her disappearance to the cold case files.

Louis rechecked the address he had for Neil Fielding. It hadn't been hard finding the guy. He was still living in the same trailer, now surviving on disability after a work accident left him a paraplegic.

Louis turned into the gate. The Lazy Lakes Mobile Home Park looked like it might have seen better days, but there were still signs that not everyone had given up—a garden gnome here, a plastic picket fence there.

At lot number 35, Louis parked and looked up at the trailer. He wondered what he was going to get from this. How much could a brother tell about a sister who had gone missing more than thirty years ago? Especially since the two apparently weren't exactly close to begin with.

Louis went up the Astroturf-covered ramp and knocked. The sound of the television, tuned to a game show, came through the door. Louis banged again on the metal door.

It jerked open. A man in a wheelchair squinted out at Louis. His eyes narrowed in fear—at the sight of a young strange black man, Louis presumed.

"Mr. Fielding? I'm here on behalf of Fort Myers police."

"What about?"

"Your sister, Emma."

Neil Fielding's pasty face screwed up in a frown. "Em? Fuck, she's been dead for thirty-four years, man."

"Missing," Louis said.

Neil shrugged. "Missing, dead. What's the difference?"

"I need to talk to you, Mr. Fielding. Can I come in?"

"Sure, why not? I'm not doing anything."

Neil wheeled away and Louis opened the door to the trailer. It was dark inside, the sun kept out by dust-coated old plastic blinds. A wall unit wheezed away over the worn plaid sofa, keeping the place plenty cold but doing nothing to disperse the smell of dirty clothes and cigarette smoke. There was an undernote of another odor that Louis couldn't place—something fusty and metallic.

"Sit down," Neil said, backing his chair in front of the TV. He picked up the remote off the TV tray and turned down the sound on the game show. "Why are cops coming round asking about Em after all this time?"

"We might have connected her disappearance to the recent death of another young woman," Louis said.

"That so?" Neil's eyes had drifted to the TV. He was a big man, or had been at some point. He still had a barrel chest beneath the stained T-shirt and his arms looked like maybe he still lifted weights. But his legs were withered like an old woman's. Louis's eyes went to his right foot. It was heavily bandaged, red, and swollen. Louis suddenly recognized the smell—decay.

Neil saw him looking at the foot. "Diabetes," he said. "Probably gonna lose it."

Louis pulled a photograph from the file. It was a closeup of the coral ring they had found on Shelly Umber. "Did your sister have a ring like this, Mr. Fielding?"

Neil took the photo, shook his head, and handed it back. "Em liked gold. Was all she ever wore."

"Were you and your sister close?"

Neil shrugged. "I was four years older. You know how that goes."

Neil's eyes drifted to the TV where Bob Barker was shoving a microphone into the face of a woman in a purple tube-top.

"She disappeared when she was sixteen. Your stepfather told the police back in 1953 that she just ran away one night."

"That's right."

"Why?"

Neil looked at Louis. "What do you mean, why?"

"Why would your sister just leave?"

"Kids run away all the time, don't they?"

"Did you?"

Neil was staring hard at Louis but finally he just shrugged and looked away. "I left, yeah."

Louis looked at Neil's 1953 police interview. "You were seventeen when you left home, right?"

"I guess."

Louis stifled a sigh. "So, why'd you leave, Mr. Fielding?"

He shrugged again. "I dunno. Didn't get along with the old man, I guess."

"How about your sister? Did she get along with him?"

Neil was silent, staring at Bob Barker. Louis was looking

at the line in the old police report about the car accident. He was thinking about a drunken Cliff Parker driving off that dark two-lane highway, plunging his pickup into the black water. But he was seeing his own mother, Lila, seeing her and hearing her and smelling her the way she was when she would come home drunk. Seeing her, and seeing his older brother, Robert, running out of the house, and seeing himself at six too little to keep up so he would hide out in the high weeds alone in the dark until the screaming stopped and he could creep back into his bed.

"Mr. Fielding," Louis said, "was your stepfather an alcoholic?"

Neil didn't answer.

"Is that why you ran away?"

Neil's eyes didn't leave the television. Louis waited.

"I got out," Neil said.

"What about Emma?"

Neil's pasty face had gone lax as he continued to stare at the game show.

"Mr. Fielding?"

"Where the hell do they *get* these cretins?"

"What about your sister, Mr. Fielding?"

"Higher, asshole!"

Louis reached over, grabbed the remote, and clicked off the TV. Neil's face swung toward him.

"Talk to me, Mr. Fielding."

"I talked to the cops thirty-four years ago." He shook his head, slowly, looking away. "I don't want to do it again. I can't."

"Why, Mr. Fielding? Emma's dead. You said so yourself. What does it matter now?"

Neil's eyes shot back to Louis's face. "Get out of my house," he said.

Louis shook his head. "Not yet. Not until we're finished."

Neil was gripping the arms of his chair. Louis watched his hands, watched the knuckles turning white.

"Mr. Fielding—"

"Look, I can't throw you out or I would. Now just leave! Please."

Louis focused on Neil's face. His pupils were jumping, like he was shaking inside, as if there were something deep inside him fighting to get out.

"Mr. Fielding, your sister is dead," Louis said.

"She shouldn't be!"

Neil drew back in his chair, looking away quickly, back at the blank television.

"Talk to me, Neil," Louis said quietly.

Neil ran a hand through his sparse, oily hair. He was shaking his head slowly, deliberately.

"Whoever killed your sister is still out there," Louis said. "We're trying to find him. You can help."

Neil closed his eyes. "He killed her," he said.

"Who, Neil?"

"My stepfather. That fucker killed Em."

Louis was silent. Finally Neil looked at him. His eyes were watery. "The fucker just wouldn't leave Em alone. He kept at her and kept at her. And I couldn't stop him. Then, one night I heard him going into her room again, heard her crying again, so I went out there in the hall and, and—" Neil drew in a breath. "He was standing there with his pants off and his dick hard."

Neil took another deep breath. "I told him to do me, to do me instead, and leave her the fuck alone. That was the only night he didn't go into her room."

Neil ran a hand roughly over his face. It was quiet except for the wheezing air conditioner.

"I left the next morning," Neil said. "It was really early. The sun wasn't even up. But Em heard me and came running out in her nightgown. She started to cry and then—"

He paused. "She started saying she wanted to come with me."

Neil stopped again, but Louis didn't prod him. Finally, Neil let out a long breath.

"I said, Em, I can't take you with me. I gotta go, Em. I gotta go. And she got so mad and screamed at me, Just go then! Just go!"

Neil looked at Louis. "So I did."

His eyes held Louis's steady for a second but then wavered and he looked back at the television.

"Fuck it," he whispered.

Louis was gripping the remote. He let go, flexing his fingers slightly. Neil was just sitting there, hands hanging limp over the arms of the wheelchair, eyes fixed on the blank television.

"Mr. Fielding, one last question," Louis said. "Did you or your sister know anyone named Frank Woods?"

Neil looked at him. "Woods? No, why?"

"Nothing," Louis said. He rose and placed the remote in Neil Fielding's lap. "Thank you for your cooperation, Mr. Fielding," he said.

Neil Fielding grabbed his pack of Marlboros and lighter off the TV tray. His hand shook slightly as he lit up a cigarette. He sucked in a quick drag and blew it out, not looking up at Louis.

Louis let himself out, pausing to take in a long, deep breath of fresh air. He heard the sound of groans and Bob Barker yelling that the woman in the purple tube-top had just lost out on winning a brand-new, all-equipped 1987 Corvette.

He got in the Mustang and started the engine. He sat there, his hands gripping the wheel. Finally, he slapped the car in gear and drove out, not looking back until the trailer had disappeared from his rearview mirror.

# CHAPTER 19

Louis went through the glass doors of the Fort Myers Police Station, his notes on Emma Fielding in his hand. He didn't have much to tell Landeta. Just that if Emma Fielding hadn't been reported missing, she probably would have run away soon anyway. The question was, had Frank Woods played any part in her disappearance? Had he been able to lure a vulnerable girl with a promise of protection and security? But if she had gone willingly, why did Frank Woods keep the newspaper clipping?

At the top of the staircase, Louis saw a uniformed officer coming out of Landeta's office, pulling the door closed behind him.

"Hey," Louis said, "tell Detective Landeta Louis Kincaid is here to see him, would you?"

The officer stuck his head back in. "Mel, Kincaid's here."

"Tell him I'll be a minute."

Louis stood at the top of the stairs, looking down at the lobby below. The minutes passed. Finally, he flipped open his notebook and read his notes on Emma, hoping maybe something would click. Nothing. Nothing but the same nagging question. Why hadn't Emma Fielding—or her body—resurfaced after thirty-four years?

He walked down the hall and took a drink of water from the fountain, then moved back to the stairwell. Landeta's door was still closed.

*Damn it. . . .*

His eyes drifted down the hall. Small white signs stuck out from doorways, labeling the offices. ANIMAL CONTROL. COMMUNITY RELATIONS. CONFERENCE ROOM. BURGLARY AND FRAUD.

At the end of the hall, there were two signs. REST ROOMS, with an arrow to the left. RECORDS, with an arrow to the right.

Louis looked back at Landeta's closed door. *Screw this.*

He walked down the hall and turned right. Four doors down, he pushed open the door to the Records Room. A plump redhead stood behind the counter. Her face was freckled and sunburned, her hair like an orange fountain on top of her head. Her uniform looked stretched to the seams. Her name tag said GEORGIA.

"Georgia," Louis said.

She smiled, her eyes almost disappearing into her face. "Can I help you?"

"I'm Louis Kincaid. I'm working with the Chief and Detective Landeta. I was hoping you could help me with something."

"Oh yeah," Georgia said. "The Chief called us a few days ago. Said to give you whatever you wanted. So, what do you need?"

"Missing persons information."

"From when?"

Louis pulled out the Xerox copies he had made of the index cards from Frank's drawer. "Sixty-four, sixty-five—"

"Oh, wow. We don't have those on computer. I'll have to get into the storage, and I really can't right now."

"I'll look."

"I don't know," she said. "Maybe I should call Detective Landeta."

"He's in a meeting. I'm doing this at his request."

She shook her head. "Boy, I know how that goes. I do lots of things at his request. Copy this, look for that, read me this. It's like the man is helpless, for crying out loud."

Louis nodded. "I understand."

She leaned toward Louis, her breasts resting on the counter. "You know what we call him? Lemon-head. Kind of a combination of the yellow glasses and the bald head."

Louis grinned. "About the files . . ."

Georgia waved him behind the counter. "C'mon. I'll show ya."

Louis followed her to the back and down one floor of concrete steps. She used the keys on her belt to open a door marked AUTHORIZED ACCESS ONLY. The door creaked and stuck, like it hadn't been opened in a while. Georgia gave it a shove with her ample hip.

"We call this place the dungeon," she said. "We don't put much stuff down here anymore, just the old junk and the cold cases."

Georgia hit a switch. The fluorescent light overhead fizzed, popped, and finally flickered on. One of the bulbs was burned out and the other gave out a feeble greenish light.

"The files are sorted by date. You should start back there by the window," Georgia said.

"Can I copy what I find?" Louis asked.

"Sure. Bring 'em up. I'll copy them for you, if there's not too many pages."

"Thanks."

Georgia waddled away, swinging her keys and humming.

Louis looked at the room. It was small, maybe twelve feet square, with pipes running overhead. It was made of concrete block that was once painted green but now had the moldy and peeled look of a water-mottled corpse. Beneath the fizz of the fluorescent light, Louis could hear a dripping sound.

He headed slowly down the rows of old black file cabinets toward the small dust-veiled window at the back, scanning the cabinet labels as he went. The dripping sound grew louder and finally he saw the old janitor's sink, black with grime and rust.

The label on the cabinet next to it was covered in dust and he wiped it clean. January–February 1964. He pulled on the drawer, but it didn't move. He had to give it a good yank, and it opened with a scrape and a cloud of dust. He waved at the air and looked inside.

All he had was the girls' first names and he scanned the file folder tabs for a Cindy or Cynthia. Nothing.

He moved to the next drawer down. There was a Cynthia Shattuck in the middle of the drawer. Louis wedged it loose and opened it. There was a single piece of paper, the responding officer's report. It was three paragraphs. Stapled to the inside of the folder was the same photo Louis had seen on the index card in Frank's office, but it was the original and it gave him a better look at Cindy Shattuck. She had been a plain girl, her thin blond hair worn in the poker-straight style favored by girls in the sixties. Her eyes were heavily lined in black and she was wearing a black turtle-neck sweater, like she was trying to look like Cher or one of The Beatles' girlfriends.

Louis scanned the police report. There was no follow-up report or disposition, so Louis assumed Cindy Shattuck had never been found.

He set the file aside. Looking around, he spotted a small stool and pulled it over and moved on to the next cabinet. After almost two hours, he straightened and rubbed his neck. He looked up to the window at the dust particles floating in the shaft of sunlight. His nose was stuffy from the mold and his head was pounding from trying to read in the flickering green fluorescent. But he had found all the girls.

Cynthia Shattuck. Born 1948, disappeared 1964. She would now be thirty-nine.

Paula Berkowitz. Born 1945, disappeared 1965. She would be forty-two.

Mary Rubio. Born, 1957, disappeared 1973. She would be thirty.

Angela Lopez. Born 1967, disappeared 1984. She would now be twenty.

If any of them were still alive.

All the files had photographs of the girls stapled to the inside of the folder, the same photos that had been given to the newspapers, the same photos Frank Woods had hidden in his office. All the folders had missing persons' reports but only two had follow-up interviews.

None had a disposition. None of these girls had been found. Not even their bones.

Louis stared at the four files. So thin. So . . . incomplete. Buried down here for all these years, untouched until now. Just like the skull. And just like the skull before he put the name Isabella to it, so sad in their disconnection to anything living and real.

He knew in his heart they were dead. But maybe he could try to bring them home. Scooping up the files, he went back through the rows of cabinets. Shutting off the light, he leaned into the door, pushed it closed, and headed back upstairs.

# CHAPTER 20

He started early the next morning, the four folders on the passenger seat of his car. He had no particular reason for starting in chronological order of the girls' disappearances, except that it seemed natural. Maybe he was looking for a pattern, a sense of what they had in common besides having vanished.

Cindy Shattuck had lived in Matlacha and had been reported missing by a girlfriend in the summer of 1964. Louis had been unable to find the girlfriend but finally traced Cindy's mother, Nancy Shattuck, to a home in Cape Coral. She was now Nancy Buckle, married to a land developer.

The Buckles lived in a new development, a place where any natural vegetation had been scraped away to make room for homes too big for their lots and too brazen to be called tasteful.

It was a yellow, two-story mini-mansion, one of the cookie-cutter homes popping up in the suburbs like mushrooms after a heavy rain. The lawn was the size of a putting green, and there was a sign in front that read ANOTHER STUART BUCKLE CUSTOM HOME.

Louis walked to the door, Cindy Shattuck's folder in his

hand. He knocked and waited. When no one answered, he rang the bell. He heard a few bars of Beethoven's "Ode to Joy" jingle inside the house.

A woman appeared behind the door, her face close to the glass. Her heavily lined eyes blinked several times when he held up his state-issued private investigator's ID card.

He leaned close. "Can I ask you a few questions?"

The door swung open. She was a small woman, dressed in emerald-green capri pants and a shiny green sleeveless top. She had reddish brown hair that sprouted from her head like unraveled cassette tapes. She was in her fifties but clearly not happy about it.

"Mrs. Buckle?"

"May I ask who you are?"

"Louis Kincaid. Private investigator."

"What are you investigating?"

"The disappearance of your daughter, Cindy."

The raccoon eyes ignited with a flash of shock that she tried to cover by blinking twice.

"Excuse me?"

"Your daughter . . . Cindy?"

"She didn't disappear."

Louis slipped the report from the folder. "According to this, she did."

Nancy Buckle tipped a bright pink fingernail toward the paper. "What is that?"

"A report taken by the Lee County Sheriff's Office in Matlacha. Her friend Doris reported her missing August twenty-third, 1964."

"Doris was a stupid girl," Nancy said, crossing her arms. "They both were."

Louis tucked the folder under his arm and pulled out his small notebook. "Mind if I take notes?"

"Not at all."

"So you're saying Cindy didn't just mysteriously disappear?"

"I threw her out. There was nothing mysterious about it."

"What was the problem? Drugs? School?"

"Men. The girl hung on every man I brought home. When she was little, they thought it was cute. Hell, even I thought it was cute. But when she turned sixteen, it wasn't so cute anymore."

"So you told her to leave?"

"Yeah. I caught her wagging her ass in front of my third husband, Larry. Like the poor man could help himself with something like that prancing around every day in that little bitty place we had."

Louis fought to keep his expression neutral. "Did she stay in Matlacha after that? Even for a while?"

"Have you ever been to Matlacha, young man?"

"Been through it."

"Exactly. It's a place you go through and keep going. I grew up there. I had Cindy at sixteen, and it was just her and me."

*And all the uncles passing through,* Louis thought.

"Did she have a boyfriend she might have gone to?" he asked.

"Probably. I was waitressing at the Snook Inn and sometimes she helped out there. Lots of guys passed through there, tourists, fisherman, locals. She could have hooked up with one of them."

"What about her father? Could she have gone to him?"

Nancy Buckle gave a harsh laugh. "You kidding me? She never knew him. I was sixteen. Boys leave. They don't hang around once they fuck up your life."

Louis stared down at his notebook. The sun was suddenly very hot on his neck. He drew a thin breath, and went on.

"Did she take anything with her when she left?"

"She had nothing to take except some old shorts and T-shirts, and I certainly can't tell you if she took any of them. I only know I threw a lot of shit out later."

"Nothing personal? Jewelry?"

"You want to know how screwy this girl was? She took her damn sock monkey."

"A stuffed monkey?"

"Yeah. Some old raggedy thing her grandma made for her before she croaked."

Louis took a step back, suddenly anxious to get the hell out of here. Nancy Buckle watched him, the humidity starting to melt her makeup.

"Hey, you okay?"

Louis nodded. "It's just the heat."

"If you see her," Nancy said, fanning herself, "don't tell her where we are now. Tell her I'm dead or something."

Louis stared at her.

"I don't want her coming around here, you know?"


Louis picked up the next folder off the car seat. Paula Berkowitz. Disappeared in 1965. She had been twenty, but still living at home with her parents on Pine Island. She worked as a checkout girl at the Winn-Dixie on Stringfellow Road. Her parents reported her missing on a Sunday morning in July after they discovered an open window and untouched bed in her bedroom. The only thing missing, besides Paula Berkowitz, was one small suitcase.

The Lee County Sheriff's office, which had taken the call, had obviously chalked it up to a runaway. Louis could tell that much from the paucity of information in the old report. The parents had insisted their daughter would never run off, but Louis knew what the police did: that kids often did things mothers and fathers never saw coming.

He rechecked the address he had for Clara and Ed Berkowitz. Lucky for him, they were still living in the same house after twenty-two years. He pulled up to the neat bungalow and cut the engine. As with Nancy Buckle, he was counting on catching the Berkowitzes off-guard. People had a way of saying things they didn't intend to if you caught them unprepared.

He rang the bell. A moment later, the door opened and a woman of about sixty answered the door. She was small, with a neat nest of blue-gray hair and blue-gray eyes, which looked out at Louis suspiciously.

"Mrs. Berkowitz?"

She nodded, half hiding behind the door.

"I'm an investigator working for the Fort Myers police," Louis said. "I would like to talk to you about your daughter Paula."

"Paula was not my daughter," she said. "My name is Ruth. Paula was my niece. I was married to her father's brother, Harvey."

"Are her parents home?" Louis asked.

"They're gone," she said. "Passed in eighty-one and eighty-three."

"I'm sorry."

"They left us this house," Ruth said. "My husband, Harvey, passed in eighty-five. I live here alone."

Louis didn't say anything, disappointed. Ruth Berkowitz pushed open the screen. "It's awfully warm today. Why don't you come inside?"

Louis stepped in, grateful for the cooler air. He pulled out his notebook.

"Would you like to sit down?" Ruth Berkowitz asked. "I was about to have an iced tea and I can make one for you."

Louis hesitated, looking at Mrs. Berkowitz's eager face. It was plain that the woman wanted some company. "That would be nice, thank you," Louis said.

He followed her into the small living room. It was done in bright blues with dozens of pieces of old blue and white china hung on the walls and lining shelves. A blue parakeet was chirping in its cage by the window. Mrs. Berkowitz disappeared into the kitchen and came back with two tumblers of iced tea. Louis took his glass and thanked her. The tea had a sprig of fresh mint in it.

"Mrs. Berkowitz—" Louis began.

"Call me Ruth, please."

"Ruth," Louis said, setting the glass on a coaster. "Did your sister and her husband talk about Paula's disappearance much?"

Ruth sat down in a blue wing chair, holding her glass. "In the early days, after her disappearance, they did."

"So they never thought she left on her own?"

"Clara never saw Paula for the way she was, not even after the thing in high school."

"What thing?"

Ruth hesitated, then took a sip of her iced tea. "It was cruel, you know, one of those things kids do. Some boys made up a game where the loser had to take the homeliest girl to some dance. Paula was the girl they chose. She found out later."

Louis was writing.

"She was overweight, you see," Ruth went on. "She had a sister who was thin as a stick, and well, you know, in the sixties, thin was everything. All the girls wanted to look like Twiggy."

"Paula worked at the grocery store, right?" Louis asked.

Ruth frowned. "She did? Oh, wait . . . now I remember. Yes, at the Winn-Dixie. Clara thought if Paula had her own money it would boost her self-esteem. I knew it would take more than fifteen dollars a week to do that, but I couldn't tell Clara that."

Louis thought about his next question carefully before he asked it. "Did she ever try to commit suicide?"

Ruth's little eyes widened. "Heavens, I don't think so. I'm sure Clara would have told me." She paused. "But then again, maybe not. Back then, we didn't talk about things like that much."

"Do you know if she had any close friends?"

Ruth shook her head. "I was living in Minnesota then. I didn't know Paula well. I'm sorry."

"Maybe a boy? One boy who she was close to?"

"I would've heard. Paula getting a boyfriend would've been big news to Clara."

"Is there anything else you can think of that might make a difference?" Louis asked.

Ruth thought for a minute, her finger on her powdered cheek. "I do know Paula desperately wanted children. When my daughter had her children, Paula would send her all kinds of baby things. She spent all of her work money on a baby she would never probably even meet."

Ruth looked up at Louis. "Kind of sad, isn't it?"

Louis pulled the Mustang into a driveway at 336 Isle of Capri Boulevard, stopping behind a monstrous RV with Florida plates. The RV was four times the size of the Chevy van that sat next to it, and much newer.

Louis climbed out of his car, and walked along the side, checking out the inside. It was prettier than most homes. Bags of groceries sat on the counter.

He looked up at the house just as a woman came out the front door. She was carrying a box of kitchen pans and utensils. She was probably forty-five, with a trim, tanned body. Her shoulder-length blond hair looked like satin and swung in sync with her hips as she walked. She saw Louis and stopped.

"Can I help you?"

"Louis Kincaid. I'm a private investigator. I'm looking for Julie Plummer?"

"I'm Julie," she said, coming forward slowly. She stopped at the RV door.

Louis opened the door for her. She hesitated, then set the box down just inside the door, turning to face him.

"Thanks." She brushed her hair back. "Now, what exactly are you investigating?"

"The disappearance of Mary Rubio. You were listed as the reporting party on the police report."

Julie looked at him blankly.

"Mary Rubio. The report says you were her foster mother."

"Oh . . . oh. Mary. Yes, I remember."

*How could she forget her so easily?*

Julie brought up a hand to shield her eyes from the sun as she stared at Louis. "Why are you asking about Mary after all these years?"

"Her disappearance might be related to a new case," Louis said. He pulled out his notebook. "Can you tell me anything about her? How she disappeared, her habits . . ."

Julie's thin brows knitted into a frown, bringing a wrinkle in her otherwise placid face. "I only had Mary for a few months."

"What was she like?"

Julie hesitated. "She was trouble. She was strange, emotionally unstable, disruptive, and depressed. In the short time I had her, she tried to harm herself at least a dozen times."

"How?"

"She'd cut herself, on the arms and thighs. Once she pushed a lit cigarette into the back of her hand."

"Did she ever try to harm anyone else?"

"No, just herself. Sometimes she would scream at the other kids for no reason. One time, she tied one of our toddlers to a chair and tried to force-feed him some oatmeal. Strange."

"What was her background?"

"Before us?" Julie pushed her hair back from her face. "Well, she was born to an alcoholic mother, who started pimping her out at twelve for drug money. She ran away the first time at thirteen and again at fourteen. That's when DCF pulled her into the system. We were her fifteenth foster home in two years. One family only kept her six hours."

Louis looked up from his notebook, rubbing the bridge of his nose. "When did she go missing?"

"Actually, she ran away the night before, if I remember right. Sometimes I give the kids a break and not report them right away. DCF slaps them down pretty hard when they take off on their fosters. They do it a couple of times and DCF pulls them out and sends them to detention."

"Did you give Mary a break that night?"

Julie sighed. "She was so emotionally draining, it was ruining the family."

Louis waited for her to continue. She let out a breath, almost as if she was embarrassed to say anything more.

"Okay, yes, the minute I discovered her gone, I was on the phone. Sometimes you can do only so much for these kids."

Louis heard a dog bark and looked to the house. He could see a huge golden retriever pushing at the screen and barking.

"Ruffus! Stop that!" Julie shouted.

"So Mary was a lost cause?" Louis asked.

Julie was looking at the dog. It was going nuts, jumping up, yelping. "Damn it, Ruffus!" Julie yelled. "Gene! Gene, come get the damn dog!"

"Mrs. Plummer—"

Julie's face snapped back. "What?"

"Mary Rubio . . . you considered her a lost cause?"

Julie swept back her hair. "In my book, yes. This job is hard enough, what with all the problems these kids have. Having a Mary Rubio in a house full of these kinds of kids only complicates the situation."

The dog was still barking. "Look, I've got to go," Julie said. "We're getting ready to go to Disney World." She started toward the house. "Gene! Come get your dog!"

"Mrs. Plummer?" Louis called out.

She stopped halfway to the house and looked back impatiently. "What?"

"Did you ever hear from Mary again?"

Julie shook her head. "I would be the last person she would contact. She knew she wasn't part of our family and never would be."

Louis walked back to the Mustang, and got in. He was about to start the engine when the front door of the house opened. A pack of kids came out, ranging from about age five to fourteen. Louis knew instantly they were all foster children, and it wasn't just because they didn't resemble either of the Plummers. They had a look about them, a darkness in their eyes that set them apart, and an odd tentativeness to their steps that didn't match their brightly colored summer clothing or the shine of their freshly scrubbed faces.

*These kinds of kids . . .*

He put both hands on the wheel, watching Julie herd them into the RV.

Foster homes. He'd had five in less than two years.

Summer, 1967. A house on Strathmore in Detroit. One of those big redbrick places with one apartment upstairs and one down. The man had been called Moe, but all Louis could remember about the woman was her rusty, wiry hair and chipped red nails. And a house littered with Pabst Blue Ribbon beer bottles, dirty clothes, and hungry children. And an old black leather belt, marked with the flesh of children.

Louis closed his eyes.

Then came one hot day when Moe loaded them all into the station wagon and announced they were going on a trip.

*What's the matter with you, Louis? You don't want to go to Whitmore Lake?*

*I want to go home.*

*You ain't got a home no more.*

*I want my mama.*

*Well, your mama didn't want you. Now get your sorry black ass in that car, or I'll lock you back in the closet and leave you here alone again.*

Louis opened his eyes, looking away from the RV, toward the street. He'd gotten in the car. And it didn't turn out to be a bad day. He had braved the water slide and learned to make sand castles. But it wasn't enough.

Whitmore Lake hadn't erased the dark depths of that closet, or any of the closets or belts that had come before or after.

He started the Mustang and drove off, watching the RV in the rearview mirror. And neither would Disney World for these kids.

# CHAPTER 21

He had been to Immokalee once before. The circumstances had been strangely similar. A long, hot drive to the scrubland of inner Florida in search of a teenager's life.

Louis slowed the Mustang at a corner and reached down, opening the Angela Lopez file on the seat. Like the others, it was pathetically incomplete.

Her last address had been listed as Building D, Farm Workers Village. He passed through Immokalee and continued south on 29, finally spotting the sign for the village.

It was nothing more than a stark gathering of white cinder block buildings baking in the sun. Brown-skinned children romped in the yards, their feet and legs covered in dust. Thin curtains floated from open windows, and a red and green Mexican flag hung from a railing, the only splash of color against a plain white canvas of poverty.

He stopped the car and got out, taking Angela's file with him. A Hispanic woman hanging T-shirts on a sagging clothesline turned to look at him.

He took off his sunglasses and forced a smile, but the woman's face only grew harder.

"Good morning. Do you speak English?" he asked.

The woman shook her head and mumbled something, turning back to her laundry. He slipped the picture of Angela Lopez from the folder and held it out to her.

She glanced at it. *"Vete,"* she muttered and turned her back.

Louis looked around. A small pack of children had gathered around his Mustang. He had the top down and the kids were running their hands over the blue vinyl seats. A young woman was pushing a crying baby in a rusty stroller across the asphalt street. An old man sat on an overturned plastic bucket, trying to reap some shade from the leafless, snake-like frangipani tree. His face was shadowed by his cap, but Louis could see that his eyes, two black beads set in a sun-weathered face, were focused on him.

He started toward the man. The man watched him approach, his cigarette dangling loosely in his short, brown fingers.

"Do you speak English?" Louis asked.

The man nodded slowly.

Louis held out Angela's picture. "Do you know this girl?"

The man looked at it for a long time, then turned his head toward the street. He pointed across the street, to a red and white cinder block building with a tin awning. "There."

Louis walked toward the building, the back of his shirt moist against his skin. He crossed the road, pausing outside the store.

The hand-painted letters outside the store read JUAN'S PLACE and under that, CAMBIANOS CHEQUES.

Louis pulled open the flimsy screen door and walked in, again taking off his sunglasses. A ceiling fan turned slowly above, stirring a heavy air-stew of frying food and spices.

A Hispanic man sitting at a table looked up at him. A woman came out from behind the counter, wiping her hands on a towel. Her hair was a brittle mixture of gray and black.

"You lost?" the man asked.

Louis shook his head. "I'm trying to find out about this

girl," he said, opening the file. He held the photo out so they could see the face. Neither said a word.

"She's been missing for almost four years," Louis said, his eyes moving across their faces. "Her name is Angela Lopez."

The woman looked down at the photo in Louis's hand. Louis could see something pass over her face, something buried and painful that she was trying hard not to let surface. She turned away.

The old man said something to her in soft Spanish; the only word Louis could make out was the name "Rosa." With a glance back at Louis, she disappeared into a room in the back. The man looked back at Louis.

"Why are you here? Why do the cops come now?" he asked.

"I'm not a cop."

"No difference," the man said. "Angela has been gone three years. No one cares now. Go away."

When Louis didn't move, he waved his hand. "Go. No one here wants to talk to you. Go. *Vete!*"

*Damn it.* Louis put Angela's picture back in the folder, and reached for his sunglasses. He hated dead ends. He hated it when people wouldn't talk him. He hated having to tell Landeta he had no new information.

He turned and walked toward the door, Landeta's voice at his ear. *Come on, Rocky, you can do better.*

Louis paused, glancing back at the couple. The man was hunched over a red can of Tecate beer. The woman was back behind the counter, writing on a small pad. But she caught Louis's eye, then quickly looked away.

Louis pushed open the door and walked back out into the hot sun. The kids at the Mustang scattered when they saw him coming. He reached in and grabbed the files on the other girls, hesitated, then picked up the one Horton had given him on Shelly Umber. He went back to the store.

"Why are you back?" the man asked.

"Whoever took Angela took other girls," Louis said. He went to the small table and laid Cindy Shattuck's photo in front of the man.

"Disappeared 1964," Louis said.

He set Paula's and Mary's right to next to it. "Nineteen sixty-five and 1973."

Then he set down Angela's picture. "Angela Lopez . . . 1984."

The man's eyes went from the pictures up to Louis's face. "Why are you doing this?" he asked.

"Because you need to know that Angela is not the only one. You need to know that there was no way the cops could've found her, even if they had started looking the next day."

The man's black eyes rose to Louis's face. "Is she dead?"

"Probably," Louis said. "But we haven't found her. We haven't found any of these girls, except one."

"Which one?" the man asked.

Louis looked down at the last photo in his hand. It was a facial shot of Shelly Umber taken at her autopsy.

"This one. They found her in Pine Island Sound a few weeks ago. She's probably victim number six."

Louis heard a sound and looked up. The woman had turned away.

The man took a drink of his beer, then spoke quietly. "Angela worked in the fields with her father. But sometimes she worked here to make extra money," he said. "She left early one day in July."

The woman was watching, silent.

"Why?" Louis asked.

"She met a boy."

"She called him a boy . . . and not a man?"

"Yes, a boy."

"From this area? From Immokalee?"

"Fort Myers," the man said, pulling Angela's picture toward him. "She told us he was going to take her to lunch in the city."

Louis was thinking about Emma Fielding, the missing woman from 1953. Frank would have been young and handsome enough to lure her to her death. But by 1984, he was in his mid-fifties. No way he could have been mistaken for a boy.

"Did she tell you his name?" Louis asked.

The man shook his head. "I do not remember, but I know it was a good Hispanic name."

*Hispanic?*

"Did she ever describe him to you?" Louis asked. "Tell you more about him?"

The man shook his head. "I think she call him . . ." He looked at his wife. "How she call him?"

The woman hesitated. *"Papi chulo,"* she whispered.

"What does that mean?" Louis asked.

"It is something young people say. It means . . . he was handsome, a hunk you would say." He took a drink from his beer. His face was hard when he put down the can.

Louis looked at the woman. Her expression had changed, too. Now she looked sad, not so much like she was remembering what Angela said but what any woman could remember feeling about any young man. She turned, disappearing into the back.

Louis gathered up his photos, stacking the papers and folders. They were damp with humidity.

"The file says her father reported her missing," Louis said. "Do you know where I can find him?"

"I heard he died last year in Texas. Angela had no one else."

Louis closed the folder and stuck out a hand. "Thanks for your time."

The man wiped his palm on his jeans, then shook Louis's hand.

Louis went out, pausing in the hot sun, watching the kids playing around his Mustang. He was surprised when the woman came out to stand next to him.

"Can I see the picture?" she asked softly.

Louis pulled it out of the file and handed it to her. The woman's worn face seemed to slowly cave in on itself. She brushed at her eyes.

"She didn't want to be called Angela," she said. "I did not call her that."

"What did you call her?" Louis asked.

"Angel."

The woman was still staring at the picture. She finally looked up at Louis. "You said she is dead."

Louis hesitated. "We don't know for sure."

She looked back at the children playing in the dust.

"When Angela became fifteen, she started working with her father in the fields," the woman said. "The same age I was when I started."

She was quiet for a moment, her eyes back on the children. "It is hard work. You wake before the sun is red and wait for the bathroom to become free. There is only one bathroom for the twelve people you live with. Then you walk the three miles to the bus so you can be chosen to work. The sun is just up when you get to the fields and you are hungry but you run and grab a bucket and start picking. You pick as fast as you can so you can eat."

The old woman brushed a hand over her hair. "You fill your bucket and it is heavy but you pour the tomatoes in and the man gives you a ticket. You put it into your pants because it is precious, worth forty cents. When the sun goes down, you stop and take your tickets to the house and you get your money. Then you get back on the bus and walk home. You take a cold shower because the hot water is all gone by now. At eleven, you eat, then go to bed. The sun comes up again the next day and you do it again."

The children were beeping the Mustang's horn. Louis let it go.

"I was lucky to marry a good man," the woman said. "I

didn't have to work in the fields. I hoped Angel would be lucky, too."

"You were close to her?" Louis asked.

She looked up at him, then down at the picture in her hand. "She was like my daughter. We used to talk at night when the store was quiet," she said. "Angel say she would get away from here someday, that she would never have her children here."

The woman paused. "I told her, good, that she should go and never come back, not even to see me." She paused again. "I want to believe that is what she did."

The woman was looking up at him again. Louis couldn't think of anything to say so he nodded.

"Thank you for your help, Rosa," he said.

She hesitated, then held out the photograph. It was a copy, not even a good one, but the original was back in the station.

"You can keep it," he said. He hesitated. "If I find out anything—"

Rosa shook her head. "No," she said softly, clutching the picture. "Don't come back here. Please. Don't come back."

# CHAPTER 22

Louis slid into the old wicker chair on the porch and propped his bare feet on the small table. In his hand was a Heineken and in his lap was the baby skull.

It was hot again tonight, the black velvet air hanging heavy and dark over the still gulf waters. The cottage next to his was empty, eliminating any nearby lights. Far out in the blackness he could see a twinkle of white. A ship. A low star. He couldn't tell.

All the girls were on his mind, but it was Neil Fielding who nagged at him, closed up tight in that tin-can trailer, waiting to die.

He took a long, slow drink of the cold beer.

How long did it take for guilt to kill a man? How long could you live with the stink of your failings until the bitterness ate away your soul?

Cliff Parker had sexually abused his step-daughter Emma. Neil knew it and couldn't stop it and then couldn't stop himself from leaving when it got to be too much.

*Just go,* Emma had told him.

*And I did,* Neil said.

Louis took another drink of beer. It had taken the entire drive back to Fort Myers for the stuff inside him to finally ooze its way to the surface. Maybe if the drive hadn't been so long or if Neil Fielding hadn't been so pathetic, he himself wouldn't be sitting here now holding a baby's skull and thinking about that gray February afternoon eight years ago when Kyla had appeared at his dorm door, her hair wet with the sleet, her eyes hard with anger.

*I'm pregnant, Louis.*

*I can't deal with this now, Kyla.*

*I'll have an abortion!*

*I don't care what you do with it.*

*Louis? Louis! Where are you going?*

*I don't know. I've got a class. I don't know . . .*

*Then go! Just go!*

He closed his eyes. It used to be easy. Easier. It used to be easier. Easier to keep the lid on the box where he hid these things. The box had been there inside him for as long as he could remember, since he was little. He could even see it sometimes, a hard, black metal thing with a rusty hinge and bolt. He could even feel it sometimes, a cold lump wedged somewhere up high in his ribs, so high that it made breathing hard. The box hurt but it worked. It held fast.

Until now. Now things were breaking out, getting loose and flying around inside him. Screaming in his ear, making him sweat at night, a babble of memory and hurt, the loudest voice screaming, *You should have done better, you should have been better.*

He opened his eyes and looked down at the skull.

Isabella Maria Carreira de los Reyes. He had memorized the name, even looked it up in a Spanish dictionary. It meant "of the kings." Such a grand name for such a short life. Somebody's daughter. *Vios con Dios, preciosa angelita. Go with God, precious little angel.*

Car lights swept the south end of the porch and Louis

drew his feet off the table. He set the skull down and moved to the screen. He was surprised to see a Fort Myers police cruiser pulling in.

The headlights went out and a tall, thin man got out of the passenger side. Louis knew immediately it was Mel Landeta from his arrogantly erect walk. The second man emerged and Louis recognized the young deputy who had helped him with the skull the day after the storm.

"Wait in the car, Strickland."

Louis watched as the young cop stopped, let out a sigh, and got back in the cruiser. Shit, now what? Had Landeta commandeered his own personal chauffeur?

"Why aren't you answering your phone?" Landeta said, coming onto the screened porch.

"I went down the road to eat," Louis said.

Landeta was looking through the open door to the living room. His eyes swept across the porch and back up to Louis. He ignored the skull on the table.

"You get down to see Fielding yet?"

"Yeah, come on in."

Landeta paused just inside the door. He was taking in the worn rattan furniture, the small kitchen, the bookcase where Louis had stowed some of his books and mementos. He focused finally on the two old prints of the cockatoos that hung over the sofa.

Louis moved past him and put the skull back on the shelf. "You want something to drink?"

"You got a Diet Coke?"

"Dr Pepper."

"Water. No ice."

Louis went to get a glass. When he came back out, Landeta was sorting through the books that Louis had left out on the table. They were the books on runaways he had checked out of the library that first day he had met Frank Woods. After leaving Neil Fielding's place earlier today he had started skimming through them, trying to find some insights into all the girls' psyches.

"Here," Louis said.

Landeta turned and took the water. "I went to get some files today," Landeta said. "Wanted to take a look at the reports on the other missing girls. Funny thing was, the records clerk said you already went through them."

Louis shrugged. "Figured what the hell."

"I told you I would take care of that."

"You didn't seem anxious to do it," Louis said.

"I don't like people going over my head, Rocky."

"I don't like to be kept waiting outside your door."

Landeta stared at him for a minute, then took a drink of water. "I ran some background checks on them. All of them, including Emma Fielding."

"And?"

"They no longer exist," Landeta said. "Not one has filed a tax return, used her Social Security card for a job, applied for a credit card, or even gotten married. There's not even a driver's license renewal for any of them."

Gone. Just vanished. Louis thought about what Rosa in Immokalee had said about Angela. *I told her she should go and never come back. I want to believe that's what she did.*

Landeta wiped his brow. "Fuck, it's hot in here. Don't you have air in this place?"

"Welcome to paradise, as you called it," Louis said. He went over and switched on the wall unit. It clattered and wheezed and finally sent out a weak stream of cool air. Landeta took his glass of water to the sofa.

Issy saw him coming and jumped down, settling into a chair across from him. Landeta sat down stiffly on the sofa. He sipped the water, his eyes on the floor.

Louis went to the kitchen and brought back a Heineken. "You didn't come all the way out here to chew my ass about those files. Why are you here?"

"The girls aren't the only ones without a past. Frank Woods doesn't seem to have one either."

"Everybody has a past."

"I mean, there are no records. No birth certificate, no marriage license, no school records. Nothing before 1952. Everything after that says Frank Woods, friendly librarian."

Louis took a drink, thinking. "He mentioned Sarasota at the campground. You checked that out, right?"

Landeta nodded. "Of course I did. He didn't attend school there or anywhere else we can find. He lied to you."

"What about Diane's mother?" Louis asked. "Can't we trace her?"

"You know her maiden name?"

Louis shook his head. "But Diane would."

"Oh, yeah, she's real cooperative. Let me tell you what happened today." Landeta picked up the water glass, downed it in one gulp. "After we finished searching Frank's house, we went to hers."

"Why?" Louis asked.

"Well, according to you, she has a coral ring. That's evidence. But according to *her,* there is no fucking ring."

"What?"

"We tore that apartment apart. She just stood there and watched us. We didn't find shit. So now we're trying to get a warrant for her office."

"She's a principal. You know what's going to happen if you go charging in there?"

Landeta shrugged. "That's her problem. All she has to do is give us the damn ring." He looked up at Louis. "If it exists."

"I saw it." Louis leaned against the kitchen doorway. "I suppose you want me to try."

"You still working for her?"

"Well, I haven't been officially fired. Yet."

"Does she like you?"

Louis wasn't sure he wanted to tell Landeta that Diane

still had hopes of him bringing Frank Woods in for questioning quietly. Landeta was looking at him, his eyes steady behind the yellow lenses.

"No, she doesn't like me," Louis said. "I'm not sure she likes anyone."

"Well, we need the ring and she knows you, at least. While you're at it, find out the mother's maiden name. Convince her it's for her father's own good."

"I'd be lying to her."

A small smile spread across Landeta's face. "I can't believe you actually said that. We lie all the time."

"Not to families. At least I don't."

"As far as I'm concerned, she's half the problem in this whole case."

"What's the other half?"

"You. You don't want to admit that Woods is probably a serial killer and his daughter is a paranoid weirdo who needs to quit playing mama to her daddy and find herself a man."

"Your compassion is overwhelming, Detective."

"And yours is overflowing," Landeta said.

The cottage was quiet. Louis could hear Issy purring.

"Are we done?" Louis asked finally.

"No, tell me what you found out about the girls."

Louis walked to the table and picked up a folder. He hadn't yet bought a typewriter, so his reports on the girls were written in longhand, formatted and dated like a police report.

He held out the folder to Landeta. "Go ahead. Take a look."

Landeta looked up at Louis, elbows on his knees. "Just tell me about them."

"I'm tired of reading and interpreting and narrating this goddamn case to you. You want the information, you read it."

Landeta stood up, taking the folder. "I'll take them with me."

"The hell you will. I'll drop you a copy tomorrow."

"They're part of the case file. They go with me."

Louis stood right in front of him. "It's my work. It stays here."

Landeta hesitated, then tossed the folder to the sofa. He moved to step around Louis, and his knee caught the edge of the table. The empty water glass toppled to the terrazzo floor, shattering.

Landeta glanced down, then continued toward the door. "Sorry about that," he muttered.

He shoved open the screen, and Louis followed him to the porch.

"You're a real jackass, you know that?" Louis called.

Landeta ignored him, continuing on toward the cruiser. Officer Strickland was standing near the gumbo limbo tree, smoking a cigarette.

"Let's go," Landeta called to him.

Strickland watched Landeta walk to the car and climb in the back, slamming the door.

"How'd you get stuck with chauffeur duty?" Louis asked.

Strickland shook his head. "Chief said a guy of his reputation gets what he needs to do the job."

Landeta's bald head appeared out the car window. "Let's see a little hustle there, Officer," he shouted.

Strickland tossed the butt to the sand and ground it out. "I hope I'm shot dead before I get that old," he mumbled, heading to the car.

Louis closed the door and walked to the kitchen. He pulled down a file he had been keeping on Frank Woods and sifted through it for Diane's address and phone number.

*Convince her it's for her father's own good.*

Right.

He glanced up at the clock. Almost eleven. It was too late now to call. He'd call her in the morning. When he was sure she was sober.

# CHAPTER 23

The rain beat against the windshield, the pounding so loud he could not hear his radio. Louis slowed when he saw the sign SCHOOL ZONE.

He hadn't wanted to come here. He tried calling Diane, starting at six-thirty A.M. But he kept getting a busy signal and then the answering machine. He figured she was pissed. And she was blaming him.

Having your home searched was the ultimate humiliation for anyone, but for Diane Woods it would be devastating. Cops were never careful. He knew her *Gourmet* magazines had been dumped to the carpet, the perfectly arranged drawers left open and tossed, her books pulled from the shelves.

Why the hell didn't she just give them the damn ring?

Louis passed the WINK-TV van sitting just off the school grounds. Heather Fox was standing under a canopy wearing a yellow raincoat. Her cameraman was soaked, his equipment wrapped in plastic.

Louis parked as far away from the van as he could and dashed toward the school entrance. Heather Fox didn't see him until it was too late. He jerked open the school door, pausing just inside to wipe his face.

The old smells of high school flooded back to him—fried chicken, dust, and musty gym clothes. He could hear the faint *thump-thump* of a basketball somewhere. There was a trophy case to his left with the usual sports paraphernalia in it. Next to it was a row of portraits of the administration—two pictures of women assistant principals and one of the male athletic director. There was a blank spot in the middle where one picture had been taken down. Underneath was a plaque that said MISS DIANE WOODS, PRINCIPAL.

He saw a glass-enclosed office with the sign ADMINISTRA-TION above the door and went to it.

A couple of students glanced at him as entered. It was a large office, dominated by a U-shaped desk and painted a cheerful blue that matched the orange and blue industrial car-peting. There was a sign over the desk that said CAPE CORAL HIGH SCHOOL, HOME OF THE SEAHAWKS. There was a big or-ange and blue stuffed bird in the corner. It was wearing a hat that said BREEZY.

The woman behind the desk finished with the two boys and sent them on their way. She looked up at Louis.

"Can I help you?"

Louis was looking over her shoulder, into the glass-enclosed office. He could see Diane in there, on the phone. She didn't see him.

"Would you tell Miss Woods that Louis Kincaid is here to see her?"

"Well, I think Miss Woods is—"

"Just tell her, please."

The woman must have heard the cop-edge in his voice because she began backing up toward the office, eyes on Louis. She turned and poked her head in the door. Louis saw Diane crane her neck to look his way. She looked like a trapped animal.

Diane said something into the receiver and then slowly put it back in the cradle. Her eyes took a long time to focus on him; then they moved slowly to the secretary. "It's okay, Maggie."

Louis went in. Maggie retreated, closing the door.

"I can't believe you came here," Diane said. "How could you do that to me?"

"I came to help you, even though you don't seem to want any help."

"You let my father become a suspect. Do you have any idea how that feels?"

"For him or you?"

She looked away, out the window. She brought up one hand to brush her hair behind an ear. Her hand trembled. "What do you want?" she asked.

"The ring."

She looked him dead in the eye. "There is no ring."

Louis came forward and leaned both hands on the desk. Diane rolled her chair back in surprise.

"Look, lady, I'm sick and tired of your shit," he said. "You told me to find your father. But you won't lift a hand to help me. I don't know what's going on between you two—I don't *want* to know." He jabbed a finger toward her face. "But I don't like being jerked around. Now where is the damn ring?"

Diane was staring at him in shock. He saw her eyes shift to the door and he knew the secretary outside had heard every word he had said.

Diane looked back at him. "I lost it."

"Try again."

Diane sat there, frozen in the chair. Then suddenly, amazingly, her eyes teared up.

"Please," she whispered. "You don't know what it's been like. The TV people won't leave me alone. I can't go out of my apartment, I can't leave my phone on the hook."

She wiped angrily at her eyes. "Today, when I got here I found out that someone took a felt-tip and wrote *wanted* on my picture outside in the hall."

That was why the picture out in the trophy case was missing, Louis thought. He stood up, backing away from her desk.

"It's going to get worse," he said. "They're getting a warrant to search this office. You know what that's going to be like?"

He nodded out toward the desk where the secretary and now two other women were clustered, whispering and looking their way. "Do you really want them watching it? You want them to see the cops coming in here, going through your desk, your trash, tearing this place up like they did your home?"

Diane looked ready to cry again. But Louis could see the boil of anger beneath it.

"Give me the ring," he said.

She rose slowly and turned her back to him. He watched as she slipped her hand inside her blouse. She turned back.

Louis held out his hand and she dropped the ring into it.

"Now get out of my office," she said.

"Not yet," Louis said. "I need some information. I need to know about your mother for starters."

Diane sat back down in her chair, shielding her eyes with a shaking hand. "I told you she died when I was little. I don't remember much about her."

"What's her maiden name?"

"I don't know." She looked up at Louis and saw the disbelief in his face. "I don't know," she repeated tightly.

"What about family records?"

"I never saw any."

"What about your birth certificate? What does it say under your mother's name?"

"I don't know. I . . . I never looked at it."

"What about your father?" Louis pressed. "Where is he from? Where did he go to school?"

Diane was frowning slightly. "I . . . He never said anything . . ."

"Is he from Fort Myers? Did he ever mention Sarasota?"

She was looking up at Louis now and he could see a change in her expression, an odd confusion, like she was looking at something that was supposed to be familiar but seeing something different.

"Diane, we can't find anything about your father's background before 1952," Louis said.

"That's the year I was born," she said.

Louis didn't respond. He just let it sink in.

"I need your mother's maiden name, Diane," Louis said.

A bell rang and Louis could hear the bustle and laughter of kids out in the hallways. He saw Diane's eyes shift and he looked over his shoulder to see a wiry teenage boy come shuffling into the outer office, his head bowed, backpack dragging.

Diane pushed herself up from her chair. "I'm sorry, I have something I have to take care of," she said.

"It can wait," Louis said.

Diane shook her head. "No, this can't. That boy out there was accused of stealing another boy's radio and I know he didn't do it." Her eyes drifted out to the boy outside. "I know Ricky didn't do it even though his father thinks he did. His father is coming in and I have to convince him his son needs some attention . . . not another slap."

Louis stared at Diane. "But you're not going to help me," he said.

"I can't trust you," she said, shaking her head.

"Little late for that now," he said.

"Yes, it is," she said. "Now please leave." Her eyes were pleading. "Please," she said tightly.

Louis turned and left the office. The boy looked up at him as he went past. At the entrance, Louis paused and looked back toward the administration office. He could see Diane leading the boy into her office, an arm over his skinny shoulders. Louis turned up his collar and darted out into the rain.

"Hey! Kincaid! Louis Kincaid!"

He saw a flash of yellow coming up on his right. Heather Fox had seen him. He kept going.

"What are you doing here, Kincaid?" she asked, falling in

step. He could see the cameraman hustling over, fumbling with the camera.

"Were you here to see Diane Woods? Did she have anything to say about her father?"

Louis kept walking.

"How did she look? Did she look upset? Did she—"

Louis spun. "Get out of my face," he said.

Heather Fox's cheeks had black tracks from where the rain had run her mascara. "Don't get testy," she said. "She won't talk to us and I'm just trying to get a feel for her. She seems like a cold fish to me and—"

"Leave her alone," Louis said.

Heather smiled. "Hey, I'm just doing a job here. Just like you."

Louis sprinted to the Mustang. He started the engine and sat there for a moment, listening to the rain beat on the convertible's top. He unclasped his hand and looked at the coral ring.

It was just a simple band but finely carved, like someone had taken great care with it. He slipped it on his left pinky. It was so small it didn't even go over his first knuckle.

Had it been worn by Emma Fielding? Or any of the other missing girls? Had Frank made them wear the rings as some perverse symbol, like he was marrying his victims before he killed them?

Louis slipped the ring off his finger and put it in his pocket. He pulled out of the lot and headed west. When he hit 41, he turned north and followed the highway out until it narrowed to the two lanes leading to Pine Island. The rain was still heavy by the time he pulled into Bokeelia. He parked the car at the marina across from Cap'n Con's Fishhouse.

He didn't know why he had come out here. Maybe to think, get a clear take on things that were increasingly less clear. He sat there, looking out at Charlotte Harbor. He could make out the outline of Bessie Levy's stilt house but the driving rain had turned everything else into just a gray expanse of sky and water with no horizon to separate the two. The gray would blur with rain and then the wipers would sweep across, giving him a moment of clarity before the blur came back.

Endless gray . . . and a few seconds when he could see the dark green islands far out in the harbor. All those countless little islands out there where Frank Woods could be hiding. All those islands where he could have buried those girls.

He knew in that second, knew that was where he would find Frank. He would be with the victims.

The wipers slapped a clear picture of the islands into view and then it was gone.

Now all he had to do was find the right island.

# CHAPTER 24

The ferry pulled into the dock and the crewman secured the lines. Louis sat up, lifting his bare legs off the sticky vinyl of the Mustang's seat. His shorts and T-shirt were almost soaked through with sweat. He looked at his watch. It was just before eleven.

He picked up the binoculars and focused on the people gathering to board. A group of old women in sunhats and a sunburned family of five, Dad laden down with a video recorder and a crying three-year-old, Mom looking like she needed a stiff drink.

Louis set aside the binoculars with a sigh. Shit, three days he had been sitting here, waiting for Frank Woods to make an appearance. All because Landeta had a half-assed hunch that Woods would show up.

"He's gone," Louis had said that morning.

"He'll show. He's a man who is scared," Landeta had answered. "Men like that need the security of the routine."

Louis wiped his face. Easy for Landeta to say. He was sitting in an air-conditioned office working the phones and computers trying to find those other missing women. Not sweating his balls off for nothing.

Louis gave the group on the dock one more scan, then set down the binoculars. He picked up the copy of that morning's *News-Press*.

Frank Woods was still the lead story, the newspaper playing catch-up on the TV reports about police upgrading Frank to a murder suspect.

He wondered how Diane was taking it, but he really didn't care enough to call and find out. She had made her own bed and now the media wanted to see her not just lying it in, but bound and tied to the bedposts. Last night, watching Heather Fox on TV, he had felt a twinge of pity for Diane. Fox was doing a remote in front of the Fort Myers Library and the letters below said BOOKED FOR MURDER? Some idiot's attempt at humor had made it seem like the serial killer librarian was finally arrested and the streets were safe once again. Louis knew it was only going to get worse for Diane. God knows what the press would do when Frank was actually caught.

*If* he was caught.

Louis's eyes wandered back out to the dock. The two crewmen were talking, waiting for the call to cast off the lines. Suddenly, Louis froze. He watched as the shorter of the two men, the one wearing a red shirt and a khaki fishing hat, calmly took the cigarette butt from his mouth, snuffed it out with his fingers, and put it in his pocket. He jumped on board just as the ferry pulled out.

Louis threw open the car door and ran to the dock. A man in the red shirt was standing at the stern, looking at him. The beard was gone, but Louis was sure. It was Frank Woods.

"Shit!"

Louis raced into the bait shack. The lanky guy in the Grateful Dead ball cap was there, leafing through a fishing magazine.

"Get that ferry back here now!" Louis shouted.

"What?"

Louis thrust out his PI card. "Get that boat back!"

The guy glanced at the ID and shrugged. "Can't do that. She's got a schedule to keep."

Louis pointed at the shortwave radio behind the counter. "Call and get it back!"

"No can do, dude."

Louis spun to the window. The ferry was heading out into the sound. He slammed a hand down on the counter in frustration. The Deadhead jumped back.

"Where's it going?" Louis demanded.

"Hey, man, chill—"

Louis grabbed the guy's shirt. "Where is it going?"

"Away So Far Island!" The Deadhead jerked out of Louis's grasp and backed up, eyeing him. "There's a tourist restaurant out there."

"I need a boat," Louis said.

"You can't take your own boat there. It's private. They only let the ferry dock." He went back to his magazine. "Your buddy will be back in about three hours."

Louis looked back to the window. The ferry was heading north, cutting a quick wake across the sound. He could call Horton, get a police boat out there. But he couldn't take the chance that Woods would slip away again. He was the one who had lost Frank, not once but now twice. And he was the one who was going to bring him in.

"You said you had a boat," Louis said to the Deadhead.

"Yeah, but I ain't taking it out there, man. When they say no trespassing, they mean it."

"Fifty bucks," Louis said.

"I told ya. They won't let me dock."

"A hundred."

The Deadhead's eyes narrowed. "I can take you as far as the flats on the east side." He glanced up at the clock on the wall. "It's low tide. Maybe you can walk in from there."

"Let's go," Louis said.

The ferry was out of sight by the time the Deadhead throttled up his beat-up skiff and headed out into Pine Island

Sound. The sun was high overhead, searing in the cloudless sky. The Deadhead told Louis that the island was owned by a family that ran a restaurant popular with tourists who wanted an "authentic old Florida" experience. "A rip-off," he added, "just conch fritters, beer in plastic cups, and no air-conditioning. Shit, I can get that at home."

Forty minutes later, the Deadhead throttled down the engine. They were coming up on a lush mangrove-ringed island. Louis could see the ferry sitting at the dock but nothing else except an old wood water tower rising above the trees. The Deadhead steered east, taking the skiff in a wide circle away from the dock. Louis saw several large NO TRESPASSING signs posted on the island. Finally, the Deadhead cut the engine.

"This is as far as I go," he said.

They were about fifty yards from the island. Louis looked down at the shallow water, estimating it was only knee-high. He was wearing sandals, so if he was careful he would be dry when he got to the restaurant. He started to ease himself over the side.

"Hey, man, where's my bread?" the Deadhead demanded.

"I'll send you a check."

Louis started toward shore, the Deadhead's expletives following him. He heard the outboard start up but didn't look back. By the time he reached the island, the skiff was gone.

The shore was similar to the place where they had found Shelly Umber's body, a dense, dank stand of mangroves that rose slightly from black mud up to dry ground thick with brush. Louis paused there to wipe his face, trying to get his bearings, then continued on. The ground rose slightly and finally, he came to a path. He stood for a moment, trying to remember which way the dock was, and finally turned left, keeping to the narrow path. A sound came to him through the trees—the clatter of dishes or pans—so he followed it and a few minutes later, he saw a fence. There was a gate and

it was open so he went through, coming around the back of
the restaurant. He could hear kitchen sounds coming from
the open windows. Keeping to the trees, he made his way
around front.

It looked like an old Florida cracker house, white clapboard with a screened-in porch. He could hear the diners inside, laughing and talking. He stuck his sunglasses in the
pocket of his shorts and went up the steps.

He paused at the entrance, letting his eyes adjust. It was a
single large room, simply furnished with long wood tables
and benches. There was a coral rock fireplace at one end and
a primitive wood bar at the other, over which hung an old
painting. Three ceiling fans turned slowly above, stirring the
air, which was thick with the smells of frying fish.

Louis scanned the diners, but didn't see Frank.

Damn, had he somehow gotten off the ferry somewhere
else? Then, suddenly, there he was, emerging from a door
with a MEN sign over it. Louis dropped back and watched as
Frank stopped and began talking to the man behind the bar.
The man nodded and disappeared. Louis braced, ready to
move if Frank ran or tried to leave. But he just looked around
the dining room, moved to a table in the corner, and sat
down.

He was wearing the fishing hat, pulled low over his face,
but Louis could see his eyes darting around the room, over
the other diners, like he was searching for someone or something. Frank wrapped his hands around a plastic glass before
him, but did not take a drink of the beer. There was a menu
lying on the table but he didn't touch that either.

Then he spotted Louis and froze. Louis went to the table.
Frank looked up at Louis, his eyes almost sad.

Louis slid into the chair across from him. Frank pulled
the hat off his head. His hair was a mess, his jaw dark with
whiskers. He was badly sunburned, his nose peeling. An
odor rose off him, like he hadn't bathed in days.

Frank dropped his head, his shoulders sagging. "How did

you get here?" he asked softly.

"Never mind that," Louis said.

"You weren't on the ferry. How did you get here?"

"Frank," Louis said, "I'm taking you in."

Frank shook his head slowly, still not looking up.

"You don't have any choice," Louis said,

Frank shut his eyes. He was still gripping the beer.

"You go back on the ferry with me, nice and quiet, or I call the police to come out here and haul you back. Either way, you are going in."

Frank didn't move.

"You hear me, Frank?"

Frank's head came up and his eyes darted around the room. For a second, Louis thought he was going to bolt, but then he sagged back into the chair. He was staring in the direction of the dusty painting hanging over the bar but his eyes were unfocused, almost dreamy.

"I haven't been here in years," he said softly. "It hasn't changed."

A young boy came up to the table. He was about ten, the strings of the white apron wrapped twice around his slender waist.

"Do you want a menu?" the boy asked Louis.

"No, we're not staying, thank you." Louis looked at Frank, who was looking at the boy.

"What's your name, son?" Frank asked gently.

The boy stared at Frank, glanced at Louis in confusion, then looked back at Frank.

"Roberto, sir."

"Roberto," Frank repeated softly.

The boy picked up Frank's menu and left. Frank's eyes followed him until he disappeared into the kitchen.

"Frank," Louis said, "who was that man I saw you talking to, the one at the bar?"

"No one." He seemed to be staring at the painting over the bar again.

"Don't lie to me," Louis said. "Why did you come out here?"

*"Non debui umquam ab hoc loco discesse."*

"What?"

*"Non debui umquam ab hoc loco discesse. Si mansissem id prohibuere potuissem."*

Frank was still staring at the painting. Louis turned to look at it. It was just a dusty old print of what looked like an orgy, a bunch of Roman soldiers and fat women. Louis touched Frank's arm.

"Frank, talk to me, man."

"It's too late now."

"What's too late?" Louis leaned closer.

"I can't bring them back." He covered his face with his hands. "I just let them die."

Louis sat back, stunned. Jesus, Frank had confessed. Just like that. He needed to get a hold of Horton fast. But he couldn't leave Frank alone for a second even to make a phone call. He looked at his watch. The ferry back was leaving in a half hour. Until then, he was going to get as much out of him as possible.

Louis leaned forward. "Who'd you let die, Frank?"

Frank's hands were still covering his face.

"Did you kill those girls?" Louis pressed.

Frank shook his head.

"Where are they, Frank?"

"Gone . . . dead, they're all dead," he murmured through his hands.

"Where did you bury the bodies?"

"I . . . oh, Jesus."

Louis leaned closer. "Damn it, Frank, talk to me. It'll be a lot easier if you do."

Frank took his hands down from his face. *"Hic solutio est,"* he said.

"What?"

*"Hic solutio est."*

"Knock it off," Louis hissed. "Tell me where they are."

Frank's eyes were darting around the restaurant. He looked like a trapped animal. The women at the next table were staring at him, whispering.

"Come on. Let's go," Louis said.

Frank looked up, his face sunken with exhaustion, resignation, and what Louis could only read as fear. It was over, the man knew it.

*"Hic solutio est . . . Hic solutio est."*

"Enough, man!"

Louis grabbed Frank's arm and pulled him to his feet. The old ladies at the next table turned to stare at them.

"Let's do this easy, Frank," Louis whispered.

Frank stiffened, his eyes searching the restaurant for something—the other man, a way out? Louis could feel Frank's biceps, tight as a coiled spring. He could feel him resisting; his strength was surprising. Louis tightened his grip.

Finally Frank gave a tight nod. Louis felt his arm relax. He picked up Frank's fishing hat and led him to the door.

# CHAPTER 25

The gulls dipped and hovered, following in the white foam of the ferry's wake. A little girl was standing at the rail tossing Cheetos at the birds. Frank stood there, hands deep in his pockets, watching her. Then, finally, he looked away, his gaze going back to Away So Far Island, quickly growing smaller.

"Come on, Frank."

He looked back at Louis.

"I need to go call in, let them know we're coming."

"I'll wait here," Frank said quietly.

"I have cuffs, Frank. You want me to use them?"

Frank just stared at him. Then he turned and headed toward the front of the boat. At the bridge, Louis rapped on the door, then slid it open before the man behind the wheel had a chance to protest. Louis flashed his ID.

"I need to use your radio," he said.

The man was in his sixties, with wild white hair and brows as bushy as caterpillars.

"What—"

"I'm arresting this man," Louis said. "Get the coast guard,

please. Ask them to patch you through to the Fort Myers police."

The man's blue eyes jumped from Louis to Frank, standing by the door. He hesitated, his gnarled brown hands gripping the wheel. Finally, he unhooked a mike and keyed it, his eyes locked on Frank.

Louis saw a crewman hovering outside and he pulled Frank inside, shutting the door. The ferry captain held out the mike.

"Got someone named Horton," he said, his eyes still on Frank.

"Al?" Louis said, keying the mike.

"Louis? Where the hell are you?"

"I got Woods. We're coming in."

"What? Where?"

"Sutter's Marina, Captiva. We'll be there in—" Louis looked at the ferry captain.

"Half hour," the man said.

"We're on the ferry. We'll be there in a half hour." Louis hesitated. "No press, Al, okay?"

"Just get him here, Kincaid."

Louis clicked off. The captain was trying to steer but kept looking back at Frank with shock, as if he were seeing Charles Manson, complete with a swastika tattooed on his forehead.

"That the guy in the newspaper?" the captain asked.

Louis ignored him and took Frank by the arm. They went back outside. Louis led Frank back to the stern.

The little girl was gone. They were alone except for two women standing at the rail. Frank sank down on a bench, elbows on knees, hands clasped, head bowed. Louis looked out over the sound. They were out in the broadest stretch of the sound now, surrounded by water. To the west, he could see the mangrove fringe of Cayo Costa. He looked east and could see the northern edge of Pine Island, where Bessie

Levy's stilt house was. And there, far away to the south, he could just make out the green that he knew was the tip of Captiva.

There was nothing else to see but water, a stunning spectrum—aquamarine, turquoise, azure—changing with the shifts of the sand bottom and the sun rays.

Louis looked over at Frank's bowed head. He was glad that the ferry's engine made it difficult to talk. Louis took a bench facing Frank a few feet away.

"Diane," Frank said after a moment. "How is she?"

"Worried about you."

"I failed her."

Louis didn't know what to say.

*"Cruoris innocentium sceleratus sum,"* Frank said.

"Frank, I can't understand what you're saying."

*"Cruoris innocentium sceleratus sum.* The blood of the innocent is on my hands."

Louis just shook his head.

Frank looked out over the water. He was squinting into the sun, his eyes moist.

"I need to fix things," he said. "Tell Diane I'm sorry."

Suddenly, Frank rose and headed to the rail. It took Louis a second before the thought hit him, and then another second to take it seriously. He jumped to his feet, rushing toward the rail after Frank.

Frank disappeared over the side in a flash of white spray. Louis grabbed the rail, screaming down into the water.

"Frank! Goddamn it, Frank!"

Frank's head bobbed away, his arms flailing against the wake of the boat.

"Motherfucker," Louis muttered.

He grabbed the wood railing and hopped over the side, sailing down into the water.

The cool water rushed over him and he could hear the dull churn of the ferry's engine close by. He struggled through the bubbles to the surface, the salt water stinging his eyes. The boat was a dark shape to the left.

But there was no sign of Frank Woods.

Louis treaded water, his head swiveling. Nothing. Just water and the ferry growing more distant. Louis pulled a full breath and dove down. The water was clear, maybe twenty-five feet, and he could see down to the sandy bottom. Nothing. Just the sand, rippled by the currents. The currents were strong, strong enough to make Louis fight to keep from getting pulled away.

Louis felt his lungs start to burn and fought his way out of the current and up to the surface. He took another deep breath and dove again, frantically searching. A flash of silver as a school of small fish darted by and then blue. Just endless blue fading away into nothing.

He broke the surface, coughed, and wiped his eyes. He could see the ferry far off to his left and he could feel the current, pulling him in the opposite direction. He felt a panic rising up inside, but he pushed it back down. He started side-stroking, trying to get out of the current's pull. Finally, he felt the pull lessen and then he was free.

He stopped, treading water, trying to catch his breath. He could still see the ferry. It took him a moment to realize it had stopped. A flood of relief passed through him. It was circling back.

He took another dive down to search but saw nothing. He could hear the chug of the ferry's engines underwater, hear it coming nearer. But he couldn't see any sign of Frank.

When he broke the surface, people were yelling. His legs and arms were tiring fast but he spat out a mouthful of salt water and kept treading water. A few minutes later, something hard and white splashed near his shoulder, a lifesaver. Louis grabbed it and felt himself being pulled toward the ferry. He wiped the water from his stinging eyes and scanned the surface for Frank Woods. Nothing.

*Sonofabitch.*

Someone threw a ladder over the side and he climbed back onto the boat. He wiped his face, still searching the water. He could feel the eyes of the tourists on his back as water puddled at his feet.

"I called in your man overboard," the captain said, coming up behind him. "The coast guard is on its way."

Louis stayed at the rail, looking for Frank's body while the ferry slowly kept circling. Finally, he saw the coast guard boat speeding toward them. He stood at the railing, rigid and angry, his neck burning from the searing sun. The other passengers were all staring at him and whispering. The little girl with the Cheetos was hiding behind her father, who was filming Louis with his video camera.

The captain approached Louis. "The coast guard says I can go take everyone back. You wanna stay here with them?"

Louis looked out over the water. "No. They won't find him."

Fifteen minutes later, the ferry pulled into the marina and Louis waited until the tourists had left before he stepped off onto the dock.

Landeta and Strickland were standing under a palm and came forward when they saw him. Landeta was wearing his usual black suit and white dress shirt, his bald head glistening with sweat. He stopped at the end of the dock, blocking Louis's way.

"I heard a rescue call," Landeta said.

"You heard right, but they're not going to rescue anyone," Louis said tightly. "He's gone. Frank's gone."

"He's gone?" Landeta said, his voice sounding as if it were being pulled through a grinder. *"He's gone?"*

"He jumped overboard," Louis said.

Landeta grabbed Louis's arm, and jerked him off the dock onto the sand. "What the hell's the matter with you? Are you fucking stupid? You can't even keep a fifty-eight-year-old man on a fucking boat for forty-five minutes?"

Louis pulled away. He started to argue, started to fight back, but he had nothing to fight with. He had fucked it up—again.

"Look," Louis said, "we need to get back out to that island. I saw Frank talk to a man there. We need to get out there and question them."

"We'll do it," Landeta said. "But you're out of the picture."

"What?"

"You heard me. You're done with this."

Louis stared at Landeta, then turned sharply. He started away, catching Strickland's look of pity as he passed.

"And don't come begging around the station for any more work," Landeta hollered. "You hear me, dumb-ass?"

Louis just kept walking.

# CHAPTER 26

He knew the currents. He knew where they would take him. So he stayed underwater until his lungs were burning, swimming near the bottom where the water ran the swiftest.

When Frank finally came up, he gasped for air and wiped a hand across his eyes. Treading water, he searched for the ferry. It was maybe fifty yards back, heading away. Then he spotted something dark in the water.

Damn . . . Kincaid. He had jumped in after him. He could hear him yelling his name.

Frank pulled in a deep breath and dove back down. He swam fast and as far as he could before coming up again for air. Then he drove down again, swimming underwater until he felt as if his chest would explode.

He surfaced, gulping in air, and scanned the water again. Good . . . he was far away now. If he was lucky, the fast-flowing, northbound current would carry him away before they could get help.

His heart was hammering in his chest. He was tired, his legs and arms heavy with fatigue. But he had to keep going. He started to sidestroke to conserve his strength, moving away from the ferry.

Stupid . . . foolish. Jumping overboard had been a stupid thing to do. He hadn't planned it. But he knew that he couldn't go back. He would have been tried and probably convicted for killing Shelly Umber . . . maybe the others, too.

No . . . no way would he rot in prison. He had spent the last thirty-five years hiding from his past, and he wasn't about to give up now. But there was no place to hide anymore, no place left to go.

Except . . .

His eyes stung from the salt water and he was exhausted. He flipped on his back to float for a minute. The sky was brilliant blue above him, cloudless, infinite blue. Beautiful . . . so pure and beautiful. He felt a sudden catch in his throat, but it was so unfamiliar it took him a moment to realize what it was. Salt, he tasted salt, but not from the water, from his tears. He hadn't cried in a long time, not since that night Sophie died. Everything had changed that night. She was the only thing that had kept him going, the only thing he felt connected to. When she died, he had gone adrift.

Diane . . . he had tried to be a good father to her, but a part of him always thought she blamed him for her mother's death. *Why didn't you go with her, Daddy? Why did you let her drive in the rain?* How did you explain things like death to a seven-year-old girl, things you didn't even understand yourself?

Frank closed his eyes to the sun, letting the current carry him.

How did things get to this point? How had it spiraled so out of control? He had always known it was wrong to kill them. Until now, he had been able to distance himself. But when they found Shelly Umber's body, he knew it was over.

*Ah, Sophie . . . I'm glad you're gone so you don't see what is happening to me. I thought I could escape it, but it's always been there, deep inside me, waiting to come out. A man can't escape what he is.*

He opened his eyes. He stopped moving his arms, then

his legs. For a moment, he just floated, looking at the blue above, waiting, waiting, waiting to be sucked down into the blue below. The water covered his face, he let it flow in. But instinct kicked in and he struggled back to the surface, coughing the water out of his lungs.

*No . . . that's the coward's way. Keep going.*

He flipped back on his side and started swimming again.

Time seemed to stop. The sun began to dip slowly in the west. The sunlight was coming in at a low slant over the water when he saw the green fringe of the island ahead. He was beyond exhaustion now, his limbs leaden in the water, his eyes swollen from the salt water. But he kept sidestroking.

Finally, his feet touched sand and he dragged himself toward the mangroves, using the roots to pull himself up.

He stood for a moment, knee-deep in water, breathing heavily. It was near dusk. He heard the shriek of a grackle, and then the odd rusted-hinge call of a limpkin. He knew birds didn't normally call at dusk; they were announcing the presence of an invader. He wiped a hand over his eyes, tried to steady his shaking legs. When he looked up, he saw a figure standing on the dock ahead.

"I knew you'd make it," the man said.

Frank staggered toward the dock.

"I heard the distress call go out on the radio," the man said. "So I came out here to see."

Frank looked up at the man's face. Thirty-five years . . . Jesus, he hadn't seen him in thirty-five years. He looked different, older, yet so familiar it was like looking in a mirror. Frank felt a sudden urge to embrace him and took a step forward. But the man's expression froze him, there in the water. And the rifle . . . he had a rifle slung over his shoulder.

"Why did you come back?" the man said.

"Emilio—"

"You were told to stay away," the man said. "She told you that. She told you never to come back."

"I left with her blessing," Frank said.

"We don't want you here," the man said. "I don't want you here. You're dead to us."

Frank let out a long breath and looked around. "Where are the others?" he asked. "Do they know about me?"

The man shook his head. "They know what you did. But they didn't hear the distress call. They won't even know you ever came."

Frank came out of the water, starting up the rise toward the dock. The man swung the rifle around, aiming it at Frank's chest. Frank froze. He felt a clutch in his gut but it wasn't from fear.

"Emilio," he said quietly, "I'm your brother, for God's sake."

"You have no brothers here. You have no family here. Not anymore."

Frank took another step. "I have nowhere else to go. You know that. You must have seen the papers."

"I've read them," Emilio said. "There was a picture of the ring. How did they get it?"

Frank shook his head slowly. "My daughter turned it in."

"Your daughter? What did you do to her to cause her to hate you so much?"

"Don't talk to me about daughters, Emilio."

Emilio snapped the lever on the rifle. "Then go now. Leave."

Frank shook his head. "I won't go. I want to talk to the others. I want to talk to—"

"No!" Emilio yelled. "The police will come here after you. Don't you know that? You made your choice when you left. We don't want you here."

Frank took a few more steps. "Emilio," he said carefully, his eyes locked on his brother's face. "I know you still blame me. But Sophie didn't love you, she—"

Emilio lifted the rifle, his finger on the trigger. "I said go!"

Frank came closer.

"I'll shoot you!" Emilio shouted.

Frank lunged for the rifle, grabbing the barrel. Emilio twisted away, falling against the mangrove roots.

Frank wrenched the rifle from his hands, but before he could get away, Emilio grabbed his legs, pulling him to the ground.

Emilio's hands wrapped around Frank's throat. Frank tried to wedge the rifle between himself and Emilio's chest, but he couldn't get a breath, couldn't find the strength to do it.

"Emilio, stop," Frank gasped.

Emilio pulled Frank forward, then slammed his head back against the tree. A split second of blackness, and then a sudden surge of adrenaline ripped through Frank's body. He jammed the rifle butt down hard against Emilio's head.

Frank felt Emilio's hands fall away from his neck, and then the weight of Emilio's body sent him stumbling backward. Frank thrust out a hand to brace himself as he fell hard back against the mangrove roots and into the shallow water.

He sat up, grabbing at his throat, gagging and gulping in air. He saw the rifle and grabbed it with a shaking hand. It took a few seconds for him to realize that Emilio had not moved. He was lying facedown, draped over the roots. Frank grabbed him and rolled him over. Emilio's eyes were open.

*No . . .*

Frank touched Emilio's throat. He felt nothing.

"No," he said, his fingers groping for a pulse. *Oh, God, no.* He pulled Emilio's limp body off the mangrove roots, laying it down in the mud, and pressed his ear to the chest. Nothing. With a cry, Frank leaned back and flung the rifle into the water.

"Emilio?" Someone was calling from beyond the trees, a woman. He knew her voice immediately.

Frank looked up. He scrambled to his feet, and stumbled up the incline through the trees. When the woman saw him, she stopped in the path.

"Emilio?"

Frank came forward. It was almost dark now and he couldn't see her. Just her small black form and the white aureole of her hair. Tiny . . . she was so tiny.

He went closer so he could see her. Her face had been stored in his mind for decades, put there by his heart for safekeeping, to be taken out only when his loneliness overwhelmed him. Her face was there, in the archive of memory, with all the other images and experiences of this place. But he could see now that his memory had been unreliable. She was different . . . her skin, once so smooth and white, was now yellowed and crinkled like old parchment. Her eyes, which once had the dark shine of onyx, were now cloudy. She was old.

He felt something tear, deep inside his chest.

"Mama," he said softly.

She took a step back, putting a hand on her chest.

"It's me, Mama," he said, "it's Frank. Francisco."

She wavered slightly and he stepped forward, ready to catch her if she fell.

"Francisco," she whispered. "Francisco." She lifted her hands, cupping his face.

"How? Why are you—" She stopped. "So many years. I can't believe you came back."

Her hands were warm against his cheeks and Frank closed his eyes. Her touch, that had not changed. It was exactly as he remembered it.

"How did you get here?" she said softly.

"I jumped . . ." He took her hands in his and looked down into her face. "It doesn't matter."

Her eyes filled with tears. He pulled her into his arms. He could feel her shoulder blades, sharp as knives, through her dress. She was so fragile, as if she would shatter into a million pieces if he held her too long or too hard. He lowered his head to hers, and breathed in her scent—not the lavender soap he remembered, but something dusty and dry. His throat constricted and he squeezed his eyes shut against it.

She pulled away to look up at him. "The police are looking for you. They will come here."

Frank shook his head. "They won't come. They don't know about this place. They don't know who I really am." He hesitated. "Mama, I have nowhere else to go."

"But the others . . . your brother won't allow it."

Frank stepped back and took her small shoulders in his hands. "Emilio is dead."

Her eyes widened. "Dead?"

"It was an accident," Frank said. "I didn't mean to do it. We were fighting, and—"

She eased himself from his grip and turned her back to him. She covered her face with her hands. Frank hung his head, rubbing his face. Emilio had been right. He shouldn't have come back. Kincaid or someone would eventually trace him here. The police would come. And they would find out about the girls and what they did here, what they had been doing here for decades.

"Francisco."

Frank looked up at his mother.

"Where is he? Where is your brother?"

Frank looked down toward the mangroves. She followed his gaze and started toward the water, but he put his hands on her shoulders, stopping her.

"I'll take care of him," he said. "Then I will go."

Her fingers curled around his forearm. "Go? Where?"

"Back. If I turn myself in, they'll leave you alone. If I don't go back, they'll come here."

"No," she said. "I lost you once. I won't lose you again. You will stay here now."

Frank shook his head. "No, Mama, there's no way that can happen now."

Her grip on his arm tightened. He was surprised by her strength.

"There is a way," she said. "I know a way you can stay and they will not come here looking for you. *Frater tuus*

*mortuus est. Voluntas dei est. Nunc ille locum tuum sumet et
tu suum sumes."*

Frank stared at his mother, too stunned to answer.

"Francisco, do you understand?" she said.

He hesitated, then nodded.

"Tell me you understand," she said firmly.

*"Sic intellego,"* he whispered.

She touched his face.

"What about the others?" he asked.

"They will do as I say. They always have."

Frank shook his head. "I'm so sorry, Mama," he whispered. "I didn't mean to kill him. I didn't—"

Her hands came up to his cheek and he felt its dry caress. "I know. Everything will be all right. You are home now."

Frank reached up and took his mother's hands from his face. He covered her small hands with his own, holding them for a moment, then turned away.

He looked down into the dark mangroves. He could just make out the white of his brother's shirt. He didn't want to look at it. He didn't want to do what he knew he had to.

*Your brother is dead. It is God's will. You must take his place and he must take yours.*

He looked back at his mother. "Go back to the house, Mama," he said. "I'll take care of everything."

He started down toward the mangroves. It was quiet, just the sound of the water lapping against the roots. He stood there for a moment over the body.

"Francisco?"

Frank turned back but couldn't see her in the dark. "It's all right, Mama, go back to the house," he said.

He looked up, out over the black void of the sound. There was nothing to break the darkness, not one light, not one boat, no sign that there was another world somewhere out there.

He knelt in the mud and began to unbutton his brother's shirt. When he had undressed him, he took off his own red

shirt and shorts, putting them on his brother. Mustering the
last of his strength, he slowly dragged the body back into the
water.

He started wading out, away from shore, guiding the body
in front of him. When the water was chest-high, he stopped.
He brought up his hand and slipped off his gold wedding
band. He put it on his brother's left hand.

Lightning flashed behind the billowing banks of thunder-
heads, but there was no thunder. There was no noise at all
except for the lapping of the water and the pounding in his
temples. The currents were swirling around him. He let go,
and his brother's body began to drift away.

*"Ave atque vale,* Frank Woods," he whispered.

# CHAPTER 27

Louis slammed the screen door to his cottage, ripping off his shirt as he headed to the kitchen. He threw the shirt in a corner and yanked open the refrigerator. No fucking beer.

His eyes lasered up to the bottle of Remy Martin that Roberta had forced on him after the storm. He pulled it down, and took off the cap.

"Louis?"

Damn it. It was Pierre. What the hell did he want?

Louis walked to the living room, looking at Pierre through the screen.

"What?"

"The Kozol family in number eight, they say they were robbed this afternoon. Someone went in and stole their boom boxer."

Louis lifted the bottle to his lips and took a drink.

"You were not here to stop them," Pierre said.

"No, I guess I wasn't," Louis said.

"You playing *flic* again?" Pierre asked, using the slang for "cop."

Louis gave a bitter snort. "Yeah, a fucking flic, that's me all right."

*"Tiens!* And they pay you enough to live here on your own?"

Louis lowered the bottle. "No, they don't."

"You should remember that next time you sit on your porch here to see the sunset, Louis."

Pierre turned away, and disappeared into the shadows. Louis looked down at the bottle in his hand. He went back to the kitchen, recapped the brandy, and put it away. He leaned against the counter and rubbed his face, his mind rewinding the scene on the boat again. Frank moving to the rail. His head bobbing in the water, then slowly sinking, along with the case and *his* reputation.

Now what?

Louis went to the television, and flipped it on, tuning it to the news. He caught the middle of a talk show, and glanced at his watch. He had ten minutes before the news.

He showered, pulled on a pair of shorts and a clean T-shirt, and went back to the television, a Dr Pepper in hand.

It was the lead story.

Landeta was at the marina, backdropped by the bay and a few boats that were still searching. Landeta's head was red, burned by the afternoon sun, and his shirt held dark circles of sweat. The gold detective shield hanging on his pocket sent off a sharp glint in the setting sun.

Landeta was recounting the afternoon's events, pointing out at Pine Island Sound. Heather Fox was barking out questions, thrusting the mike in Landeta's face. He didn't have many answers.

"Why did Woods go out to the island?"

"We don't know."

"Why did he jump overboard?"

"We don't know."

"Do you believe him to be the killer of Shelly Umber?"

"We just wanted to talk to him."

"Who was with Woods on the boat?"

Landeta stared right into the camera. "A private investigator named Louis Kincaid."

"Is Kincaid working in an official capacity with the Fort Myers police?"

Landeta drew in a breath. "Not anymore."

The camera switched to a view of the sound. Louis watched the police and coast guard patrol boats, hoping to see Frank's body being hauled on board. Heather Fox was talking about the search and how many agencies were involved.

"So far, no body has been found," she said. "And with police unwilling to speculate on Frank Woods's mental state, some sources are saying that Woods's jump off the ferry was simply an escape attempt." She gestured back at the sound. "Apparently, a successful one. This is Heather Fox, live on Captiva Island for WINK-News."

His phone rang and he reached for it, then hesitated. Damn, who was this? Another reporter? He let it ring, but then realized it could be Chief Horton. He answered it.

"You killed him!" she screamed.

Louis sat forward. "Diane—"

"Why didn't you stop him? I told you he would do this! I told you!"

He moved the phone farther from his ear.

"I paid you to protect him!"

"I'll give your damn money back."

Silence. He could hear her crying now.

Louis dropped onto the sofa. Jesus, here he was pissed off because he had lost a suspect again. Diane had lost a father. His eyes went to the TV. Frank's picture was displayed behind the anchorman's head. Louis muted the sound.

"Diane, listen to me," he said. "They haven't found his body. He could have . . ."

She was sobbing now. She knew he was lying. She knew just as well as he did that Frank Woods wanted to die.

"Diane, I'm sorry." It sounded weak, almost pathetic. It was all he had to offer her.

"Diane, if a person really wants to kill himself, no one can stop him," Louis said. "You know that, don't you?"

She didn't answer. It was quiet. He wondered if she had put the phone down and walked away.

"Diane? You still there?"

Silence. Then, "Yes" in a whisper.

"Diane . . . I still want to know if he killed those women."

"Why? What difference does it make now?"

"Reputation," Louis said. "Getting it back. That's worth something."

"You don't really care whether he did it. It's your own damn reputation you care about."

Louis put his head in his hand, holding his temper. "It's not that. I've looked stupid before."

She gave a short, bitter laugh.

"Diane—"

"What the hell do you want from me? What else can I possibly give you?" She was crying again.

"Your mother's maiden name."

She made a strange sound. He couldn't figure out if it was a laugh or a sob.

"Screw you, Louis Kincaid," she said. "You've killed my father. I'm not letting you near my mother."

She hung up.

# CHAPTER 28

He flipped to his back and closed his eyes again, hoping this time sleep would come. He lay in the darkness of his bedroom, stripped down to his shorts, listening to the rattle of Pierre's fan.

Every once in a while, he could feel the breeze of the gulf wash over his bare skin, bringing temporary relief from the heat.

It was hopeless. He opened his eyes and stared into the darkness.

What time was it? Had he slept at all? Was it the brandy keeping him awake or this damn case? Or was it the burning embarrassment of stupidity?

The soft light of dawn started to rise in the window.

He hadn't become a cop for the attention . . . few did. But the last few years had brought some headlines and accomplishments. He still didn't like reporters, or the spotlight, but he was proud of what he had done. He liked having the reputation as a dogged, smart investigator whom the cops trusted. It meant something. Until yesterday.

*Forget it, Louis. It's not the first time. Go back to sleep.*

He closed his eyes just as the phone rang. Something told

him the call was about Frank, but he wasn't sure why anyone would be calling to tell him anything about Woods. It was probably just Pierre wanting him to quiet down some drunken tourist.

He grabbed it without rolling over.

"Yeah?"

"Louis?"

"Who's this?"

"Strickland. Officer Strickland."

Louis sat up. "What happened?"

"He's washed up. Woods is in the water just off Monkey Island. I'm heading out now to pick up Landeta."

Louis rubbed his eyes with his free hand. "Strickland, why are you calling me? Didn't you see the news?"

"I heard what Landeta said, but I also know he's a moron. And when we got back to the station, the chief took him behind closed doors and Landeta's head was red as a frickin' beet when he walked out of there. He was pissed."

Louis was quiet.

"Look," Strickland said. "I just thought maybe you weren't so ready to give up, that's all. I gotta git." He hesitated. "You won't tell the chief I called you, will you?"

"No. Thanks for the tip."

Down at the Fort Myers yacht basin, Louis caught a ride from the mainland with a couple of crime scene techs he had worked with before, guys who knew who he was and what had happened but didn't seem to care.

The sun was still low in the eastern sky but the tide was high by the time they got to the island. No wading in this time. Louis stepped off the boat and headed up the small rise to where he could see the yellow crime scene tape. A couple of uniforms stood talking, and two fishermen were pointing toward the water.

He was surprised to spot Heather Fox standing a little ways off, working to set up a remote with her cameraman. She was wearing worn jeans and bright yellow rubber boots like a kid might own, but above the waist she looked picture-perfect right down to a white silk blouse and lacquered hair.

On the other side of the tape was Chief Horton. He stood, legs wide, hands on hips, looking down at the water. Out in knee-deep water, Landeta and two other men stood in a tight knot. The photographer moved and Louis caught a glimpse of bright red that he recognized as Frank's shirt.

With a glance back at the uniforms, Louis ducked under the tape and went up behind Horton.

He could see Frank's body now, the red shirt billowing like a flag in the pale shallow water. Frank was curled against the tree roots, as if he were being rocked asleep by the gently rippling current. He looked almost peaceful lying there, nothing like Shelly Umber had looked, twisted and tortured in her mangrove cage.

"He couldn't swim," Louis said.

Horton's head swiveled back to him.

"What the hell are you doing here, Kincaid?"

Louis couldn't think of an answer. And from the expression on Horton's face, he wasn't even sure he needed one. In fact, Horton looked almost glad to see him.

"Frank's daughter, Diane, told me he couldn't swim."

"Why didn't you tell me that before now?"

"I just remembered it."

Horton looked back at the body. "Suicide?"

"Diane thinks so."

Horton's eyes came back to Louis. "You don't?"

Louis didn't answer. He was looking around at the mangroves, at the proximity of the other islands.

"Strange," Louis said.

"What is?"

"Frank ending up close to where Shelley Umber did."

"Maybe he planned it that way." Horton let out a tired sigh of frustration. "Sick fuck."

The crime techs were finished. The body was lifted into a bag. Landeta was still standing in the water, pulling off his gloves as he talked to the other Fort Myers detective. Horton was watching them both closely.

"How'd you find out about this, Louis?" Horton asked.

"I have friends."

"In my department?" When Louis didn't answer, Horton added, "Friends who don't think we can handle this without you?"

"Friends who think Landeta's lost it."

Horton drew in a slow breath. He looked at the other cops, the crime tech guys, and finally at Heather Fox. He ducked under the tape and started away, nodding at Louis to follow. The sun was high in the heat-hazed sky now, baking the mucky earth and unleashing all the primordial smells. Horton finally paused under the thin shade of a strangler fig tree.

"I didn't think it was that obvious," he said.

"You knew?" Louis asked.

"I had a suspicion so I started watching," Horton said. "Out in the field, Mel can't seem to get a feel for things and he's missing stuff." Horton was still looking out at the water. "This is a guy who had great instincts, who could find evidence fibers on a gnat's ass."

Horton let out sigh. "I don't know what happened."

"He's an alcoholic. You know that, don't you?"

"He's been off the sauce for years."

"I saw him take a drink at O'Sullivan's."

Horton looked back at Louis. "Shit," he said softly. "I don't suppose it matters much now. This case is about done."

"Done?" Louis asked.

Horton nodded. "Woods is our killer. Not being able to prove it doesn't change anything. I wish we had more than that ring to link Woods to Shelly Umber, but we don't. And I don't have the manpower or money to keep looking. We'll just have to call it closed with what we got."

Louis looked over toward Landeta and Frank Wood's body. "I think I'll stay with this awhile longer," Louis said.

Horton squinted at Louis, the sun in his face. "Louis, this

case hasn't been one of your best pieces of work. You're not looking just to redeem yourself, are you?"

Louis glanced out at the water. "I just want to be sure."

Horton nodded. "Well, I can't stop you, but do me a favor. Work with Mel. I don't want him fumbling around for weeks trying to close this thing down."

Louis gave him a look of disgust.

Horton leaned close. "Look, Louis, you're a PI. Most PIs don't even get within smelling distance of a homicide, let alone allowed access to the things I've given you. I do it because I like and respect you. But don't think I don't take shit for it among my own."

Louis was silent.

"I can't force you to do anything," Horton said. "But I'm asking."

"Then what?" Louis asked.

Horton let out a big breath. "Then I think Mel is going to have to resign."

Horton heard Landeta coming up behind him and he threw Louis a pleading look. Landeta stopped near them, pulled out a handkerchief, and wiped his head. "It looks like Woods but no beard," he said.

"He shaved it," Louis said. "And he was wearing that red shirt at the restaurant."

Landeta stared at Louis, as if he had just noticed he was there. Then he turned his back on Louis to face Horton.

"We'll need an ID," Landeta said, taking off his glasses to clean them. "I'll call his daughter and get her in—"

"No," Horton interrupted. "Let Louis do that."

Landeta's hands froze and he lifted his gaze to Horton. His eyes looked bugged, glassy, and red. Louis wondered if he had been drinking again.

Horton waited for a reply and Landeta finally replaced his glasses, his neck twitching. "Yes, sir."

"I want this whole thing wrapped up real quick, Mel," Horton said. "I'd like something stronger between Woods and

Shelly Umber but if we don't get it, we wrap it up by the end
of the month."

Landeta inhaled slowly, his eyes focused hard on Horton's
face. "What about the other women?"

"There's no evidence Frank Woods had anything to do
with them except cutting their pictures out of a newspaper,"
Horton said. "Just concentrate on Umber."

"What about him?" Landeta asked, nodding toward Louis.

Horton glanced between Louis and Landeta. "Nothing's
changed, in spite of your comments on TV yesterday. Work
with him, Mel. That's an order."

Landeta watched Horton move into the crowd, then looked
out at the bay. He said nothing but there was an emptiness in
his gaze, a small slump to the shoulders. Louis wondered if
Landeta knew about the talk behind his back. He wondered
if Landeta knew how close he was to not being a cop anymore.

He remembered suddenly what Landeta had said back in
his office that day he came in to pick up the baby skull.

*So how long did it take before you didn't miss it anymore?*
And his thought at the time: *Try a lifetime.*

Louis drew in a breath. "Look," he said, "if it makes you
feel any better, I agree with you on the other women. If you
want—"

Landeta's head jerked back to Louis. "You think I need
*your* shit-ass opinion to make me feel better?"

Louis tightened. *Try again.*

"I only meant I understand how you must feel, with the
chief shutting you down like that, that's all," Louis said.

"You don't understand shit."

"Okay. You're right," Louis said. "I don't understand *you*
or *him*. But how can you not pursue the other women? Or
maybe you're just not seeing the connection. Is that it?"

"I see more than you think," Landeta said. "I see a hot-
shot private eye who doesn't have the guts to even try to put
on a badge again."

Louis leaned into him. "And I see a burnout playing it easy just to keep his job."

Landeta curled a fist, his body rigid. "You sonofabitch."

Louis stared at him for a second, then stepped back. He opened his mouth to apologize, but he couldn't. The man deserved every word.

"I'm out of here," Louis said, turning away.

"Where you going?" Landeta called out.

"To the morgue with Woods," Louis shot back over his shoulder.

"Make sure he doesn't get away from you this time," Landeta yelled out.

# CHAPTER 29

"He couldn't swim."

Vince looked up at Louis but then the medical examiner just shrugged and went back to weighing Frank Woods's heart.

Louis was staring at Frank's body lying on the stainless steel table.

"Louis, he committed suicide. He wanted to die. You didn't kill him, for crissake."

"I didn't save him either." Louis shook his head slowly. "How in hell does a person drown himself?"

"Easy," Vince said. "You just take a deep breath and give up. It's more common than you think. People drown themselves all the time—bathtubs, lakes, pools. Hart Crane jumped off a steamship. Virginia Woolf walked into a river. Tchaikovsky, Ophelia, Jerry Baskin."

"Who's Jerry Baskin?"

"The bum in that movie *Down and Out in Beverly Hills*. Tried to off himself in Richard Dreyfus's pool."

"This isn't funny, Vince."

"It rarely is. *Nemo ante mortem beatus*."

Louis just stared at him, waiting.

"Nobody is happy before his death," Vince translated. He put his earphones back on and returned to his work. Louis was close enough to Vince to hear Janis Joplin singing "Summertime." He moved away, going up to stand at the head of the stainless steel table.

It struck him again how different Frank looked from the first time he had seen him in the library. Then, with his salt-and-pepper beard, badly chopped haircut, pale skin, and stooped posture, Frank Woods had looked every inch the hermit bookworm he had been. But the three weeks he had spent as a murder suspect and then a hunted man had changed him. His hair was longer, his skin made leathery by the sun. His body looked almost sinewy, and even in death his face wore an odd expression of what—puzzlement? Confusion over what had happened to his life?

Why had he done it? Guilt over killing those women? Fear of facing his daughter? *Nobody is happy before his death.* That was certainly true of Frank.

Louis glanced down at Frank's left hand, at his gold wedding band. For the life of him, he just couldn't see this man killing six women. But why had he confessed?

And those strange foreign words Frank had said in the restaurant. What was that all about?

Shit, what had he said? Something about hicks loot . . . hicks looties?

Louis was thinking about all the books in Frank's house, all those language books, but he couldn't recall seeing books on any one particular language. Linguistics, language origins, that kind of stuff.

Hicks looty . . . was it Latin?

"Hey, Vince," Louis called out.

Vince's head was bobbing rhythmically. Louis picked up a towel and tossed it across the table, hitting Vince in the chest.

Vince snatched off the earphones. "What? Jesus . . ."

"Vince, Frank Woods said something to me in a foreign language. It might have been Latin. What does this sound like to you—hicks looty?"

Vince grimaced. "You sure you heard him right?"

"I don't know, man. It sounded like hicks and then looty . . ." Louis paused. "No, it was lootio. And then es, like the letter S."

Vince repeated the phrase several times under his breath, then shook his head. *"Lapsus linguae,* Louis. You must have heard him wrong."

"Shit," Louis murmured.

A sound of a door made Louis turn. It was Octavius, the diener.

"Vince, the guy's daughter is outside," he said.

"His daughter? What does she want?"

"Says the cops told her to come over and identify her father."

"Identify him?" Vince said. "I thought they already did that." He glanced at Louis. "Don't tell me somebody screwed this up."

Louis glanced at the door, hoping Diane wasn't nearby. "I don't know, Vince. I tried to call her at her school but they told me she wasn't available. I don't know who told her to come here."

"Damn it," Vince muttered. He went over and glanced at a clipboard, holding his bloody-gloved hands aloft. "This says he had already been ID'd and released."

He came back to stand by the body. "If I had known this, I wouldn't have cut him. How does this shit happen?"

Louis didn't respond. He wondered if Landeta had screwed up somehow. Or had he done an end-around and contacted Diane Woods after Horton had told him to let Louis handle it?

"Octo, get him covered up," Vince said, snapping off his gloves and tossing them in the trash. "I'll go out and talk to her."

"Let me do it," Louis said quickly.

"Why?"

"I need to."

"Be my guest. Give me five and then you can bring her in."

Louis went out into the hallway. Diane was standing by the receptionist's desk. She was dressed like she had just come from school. She was biting her nails.

Louis pushed open the doors. She stiffened when she saw him.

"What are you doing here?" she demanded.

"Diane, I have to talk to you."

Her eyes went to the double doors. "Is he in there?"

"Yes, but—"

She started to go by him and Louis caught her arm. "Wait, Diane—"

She pulled away, glaring at him. "Stay away from me."

She hurried through the doors. Louis followed, catching up to her before she got to the autopsy room. He caught her by both arms and spun her away from the door's window.

"Diane, listen to me."

"Let go of me," she said. It came out as a whimper and Louis realized she was shaking. She bowed her head, her body growing heavy in his hands. He backed her up and gently lowered her onto a bench. She covered her face with her hands.

He thought she was going to cry, but when she lowered her hands, her face was dry, her eyes strangely empty.

"I can't do it," she said.

"It's all right," Louis said. "He looks . . . asleep."

She didn't seem to hear him. "You don't know what it's like," she said quietly. "You don't know what it's like to get the calls from the parents, the school board. Or to go in there every day and hear them whispering, knowing they are talking about it, and then you walk into the lounge and they shut up." She looked up at Louis. "My car, when I went out to the parking lot today, my car . . . there was red paint on the windshield. I think one of the kids . . ."

Her voice trailed off and she shook her head. "I can't *do* it. I just can't . . . do . . . it."

Louis leaned back against the cold tile wall, looking down at Diane Woods. Any pity he had felt for her was fading fast. Her father—her only living relative—was lying in there dead. And the only thing she could mourn was her own reputation.

"They need an ID," he said.

She looked up at him and then the door. She rose, smoothing her hair. She followed Louis into the autopsy room.

She stopped when she saw the body, her eyes going up to Vince and then back to the table. Vince had taken off his bloodied apron and was standing at the top of the stainless steel table. A plastic sheet had been draped over the gaping Y-shaped incision in the chest. Louis was relieved to see that Frank Woods did, in fact, look asleep. He leaned back against the wall, watching Diane.

She hadn't moved. She was just standing there, maybe five feet away from the table, her eyes locked on Frank's face.

"Yes, it's him," she whispered. She looked at Vince. "Can I go now?"

Vince came forward and held out his hand. "I thought you might want his wedding ring back," he said.

Diane looked down at the gold band and then took it from Vince. She looked at it blankly for a moment, putting it on the tip of her right ring finger, just above her mother's wedding band. Then she slipped off Frank's ring and balled it up in her fist. She turned quickly and pushed open the doors, almost running down the hallway.

Louis followed, catching up with her in the lobby. She was fumbling in her purse. She pulled out her keys with shaking hands, dropping them and the wedding band. The ring rolled away on the tile. Louis bent to retrieve it.

Diane had picked up her keys and was just standing there,

a hand over her eyes. She took in several deep breaths and looked at Louis.

"You dropped this," he said, holding out the ring.

She took it and put it in her purse. "Is there anything else?" she asked. "Do I have to sign something, do anything else?"

Louis shook his head.

"I guess I have to call a funeral home," she said. It came out almost like a question.

"Diane," Louis began. "I'm not convinced your father killed anybody."

She just stared at him.

"Maybe it's just a feeling, I don't know," Louis went on. "But I'm going to try to keep this case open and find out who did kill those women."

Louis could tell from the look in her eyes that Diane Woods didn't share his feeling. She had already accepted the fact that her father was a murderer and all she wanted to do was to bury him and find a way to live with his ghost.

"Help me clear his name, Diane."

Her eyes flicked to the hallway. "The other day," she said quietly, "when you came to my school and you said that thing, you know, about my father not having a past before I was born?"

Louis waited. Finally she looked back at him. There was something in her expression that he had never seen before. It was as if the principal, the professional woman, the careful daughter who drank her gin from crystal goblets suddenly didn't have the faintest idea who she was.

"You have something you want to tell me?" Louis asked.

She hesitated. "I found my birth certificate," she said. "It said . . . there was no hospital listed. It said I was born at home."

"So?"

"That's strange, don't you think? Like, like . . . primitive."

Louis didn't tell her what he was thinking—that he himself had been born at home. But home was a shack in Black Pool, Mississippi, something Diane surely would have no empathy for.

"Lots of people are born at home," he said. "Did your birth certificate list your mother's name?"

When she didn't answer, Louis went on. "Look, Diane. If you know the name, give it to me. If I can track down something about your father's past, maybe I can clear him." He paused. "And you."

She pulled in a deep breath. "I barely knew my mother. I was so young when she died." She hesitated. "Sophie Reardon. I think she was from St. James City."

She quickly dug in her purse, pulling out sunglasses and putting them on. "I have to get back to school," she said tightly and started to the door.

"Thanks," Louis said.

She didn't answer him or look back as she hurried out into the sunlight.

# CHAPTER 30

Louis paused on the porch of Frank's house. He looked back out at the empty street, then reached up into the planter for the key. He unlocked the front door and slipped inside.

The house was hot and smelled bad. It had been closed up since Horton's men had finished and Louis doubted Diane had been here since her father's death.

He remembered seeing a lamp near the recliner and went to it, switching it on. The room came to gloomy life. He stood, hands on hips, looking around but not at all sure what he was looking for.

Some sign of Sophie Reardon maybe? Diane had told him her mother had died when she was seven. Maybe that was why this place had the feeling that no woman—no wife—had ever cared for it.

He went to the bedroom, switching on the overhead light. The place was such a mess he wasn't even sure where to start.

At the dresser, he opened the top drawer. That is where he kept his own cache of personal stuff—the pictures of his brother and sister he hadn't seen since he was seven, and the blurry snapshot of the man who had abandoned them. But there was nothing in Frank's drawer but a tangle of socks and underwear.

The other three drawers were the same—faded pajamas, T-shirts, and shorts, a couple of old cardigans. Louis closed the bottom drawer and stood up, surveying the room.

He went over to the bookcase. It was a cheap, assemble-it-yourself job, and its particleboard shelves were sagging under the weight of all the books. But as messy as it was, there seemed to be a certain logic to the books' arrangement.

The top shelf was all books on language origins, etymology, and a huge two-volume set of the Compact Edition of the Oxford English Dictionary.

Louis's eyes paused on the second shelf. *New Latin Grammar, Wheelock's Latin, Grote's Study Guide to Latin, Aeneas to Augustus: A Beginning Latin Reader for College Students.* There were more than twenty textbooks and dictionaries, some of them with little flags of colored paper sticking out, marking certain pages.

Louis extracted a well-worn paperback called *Teach Yourself Latin* and flipped through the pages. He put it back with a sigh.

He could barely read college French. What in the hell did he expect to find here? A word-for-word translation of what Frank had said back in the restaurant?

He bent to look at the third shelf. Copies of *The Iliad* and *The Odyssey. The Early History of Rome* by Titus Livy. *Our Roman Roots: A Student's Guide to Latin Grammar and Civilization.* He pulled out one well-worn paperback. It was another copy of *The Iliad*—this one a Latin translation.

Diane had said her father hadn't gone to college. Landeta hadn't even been able to find a high school record for the man. So what in the hell was all this? Louis thought of his partner Jesse up in Michigan. Jesse had prided himself on being an autodidact. Well, reading *The Great Gatsby* was one thing, but teaching yourself to read classics in Latin was another.

Louis spotted a copy of *Bullfinch's Mythology*. He remembered having to buy a copy of it back at the University of Michigan for a freshman literature course. There was a yellow bookmark sticking out of it. He pulled the book out and opened it to the marked page.

The Legend of Romulus and Remus, the founders of Rome. There was a picture accompanying the chapter. It was a bronze sculpture of a wolf nursing two baby boys. The caption said ROMULUS AND REMUS WITH THEIR WOLF FOSTER-MOTHER, BRONZE SCULPTURE, C. 500–480 B.C. IN THE CAPITOLINE MUSEUMS, ROME, ITALY.

Louis stared at the photograph, transfixed by its weirdness. He closed the book and set it aside, turning his attention to the bottom shelf. It held only four books, stacked on their sides. Louis pulled them out, scanning the titles.

*Of Wolves and Men* by Barry Lopez. *Mother Was a Lovely Beast* by Philip Jose. *The Wolf Children: Fact or Fiction?* by Charles MacLean. *Man Into Wolf: An Anthropological Study of Sadism, Masochism and Lycanthropy* by Robert Eisler.

Louis stood slowly, holding the four books. He wiped a sleeve over his sweating face.

*Jesus . . .* What in the hell was this?

Wolf mothers? Werewolves? Had Frank Woods been some sadistic animal who hunted down women and killed them? Is that why he had bookmarked that photograph of the weird wolf statue? Was that what he had been trying to tell Louis with the Latin?

Louis went to the bedside table. There was a single book there and he picked it up. *The Myths and Customs of the Asturian People*. There was something sticking out of the book that didn't look like one of Frank's color-coded bookmarks. Louis slipped it out.

It was a picture of Frank and Diane. Diane was smiling and had her arm linked through Frank's, her head lying on his shoulder. Louis stared at the picture, trying to reconcile the affection he saw in the picture with the reality he had seen between Diane and Frank. He turned it over. Someone had written in pen *Sophie, October, 1952*.

Of course it wasn't Diane. She had probably never felt close enough to her father to touch him like that. Louis slipped the picture into his pocket. At least now when he went to St. James City, he had a picture of Sophie Reardon to show. And if he found Sophie's past, maybe he could find the real Frank Woods.

Louis added a Latin dictionary and the *Bullfinch's Mythology* to his pile of books. He left the stifling bedroom.

It was past four by the time he reached Pine Island. At Stringfellow Road, Louis turned south, heading in the opposite direction of Bessie Levy's home up in Bokeelia. The sun was sinking in a pale orange sky when he pulled into St. James City.

It was more a village than a city, a motley but pleasant collection of small homes clinging to the edges of canals like some Florida cracker version of Venice.

Louis had found a James Reardon listed on Carombola Lane. He pulled up in front of the neat white house and got out. Lights were on inside, a car parked in the drive. Louis went up to the open front door and rang the bell.

A white-haired woman came to the screen door, wiping her hands on a towel. She stiffened slightly seeing Louis. He had his private investigator ID ready.

"Yes?" she asked warily.

"I'm looking for James Reardon," Louis said, holding the ID against the screen so she could see it. "I'm working with the Fort Myers Police Department."

"Oh . . . dear. Is there something wrong?"

A man was coming up to the door. He was tall, white-haired, using a cane. "Who is it, Nan?"

"The police, Jim."

James Reardon stared at Louis and then his ID through the screen. "That doesn't look like a real badge," he said. His hand moved to the latch on the screen. Louis heard it click into lock.

"It's not a badge, sir. It's an ID. I'm a private investigator. I just want to ask you a few questions."

"About what?"

"Your daughter Sophie."

The man frowned. "Sophie?" He waved his hand, like he was dismissing the name and memory. "She left here more than thirty years ago. Why you coming around now?"

"Mr. Reardon, if I could just come in for—"

"You here to see if I'm dead yet?" Reardon asked, leaning into the screen. "Tell her I ain't and even if I was, I have nothing to leave her."

Mrs. Reardon was hovering behind her husband, her eyes wide.

"Mr. Reardon, please. This is important. Maybe if I could talk to Sophie's mother," Louis said gently.

"Sophie's mother is dead," the old man said quickly.

The woman behind him stepped forward. "I'm Jim's second wife," she said, taking her husband's arm. "I think you should go. Please."

Jim Reardon hadn't budged. He didn't seem so quick to stop talking. "You tell her I got nothing to offer her. No money and no time."

Louis took a breath. "Mr. Reardon, Sophie's dead. She died in 1959."

Reardon's eyes went liquid, like milk. The sagging skin along his jaw quivered a little as he lifted a hand to the door frame. His wife stepped forward and took his arm.

"You have a granddaughter," Louis said. "Her name is Diane."

"Granddaughter? I never heard about no granddaughter,"

Reardon said. "No one ever told me about it. I don't believe it. It's probably just some scam, someone trying to take advantage of an old man—"

"Jim, please," his wife interrupted, pulling his arm.

He shrugged out of her grasp. No one moved. Louis could feel the sweat trickling down his rib cage, and ran a hand across his brow.

"So is that spic dead too?" Reardon asked bitterly.

"Who?" Louis asked.

"That damn boy she ran off with."

"What boy, Mr. Reardon?" Louis pressed.

"That damn Mexican boy who used to come in the store. The one that took her away."

*Mexican?*

Louis reached into his pocket. He held the picture of Frank and Sophie up to the screen.

"Is this the boy, Mr. Reardon?" he asked.

James Reardon peered at the picture. "Yeah. That's the damn spic who hung around my store." His face hardened. "I knew he was no good. Damn Mexicans . . . like heathens they are."

"Jim, please . . ." His wife glanced quickly at Louis. "I'm sorry, he's—"

Louis ignored her. "Mr. Reardon, what makes you think the boy was Mexican?"

"All that black hair and that spic name and talking those words I didn't understand . . . just to gall me."

Louis pressed the photograph of Frank and Sophie back on the screen. "Mr. Reardon, you're *sure* this is the boy?"

"Yeah, I'm sure. I'm old but I still got my mind, young man." Reardon wagged a finger at the picture. "He came in my drugstore every month. I was back there filling his damn prescription and he was always out at the counter, talking to my Sophie." He was staring at the photograph.

"What was his name, Mr. Reardon?" Louis pressed. "Do you remember the boy's name?"

"I don't know. It was like Mexican or Puerto Rican. Probably one of those damn migrant workers. So is he dead or not?"

Louis nodded. "Yes, he is."

"Good." Reardon turned from the door and disappeared back into the shadows of the house.

His wife glanced after him. Louis wiped his brow again, slipping the picture back in his pocket. "I'm sorry if I upset him," Louis said. He paused. "Does he still have the drugstore? Maybe there are records—"

"Oh, no, he closed it years ago."

Back in the living room, Louis could see Reardon slump down in a chair, tossing his cane to the floor.

Mrs. Reardon opened the screen, speaking quietly. "I was a friend of Sophie's mother, see, and I don't think Sophie ever forgave me for marrying her father. You know, the wicked stepmother and all that."

She tried to smile but it came out as a sad tremble. "But Sophie was a good girl, I do know that. After her mother died, Jim kind of closed down, like he didn't want anyone to touch him. It was hard on Sophie. Too hard. All the girl wanted was someone to love her. Jim had a hard time showing that."

"I understand," Louis said.

Mrs. Reardon leaned closer. "What did you say the granddaughter's name was?"

"Diane."

"Are you going to tell her about Jim? Maybe I could convince him to see her."

Louis tried to picture Diane Woods in this place, on this porch, giving James Reardon an embrace. Or him giving her a grandfatherly one back. But he knew there were no bridges that could be built between them.

"I'm sorry," Louis said. "I don't think she'd come."

"He's dying," she said softly.

Louis drew in a small breath, his chest tightening. "I still don't think she would come, but I'll ask her."

Nan Reardon glanced back at her husband sitting in the shadows and then looked back at Louis. "He never talks about Sophie. I don't think he ever forgave her for leaving. Or himself for pushing her away."

Louis noticed she was looking at the photograph in his hand.

"Jim got rid of all her pictures when she left," Nan Reardon said. She hesitated. "I don't suppose I could have that one?"

"No, I'm sorry," Louis said.

"Nan!"

She turned to look back at her husband.

"I'm sorry, I have to go," she said softly. She shut the door.

Louis stood there on the porch, gathering his thoughts. He held the picture up closer to the porch light, studying Frank's face. Frank's hair was thick and dark, his facer thinner, almost pale. He didn't look Mexican, at least not like the brown-skinned people Louis had seen in Immokalee.

But Reardon had been sure that Frank spoke in a foreign language and had a Spanish name.

There was only one answer. Frank Woods wasn't his real name. Which was why Landeta hadn't been able to find any history on the guy. And without even a real name to go on, it was a sure bet they weren't going to find any now. Or anything concrete to connect Frank to the Umber case.

Louis slipped the picture back in his pocket and started down to the Mustang. It was going to be a long drive home— all the way back to square one.

# CHAPTER 31

It was past seven by the time Louis headed the Mustang back over the Caloosahatchee Bridge. On Cleveland Avenue, he stopped at a 7-Eleven and called Landeta.

"Why are you calling me at home?" Landeta said.

"I found out something important about Frank Woods." Louis waited. He could hear Landeta breathing heavily. "You want to know what it is or not?"

"So tell me, Rocky."

Louis shook his head slowly and took a breath. "Look, I haven't eaten all day. I'm going to grab something at McDonald's and then I'm heading over to the station. Meet me there and we'll go over it."

"No," Landeta said. There was a pause. "Why don't you just come over here?"

"Your place?"

"Yeah."

Now Louis hesitated. Landeta inviting him to his home? What was this, some new attempt at making nice?

"All right," Louis said finally. "Give me your address."

The address turned out to be nearby on First Street, only about a mile from the Fort Myers Police Station. The Babcock

Apartments were above an empty store. Most of the old storefronts had FOR RENT signs in the windows. The street was empty of people and traffic. Louis grabbed a couple of Frank's books and went into the lobby.

He scanned the mailboxes for Landeta's name, and pressed the buzzer for Number 1. When nothing happened, Louis peered through the second locked glass door into the plain hallway. He buzzed again. Nothing.

He was just about to give up when he saw Landeta coming down the stairs. Landeta jerked open the door.

"Sorry," he said, "I was on the phone."

Louis stood in front of him, the books from Frank's apartment in his arms. Landeta didn't move, didn't seem interested in inviting Louis in.

"I saw Sophie Reardon's father this afternoon," Louis said.

"Who?"

"Sophie Reardon. Diane's mother . . . Frank's wife. I finally got Diane to give me the maiden name."

"And?"

"I have some stuff I need to tell you. You going to ask me in?" The lobby was hotter than an oven.

Landeta didn't budge. "Tell me here."

Louis drew in a breath. "Look, I'm tired of this shit. I've been your errand boy long enough. You asked me to come over here. Either you let me in and we talk or I take what I have to Horton."

Landeta hesitated a moment, then stepped back. "Okay. Come on up."

Louis followed him up the narrow stairs to the second floor. Landeta was wearing plain black pants and what looked like just an older version of his usual white dress shirt, neck unbuttoned, sleeves rolled above the elbows. He was wearing only black socks on his feet.

Landeta closed the apartment door behind Louis. "Have a seat," he said, moving into the living room.

It wasn't a big place, but its spareness made it look as if it were. The walls were all white, the wood floor left bare, the windows that looked out on First Street were covered with white blinds. There was a beat-up black leather sofa and a couple of plain black wood tables. A black Ikea entertainment center dominated one wall, holding a TV and a good stereo system. A well-worn black Eames chair was positioned close in front of the TV and there was a sleek black desk with a black drafting table lamp hovering over it. There was nothing on the walls, no books, no plants, no knick-knacks, nothing to relieve the black-and-white decor. No color anywhere in fact, except for the rows of albums, tapes, and compact disks carefully arranged on the shelves of the entertainment center.

The room was lit up like a hospital operating room, and it smelled of acrid cigarette smoke with an undernote of lemon Renuzit. It was all bare-bones style, and as charmless as the man who lived in it.

Except for the music coming from the stereo. Louis recognized it immediately—Clyde McPhatter singing "Let's Try Again."

"You want a drink? I got Diet Coke," Landeta said. A second's pause. "And I think there's a beer in there somewhere."

"Beer," Louis said. He sat on the edge of the leather sofa. He set Frank's books down on the coffee table, next to a boomerang-shaped glass ashtray overflowing with butts. He heard Landeta moving around in the kitchen.

"I found out something interesting about Sophie," Louis called out over the music. "She ran away from home when she was eighteen."

No answer from the kitchen. Just sounds of drawers opening, clanking metal like spoons and knives.

"Sophie's old man told me she ran off with Frank and that he used to come into his drugstore," Louis said, raising his voice over the noise. "He said Frank was—"

There was a sudden deafening crash in the kitchen.

"Fucking motherfucking sonofabitch!" Landeta screamed.

Louis jumped up and went to the door. Landeta was standing in the middle of the kitchen, holding his left hand. A drawer lay on the floor, surrounded by knives, forks, spoons, and kitchen utensils.

Landeta's face was red. So was his left hand, blood dripping onto the white tile. He stared at Louis.

"The fucking knife was in the drawer! I didn't see the fucking knife in the drawer!"

Suddenly, Landeta drew back a foot and kicked the wooden drawer, sending it crashing against the refrigerator. Landeta just stood there, chest heaving, eyes closed. The bouncing blues of McPhatter's "I Can't Stand Up Alone" filtered in from the living room.

Louis took a step into the kitchen. "Hey, man, take it easy."

Landeta was holding his hand, the finger dripping blood. He seemed lost, glancing around the kitchen for something. He took a step, then began groping around the white tile countertop for a towel. Louis could see the white towel, several feet from Landeta's outstretched right hand.

"Goddamn it."

Louis watched him. He was looking around, down at the floor, still holding his bloody hand.

What the hell was going on?

"Can I help you?" Louis asked.

"The towel. Hand me the towel."

Louis held out the towel. Landeta grabbed it and wrapped it around his finger. He walked slowly to the sink, picking his way over the spilled silverware, recoiling when he stepped on a fork tine. Louis watched in silence as Landeta turned on the faucet and held his bleeding hand under the water.

Landeta again pressed the towel to the cut, his back to Louis. He turned off the water, but didn't move from the sink.

"What's going on?" Louis asked.

It took Landeta a few seconds to answer. His voice was as rigid as the muscles in his shoulders.

"I can't see," he said.

"What?"

"I can't see," Landeta repeated. "I'm going blind."

Louis felt himself tighten. *Blind?*

"You should have asked for the Diet Coke," Landeta said.

Louis's eyes went from the green bottle of unopened Heineken on the counter to the mess of flatware on the floor. He bent down and picked up the bottle opener, holding it out to Landeta.

"Open it yourself," Landeta said. He trudged out of the kitchen.

A moment later the music stopped. Louis set the opener on the counter next to the beer and followed Landeta back to the living room. Landeta was standing at the stereo. He went to the Eames chair and sat down, holding his towel-wrapped hand.

"You're blind?" Louis asked.

"Going blind. There's a difference."

Landeta unwrapped his finger, looked at it, and wrapped it again. "You ever think how ironic that sounds? *Going* blind? Like it's a good thing, like you're going somewhere you can look forward to?"

Louis came back to sit on the edge of the sofa. "How long?" he asked.

Landeta gave a small shrug. "About ten years now. Retinitis pigmentosa is a kind disease. Your eyes commit suicide, but it takes a long time." He unwrapped his hand to stare at his finger again. "Gives you plenty of time to . . . adjust."

Louis let his eyes wander around the spare room. No rugs to trip over, no knickknacks to knock off tables, no shadows to get lost in, no pretty pictures on the walls. Suddenly the place didn't look so stylish anymore. It looked like survival.

He started thinking back, his mind clicking on images of Landeta, trying to remember what the guy had done to cover up his problem. Back in the mangroves, asking all those questions about Shelly Umber's body. Back in the office, asking him to read him the autopsy report, and at the cottage, telling him to read him the reports on the missing girls and then knocking over the glass of water.

When they had been talking at O'Sullivan's about making your own luck, and Landeta saying something about fate taking it away. And all those questions that had seemed so arrogant: *Why don't you read me the report while I clean off my desk, Kincaid? What do you see, Kincaid? What does the scene look like?*

Louis felt a twinge of anger at being used. And something else, a heat moving up the back of his neck, as if it were radiating off of Landeta—the heat of embarrassment, swirling around them both like the cigarette-stale air.

"You want to leave," Landeta said. He nodded toward the door. "Go ahead. Get out of here."

*Go, just go.*

*Don't make me part of this.*

*Just go, Louis . . .*

Louis rose. Landeta didn't look up. Louis went into the kitchen, picked up the bottle opener, and popped off the Heineken cap. He came back and sat down on the sofa.

"You want one?" Louis asked.

Landeta raised his yellow lenses. "I told you. I'm an alcoholic."

Louis took a long pull of the beer. It was warm. He didn't care. "Does Horton know?" he asked.

Landeta shook his head slowly. "He called me right after the thing in Miami. I was going to tell him then. But then he offered me the job over here. Once I got here and started working again, I figured I could pull it off."

"This why you get Strickland to drive you everywhere?"

Landeta nodded.

Louis hesitated. "This why you left Miami PD?"

Landeta sank back in the leather chair. The front of his

white shirt was splattered with blood. He took off his glasses and rubbed his eyes. Louis could almost feel the man's wariness.

"Look, if you don't want to talk about—" Louis began.

"Nah, I should. That's what the shrink said." He looked at Louis. "You ever seen one?"

Louis hesitated, then nodded. "Yeah, once. Up in Michigan after my partner got shot. Department policy, that kind of shit."

They were quiet. Landeta put his glasses back on and leaned his head back in the chair.

"So what happened in Miami?" Louis asked.

"I was still driving some then," he said. "I knew the way to work by heart and if we had to go out at night, I'd have my partner drive. I knew I had to stop. I couldn't even read the signs anymore. But giving up your wheels, shit, it's like admitting you're an old man."

Landeta paused. "Then one morning, I was driving into the station and the pursuit call went out. It was instinct. I took off after the guy. I never saw the kid in the other car."

"Horton told me the kid ran a light," Louis said.

Landeta shook his head slowly. "I don't know. I didn't see him." He took a deep breath. "The kid ended up in a wheelchair and the family sued. My chief found out about the RP. He told me he'd keep it quiet if I resigned. It was almost a relief."

The room was quiet. Outside, a siren wailed and faded. A mile from the station, an easy walk, Louis thought.

"You want another beer?" Landeta asked.

Louis shook his head.

"I said do you want another beer?"

Louis started to shake his head again, then realized Landeta hadn't seen it. "No, no, thanks," he said.

"So how much . . . ?" Louis faltered.

"How much can I see? I've got tunnel vision and what's there is like looking through a shower stall that's got soap scum all over it." He held up his glasses. "The yellow lenses give me more contrast. So does having things in black and white. Like my clothes. Makes getting dressed easier."

He gestured to the televison three feet away. "If I sit right in front of it and turn the contrast and brightness buttons on high I can see some TV, but lately it makes my eyes hurt."

Louis looked down at the beer bottle in his hands.

"You're just a flesh-colored blur," Landeta said.

Louis looked up.

"What color are your eyes?" Landeta asked.

"Gray."

"I was guessing blue for some reason."

Louis hesitated. "I'm black."

Landeta stared at him. Then he let out a huge bark of a laugh. "No shit? I thought you just had a good tan."

Louis laughed. The room grew quiet again. A clock chimed nine times. Louis looked for it but didn't see it.

"You going to tell Horton?" Landeta asked.

Louis could hear it in the man's voice. It was buried, somewhere deep under the layers of pride and macho crap, deep under all the stuff that started accumulating the moment you understood you were a boy, male, a man. It was buried there underneath the scar tissue around the heart, underneath that veneer they painted on you at the academy that eventually hardened over you like a tough blue shell. Buried there, underneath all of it, Louis could hear the vulnerability.

"It's not up to me," Louis said.

Landeta paused. "Did Horton ask you to baby-sit me?"

The question was so unexpected Louis couldn't think of a quick answer.

"Don't bullshit me," Landeta said. "Did he?"

Louis thought of what Horton had said about Landeta when they found Frank's body. *He can't seem to get a feel for things and he's missing stuff.*

Landeta let out a long slow breath. "Never mind."

"You have to tell him," Louis said.

Landeta didn't answer. He was just sitting there, holding his towel-wrapped hand. Louis set the beer down on the coffee table. He rose slowly.

Landeta looked up. "You're going," he said.

"To get another beer," Louis said.

Landeta looked up at him, then concentrated on unwrapping the towel from his hand. The bleeding had stopped. He seemed to notice the blood on his shirt for the first time.

"You need anything?" Louis asked.

"Yeah, for you not to treat me like a fucking blind man."

"Shit, man. If we're going to work this case together, you got to stop being a prick." Louis shook his head. "All I'm asking is, can I *do* anything for you?"

Landeta just stared at him. And in the bright light of the white room, Louis could see his eyes clearly for the first time. They were a cloudy blue white, and rimmed in red, like someone's eyes might look if they had been crying for years.

But Landeta was smiling, an odd half smile that was closer to a grimace.

"Can I do anything for you?" Louis repeated.

"Yeah," Landeta said. "Bring me back a Diet Coke with lemon. Then tell me what the sunset looked like tonight."

# CHAPTER 32

Louis just stared at Landeta. Sunset? Was he kidding? Man, this guy was hard to read. But before Louis had a chance to answer, Landeta pushed himself out of the Eames chair and disappeared into the bedroom. A few minutes later, Louis heard the flush of a toilet and running water. Louis rose and went to the kitchen, getting a beer and a Diet Coke. When he came back, Landeta was standing there. He had changed into a clean white shirt and there was gauze wrapped around his left hand.

"Okay, let's get started," Landeta said.

Louis hesitated. That was it? *The guy just says he's blind and that's his excuse for being an asshole?*

"Here's your Diet Coke. I couldn't find the damn lemon," Louis said tightly, setting it on the table by the Eames chair.

Louis went back to the sofa and sat down. He took a drink of the beer, pulled out his notebook, and slapped it down on the coffee table.

Landeta heard it and looked over at him. "What's your problem all of a sudden?"

"Nothing."

"Oh, I get it. You want an apology, right?"

Louis didn't respond for a moment then he nodded. "Yeah, yeah, I do. You treated me like a piece of shit."

Landeta just stared at him.

"I know things are bad for you right now, but I was trying to help you," Louis said.

"I told you I don't need help."

"With the case, man," Louis said, "with the fucking case, that's all. And you did need help with that."

Landeta turned away. He hit a button on the CD player, popping out the disk and putting it back in its case. "I'm used to working alone," he said.

Louis waited, but Landeta was busy putting a new CD in the player. A second later, the sound of Ray Charles singing "Lonely Avenue" poured out of the speakers. Louis shook his head and started to pack up his notebook and books. He rose and started to the door.

"Maybe it's time I had a partner," Landeta said.

Louis turned. "What?"

Landeta turned down the music's volume. "I said, maybe it's time I had a partner."

Louis hesitated, then came back to the sofa. He set the books down on the coffee table. "I haven't eaten all day. Is there a pizza place around here that delivers?" he asked.

"Yeah, Fast Eddie's down the street."

"Pepperoni and extra cheese. No anchovies. And you're buying. Where's your john?"

Landeta pointed to a door. Louis went to the bathroom. When he came back, Landeta was hanging up the phone.

"I got green peppers," Landeta said.

"I hate green peppers," Louis said.

"You can pick them off."

The music stopped and for a moment, the room was quiet, just the drone of the air conditioner in the window and a car horn somewhere outside. Ray Charles started in "Them That Got." Landeta turned the volume down until the music was just a whispering stream.

"Where do you want to start?" Louis asked.

"With the missing girls," Landeta said. "You never made me copies of your interviews with their families. I'm in the dark, so to speak."

Louis remembered back to the night Landeta had come to his cottage. Landeta had refused to look at them and wanted to take them with him. "Who do you want to start with?" he asked.

"Emma Fielding," Landeta said, settling into the Eames chair.

Louis pulled out the reports he had written on each girl. "Emma disappeared in 1953. She was sixteen."

"So Frank was already with his wife then," Landeta said. "It was a year after Diane was born, in fact."

"Serial killers often have wives or girlfriends," Louis said. "Some have families and lives that look normal."

Landeta was staring off at the white wall. "Families," he said quietly. "What was Emma's family like?"

"She was sexually abused by her stepfather," Louis said. "Her mother and older brother both knew about it, and when the older brother finally ran off, Emma wanted to go with him. He kind of abandoned her."

Landeta nodded thoughtfully and said, "Let's move on to the others."

"Cindy Shattuck, 1964." Louis looked at his notes. "She lived with her mother in Matlacha. The mother kicked her out of the house because she thought she was flirting with her husband. No boyfriend, but Cindy worked in a restaurant in town where she could've met someone."

"That's all? You can do better."

Louis shrugged. "Well, her mother is a piece of work. Told me if we ever found Cindy to tell her she was dead. And she said Cindy took only one thing with her—an old sock monkey."

"Good. Go on," Landeta said.

"Paula Berkowitz. 1965. High school graduate, honor student, lived with her parents until she left home suddenly at age twenty without telling anyone. She only took one suitcase and they never heard from her again. Her aunt said she was overweight and possibly depressed or suicidal."

"Job?"

Louis scanned his notes. "Cashier at a Winn-Dixie near her home on Pine Island."

Landeta looked over at him, as if expecting more.

"She desperately wanted kids."

"Next."

"Mary Rubio. Vanished in 1973. She was a foster kid, who was placed in fifteen homes in two years. The foster mother I talked to only had her a few months but told me the girl was strange. Said Mary used to cut herself."

"Really?" Landeta said.

"Her foster mother said it was a cry for attention."

"It is and it isn't. Kids who do that are looking for a sense that they are alive and to prove it, they cut their skin."

"To see if they bleed?"

"I think it's more to see if they *feel,* but either way, they are troubled. What else?"

"The foster mother told me Mary would never have a real home with her and Mary knew it, so she left."

Landeta's eyes closed briefly. "Tell me about Angela."

Louis picked up the last report. "Angela Lopez, disappeared in 1984. Daughter of a Mexican migrant worker in Immokalee," he read. "She was close to a woman she worked for, a woman named Rosa, who told me Angela made a date to go to Fort Myers and never came back."

Landeta looked at him and Louis could read the message: You can do better.

"Angela told Rosa once that she never wanted her kids to grow up in Immokalee," Louis said.

Landeta nodded slowly. "So, what do you see? What do you see in all these girls?"

Louis thought for a moment. "They were all running away from something," he said.

"And they were all desperate to feel connected to someone." Landeta paused. "That's a powerful human need."

"Except Shelly Umber," Louis said. "She wasn't running away from anything."

Landeta nodded. "But she was not vulnerable like the others."

"Explain," Louis said.

"You have to look at the times in each case," Landeta said. "Emma disappeared in the fifties. Things were different then. Women were usually looking for someone to take care of them."

Landeta got up from the chair. "But by the sixties, girls were a little different. They weren't all looking to get married. They were looking for other things—excitement, a feeling of belonging to a family—so they ran off to communes or Haight-Ashbury."

Louis was watching Landeta as he paced slowly around the room.

"Take Cindy Shattuck," Landeta went on. "In need of affection, especially from men, with a stuffed monkey as her favorite possession. She was a baby, put out on the street by her mother. And Paula . . . fat, unhappy, working in a dead-end job and dreaming of having a baby she could love."

"And Mary Rubio," Louis said. "Looking for a family . . . any family."

"But now, times are different. Young women now are more independent," Landeta said, "which brings us to Shelly Umber. A strong woman who wanted to be a doctor and climb mountains. She was the only one who didn't go willingly. She might have been the only one who tried to escape. So Woods had to shoot her."

A sharp buzz made Landeta pause. "Pizza," he said, moving to the door.

He left and came back a minute later with the pizza box. He set it on the coffee table in front of Louis, flipping open the lid. The aroma made Louis's stomach churn with hunger and he eagerly dug out a slice. Landeta did the same, taking it back to the Eames chair. Neither said a word as they devoured their food.

Finally, Louis tossed down a crust and finished off the Heineken. "So except for Umber, you think they all went willingly?" he asked.

"Not exactly. I think Woods seduced them into thinking he could give them what they needed," Landeta said. "He was Daddy, the white knight, Prince Charming, and Mr. Goodbar—whatever the girls needed him to be."

Louis was shaking his head. "Okay, I can buy that for Emma Fielding. Frank was young then. But he would have been in his thirties when he met Cindy and Paula. And in his forties for Mary Rubio."

Landeta nodded. "Yeah, and fifty-five when Angela Lopez disappeared."

They were both quiet for a moment. Landeta got another slice of pizza and went back to his chair. Louis did the same. When he had finished it, he looked at Landeta. He started to call to him but hesitated, unsure what to call him. Suddenly "Detective" seemed too formal, yet "Mel" wasn't quite right either.

"Hey," Louis said.

Landeta turned.

"The old woman in Immokalee? She told me Angela was meeting a boy, not a man. Angela called him some Spanish name for 'hunk.' And she also said the guy was Hispanic."

"Well, what do you—"

"Wait, wait a minute," Louis said. He sifted through his papers, pulling out his notes on Jim Reardon. "Sophie's father told me she ran off with Frank but he called Frank Mexican."

"He's sure it was Frank?"

Louis unclipped the old photo of Frank and Sophie from the report and held it out. "I showed him this picture. Reardon said this was definitely the guy Sophie ran off with. And he said Frank spoke a foreign language and had a Spanish-sounding name."

"Give me the picture," Landeta said, rising. He held the photo up to his face and stared hard at it. Louis rose and went to the kitchen, tossing his empty beer bottle in the trash can. When he came back, Landeta had moved to a desk in the corner and switched on the black drafting lamp. As he pulled it closer, Louis saw it had a large built-in magnifier. Landeta was hunched over, peering at Frank's picture.

Landeta looked up. "Well, at least we know now why we couldn't find Frank's past. He must have changed his name."

They were quiet for a moment, both of them trying to figure out the Hispanic connection, trying to reconcile a middle-aged Frank Woods with Angela's supposed date.

"Do you think Frank could have taken on an accomplice?" Louis asked. "Someone younger who could have lured Angela?"

"Beats the shit out of me." Landeta took off his glasses and rubbed his eyes, then looked back at Louis. "When did you talk to Sophie's father?"

"Earlier today," Louis said. "He's a bitter old man, and Sophie's stepmother told me he drove Sophie way. She fits your theory about running off with Prince Charming."

Louis realized Landeta was looking at the picture again with the magnifier. "What the hell are you looking for now?"

"Trying to see if Sophie is wearing a coral ring in this picture. But her left hand isn't visible." Landeta looked up, pushing the lamp away.

"She wore a gold band. Diane wears it now. I saw it." He came over to look over Landeta's shoulder at the photograph.

"I don't think Frank looks Mexican," Louis said.

"He doesn't," Landeta said. "Spanish, maybe, Castillian Spanish." He looked up at Louis. "Didn't you say Frank spoke Spanish to you at the restaurant?"

Louis shook his head. "It was Latin."

"You sure it wasn't Spanish? Latin is the basis for all the Romance languages."

"Hell, I don't know. I ran it by Vince, the ME. He said it sounds like Latin."

"What exactly did Frank say to you? What'd it sound like?"

"Hicks salute something. I tried to find it in these books, but I can't figure it out."

"What books?" Landeta asked.

Louis set the pizza box aside, pulling the stack of books closer. "I found these in Frank's house. He was self-educated, and into all kinds of weird shit."

"Self-educated? In what areas?"

"Language, for one. Listen to this." Louis read off the names of the language books. When he got to *Teach Yourself Latin,* Landeta held up a hand.

"How in hell does someone teach himself Latin?" Landeta asked.

Louis shrugged. "Diane said he always wanted to go to college and the girl at the library said he was head of the research department."

"Let me see that book."

Louis handed Landeta the Latin book. Landeta pulled his lamp closer and thumbed through the book. But after a few minutes, he straightened and took off his glasses, rubbing his eyes. He rose and headed toward the kitchen. Louis picked up the Latin book Landeta had been reading and started looking through it again.

A few minutes later, a fresh Heineken appeared by Louis's elbow. Louis muttered a thanks and watched Landeta settle back at the desk, a different one of Frank's books in his hand. Louis went back to his own reading, repeating Frank's expression over and over in his head.

*Hicks allude? Hick salude? Salute? What the hell had he said?*

For a long time the only sound in the room was Ray Charles singing a soft accompaniment to the hum of the air conditioner. Finally, Landeta broke the quiet.

"This is great," he murmured, almost to himself.

Louis looked up. "What is?"

"This man-into-wolf stuff."

"Frank had a thing about werewolves," Louis said. "He had a bunch of books about it."

"Lycanthropy's not really about werewolves."

"What is it then?"

Landeta pursed his lips. "According to this, it's a mental disorder where a person believes he has turned into a wolf."

Louis just stared at him.

Landeta poked a finger at the book spread open beneath the magnifier lamp. "This shrink, Robert Eisler, had a theory that violence, war, especially murder, could be traced back to man's primal urges as a member of his animal pack. Woods underlined a bunch of shit in here and wrote a couple of things in the margins."

"He did?" Louis rose and went over to Landeta.

"Yeah, there's this passage about how modern man is descended from a mutated wolf species that raped and sometimes even cannibalized females." Landeta looked up. "Woods underlined it twice and wrote next to it 'see Asturian rite.' "

Louis came closer. "Asturian? There was a book in Frank's room with that word in the title."

"You got it with you?"

"Yeah, but I left it down in the car."

"Bring it in tomorrow. Here's another passage he underlined," Landeta said. He started reading out loud. " 'The aggressive pack would, whenever occasion offered, kidnap and carry away the females of the weaker tribes.' "

"Jesus," Louis said. "Abduction by wolves?"

"Or a man who thought he was," Landeta said. He went back to his reading.

Louis went back to sit on the sofa, shaking his head

slowly. Shit, eating the victims? Is that why they never found the women's bodies?

"Listen to this," Landeta said. "Jung had a patient with this disorder. The guy dreamed he was part of a herd that he had to leave. So in the dream he puts on a wolf-head disguise and goes off into the woods, becoming an outlaw from his herd. He dreams he is alone on a desert island."

"Like Cayo Costa, the place where Frank hid out," Louis said.

Landeta kept reading. "Then the guy feels the need to go back to the life he broke away from. When he does, he is surrounded by women from his original herd but he doesn't recognize them."

"Frank underlined all that?" Louis asked.

Landeta nodded.

"You should have seen him," Louis said. "Out on that island. It was like he was right at home, like he was . . ."

"An animal?" Landeta asked.

Louis stood up suddenly, pacing a slow tight circle. "This is nuts," he muttered.

Landeta was reading something. He looked up. "Listen to this," he said. He began to read another passage from *Man Into Wolf.*

" 'Murderous sadistic assaults are sometimes committed by well-educated, highly intelligent persons with no previous convictions or with a record showing no more, at worse, than minor sexual irregularities.'

"Or so says the good doctor Robert Eisler." Landeta closed the book.

"Shrinks . . . It's all bullshit," Louis muttered.

"Not always," Landeta said.

Louis was shaking his head slowly. Landeta pushed the magnifier lamp away and sat back in his chair, looking at Louis.

"All of us get desperate enough to do bad things," he said. "For most of us, it's just selfishness, but for a few, it's something darker at work. Face it, we're all just a couple of genes removed from the things that crawled out of the slime."

The clock chimed again, ten times.

Landeta rubbed his eyes, pinching the bridge of his nose. "I'm tired," he said. "My eyes have had it."

"Mel, come on—"

"No," Landeta said firmly. "Tomorrow. We'll pick this up tomorrow."

Louis hesitated, then nodded. He pocketed his notebook and started to gather up the reports and books he had brought.

"Leave the books, okay?" Landeta said.

Louis put the books down and began picking up the empty bottles and the pizza carton.

"Leave that, too. I can do it."

"Okay. We'll get back on this tomorrow at the station."

Landeta's eyes were shut but he nodded. The man looked bone tired. Louis started to the door.

"Kincaid."

Louis turned.

"Look, you're right," Landeta began, "about the way I've been acting."

"Forget it," Louis said.

Landeta shook his head. "I have a lot of shit to deal with right now. You were just in the line of fire. I'm sorry."

Louis just nodded.

"See you at the station," Landeta said.

He shut off the magnifying light and his face fell into the shadows. For a brief moment, Louis found himself thinking about Landeta's own selfishness, how it had driven him to hang on to his badge. He wondered what it must be like for him. It was one thing to stop seeing yourself as a cop. It was another thing altogether to stop seeing anything at all.

Louis let himself out of the apartment and went down the hall into the lobby. The door banged shut behind him and he paused on the steps. A heavy shroud of humid night air

wrapped itself around him, smelling of the river close by. He
drew in a deep breath and looked up.

There was no moon tonight. A moment later, he heard a
sound, like a low wail, coming from Landeta's apartment. It
was Ray Charles again, singing "Blackjack."

Louis looked back up at Landeta's window, then started
down the empty street.

# CHAPTER 33

Louis glanced up at the clock. It was nearly two A.M. He had left Landeta's apartment more than three hours ago, but he was still pumped up.

He looked back down at the book he had been reading, but the words seemed to blur and hover on the page. He took off his glasses and rubbed his eyes. He was tired of looking at Latin, tired of trying to decipher words he didn't understand.

He looked at Issy, who was sitting on one of the books, staring at him. He reached out and ran his hand along her back. The cat arched under his touch and rose, stretching and moving away. Louis picked up the book she had been lying on and looked at the spine. *The Myths and Customs of the Asturian People.*

Asturian? He had forgotten about this, that Frank had written something about Asturian in one of the wolf books. Louis leaned back in the chair and opened the book.

One of the first pages was a map of Spain, with a blue section in the north that identified Asturias. Louis opened to the first chapter and read:

*Once an ancient kingdom, now the principality of Asturias remains somewhat isolated from the rest of the world. It is one of most beautiful yet least known areas of Spain. Flanked by mountains in the south and the sea to the north, Asturias has been protected from the influences of the invaders that have flowed through Spain throughout the centuries. The result is a folk culture distinct from that of the rest of Spain, with a strong Celtic and Roman tradition stretching back over thousands of years.*

Louis thumbed through the book. He stopped at a chapter Frank had dog-earred, titled "Asturian Rites of Passage." Louis scanned the chapter, stopping when he came to a section called "The Festival of the Wolf." He read slowly:

*In classical Rome, February 15 was celebrated as Lupercalia—or festival of the wolf. Teams of young men gathered in a cave on Mt. Palatinus where they sacrificed dogs and goats. They would then smear the blood on their bodies, dress themselves in the animal skins, and then competed in a race, which drew huge crowds of observers. The ritual involved the men running through the villages and attacking women in the crowd, whipping them with narrow strips of goat skin, which was supposed to appease the gods and encourage fertility. But for the immense majority, the ceremony was merely a venting of emotional passion. The enormous crowds, the impatient suspense, and the watching of the naked men made for an occasion of wantonness.*

Louis turned the page. Frank had underlined the next paragraph:

    *Nowadays, along the old borders of the Roman empire, remnants of the lupercalia still persist. In Asturias, villagers still celebrate "Beleno Ride" where the single young men descend from the mountains down to the village on horseback, following a leader who wears a wolf costume and is allowed to indulge in bold actions such as whipping village girls with a swollen animal bladder tied to a stick. Anthropologists call it a rite of passage, which marks the difference between the "mozos" (the unmarried men) and the "paisanos" (the adult men with families).*

Louis closed the book. *Jesus.*

He rose slowly and went to the kitchen. He started to the refrigerator to get a beer, then changed his mind and just filled a large glass with tap water and gulped it down. He stood in the dark kitchen, trying to gather his thoughts. The air seemed as thick as his mind. Images of wolves speaking some gibberish language, bodies caged by dark mangroves, and blind detectives feeling their way around one last case.

And the damn Latin was swirling in his brain, like a fog obscuring everything.

*Hicks . . . hicks salute . . . no, no, that wasn't it. Think . . . try to hear him saying it. Hick solute . . . solutio. Solutio. Solution? Could that be what Frank meant?*

Louis went back to the table and pulled out the large Oxford Latin Dictionary and put on his glasses. It only took a minute to find *solutio* under the Ss.

He ran a finger down the long entry of definitions: *1. Loose or relaxed state; 2. The discharge of a debt or breaking up of a structure.* His finger stopped at the third definition: *The unfastening of a knot . . . the solving of a puzzle or dilemma; the answer.*

He flipped quickly back to the Hs. *Hick solutio . . .*

Hic. *Here.*

The answer is *here?*

Louis snatched up the phone and punched in Landeta's phone number. It rang six times before Landeta answered.

"What?" His voice was groggy.

"Mel. I found it. The answer is here."

"What? Who . . . ? What the hell? Louis?"

"Yeah."

"I was sleeping."

"I'm sorry. The answer is here."

"What? Where?"

"Here! That's what Frank was trying to tell me. *Hic solutio est.* The answer is here! On the island."

"You're on an island?"

"No, I'm at home. The answer is on the island."

"Cayo Costa? The island Frank was hiding out on?"

"No, no. The other one."

"What other one?"

"The one he went to before he drowned himself," Louis said. "The one with the restaurant. You questioned them. What did they say?"

Landeta was quiet.

"Mel, what did they say?"

Landeta still said nothing.

"Mel? You there?"

"Yeah." Louis heard him pull in a deep breath. "I didn't get out there."

"You didn't—" Louis stopped. He knew why Landeta hadn't gone back out there. He couldn't go alone; he needed help.

"All right, all right," Louis said quietly. "Forget it. Let's get back to Frank and what he told me."

"What do you think he meant?" Landeta asked.

"I don't know. I called you before I thought about it. Maybe it's where he buried the women."

There was a long pause on Landeta's end. Louis figured

he was about to tell him to hold his thoughts until tomorrow, and he was about to apologize again for waking him, but Landeta spoke first.

"Tell me about the island."

"Now?" Louis asked.

"Yeah. Tell me what it looks like."

"Well, it's all mangroves. There's this old restaurant out there and you can only get there by ferry. The tourists unload at the dock and after lunch, they make you get right back on the ferry."

"It's privately owned? Who owns it?"

"I don't know."

"What's the restaurant like?"

"It's just an old house, white weathered wood, real rustic, a coral rock fireplace, fishing nets, stuffed fish on the walls. It almost looked neglected, but I think they want it like that for the tourists."

"Did you see Frank talk to anyone there?"

"Yeah, a man working at the bar. And there was a kid, about ten, who brought us menus. His name was Roberto."

"How did you learn the kid's name?"

"Frank asked him."

"What else, Louis?"

"Nothing."

"There must be something else."

Louis jumped up and began to pace. "I didn't look at anything else," he said. "I was keeping my eye on Frank."

"What was Frank keeping his eye on?" Landeta asked.

Louis paused, his mind working hard to retrieve the image of Frank sitting across from him. Frank's sunburned nose, his jaw shadowed with whiskers, his sad brown eyes moving from the tabletop to the boy, and up to . . .

"Mel . . . there was a painting. This big, old ugly painting hanging over the bar. I thought it looked out of place and Frank made some comment about it, but I don't remember . . . Damn, what did he say?"

"Forget it. What did the painting look like?"

"Shit, I don't know. Some Roman guys having an orgy or something with a bunch of fat women."

Louis heard a clank as Landeta set the phone down. "Mel? You there? Where'd you go?"

Mel's voice suddenly came back. "I went to get one of Frank's books you brought over, the mythology book. I was looking through it after you left and I remember seeing something. I think Frank marked it. Hold on."

He could hear Landeta turning pages. "Yeah, here it is. And he had it bookmarked."

"What?"

"A painting. Roman guys and fat women, as you called it. Hold on. Let me get set up under the light."

Louis pulled up the phone and went to the kitchen. Holding the receiver with his shoulder, he opened the refrigerator, pulled out a Heineken, and popped off the top. He was taking the first swig when Landeta came back on.

"Okay," Landeta started. "This painting I'm looking at shows Romans carrying off fat women . . . in front of a Colosseum type of place."

Another pause. Louis knew Landeta was struggling to see the photo. "And there's some guy in a red cape overseeing all this."

"Yeah, that's it," Louis said.

"It's by somebody named Poussin. It's called *The Rape of the Sabines.*"

"Rape of who?"

"Listen, damn it. Don't say a word." Landeta's voice slowed, and Louis knew he was using his magnifying glass again to read.

"Okay, it's based on the Romulus and Remus myth . . . The two brothers were building a city . . . and one of them ended up killing the other one over the size of a fence or something . . ."

Louis took a drink, growing impatient at Landeta's slow

flow of information. Things were starting to fall into place, the picture coming into focus, and he wanted to know the rest of it now. He began to pace.

"Okay, they were the guys who built Rome," Landeta continued. "But they didn't have enough women for all the men to have wives—"

Louis interrupted Landeta. "So they took them from somewhere else and raped them."

"Yeah . . . no, wait." Landeta paused. "Listen to this. In Roman days, rape didn't mean what it does now. It comes from the Latin word *raptus,* which means to carry off by force."

Louis stopped pacing. His mind was whirring.

"Louis? You there?"

"Yeah, yeah, I'm thinking."

"About what?"

"That guy Jung was treating for mental illness." Louis began pacing again. "He had dreams about leaving his wolf herd behind but when he does, he feels isolated and tries to go back, where he is surrounded by women from his herd he no longer recognizes."

"Yeah, Frank underlined it," Landeta said.

"And tonight, I found something else about wolves in another one of Frank's books, something about a fertility rite where unmarried men dress up in wolf skins and beat the village women with animal skins and—"

"What?"

"Never mind. I'll show it to you tomorrow. The important thing now is that island." Louis stopped pacing. "Mel, he went back there for a reason."

"Maybe he was from there. What's out there besides the restaurant?"

Louis was quiet, trying to remember. "I only saw the restaurant. But there could have been houses on the other side."

"Well, like what? A private community thing, like Useppa or North Captiva?"

"I don't know. . . ."

"Or like out on Sanibel?"

"I told you, Mel—"

"C'mon, Louis. What was your sense of it?"

"Sense? What do you mean?"

"What did the place *feel* like?"

"Fuck, Mel. I saw trees. That was all!"

"Think. Use your other senses."

Louis was quiet. "Okay, it was way the hell out in the sound. It felt isolated."

"Try again."

"It felt . . . forgotten."

Landeta was silent. "By who?" he asked finally.

Louis ran a hand over his face. "Time? I don't know," he said.

There was another silence. Louis could hear Landeta breathing.

"What's the name of the island again?" Landeta asked finally.

"Away So Far."

"We need to find out more about the place before we go to Horton. Any ideas?"

"You can only go there for lunch and they want you back on the ferry in two hours." Louis was pacing and stopped abruptly, his eyes focusing on the baby skull sitting on his bookshelf.

"Louis? You there?"

"Yeah," Louis said. "I just figured out where to get some answers."

# CHAPTER 34

The sun was still low and the morning air still cool as the boat sliced through the calm water of Charlotte Harbor. The old man let them off at Bessie Levy's stilt house and Louis helped Landeta climb the ladder.

Louis had called ahead and Bessie was sitting out on the porch, coffee mug in hand, when they came around to her front door.

"Gonna be another scorcher today," she said, taking her feet off the railing and rising. She looked up at Landeta.

"Who's this? Dr. Mid-Nite?"

"Old comic book hero," Landeta said to Louis and then extended his hand. "I'm Detective Landeta, Mrs. Levy."

Bessie wiped her hand on her trousers and shook Landeta's hand. "Take a load off," she said, gesturing toward the old aluminum lawn chairs. "You want some coffee?"

"That would be nice," Landeta said.

Bessie went inside and Landeta folded himself into one of the chairs. Louis stood by the railing staring out at the silvery water. He was trying to figure out where Away So Far Island was, but there were a dozen green clumps out there, each with another one hiding behind it.

Bessie brought out a tray, setting it on a lobster trap next to Landeta. "So what's this about some island?" she asked Louis.

"Away So Far," Louis said. "We need to know about it."

Bessie arched an eyebrow as she poured coffee into a mug and handed it to Landeta. "Why you want to know about that place?"

"Did you hear about the man who jumped off the ferry last week and drowned?" Louis asked.

Bessie shrugged. "I don't have a TV and I don't bother with the papers anymore. But I heard them talking over at Cap'n Con's. Some crazy tourist, right?"

"No, he was local," Louis said. "He was coming from Away So Far. We just need to check it out."

Bessie looked dubious but she finally gave a shrug and handed Louis a mug of coffee. "Well, for starters, that ain't its real name," she said. "It was originally called Isla des Huesos."

"Island of . . ." Mel began.

"Island of Bones," Bessie said. "This whole place was crawling with the Spanish once and that's what they called the island. *Hueso* is the word for bone and it sounds like 'away so.' Someone else added the 'far,' I guess 'cuz it's so far out there. Folks round here just always called it Away So Far."

Louis stirred sugar into his coffee. "Who owns it?"

"A family named del Bosque," Bessie said. "Nobody knows much about 'em really. They've owned the place for generations and they've always kept to themselves, living off their fishing and oystering plus what they could hunt and grow out there. The restaurant started out as a shack back in the fifties, just a tiki-hut kind of place up on the hill where local fishermen would stop in for a beer. But then the Topsider crowd starting showing up, looking for a place to slum, so the family figured they could make some money off 'em."

"It looks like a house," Louis said.

Bessie nodded. "Yeah, they built the restaurant sometime in the sixties." She curled her lip. "Tourist trap, that's all it is."

"So no one from there has much contact with the mainland?" Landeta asked.

Bessie just shook her head. Louis was sure Landeta had not seen it, so he asked, "Not even the kids? What about school?"

"Home schooling, I hear," Bessie said, sipping her coffee. "Poor kids. Can you imagine what their life must be like?" She shrugged. "But then, lots of folks round here like to keep to themselves. I guess that's why no one ever thought twice about Isla des Huesos. As long as they pay their taxes and get their health department certificate approved every year, nobody gives a damn what goes on out there."

It was quiet for a moment. Just the gentle lapping of the water on the pilings below and the screech of a gull overhead.

Louis was trying to connect the dots. Del Bosque was a Spanish name. Frank had that book on Asturias. Was he from the Island of Bones? Is that why he went back?

*"Hic solutio est,"* Louis said under his breath.

Louis looked over at Landeta. He was staring out over the glittering waters of Charlotte Harbor. Louis knew Landeta couldn't see what was out there, but he knew his thinking was on the same track as his own. But they still had no proof to take back to Horton.

"Is there anything else you can tell us about the family?" Louis asked.

Bessie shook her head slowly. "Like I said, they keep to themselves. They come over here or go down to St. James City for their supplies, but I never seen any of them myself." She frowned. "Hold on a sec. Let me go check my library." She got up and went inside, coming back out with a book. Louis recognized it as a copy of the same book he had checked out of the library that day he had first begun surveilling Frank, the book about the settlement of the outlying islands in the 1800s.

Bessie put on her glasses. "Okay . . . Isla des Huesos. Well, says here it's 125 acres and was originally nothing but mangrove forest. But the interior is man-made."

"How can that be?" Louis asked.

"Back in prehistoric times, it was nothing but a flat oyster bar island," Bessie said. "But when the Calusa Indians settled this area around a hundred A.D., they used it as one of their main camps. They started building it up with discarded shells, bones, pottery, and junk, mainly as protection against tides and hurricanes. And over the last two thousand years all the stuff piled up and the island grew higher and bigger." She smiled. "Kind of like a big Indian landfill."

"How did the del Bosques family get it?" Louis asked.

Bessie ran a finger down the page. "Here it is. A Spaniard named Marcelo Leon del Bosque and his wife, Bianca, came to Florida during the second wave of Spanish settlement, probably in the late 1800s. They got the island on a land grant thing. They were the ones who named it Isla des Huesos because of the Indian mounds. They were from Asturias, a region in northern Spain."

"Asturias?" Landeta looked at Louis.

They were both silent. Louis had filled him in on the Asturian lupercalia rite on the drive out. Louis noticed Bessie staring at him over the rim of her glasses.

"Do they speak Latin in Asturias?" Louis asked her.

"How the hell should I know?" Bessie said.

"Latin was spoken in most of Spain at one time or another, and survived for centuries in isolated places," Landeta said. "I read that in one of Frank's books."

Now Bessie was eyeing Landeta. "Okay, what is this all about? What are you boys really after?" she asked.

Louis glanced at Landeta but said nothing.

"C'mon," Bessie said. "They're just a little strange. Every town has a weird family. What do you think is going on out there anyway?"

The sun was high in the sky now, blazing down on the stilt house. Louis felt the sweat trickle down his back.

"I can't say, Mrs. Levy," he said. "All I can tell you is we're investigating any possible connection between that island and Frank Woods."

Bessie pushed her fuzz of red hair away from her face. "Woods? That the dead man's last name?"

"Yes, Frank Woods. Why?"

"Del Bosque. That's Spanish for 'of the woods.' " Bessie snorted. "Some detective you are."

Louis and Landeta exchanged a look, and then Landeta held out his hand to Bessie.

"You've been kind. Thank you," he said. "And thank you for the coffee."

"You're welcome," Bessie said.

Bessie went to the railing, stuck her fingers in her mouth, and let out a shrill loud whistle. Louis could see the old man back on the dock at Bokeelia look up. The old man waved and got in his boat.

Louis could hear the putt-putt of the boat as it slowly made its way out to them. He brought up a hand to shield his eyes and looked back out over the sun-silvered water. Far away, out on the very edges of the northwestern horizon, he could make out the ghostly gray green of the most distant islands. In the heat-hazed air, the islands seemed to be floating, like a mirage.

As Bessie busied herself gathering up the coffee mugs, Landeta came up to Louis's side. "Now we know why Sophie's father thought Frank was Mexican."

Louis nodded slowly. "And why Frank went back to the island."

"Maybe it's time to bring Horton in on this," Landeta said.

Louis squinted out at the water.

"Louis, did you hear me? We need to talk to the chief."

"Not yet. We still don't have anything linking Frank Woods to the other missing girls," Louis said.

Landeta let out a breath. "Well, we can run a background check for him under del Bosque, see what comes up."

Louis shook his head. "Diane told me she was born at home. Chances are her father was, too. Whatever past Frank Woods had is out on that island."

"Okay, any other bright ideas then?"

"Yeah," Louis said. "Let's go get some lunch."

# CHAPTER 35

As the ferry neared Away So Far island, Louis went up to the bow. He saw the same fringe of dark green, broken by tall palms, and the jut of a weathered wooden dock. As they drew closer, he could see the dirt path that led up the gentle hill and a moment later, the white clapboard restaurant came into view. It looked exactly as it had on his first trip. But this time, he knew it was different.

He was seeing things through new eyes, eyes that saw the dense mangroves with their clawlike branches, saw the thick tangle of brush, and saw—for the first time—how far out in the sound they were, how isolated the island really was.

"The boat is slowing," Landeta said. "Are we pulling in?"

"Yeah."

"What can you see?"

"Not much from here. Heavy mangroves, the restaurant, lots of brush," Louis said. "There's also a small skiff tied up at the dock."

The ferry docked and Louis nudged Landeta to his feet. A dark-haired man on the dock roped the boat in and the motor died. Louis and Landeta waited while the tourists filed off.

Louis stepped off first, then extended a hand back to

Landeta. But Landeta ignored it, stepped over to the dock, and started away.

"When I need a Seeing Eye dog, I'll be sure to call you," he said to Louis.

Louis let it go, following Landeta up the dock.

"Enjoy your lunch on Away So Far Island," the man said as Louis passed. "The ferry back leaves in two hours. Please be prompt."

Louis and Landeta trailed the rest of the group up the path toward the restaurant.

"Did you see any other place a boat could pull into?" Landeta asked as they walked.

"No, it's all mangroves. Why?"

"Just wondering," Landeta said. He stopped walking, catching Louis's arm. He looked off toward the right side of the restaurant. "What's over there?"

Louis started walking, angling away from the restaurant toward the water. "Nothing much . . . some more mangroves and a garbage bin. Wait a minute."

Louis started across the brush, but when he heard Landeta coming up behind him, he stopped. "There's a fence," Louis said. "It's wood, about six feet high."

"Can you get a look over it?" Landeta asked.

Louis climbed atop the garbage bin. On the other side, he could see what looked like a jungle—twisted vines, rotting stumps, fallen trees, and a glimpse of a narrow dark creek, covered in a thin layer of algae.

"Hey, you there!"

Louis turned to see the man from the dock coming toward them. The man stopped, his hands on his hips. "That's private property."

Louis jumped off the garbage bin, dusting his hands. "We were just looking for a nature trail or something. Thought we'd take a look around."

The man pointed to the restaurant, up the hill. "You'd better get up to lunch. There's no time for walking."

Louis and Landeta headed back toward the restaurant. As they started up the wooden steps, Landeta caught his arm. "Did you see anything back there?"

"Not a thing. It's all brush and trees, so thick you can't see five feet ahead of you."

They were met at the door by the same young boy who had spoken to Frank Woods. He looked up at them with long-lashed brown eyes. "How many?"

"Two."

"Yes, sir." The boy led them to the back of the restaurant, and laid the menus on the wooden table. "Can I get you a drink or some water?"

"Water, please."

Louis slid into the chair, watching the boy. "That was Roberto," Louis said to Landeta. "The same kid Frank spoke to. You know, I didn't see it the first time but the kid looks like Frank when he was younger, that same pale complexion, black wavy hair."

Louis looked around. The bartender was a tall man, about forty, with a bushel of black hair. Louis could see two other men in their twenties, both dressed in white T-shirts and long white aprons. Back in the kitchen, his face barely visible in the small window, he saw another man who looked to be in his mid-forties.

He leaned back toward Landeta. "They all look the same. Black hair, dark eyes."

"What about the women?" Landeta asked.

"I don't see any women." Louis leaned over the table. "Come to think of it, I didn't see any the first time either."

"Where do you think they are?"

"They're dead."

"The boy came from somewhere, Kincaid. He wasn't hatched."

Louis could feel eyes on his back and he turned to see the two waiters staring at them. Roberto appeared with their water.

"You're Roberto, right?" Louis asked.

The boy seemed surprised Louis knew his name. "Yes, sir," he said, setting the water glasses down.

"Do you live here on this island, Roberto?" Louis asked.

The boy blinked and took a step back. "Yes, sir," he said.

"Just you and your family?"

Roberto grinned, his cheeks reddening. "It's a big family, sir."

"Really?" Louis said. "How many people?"

Roberto looked at the floor. "There's my father and Uncle Pedro and Uncle Orlando, and I have—"

"Roberto!"

Louis turned to see one of the waiters motioning for Roberto to come away from the table. Roberto slunk away, and the waiter came forward, a dish towel in his large hands.

"The boy has work to do. Can I take your order?"

Louis glanced at him. No name tag. The man's eyes were dark, deep-set, and black as coal, and they were fixed on Louis's face. Landeta drew his attention by ordering the blackened grouper and a Diet Coke. Louis did the same and the man drifted away, disappearing into the kitchen.

"That guy looks like he's wound a little too tight," Louis said.

"Who, the waiter?"

"Yeah." Louis watched the man with the black eyes. He was over at the bar. "He's staring at us."

Landeta took a drink of his water. "Relax. We're just tourists, here for some lunch and a little local color."

Louis looked out the window, trying not to stare back at the waiter.

"You know, I was thinking we might be dealing with a cult here," Landeta said.

"I was thinking the same thing."

"When you were a cop, you ever have any experience with cults?" Landeta asked quietly.

"No," Louis said. "You?"

Landeta nodded. "You ever hear of the Yahwehs?"

"No," Louis said.

"It's a cult of black racist extremists led by this wacko named Hulon Mitchell. He calls himself Yahweh Ben Yahweh and they have a headquarters over in Miami's Liberty City called the Temple of Love. Before I quit Miami PD, I was one of the guys assigned to work the case with the FBI for a while."

Louis heard a note of pride in Landeta's voice. "What was it like?" Louis asked.

"We had all this shit on Mitchell, like he was forcing minors to have sex with him and that he had this squad he called the Death Angels, who were going around murdering white people. It was an initiation thing to get into the brotherhood, and you had to bring back severed heads or ears as proof."

Louis shook his head slowly.

"The thing is, people think shit like that doesn't happen in their nice little towns," Landeta said. "They don't want to believe it. Like Bessie Levy said, every town has a weird family. Question is, where does weird leave off and cult begin?"

Louis was staring at the black-eyed waiter again.

"You remember that case out in Salt Lake a couple of years ago?" Landeta asked.

"That Mormon guy with ten wives?" Louis asked.

"Four wives," Landeta said. "He had four wives and twenty-nine kids who he kept like slaves. The girls were married off at fourteen and then lived in poverty and abuse with their babies. They finally busted the guy for welfare fraud. Maybe something like that is going on here—polygamy, slavery."

Louis leaned forward. "There are no women here, Mel."

"Just a thought."

The waiter returned with their Diet Cokes, his eyes still on Louis.

"Could I have a lemon wedge, please?" Landeta asked.

The waiter's black eyes flicked to Landeta. "You'll get lemon with your fish," he said, and moved away.

"Service just isn't what it used to be," Landeta said, taking a drink of the Diet Coke.

Louis sat back, his eyes drifting out the window to the dock outside and the water beyond. Polygamy, slavery, cults. It was all one big swirling mess of images in his brain now, images of rape, torture, sexual sadism, ritualistic sacrifices held in the deep of night, miles from anywhere, out of sight of anyone who cared.

He sat still, staring out the open front door. He thought about what Landeta had asked him last night. *What did the island feel like?*

He could feel it now, feel the emptiness of this strange place, the emptiness that he now knew was the absence of anything good, warm, or normal.

"Louis, what are you thinking about?"

Louis cleared his throat. "That thing you read me last night, the wolf-into-man thing."

"About the raping and cannibalizing?"

"Yeah. And that rite-of-passage thing in Asturias." Louis glanced at a waiter as he delivered a plate of food to a nearby table.

"Maybe that's what we're dealing with here," Louis said. "A warped old family tradition or religion of some kind. Maybe they worship the wolf and are killing the women in some sacrifice or something. Maybe they actually *think* they turn into wolves."

"Like Michael Landon."

"That's not funny, Mel."

"No, it isn't," Landeta said. "But *we* sure the hell are. Are you listening to us? Mormons, cults, werewolves."

Louis nodded. "How in the hell are we going to tell Horton this?"

Landeta was silent for a moment. "We can't. We don't have one shred of anything real to go on here. We can't even prove Frank Woods was once a part of the del Bosque family. Case closed, just like Horton said."

Louis shook his head slowly. "No, there's something bad going on here and we have to get Horton to believe it."

At that moment, the waiter came to the table, bringing their lunches. It was one of the older men this time.

Louis studied the man's face. He had Frank's square jaw and wide forehead, but his face was more lined and sunken, like he had been living outdoors all his life—like Frank had looked on the autopsy table.

The man sensed Louis's stare and took a step back. "Do you need anything else?" he asked.

Louis shook his head and the man walked away, disappearing behind the bar. Louis looked up into Landeta's yellow glasses.

Landeta picked up a lemon wedge from his plate and squeezed it into his Diet Coke. "Eat your lunch," he said quietly.

They ate in silence, uncomfortable under the weight of dark eyes and whispered conversations. The boy Roberto was nowhere to be seen.

When they were finished, Landeta drew his wrist close and peered at his watch, a white, wide dial with large black numbers.

"Let's go outside. I need a smoke."

Louis followed Landeta back out to the porch, and down the steps. They stood on the dirt path while Landeta lit a cigarette. The ferry sat at the dock, the captain busying himself on deck for the return trip. Louis put on his sunglasses and looked out over Pine Island Sound. The nearest island was just a distant clump of green, too far away to even gauge the distance.

"Damn, it's hot," Landeta mumbled.

"Let's go sit by the water," Louis suggested. "There's a bench there."

"I saw it," Landeta said, heading toward it.

Louis started to follow but the sound of a screen door slapping shut drew his attention to the side of the restaurant. He saw the boy Roberto lugging a trash can to the bin over by the fence.

Louis looked at Landeta, who had gone to sit on the bench, smoking his cigarette. Louis started over to the boy. As he neared, the boy lost his footing and the can tipped, spilling garbage onto the sand. Louis took off his sunglasses and drew up next to him.

"Can I help?" Louis asked.

Roberto looked up at him, then shook his head quickly. "No, thanks."

Louis squatted and started picking up the trash, tossing it in the can. "So, your family owns this place?"

Roberto didn't answer, his hands working fast to get the trash up.

"This is a nice island," Louis said. "Reminds me of Sereno Key, except there's no houses here."

"Where's Sereno Key?" Roberto asked.

"It's an island just off Fort Myers."

"Where's Fort Myers?"

Louis hesitated. "It's a city, over there." He pointed vaguely out at the sound. "It's a pretty big city. You've never been there?"

Roberto paused, thinking. He threw some napkins in the can. "I've never been anywhere. But Uncle Edmundo says I can go off the island with him when I'm sixteen," Roberto said. "Maybe."

"What's your mother's name?"

The trash was picked up, but Roberto didn't seem in a big hurry to dump it. He squinted up at Louis, his brow wrinkled, a few dark curls stuck to his forehead. Louis thought again how much he resembled the young Frank Woods in the old photo.

"Her name was Mary. But she died."

Louis felt his heart kick. "I'm sorry. Was it a long time ago?"

"Yeah, when I was real little."

"Do you remember what your mother's last name was?"

The boy frowned. "Del Bosque, like me."

Louis stared at the boy. He hadn't seen it the first time, but now he did: a faint but definite resemblance to the picture of Mary Rubio. It was there in the boy's large dreamy eyes and his full lips. Louis could feel the back of his shirt growing damp with sweat, and the smell from the garbage was making him sick.

"What about your father? What's his name?"

The boy was looking at Louis now as if he were crazy. "He's a del Bosque, too. His name is Carlos."

"Is he alive?"

Roberto started to nod, but the bang of the screen door again made him turn.

"That's him," Roberto said, pointing. "You want to talk to him, too?"

Carlos del Bosque reached them in three long steps. He was a big man, his arms straining the short sleeves of the white T-shirt. His dark eyes snapped beneath a tumble of black curls as he grabbed hold of Roberto's T-shirt, and slung him toward the door.

"I told you not to talk to the customers. Get inside."

"You don't have to be so rough," Louis said. "I was just being friendly."

"We don't need friendly. Go get on the boat."

Carlos del Bosque grabbed the trash can and easily lifted it up and over the edge of the bin. He shook the garbage loose, then turned back. When he saw Louis still standing there, he edged forward.

"I said go get on the boat."

Louis threw up a hand. "Okay, okay. No problem."

"And don't come back. We don't want your business."

Louis walked away, running his arm across his brow. He slipped his sunglasses back on, and glanced back at Carlos del Bosque. The man hadn't moved, his eyes fixed on Louis.

Louis looked at the restaurant. He could see Roberto on the porch, his face pressed against the screen. Louis started to the dock. As he approached Landeta, the sound of his footsteps on the dock made Landeta look up.

"You stink," Landeta said. "Where the hell you been?"

"Helping the kid with some garbage. He told me his mother was named Mary and that she's dead."

"Mary Rubio?"

"He didn't know. But he's about ten years old, and Mary Rubio disappeared in 1973. That means he could be her kid. And, Mel, he looks a little like her."

"What about Frank? Did you ask him if he had an uncle Frank or anything?"

"Didn't get a chance. The father came over."

"What did he say?"

"He told me not to come back."

Landeta was quiet, looking back at the restaurant. "You're right," he said. "Something's wrong here. I can't see it, but I can feel it."

"The name Mary is a real connection," Louis said. "You think it's enough to take to Horton?"

Landeta nodded. "We'll go see him as soon as we get back. If Mary Rubio died on this island, she's probably buried here somewhere. Maybe we can get a search warrant."

He pulled out his cigarettes and lit another one, drawing hard on it as he looked back at the restaurant.

*"Hic solutio est,"* he said.

# CHAPTER 36

Louis and Landeta walked across the grass of Centennial Park. They could see Horton sitting on a bench near the river, a small brown dog jumping at his feet. Occasionally, the dog stopped jumping long enough to eat something out of Horton's hand.

"I didn't know he had a dog," Louis said.

"I did," Landeta said.

"Did he tell you?"

"No, I smelled it on him."

"Bullshit."

"Just like I knew you had a cat."

"You *saw* my cat."

"I smelled it long before I saw it."

"Cats don't smell. You must've smelled the litter."

"Maybe you should change it more often."

"Fuck you," Louis said.

Horton was dressed in baggy yellow Bermuda shorts and a loose-fitting blue shirt. It was odd seeing him out of uniform, Louis thought. Uniforms always added a certain stiffness to a man, but Horton looked relaxed. His eyes, fixed on

Louis and Landeta, were shadowed by the bill of a Buccaneers cap.

They stopped in front of him.

"Well, isn't this the picture," Horton said.

"We've come to a few conclusions," Landeta said.

"About what?"

"Frank Woods and the dead girls."

"The only dead girl we got is Shelly Umber," Horton said. "You haven't proven to me that any of the others are dead."

"We haven't proven they're alive either," Landeta said.

"Then where are the bodies?" Horton asked.

"On Away So Far Island," Louis said.

Horton frowned. "You mean that place out in the sound with the old restaurant?"

"Yeah," Landeta said.

The dog was straining against his leash, edging toward some bushes. Horton pulled him back a bit, eyeing them. "Okay, let me hear what you got."

Louis went first. "Away So Far is owned by the del Bosque family and they don't let anyone out there except for lunch."

"I know that," Horton interrupted. "They like their privacy. So do I."

"The name del Bosque means 'of the woods' in Spanish," Louis went on, "and it's a logical jump that Frank Woods's real name could be Francisco del Bosque. We found out that Sophie Woods and one of our missing girls, Angela Lopez, were both thought to have a Hispanic boyfriend."

Horton was silent.

"We can't find any history on Frank Woods before 1952—no school, no records, no childhood," Landeta said. "We suspect his childhood was on the island."

"Okay," Horton said slowly.

"Frank went to Away So Far the day he jumped into the water," Louis said.

"So? It's a tourist joint," Horton said.

"Exactly. Why would Frank Woods go out there?" Louis said. "Especially since he was already a suspect by then—he was running," Louis said. "He was going home."

Horton held up a hand. "So you're saying that over the last three decades, Frank Woods abducted girls and took them out to that island . . . where his so-called *family* lives?"

Louis and Landeta were silent.

"Well?" Horton asked.

"We think the whole family might be involved somehow," Landeta said.

"How?" Horton asked.

They were silent again. "We're not sure. It could be some kind of cult thing," Louis began.

"Cult?" Horton laughed. "Look, that family out there might be a little strange, but no stranger than a lot of folks who've lived around here a long time. I've been out there and never saw anything weird. They just pay their taxes and run their shitty restaurant."

"We think the women were abducted and taken to the island, raped, maybe tortured," Landeta said.

Horton frowned. "What makes you think they were tortured?"

"Shelly Umber had bruises and ligature marks. She was restrained by the neck and ankles," Landeta said. "And she was wearing a coral ring, the same kind of ring that was found in Frank Wood's house, which probably belonged to his wife. The ring could be some kind of cult symbol."

Horton looked at Landeta for a long time, then reached down and rubbed the dog's head. "What else?"

"Frank told me himself there was something going on out there," Louis said.

"He *told* you?" Horton asked, looking up.

"When we were on the island, he said, *'Hic solutio est.'* It's Latin that means 'the answer is here.' "

"Latin?" Horton asked.

"Yeah," Landeta said. "Louis translated it."

Horton looked at Louis. "You know Latin?"

"No, no," Louis began.

"But Frank Woods did," Landeta added quickly. "He taught himself."

Horton shook his head slowly. "That it?"

"No, there's the painting," Landeta said.

"A painting? Like an oil painting?"

"The painting is on the wall in the restaurant. It's called *The Rape of the Sabines*," Louis said. "It's a picture of Roman soldiers carrying off women. It's part of the legend of Romulus and Remus."

"Who?" Horton asked.

"Romulus and Remus, Roman brothers suckled by the she-wolf," Louis said. "There's a photo of them sucking on a wolf's tit."

"There's a painting out on that island of someone sucking on a tit?" Horton asked.

Landeta held up a hand. "Wait, we're getting ahead of ourselves."

Horton was just staring at both of them.

"Frank Woods was into lycanthropy," Landeta said, speaking more slowly. "Lycanthropy is a mental disease where a person thinks he is turning into a wolf."

"A werewolf?" Horton asked.

"No, no," Louis said. "A real wolf."

"What the hell makes you think Frank thought he was a wolf?"

"The books in his office." Louis dug for his notebook and flipped the pages. He read off the titles of the books he had taken from Frank's house.

When he was done, he waited for Horton to say something. Horton was still staring at them both.

"That's it," Landeta said.

Horton looked from Louis to Landeta and back. Then he

got up slowly and walked a few paces away with the dog. He stood there for a moment, looking out at the river, then turned back.

"What a crock of shit," he said.

"Chief—" Louis began.

"I don't believe I'm hearing this from two grown men— no, two experienced investigators."

"Al," Louis said. "C'mon. Let's go back to the station. We'll lay it out on paper. It'll make more sense."

"Writing it down isn't going to make it do anything."

"Angela Lopez even told someone she had a lunch date," Louis said. "That's the only time people can go out to that island."

"That's good, Kincaid. A lunch date in 1984."

"There's one more thing," Louis said. "There's a kid out there whose mother's name was Mary. He said she died."

Horton hesitated but then shook his head. "Common name, Kincaid. You get anything solid to connect it to Mary Rubio?"

"No, but—"

"It's not enough," Horton said.

Landeta stepped forward. "Louis—"

"Chief, I know there's something going out there," Louis said. "I can feel it."

"Then feel your way toward some solid evidence, Kincaid," Horton said.

"Chief, let us just try for a warrant—"

"No!" Horton leaned into Louis. "I'm not going to a judge with some shit about Roman soldiers and werewolves."

Louis fell silent. He was right. He was absolutely right. He looked over at Landeta, suddenly aware that he had been quiet for the last few minutes. He seemed to be staring off toward the river.

"Go on," Horton said, "get the hell out of here. If you want to pursue this island angle, bring me back something I can use. Not paintings and wolf tits."

Horton walked away, the little dog dragging him toward a flock of pigeons at a fountain.

Louis let out a breath. "He's right."

Landeta was still silent. Louis looked at him. Landeta's face had gone slack.

"Mel, we'll get more evidence."

"From where?" Landeta said. "All the evidence is on that fucking island. Behind that *fucking* fence."

"We'll dig deeper," Louis said. "We'll find someone who knows the family, find someone who knew Frank in 1952. We'll find *something* that will get us a warrant to search that island."

Landeta shook his head. It was getting late and the afternoon light was fading. Landeta took a few cautious steps away from Louis, turning his back. He seemed to be staring out at the river again, even though Louis knew he couldn't see it clearly.

Landeta turned back. He hesitated, then reached inside his black jacket. He pulled out a small leather holder and flipped it open.

Louis saw the glint of the gold badge in the fading light. Landeta was just standing there, running a thumb over the embossing.

"Where'd Horton go?" Landeta asked.

Louis froze. He knew what Landeta was thinking.

"Jesus, Mel, no," he said.

"I said, where's Horton?" Landeta asked again.

"Over there by the fountain."

Louis watched as Landeta followed the sound of the water over to the fountain. He watched as Landeta touched Horton's shoulder and said something. Horton looked down at Landeta's hand, but he didn't move.

The two men talked for several more minutes. Finally, Horton took the gold shield.

Horton walked away, the dog tugging him toward the

parking lot. Landeta was just standing there. Louis knew he couldn't see him so he went over to him.

"Why did you do that?" Louis asked.

"It was time." Landeta was still looking off in the direction that Horton had gone. There was something different about Landeta suddenly. It was small but Louis could see it there in the slight drop of his shoulders, the laxity in his face. It was as if the damn gold badge had been the only thing holding him upright.

"Mel, look, I know—" Louis began.

Landeta's eyes came back to Louis. He smiled slightly. "Come on. I'll buy you a beer."

# CHAPTER 37

Landeta looked at him from across the table, his long fingers wrapped around the glass of Diet Coke. They had driven to O'Sullivan's in silence, Louis leaving Landeta to his thoughts. But they had been here for five minutes and the man still hadn't spoken.

"Mel, we need to talk about this," Louis said.

"It was my decision. Don't feel sorry for me."

"I wasn't . . ." Louis stopped. Truth was, he was feeling sorry for Landeta.

"I'm concerned," Louis said.

"I'm not Frank Woods, Kincaid. I won't jump into the sound on you."

"What will you do then? Go back to Miami?" Louis asked.

Landeta shrugged, his gaze wandering over to the two off-duty cops sitting at the bar. He twirled the ice in his glass. "Do you remember that day in my office, when you stopped by to get the baby skull?"

Louis nodded.

"I asked you how long it took before you didn't miss being a cop anymore," Landeta said. "Do you remember?"

"I didn't really answer you," Louis said.

"You didn't have to. I already knew. I knew the answer that day back in the mangroves when we found Shelly Umber's body."

Louis waited until Landeta took a drink and set the glass down on the cocktail napkin.

"You knelt there, down by Shelly Umber's body, and told me what you saw even though you were choking on the damn smell," Landeta said.

Louis shrugged. "Yeah, well, I guess you never stop wanting to be a part of it. Even the bad parts."

"What was it you liked most?" Landeta asked.

Louis shifted, uncomfortable. There was an unfamiliar sense of intimacy hovering over the table, and he wasn't sure he liked it. He had talked shop with lots of guys, but it was always bullshit, no real words or emotions. And he sure as hell wasn't used to anything personal coming from Landeta. He suspected the admission about the blindness that night in his apartment was nothing but a temporary slit, an emotional wormhole opening into a black space for a millisecond before closing up again.

But now Landeta wanted to talk. He needed to talk. More than that, he needed someone to sit here and listen.

"Well?" Landeta asked.

Louis wet his lips, staring at his Coke. "I liked the mystery," he said. "I just liked solving the damn mystery. And even in cases where there was no mystery about who, I always wanted to know why."

Louis waited to see if Landeta laughed. But Landeta was just looking at him through the yellow glasses. Finally, he picked up his sweating glass. The cocktail napkin stuck for a moment, then fell to the table. Landeta reached for the salt, shook some out onto the napkin, and set the glass down. When he picked up the glass again, it didn't stick.

"Old bartender's trick," he said when he saw Louis looking at him. Louis looked over at the two off-duty cops. They were sitting there, both staring silently into the mirror over the bar, sipping their beers.

Louis looked back at Landeta. "So what about you?"

"What did I like best?"

"Yeah."

Landeta leaned forward on his elbows. "A lot of guys say it's the power, the authority trip, you know? And there's the whole thing about wanting to help people, but that wears off real quick."

Louis nodded slowly. "So what was left for you? I mean, when it wore off?"

Landeta was looking down into his glass, but his brows were knit, like he was thinking about the question for the first time and not coming up with anything that made sense.

"You got any brothers or sisters?" he asked finally.

Louis hesitated. "Yeah, one of each, both older." *But I haven't seen them since I was seven and I don't know where they are or even if they are alive.*

"I was an only child," Landeta said. "My father died when I was eleven. A couple of months later, my mom dropped me off at my aunt Shirl's and left for the bright lights of Indianapolis. I went out on my own at seventeen, bummed around the country for a couple of years until I ended up down in Pensacola. Worked on an oyster boat for a year and eventually joined the police force there when I was twenty."

Landeta took a drink and set the glass down. "I remember my first roll call, sitting there in that room of blue shirts. It was the first time in my life I felt I was part of something."

"A family," Louis said.

Landeta smiled. "Yeah, but a family you could get away from when you went home at night. That's what I liked most about it."

Landeta's smile faded and he picked up his glass, swirling the ice around. "Aunt Shirl. Haven't thought about her in years. What a tough old bird, about as tender as those damn skinny chickens running around out in her yard. But I did learn one thing from her—that there were no free rides in life, that I had to earn my keep."

They fell into silence again. Louis watched as the two cops at the bar got up and left. He looked back at Landeta and saw that he had also been watching the cops.

"Did you tell Horton?" Louis asked. "About your condition, I mean?"

Landeta nodded. "At least he doesn't think I'm a burnout anymore. I don't know what's worse, pity or contempt."

Louis looked down into his own glass.

"Horton said he'd try to find me something on a desk," Landeta said. "I said thanks but no, thanks. I don't need any free rides." He gave a wry smile. "Aunt Shirl would've been proud."

"Shit, Mel, is that why you quit? Because you think you're useless now?"

"I didn't say that."

"Then what?"

Landeta's lips drew back in a small smile. "Now I can do everything you can do."

Louis just stared at him. Then slowly, it hit him. That day back in Horton's office, when the chief had asked him to work on this case with Landeta "unofficially." No pay, no badge, but with the implicit understanding that with fewer legal restraints, Louis could do things that Landeta could not.

"I want to finish this," Landeta said.

Louis was stunned. "You quit so you could freelance?"

"Why not? You do. It's why Horton put you on the case," Landeta said. "Besides to baby-sit me, I mean."

Louis put up a hand. "Okay, there are things I can do that a cop can't. But you think me waving my PI license in their faces is going to make those people let us search their island?"

"I didn't plan on asking them."

It took Louis a moment. "Wait a minute. You plan on just

cruising out there, pulling in to some shady little inlet, and just taking a look?"

"Yeah."

"That's trespassing."

"Actually in Florida, you can't be charged with trespassing until you've been warned at least once. I didn't see any signs posted anywhere out there, did you?"

When Louis started to answer, Landeta held up a hand. "Don't answer that."

Louis was shaking his head. Landeta leaned close over the table.

"Look, we just take a boat over there at night and pull in somewhere away from the restaurant. We take a camera, we look around a little, eavesdrop a little. Maybe we hear or see something we can take back to Horton. Like the name Mary Rubio."

Louis was still shaking his head.

"We'll be in and out in an hour."

"No way, Mel. Count me out."

Landeta leaned back in the booth. He paused, then pulled out his cigarettes. He lit one and took a long drag, blowing the smoke out slowly.

"Look, they took me off the Yahweh thing over in Miami," Landeta said. "I just want this one last chance to finish something."

Louis wouldn't look up, but he could feel the pull of Landeta's eyes on him.

"Remember when Woods floated up? You remember what you told me? You told me I didn't care about finding the other girls."

"I was pissed," Louis said, shaking his head. "I know you want to find them."

"So do you. Let's do it, damn it."

Louis stared at the table, his chest tight. He couldn't deny he felt a spark of interest. And more than that, a bizarre sense of excitement at the recklessness of it. But he was remembering the long night spent in Frank Wood's tent, so stiff with irrational fears that he couldn't move.

Louis looked at Landeta across the table. But he also knew that if they didn't go out there, it was over. Frank Woods was dead. Horton would let the case fold up quietly with no official resolution, and eventually, Shelly Umber's file would be sent down to that storage room to collect dust and mold like the five others.

Landeta was waiting.

"Okay," Louis said softly. "When?"

"Tonight." Landeta set a couple of dollars on the table and stood up. "We've got things to do. Let's go."

Louis slid out of the booth, and let out a long breath. Landeta heard it and turned.

"Look at it this way, Rocky," he said. "We're earning our keep."

# CHAPTER 38

The moon hung low over the water. The boat's motor gave out a low gurgling as they headed out into the middle of the sound. The lights of Captiva were growing smaller, dimmer, and Louis watched them, his hand gripping the throttle, his head filling with things he didn't want to think about.

Like what they were doing. It was illegal, no matter what kind of a spin Landeta tried to put on it.

He looked up to the bow, where Landeta sat quietly, face turned up to the warm night breeze. *Look around a little, eavesdrop a little. We'll be in and out in an hour.*

Louis tried hard to relax his hand on the throttle but it was no use. His whole body was one giant knot. He let out a long breath.

"What's the matter?" Landeta asked.

"Nothing."

"Bullshit. What is it?"

"Nothing, I said."

Louis strained to watch the water ahead of them. He could barely see it in the thin light of the rising moon. He couldn't see any land ahead.

"Mel, are you sure—?"

"Yeah, just watch the channel markers. Keep the red ones to your left."

Landeta had told him he could find the island, that he knew enough about navigation from his days working on the oyster boats. But it was so dark, so far away from anything. And they were depending on Landeta's ability to read a map of the sound that they had gotten at Sutter's Marina when they rented the boat.

A flashlight flicked on up at the bow. "Head her left," Mel said. "About eleven o'clock. The guy at the marina said there was a light on the dock. Keep an eye out for it."

*Jesus . . .*

The moon slipped behind a cloud, plunging them into darkness. Something splashed in the water and Louis jumped.

"It's a fish, Kincaid. For Christ's sake, it's nothing to be afraid of," Landeta said.

He knew it was a fish, but his body didn't. It had gone into some weird automatic response mode, the same way it had that night he spent in Frank's tent. He had sat there, the darkness and heat wrapped around him, the sounds, the snaps, the cries of the night murmuring outside the thin nylon, growing ever louder in his ears.

"We've gone far enough," Landeta said. "You should be able to see the light."

Louis was silent, his eyes straining in the darkness. The moon emerged and he saw its glint on the water. And then something else.

"I see something," he said.

"Where?"

"Over there, to the right, about two o'clock." He leaned forward, squinting. "It's a light. I'm sure it's a light."

"Okay then. All you gotta do now is aim at it."

They fell quiet. The light was growing larger. Louis could now make out the dark outline of the mangroves.

"Where's the Deets?" Landeta asked.

"In the backpack," Louis said.

"Put it on now. We're going to need it when we get close."

They had tried to think of everything they would need for a few hours of surveillance. Mosquito repellent, gloves, flashlights, a pocket knife, a camera with low-light film, and Landeta's portable police radio. Each had a gun strapped to his hip.

It hadn't even occurred to Louis to question Landeta about his .45. He knew Landeta would probably never pull it tonight, let alone shoot at something he couldn't see. What he needed was what all cops needed, the *feel* of it, on his hip. At his fingertips.

"Kill the motor," Landeta said softly. "Island people know the sounds of their home, especially at night. We don't want them to hear them anything out of the ordinary."

Louis cut the motor and Landeta picked up an oar. Louis did the same, and they paddled quietly in toward the mangroves. As they paddled past the dock, Louis tried to find the restaurant in the gloom of the trees and brush. Finally, he picked out the white boards, but all the lights inside were out.

They were heading to the western side of the island, looking for some place behind the fence where they could pull in. But Louis could see no dry land, no way into the tangle of mangrove roots. If they could just get off the water and under the cover of brush, they would have a chance of pulling this off. But out here in the open water, with the moon moving among the clouds, they could easily be spotted.

Landeta was quiet. Louis knew Landeta wanted to ask what Louis was seeing. But any sound they made now could be heard.

Finally Louis saw a break in the black mangroves. He made a correction with his oar to move them in and Landeta picked up the hint immediately, matching his movement.

"Mel, duck," Louis whispered as they entered the tiny inlet.

Landeta hunched just in time before a mangrove branch

raked across his back. He stayed down as Louis paddled into the dark tunnel. About twenty feet in, the boat bumped on ground.

"Stay here," Louis whispered. He could see just enough to avoid tripping over the high-arching roots as he stepped out of the boat. Mud sucked at his boots. He looked around in the spare moonlight. Up a slight incline, he could see dry land where the mangroves stopped.

There was a cloud of mosquitoes in his ears, around his nostrils and mouth.

He went back to Landeta and leaned close. "You've got about six feet of mangrove roots, and then it's dry land," Louis said.

Louis helped Landeta climb from the boat, following as Landeta felt his way across the twisted roots. Landeta slipped once, his boot sinking into the black mud. He whispered something and kept going.

"You got the backpack, right?" Louis asked.

"Yeah."

Louis led him up the incline. When Landeta's feet hit the flat ground, he stopped, drawing in a breath. He pulled a black ball cap from his back pocket, and slipped it on his head. Then he pointed to the moon as if to tell Louis he was covering the shine of his bald head.

They stood there, perfectly still. At first, Louis heard only the silence. Then the small noises crept up out of the darkness. The whine of the mosquitoes, the murmur of the water, the hiss of the wind in the trees.

He could feel his heart quickening as the sounds grew. The scurry of something at his feet, the rasp of something ahead of him. A bird? A branch against another? His heart seemed to be pulling his muscles inward, pulling them into a tightness across his chest.

He felt something on his back and jumped. It was just Landeta's hand.

"What do you see?" he asked.

"Nothing . . . nothing."

"Look again."

Louis pulled in a deep breath. "There's a path. I think it rims the water." Louis was looking down the path, looking into the tunnel. The moon slipped behind a cloud, and the darkness engulfed them.

His skin hurt, as if he were being burned. It was the same thing he had felt that night in the tent. As if every nerve in his body was on fire.

He couldn't think. He couldn't move.

Landeta's hand was still on his back. "Louis?"

He couldn't breathe.

"Louis, I can feel you shaking."

"I'm okay . . . I'm . . ."

"You're afraid."

Silence.

"Of what?"

"I don't know. . . ."

"It's darkness, that's all, Louis. That's all it is."

Silence.

"Take a breath."

Landeta pressed on Louis's back. Louis slowly inhaled.

"Take a step."

Another press on the back, pushing him gently forward. Louis moved toward the tunnel.

"You can't trust your eyes now," Landeta said.

Louis drew in another breath, deeper this time. He felt the pressure of Landeta's hand on his back lessen slightly but not drop away. He knew Landeta was waiting for him to move them forward. He walked toward the tunnel, Landeta's hand on his shoulder.

# CHAPTER 39

They stopped to tie a small piece of white cloth to a tree. It was Landeta's idea, a way of marking the opening in the mangroves where they had left the boat. Then they followed the path as it wound along the mangrove shoreline. The moon slipped in and out of the clouds, giving them a chance to get a sense of their surroundings.

To the left were the mangroves, creeping out into the open water. To their right was a jungle of heavy brush, vine-tangled trees, and stands of shallow black water.

"I still haven't seen anything, no buildings, no houses," Louis said.

"We've only come about a half mile," Landeta said. "We're still running parallel with the water. My guess is the family lives inland."

"It's uphill," Louis said. "And I haven't seen any paths or anything going in."

"So I say we stay near the water for now."

"No argument from me, man," Louis said.

They went a little farther and Louis drew up short. Landeta stopped.

"What is it?" he asked.

"I'm not sure. Hold on." Louis got out his flashlight and flicked it on, aiming it inland. About ten feet into the brush, the beam picked up a white mound about five feet high.

"What do you see?" Landeta asked.

Louis let out a breath. "I think it's an Indian shell mound."

He flicked the light off and they moved on. Finally, the tunnel opened onto a clearing. Louis stopped.

"Shit," Landeta whispered.

Louis turned back. Landeta was rubbing his temple. He had walked into a board nailed to a tree. Louis flicked on the flashlight.

"Is it a sign?" Landeta asked.

"Yeah. It's in Latin. It says *Agni Dei.*"

"That's it?"

"Yeah," he said, clicking off the light.

Louis turned back to the clearing just as the moon came out from a cloud. It swept the sand and trees like a soft spotlight. A wall of mangroves formed the outer barrier, the roots looking like snakes against the shimmering water. A canopy of oak trees arched high overhead, hung with what looked like heavy black rags. The sandy ground was carpeted with dead leaves. Embedded in the sand were a half a dozen or so round stones, slightly larger than a human head.

Louis drew in a sharp breath. "Jesus," he whispered, moving forward. "Jesus."

"What?" Landeta asked.

Louis turned on the flashlight, sweeping it slowly over the round stones. They were carved from white coral and spaced about three feet part. They ran from the center of the clearing, down toward the water. He counted them. Five.

"What?" Landeta hissed.

"It's a cemetery of some kind."

Louis's eyes moved over the markers. This was it. This was the reason they had come. Even though he had expected this, it was hard to think about. The faces of the five missing women hovered in his mind and he tried to remember something he had learned about each of them, but nothing was coming, not even their names.

They were too late. *Years too late.*

"What are those things in the ground? They look like markers," Landeta asked.

"They are. They're made of coral, I think."

"Names?"

"No. I don't think so. Let me look." Louis moved closer, kneeling. He shined the light on the coral, hoping to see some writing or carvings, but there was nothing. The coral was too rough and covered in moss and mold.

"No names. But there are five of them, Mel."

The moon disappeared again. Louis felt Landeta's hand and turned to see him holding out the camera.

Louis stepped into the graveyard, glancing around. He hoped he could take a photograph without the flash. But he needed to wait for the moon to reappear. He looked up. It wasn't going to happen any time soon. He flicked the button for the flash and snapped the picture.

In the instant the flash lit up the graveyard Louis thought he saw something else—something dark and boxy on the edge of the graveyard that he hadn't seen before. He walked toward it.

"Mel, there's a table over here."

Landeta came up next to him and Louis clicked on the flashlight, running the beam over the table.

It was a small, rough, wooden table. A dark red cloth was spread over the top.

"Do you see any candles? Knives? Anything for a ritual?"

"No," Louis said, "just the table and the cloth."

"Take a picture of it."

"Jesus, Mel . . ."

"Do it."

The flash lit up the cemetery again, hanging in the air like lightning. Louis heard a sound behind him.

"Shit," Landeta muttered.

"What's the matter?"

"I stepped in a fucking hole."

Louis clicked on the flashlight. He froze. Landeta was sitting on the edge of an open grave. There was a small mound of dirt with a shovel lying on it.

"Christ, Mel, it's a grave."

"What?" Landeta pulled his leg out and scrambled to his feet.

Louis shined the light directly down into the hole. It was about two feet long, maybe a foot deep.

"You're sure it's a grave?" Landeta asked.

"Yeah, but there's nothing in it and it looks like it's only half dug. There's a shovel here."

"What else do you see?" Landeta asked.

"Nothing," Louis said. "That's it, man. We've got to call this in now."

"Horton's going to be pissed," Landeta said.

"I don't care. Call it in."

Landeta got the police radio out. Louis moved away, his flashlight scanning the brush, looking for anything that could tell them what was going on here. The flashlight beam picked up a break in the brush. It was another path and it seemed to head uphill and inland. Louis heard Landeta's voice and then a low burst of static.

Landeta clicked the radio off. "I'm not getting anything. We must be out of range."

"Shit," Louis muttered. "All right, we'll try again when we get out in the sound."

Landeta was quiet. "You're sure there are only five markers here?"

Louis flicked on the light and swept the small cemetery. "Five, that's all." He turned off the light. "Maybe they were digging this grave for Shelly Umber."

Landeta went over to the wooden table, running his hands

over the red cloth spread over the top. Then he came back and knelt by the hole. He grabbed a handful of dirt, bringing it up to his nose.

"The dirt is too fresh," he said. He stood up, throwing the clot to the ground. "And there are no leaves on the cloth."

They stood motionless in the dark, listening, attuned to the smallest sounds in the brush and trees. But there was nothing except the whine of the mosquitoes and the lapping of the water. Five girls were buried here. But who was meant to go in this half-dug grave? Was someone still alive, someone they didn't even know about?

Louis wiped his forearm over his sweating face. His brain was screaming to get the hell out of there. But suddenly he could see the faces of all the girls. Cindy, Emma, Paula, Mary, and Angela. He could see each one of them clearly, as if they were standing there in front of him.

"Mel," Louis said quietly, "if this is a new grave, someone could still be alive somewhere."

"I was thinking the same thing."

Louis hesitated. "I saw another path," he said. "It heads inland. I say we go up and look around."

"You're reading my mind."

Louis switched the flashlight back on, aiming the beam into the break just beyond the wooden table. He went to the path and hesitated.

"Better turn that off," Landeta said, coming up behind him.

He felt Landeta's hand on his back. It was pushing him forward. Louis started up the path, Landeta behind him.

"Well, it's all uphill now, Rocky," Landeta said.

# CHAPTER 40

Louis saw the lights first, and then the house emerged, coming out of the dark trees. It was large, two stories, and made of wood. It looked like the restaurant, but without the white paint.

As they crept closer, Louis could tell they were at the side of the house. The path continued on to the front, opening onto what looked like a large yard. Louis could see the vague outlines of other, smaller buildings arranged in a semicircle facing the big house. The light had been coming from the ground floor of the big house. It had the soft glow of lanterns. There were lights on on the second floor, too, but none of the cabins surrounding the house were illuminated.

"There's a house," Landeta said.

"Yeah, other smaller ones around it like a compound," Louis whispered.

"People?"

"No one."

"Wait. I hear someone," Landeta said.

"Okay, we're going closer," Louis said.

Louis led Landeta up to the house. They flattened themselves against the weathered wood, moving toward a lighted window. Now Louis could hear the voices.

"Tomas, I don't want to talk about this."

Louis looked at Landeta. Female.

"He's causing trouble," the man said. "He's trying to change things."

Louis eased up to the window. In the glow of the lantern, he saw the woman. She was old, gray-haired, and small, wearing a black dress. She was sitting in a carved wooden chair in front of the cold, stone fireplace, which framed her like a primitive throne. The man's back was to Louis; he could see only his long dark hair and the rifle slung over his shoulder.

"He's been talking to Rafael," the man said. "He's telling him we're living like animals, that we—"

"Stop," the woman said. "I won't hear you talk like that."

Landeta was tugging at Louis's shirt and pointing back to the path. But Louis shook his head.

He heard a door open, and ducked back down. Another man's voice.

"It's time. Angel's ready."

*Angel?* Louis felt Landeta's hand tighten on his shoulder.

"Tomas, go with Rafael," the old woman said.

"I can do this alone," Rafael said.

"No, let Tomas go with you."

A moment later, Louis heard a screen door open and bang shut. Two men came out of the house, pausing in the yard while one of them turned up the Coleman lantern he was carrying. They walked across the dark compound and one of the men disappeared into a cabin. When he emerged, he had his arm clamped around the shoulders of a dark-haired woman. She was hunched over and Louis could hear her whimpering.

"Where is he taking her?" Landeta asked.

"Down the path we just came up," Louis said. "Come on. Stay behind me."

The man with the rifle led the way, carrying the lantern.

The other man followed, his grip firm around the woman's shoulders. They didn't speak. The woman's soft sobbing was the only sound Louis could hear as he followed the soft glow of the lantern's light down the dark path.

About halfway to the cemetery, the trio veered off to another path. Louis realized he had not even noticed the fork in the path when they came in. He motioned to Landeta that they were heading right. The path led to a cabin settled into some twisted trees. The cabin was smaller than the ones in the compound, more primitive looking, and it was dark.

The trio stopped. Louis touched Landeta's arm and motioned for him to hide in the brush.

The man the old woman had called Rafael still had his arm tight around the woman's shoulders. Her whimpers were growing louder, more like short cries now. Louis could see she was having trouble walking. She looked badly hurt, and Louis fought the urge to jump out and stop this now, whatever it was. But he knew it wasn't time.

"You don't have to come inside, Tomas," Rafael said.

The other man mumbled something Louis couldn't hear and handed Rafael the lantern. Rafael pulled open the screen door and took the woman inside. Louis could see the glow of the lantern in a window.

In the dim moonlight, Louis watched as Tomas pulled the rifle off his shoulder, and set the butt on the ground. He rested the rifle against his body and pulled out a cigarette. As he cupped his hands to light it, Louis could see his face. He looked to be in his twenties and his dark hair flowed past the collar of his shirt. Louis recognized him as the man who had waited on them at the restaurant, the one with the piercing black eyes.

A woman's scream split the silence. "Oh, God, no!"

Louis bowed his head. Another scream, followed by a low moan.

"We've got to get in there now," Landeta whispered in his ear.

Louis wiped his hand on his shirt and slipped his gun from the holster on his hip. He could feel Landeta do the same. Tomas was still standing there, smoking the cigarette. With the rifle on the ground, they could take him.

Something snapped in the brush. More footsteps.

Tomas picked up the rifle, his eyes trained on the path. A man came to a stop about ten feet from Tomas.

"Go home, Uncle Francisco," Tomas said.

*Francisco?* He heard Landeta pull in a quick breath. He had heard it, too.

The man came closer toward the cabin, and Louis peered into the dark.

*Jesus.* It was Frank.

He was thinner, his hair was longer and ragged, and he had started to grow a new beard. But it was definitely Frank Woods.

Another scream came from the cabin, and then faded off into ragged breathing. Frank looked at the cabin, then back at Tomas.

"Tomas, just listen to me," Frank said.

"You've talked enough," Tomas said.

"This doesn't have to happen. We can stop it. Now, right here."

"It's the way it's done," Tomas said. "It's the way we've always done it."

"No," Frank said. "Not anymore. I'm in charge now."

"Bullshit!" Tomas said. "You come back after thirty-five years and you think you can bring the outside world with you. We don't want it!"

"Tomas, listen—"

"You're not one of us anymore, old man."

The woman screamed again, a long, guttural scream that hung in the thick wet air.

Frank started toward the cabin. Tomas grabbed the rifle and jammed the butt into Frank's belly. Frank doubled over, gasping for breath. Tomas hit him again on the shoulder, sending him to his knees.

"I'm moving," Louis whispered to Landeta. "When you hear my voice, step out and point your gun at the light inside the cottage. I want them to know there are two of us."

Landeta nodded.

The woman's cries were now a steady stream of whimpers that would build to sharp little shrieks, then die away again.

Louis stepped toward the path just as the door to the cabin opened. Rafael came out, holding the lantern high in his hand. He was sweating and breathing hard. His hands were covered with blood.

"Tomas, something's wrong. I can't—" he began.

Tomas turned toward the cabin.

Louis moved into the open. "Everyone freeze!"

Tomas swung back toward Louis. He started to raise the rifle but when he saw the Glock, he stopped.

Landeta stepped from the brush, his gun aimed dead ahead of him.

For an instant, no one moved.

"Drop the rifle," Louis said.

Tomas looked at Landeta, then back at Louis. He took a step back, planting his feet apart. Rafael was frozen in place.

"Drop the fucking rifle!"

Tomas didn't move, the rifle pointed down.

Sweat was trickling into Louis's eyes and he blinked it away. "You," Louis said, indicating Rafael with his gun barrel. "Come forward."

Rafael took two steps forward, then stopped.

"Closer!"

Rafael just stood there, holding the lantern.

"Damn it, do it!"

"They won't," Frank said softly.

Louis glanced quickly at Frank, still on the ground.

"Frank, get over there with them," Louis said.

"You know him?" Tomas demanded. He was staring at Frank. "You *know* him? You *brought* him here? Is he a cop?"

"I didn't bring them," Frank said through gritted teeth.

"You're lying, old man!" Tomas yelled, gripping the rifle. A scream came from the cottage.

"Louis," Landeta said quietly, "I can go to her."

Louis hesitated, his eyes locked on Tomas and Rafael. Landeta was standing just clear of the brush, about ten feet off to Tomas's left.

"Go," Louis said.

Landeta started slowly moving sideways. He had his gun still pointed at the lantern in Rafael's hand. But his other hand was outstretched, held low, the fingers spread.

Louis watched out of the corner of his eye. He could tell Landeta couldn't see where he was going, that he was trying to fake it. But the ground was too uneven, there were too many branches in the way. And he was moving too slowly.

Landeta inched his way toward the cabin. Tomas was watching him carefully, watching his outstretched hand. Suddenly, Louis saw Tomas's eyes narrow.

"Rafael," Tomas said, "turn off the lantern."

"Don't do it, Rafael," Frank said.

Louis saw a flicker of confusion cross Rafael's face and he started toward him.

"Turn it off! Now!" Tomas yelled.

The clearing went black. Louis saw a shadow rush toward Landeta and he swung his gun toward it but held his fire.

A shot cracked the silence.

Louis froze in a crouch, his gun sweeping the darkness. The shot—a .45. That's what he had heard. Not a rifle shot. Mel had fired his gun.

"Mel!"

Louis heard breaking branches, sounds of a struggle, and the crack of a fist against hard flesh. Then the scurry of footsteps in the brush.

"Mel!"

The footsteps were gone. It was quiet.

A low moan led him to Landeta. He was on his back, his hand on his face, blood seeping between his fingers.

Louis grabbed Landeta's shoulder. "Are you shot?"

Landeta shook his head. "No, I got a shot off and then the fucker jumped me. Shit, I think he broke my nose." He grabbed Louis's arm to pull himself up. "Where are they?"

"I don't know. Stay here."

Louis edged back to the clearing. He saw the lantern on the ground. Rafael was gone. He knelt to pick up the lantern and saw dark spots in the dirt. He touched the spots and his hand came up bloody. But whose blood was it—Angel's or Rafael's?

Still kneeling, gun drawn, he scanned the brush. He saw no one. He heard nothing. Not even from the cabin.

# CHAPTER 41

Louis pushed open the screen door of the cabin. Just one room and a dark form on a narrow bed. He lifted the lantern and light flooded the room.

Blood. A dark pool of it in a tangle of white sheets. Then he saw Angel, lying on the small bed, curled on her side, her face to the wall. She was wearing a thin white gown, but it was pulled up, exposing her from the waist down. Her buttocks and thighs were streaked with blood. Blood had soaked into the sheets beneath her.

Louis couldn't see her face, just her hair, a tangled, damp mess. Her bloody fingers clutched the sheet, bunching it between her body and the wall.

*Animals . . .* he should have just shot the fuckers where they stood.

A low moan.

Jesus, she was still alive. Barely, but alive and trembling. He touched her shoulder and she cringed, drawing away.

"Angel?"

He heard her draw in a quick breath at the sound of his voice.

"Angel Lopez?"

She turned her head toward him slowly. Her eyes lit up with fear and she tried to sit up, but she couldn't find the strength in her arms.

He set down the lantern and moved to help her, but she pulled back. "No, no, don't touch me. Leave me alone," she whimpered.

Louis put up his hand. "I'm not going to hurt you."

She was trying to cover herself with the bloody sheet. She was so pale, her dark hair plastered to her face with sweat. And she was looking at him with terror, as if he had come to kill her, not save her.

"I heard something," she said. "Rafael? Is he all right?"

Something was wrong here. She was lying in a pool of blood, but he couldn't see a mark on her. And why was she asking about Rafael?

"Rafael . . . Is my husband all right?"

Husband? His eyes went to her left hand. She was wearing a coral ring.

He heard a weird sound. It sounded muffled, weak, almost like a cat. His eyes moved to the bunched-up sheet between Angel and the wall. He reached down. She grabbed his wrist.

"No," she said, "please, please."

He eased his wrist from her hand and pulled back the sheet.

A small red body squirmed in the bloody folds. Tiny, white-knuckled hands trembled in the air.

*Jesus.* It was a baby.

Louis looked at Angel. She reached weakly for her baby and gathered it to her chest. The pool of blood under her was spreading.

"Angel," Louis said, "we've got to get out of here."

She shook her head violently, pulling the child closer. Louis reached for the baby, but she turned away from him.

"Angel, come on!"

She didn't move.

*Damn it.* He had to get her out of here now.

He bent and tried to pick them both up, but she twisted from him, whimpering.

"Look," Louis said, glancing at the door, "these people are crazy. They're going to kill you."

She was trying to get away from him, inching toward the wall. He understood. He understood that she was afraid of him, that she couldn't make any distinction between him and the others.

"Angel," Louis said softly, "Rosa sent me. She wants you to come home."

She looked up at him, her dark eyes moving across his face. "Rosa?" she whispered. "Rosa?"

He sensed a lessening in her tension. Maybe she was just on the verge of passing out. He didn't care. He picked her up, bringing her body tightly against his chest. He pulled her away from the bed, the sheets dragging behind. She wrapped her arms around her baby and let him carry her to the screen door. He kicked it open.

Landeta was standing by the porch, gun drawn. "Louis? Jesus, is that her?"

"Yeah. She's still alive." Louis hoisted Angel up to get a better grip. The baby let out a cry.

"What the fuck?" Landeta said. "What the hell is—"

"She had a baby," Louis said. "I've got them both."

"A baby! Jesus H Christ . . ."

Louis was frantically scanning the dark, but he still didn't see any of the del Bosque men—or Frank. They needed to get back to the boat. Fast. His sleeves were already soaked with blood. When he looked back at Landeta, he saw the police radio in his hand.

"Nothing, still nothing," Landeta said.

Louis shifted Angel in his arms. "All right, we're going back to the boat. Stay close behind me and keep your gun out. If I say shoot, shoot."

At the fork in the path, Louis felt Landeta grab his arm.

"They'll be looking for us if we go back this way," he said.

Louis looked down at Angel's face. She was having trouble keeping her eyes open.

"Angel, can you hear me?" Louis said.

Her eyes fluttered open and she clutched the baby tighter.

"Is there another way to the path that goes around the island?" Louis asked.

She didn't answer.

"Talk to me, Angel. Is there another path?"

She drew her hand from under the sheet and pointed left. He saw no path. Just trees and brush.

"I can't take you through there," he said.

Her hand waved toward the thicket.

"Go through the trees?" he asked.

She nodded weakly.

Louis shifted her weight, his arms starting to burn. "Mel, hold on to my belt and keep one hand above you so you feel the branches."

"Louis, we need to know what we're up against. Ask her."

"No! Let's get back to the boat first."

Louis ducked under a branch, and stepped into the thicket. He kept his head down, using his shoulders to push the brush. The branches tore at his face. He was drenched in sweat and blood and could barely hang on to Angel. But he moved on, Landeta's hand tugging at his belt.

Louis's foot hit flat ground. Another path.

"I hear water," Landeta said.

Louis braced himself against a tree, using his knee to boost Angel up into his arms. His lungs were burning. He could smell her blood on his sleeves, thick and heavy.

"We came up with the water on our left. We go back with it on the right," Landeta said.

"I agree."

They had to go more slowly now. Angel and the baby were so heavy Louis had to stop every twenty feet or so to hoist them back up into his arms.

"I see the white cloth," Louis said.

They made their way to the cloth they had left on the tree. Louis peered down into the mangroves, out to the water.

"Mel, I can't see the boat. They must have found it."

He carefully laid Angel on the ground. The baby was fussing in her arms.

"Watch them," Louis said.

Landeta nodded, knelt, and put one hand on Angel.

Louis skidded down the incline, catching himself on a mangrove limb. When he reached the mud, he stopped and ripped the flashlight from his back pocket.

The beam picked up something white. The boat was there. But there was no water.

He directed the flashlight out toward the bay. The beam caught the water, a good thirty feet out from shore.

*Motherfucker! The fucking tides!* Why hadn't they figured that into this whole stinking mess?

He felt his entire body tighten. He threw the flashlight down to the mud.

This whole thing was stupid. Stupid! They shouldn't have come here in the first place.

"Louis, what's wrong?" Landeta called.

Louis closed his eyes, drawing in heavy breaths. *Calm down. Calm the fuck down.*

"Louis?"

He picked up the flashlight and pulled himself back up the incline.

"The tide went out and the fucking boat is in the mud," Louis said. He saw Landeta was holding the baby, a torn piece of the bloodied sheet wrapped around it.

"I had to cut and tie off the cord," Landeta said quietly. "It was still attached."

Louis turned and looked down at Angel.

"She's dead," Landeta said.

Louis knelt and felt at her neck for a pulse. Nothing. His hand lingered on her neck. He hung his head.

"We're stuck here until high tide," Louis muttered.

"When is that?"

"How the fuck should I know?" Louis said angrily.

Landeta didn't respond. In the quiet, Louis could hear a squeaking sound and looked at the baby in Landeta's arms. A tiny foot was sticking out of the sheet.

"There's the ferry at the restaurant dock," Landeta said. "Or maybe that skiff is there."

Louis shook his head. "No, that's where they'll expect us to go." His eyes searched the darkness. "We have to go back to the compound. Maybe there's a phone there. They won't be expecting us to go there."

He looked down at Angel.

"You have to hide her," Landeta said.

Louis ran a hand over his sweaty face.

"Now," Landeta said.

Louis knelt and gathered her body into his arms. He stood and stepped over into the mangroves. He gently laid Angel down among the arching roots. He paused, then smoothed her white nightgown down over her bare legs. He placed the remaining portion of the sheet over her face.

He turned back to Landeta. "Let's go," he said quietly.

Louis knew they couldn't stay on the path, so he led Landeta straight up into the brush, keeping the water at their backs. If they kept going uphill, they had a good chance of reaching the compound. They had to move slowly, and the heat was unbearable. Landeta was doing his best to keep the baby covered with the sheet to protect it from the mosquitoes, but Louis could hear the baby's small cries.

A yellow light glowed in the darkness ahead. It was the house. They moved toward it and soon the shapes of the other cabins in the compound came into view.

Louis saw the beam of flashlights and waved Landeta down

into the bush. Two men emerged into the compound, one carrying a rifle. They stopped and began to talk. One of them was clearly angry, but the other was just listening. Louis couldn't see their faces or hear what they were saying.

"What's going on?" Landeta whispered.

"I don't know. Two men . . . Wait." Louis watched as one of the men shined the flashlight in the face of the other man. It was Frank. They argued again and finally Frank swatted the flashlight away and went up into the house. The other man shouldered his rifle and followed.

Louis pulled out the Glock. "I'll be right back."

"Where you going?"

Louis could hear the anxiety in Landeta's voice. "Up to the house. Something's going on in there and I want to find out what."

Louis crawled to the house, sliding up against the wood. The window was open, and he could hear voices. He took a quick peek inside, scanning the room. Five men, and the old woman.

He slipped down against the house and listened.

# CHAPTER 42

Ana del Bosque ran her hand over the smooth wood of the chair. The chair had belonged to her mother, her grandmother, and her great-grandmother before that. She had never known her great-grandmother; she had died many years before Ana was born. But Ana knew her name—Bianca Quinones Marquez del Bosque. The name was written in the family Bible alongside her great-grandfather, Marcelo Leon del Bosque. All the names of the del Bosque women were written there: Great-grandmother Bianca, her grandmother, Esperanza, and her mother, Lourdes.

Ana's thin fingers explored the indentations of the old chair's carving, all its small nicks and holes. She could barely remember her mother's face anymore, just her long black hair. She had died of fever when Ana was only nine. After that, her father had drifted into madness until he walked into the water one night and drowned. Ana was eleven when it happened. After that, there were just the four of them on the island—Ana, her grandmother, her older brother, Alfonso, and her younger brother, Mateo.

Abuela Esperanza . . . Ana could remember her. She could remember coming in from playing and sitting on the wood floor, looking up at her grandmother as she sat in the chair. Ana loved the big chair, with its shiny wood and swirling carvings. And she loved her *abuela,* loved hearing her tell her stories about a magical place called Asturias. A place of high mountains and cool forests, where silver fish jumped in the water and the wolves sang in the night.

*We come from a family that is very old, Analita, a family that descended from the great Roman soldiers, a family of the purest blood.*

And then her grandmother would talk to her in the old language. Not the Asturian Spanish that her mother and father had spoken, but the old Latin tongue of the Romans. Ana would try hard to learn the odd sounds and words. When she had finished with her lesson, Abuela Esperanza would let her sit in the chair. It was so big, big like a throne, and it made her feel like a princess.

Ana eased her seventy-seven-year-old body into the chair. She was still small, but the chair fit her now.

Abuela Esperanza had been gone for a long time now. And her brothers—they were both gone now, too, buried in the family graveyard with the others.

She looked around the room at her family. Her eldest son, Edmundo. Her grandsons Pedro and Carlos. And standing off to the side, her nephew, Orlando. She had devoted her life to keeping the del Bosque family alive, keeping the Isla des Huesos the way her ancestors had wanted it to be. But it struck her now, an idea that pierced her heart.

She had failed. The outside world was closing in, and she couldn't stop it.

*"Tempora mutantur, et nos in illis mutamur,"* she whispered.

Frank was standing at her side and looked down at her. "Mama? You said something?"

She shook her head and reached for his hand. She felt eyes and looked across the room to see Orlando staring at her. She looked across the room to her grandsons Pedro and

Carlos. Like Orlando, they stood stone-faced and rigid. All of them were staring at Francisco, as if he were a stranger, an invader. *Which is exactly what he is to them,* Ana thought. They had grown up hearing only the sketchiest stories about the uncle who had left. She had never told any of them why.

The only thing they knew was that Emilio was dead, and that a man with his face was now taking his place.

Ana's gaze went to her oldest son, Edmundo. He was sitting at the table, his eyes red from crying. He had been close to Francisco and Emilio when they were boys, playing the role of father, teaching them the ways of the island, about the tides and the winds, about the ospreys that nested in the highest dead trees and the manatees that cradled their calves in the salt shallows. It had broken his heart when Francisco left. And now Emilio was dead by his twin brother's hand.

Would they listen to her? Would they stand behind one of their own or treat him like the stranger he was?

A bang of the screen door made Ana look up. Tomas came in, his long dark hair matted to his forehead with sweat.

"There's no sign of them," he said. He slumped in a chair, propping his rifle next to it.

"Where's Rafael? I thought he was with you," Carlos said.

"I don't know," Tomas said. "I think he went back to get Angel."

Ana drew in a deep breath. "What about the strangers?"

Tomas looked around at the other men. "I lost them. But they can't get far."

Ana looked at her grand-nephew, Tomas. His eyes glittered with anger in the soft light. Tomas . . . as unpredictable as the hurricane winds that had torn across the island three weeks ago.

"Do we know who they are?" Ana asked.

"They came here to get Francisco," Tomas said, sitting up. "The newspapers said he killed Shelly. Why else would they be here?"

Ana looked up at Francisco. "Is that true? Are they police-men?"

All eyes turned to Frank.

"The black man is a private investigator," Frank said. "I don't know the other one. He may be a policeman."

"He's no cop," Tomas said quickly. "He can't be. He's blind."

"Then they pose no threat," Ana said.

Tomas stood quickly. "No threat? If you—"

"Tomas," Orlando interrupted. "Watch your tongue."

Tomas glared at his father, then sat back down. Orlando turned to Ana.

"You're wrong, Abuela Ana," he said. "They will bring others."

"They don't know anything," Frank said.

Tomas spun to face Frank. "They know about *you!* They know you are here, old man."

"Tomas!" Ana snapped.

Tomas raked a hand through his hair and looked away.

Frank stepped toward the center of the room. "This is no good. I'll give myself up. We'll leave quietly."

"What good will that do now?" Tomas said. "They know you came here. They won't leave until they know why!"

"I can keep them from—" Frank started.

"How?" Tomas shouted. "Do you really think they'll be-lieve you now and leave the rest of us alone? They saw Angel! They saw what was happening!"

"They saw a pregnant woman, that is all," Frank said.

"How do you know? How do you know for sure?"

Ana looked around the room. She could see it in their faces, see that they were listening to Tomas.

Tomas saw it, too, and he stood up. "We need to kill them."

"No," Frank said.

"We need to kill them and bury them here so they don't float to the mainland like Shelly did."

"No," Frank said.

"You have no say in this, old man," Tomas said.

"We can't kill them," Frank said.

Tomas laughed coldly. "Did you hear him?" he asked, his eyes scanning the faces. "He killed his brother but he won't kill strangers?"

"It was an accident," Ana said.

"Accident?" Tomas said. "He killed Emilio, then threw him in the water so they would find him!"

The room was quiet for moment. Then Carlos stepped forward, resting the butt of his rifle on the floor. "Tomas is right. They cannot be allowed to leave."

Ana looked at him; then her eyes moved to the man standing next to him.

"And you, Pedro?" she asked.

Pedro's chest rose with a deep breath. "The police might know they are here," he said slowly. "If they don't return, we could bring ourselves even more trouble."

Tomas shook his head, his voice tight. "I'm telling you, they are alone. If they had any authority or backup, they wouldn't be sneaking around and hiding in the bushes."

Ana's gaze moved to Tomas's father. "Orlando?"

Orlando lifted his head, his hard, dark eyes sliding to Tomas. He held them there for a moment, his lips drawn tight.

"This is my son's fault," he said, looking at the rest of them. "I apologize for what he has done to this family." He took a deep breath. "But Tomas is my son, and I will do what is necessary to protect him and the rest of us."

Ana felt Frank's hand slip from her own. She looked back at Edmundo. He was still sitting at the table, his back to them. He had not moved or said a word.

"Edmundo?" Ana asked.

Edmundo turned. He looked older than his sixty-two years, and his creased face was sunken with despair. His eyes were red as he looked first at Ana, then up at Frank.

"Francisco has been gone for many years," he said. "But

that doesn't make him less of a brother or a son to us. He has done nothing wrong."

He looked at Tomas. "You are the one who must go, Tomas. You should go to these men and take responsibility for what you did. Then maybe they will leave the rest of us alone."

"You're crazy!" Tomas said, hefting his rifle to both hands. "I'm not going anywhere."

Ana started to rise, but a noise drew all their eyes to the door. Rafael came in, gasping for breath. He was dirty, his shirt soaked with sweat, his right shoulder bloody.

"She's gone," he panted. "Angel's gone!"

"What about the baby?" Tomas asked.

"I don't know . . . the baby's gone, too. They've taken them."

Tomas looked back at Edmundo. "That's it. They won't leave us alone now. Angel will tell them everything."

"He's right," Carlos said.

Pedro nodded. "We need to find them now before they get back to the dock."

Ana's eyes went to Orlando, but it was clear that he would side with his son. Edmundo was just sitting there, shaking his head.

Ana stood slowly, pushing herself out of the chair with her thin arms. "God forgive me," she whispered.

"No, Mama, no," Frank said.

She looked back at the men. "All right. Go, and be quick with it."

The five younger men hurried out. Edmundo didn't move from the table. Ana sank back down in the chair and Frank knelt in front of her, taking her hands.

"This is wrong," he said.

"There's no other way," she said.

Frank looked toward Edmundo. His brother looked back at him with welling eyes. "You've been gone too long, Francisco," he said. "If you want to stay now, you must do what is necessary, not what is right."

Frank rose slowly. He looked around the room and then

walked to an old wooden cabinet near the fireplace. He opened the doors, stared at the rifles, then took one down. From a drawer, he pulled out a handful of bullets. He cracked open the rifle and loaded it. He snapped it shut and with a final look at Edmundo, he left the room.

# CHAPTER 43

Louis stayed crouched beneath the window and watched as five of the del Bosque men came out the front door. They stood in a knot, talking for a moment, then dispersed. A moment later, Frank emerged from the house.

*Christ . . .* He was carrying a rifle.

Frank paused for a moment, looking around the compound, then disappeared down a path. Louis crept back to the place where he had left Landeta. He heard the small cries of the baby before he saw Landeta.

"Can't you keep it quiet?" he hissed.

"What the fuck you want me to do?" Landeta snapped back.

Louis inhaled deeply. "They aren't going to let us leave here alive. They're going to hunt us down and kill us."

He could hear Landeta breathing hard. Shit, he could hear his own heart hammering. The baby let out a cry.

"Louis—"

"Yeah, yeah. I'm thinking." Louis looked back at the compound. No one else had come out of the house.

"All right," Louis said. "I think the old guy is staying in there with the old lady. Everyone else is out looking for us, including Frank. I say we find a place here to hide. Stay here, and keep that baby quiet."

Louis crept toward the back of the nearest cabin. Its screened windows were dark. There was no sound coming from inside. He pulled the pocket knife from his jeans, sliced the screen, and slipped inside.

He stood for a second, trying to get a sense of his surroundings in the dark. The room was small, furnished with a bed, a dresser, and something that looked like a desk in the corner. The room smelled of old cigar smoke and gunpowder. He moved to the short hall, pushing open a door with his hand. He peered into the dark and saw the outline of a smaller bed and dresser. He moved on.

On his right was a living area with just enough room for a sofa, a wooden chair, and a coral fireplace. A lantern was on the table, but there was no phone or television, no sign that there was even electricity.

He heard a faint humming sound and turned. A dark, narrow kitchen with a wood table, a sink, and . . . an ancient refrigerator.

*Milk for the baby? Something, anything to keep it quiet?*

He retraced his steps and slid back outside. As he neared the brush, he could hear a muffled cry. When he reached Landeta, he saw Landeta's hand over the baby's mouth.

"Jesus, don't smother it," Louis whispered.

"I had to do something," Landeta said. "You think you can do better, then you take it, damn it."

"Never mind. Follow me," Louis said.

Louis took them back to the cabin, taking the baby while Landeta crawled in through the sliced screen. Once they were all inside, Louis left Landeta and the baby in the larger bedroom and went to the kitchen.

He hesitated in front of the refrigerator. Damn, there was no way around it. He opened it a crack and light split the darkness. He spotted the button and held it down. In the dark again, he scanned the shelves.

A milk carton. He grabbed it, shut the refrigerator, and went back to the bedroom.

"Here," he said, thrusting it at Landeta.

Landeta took the carton. "What do you want me to do with this?"

"Give it to the baby."

"With *what,* goddamn it?"

"Can't you figure out some kind of nipple or something?"

"The only nipples I got won't work."

The baby's cries grew louder. Louis walked a tight quick circle, then went back to the kitchen. No way was he going to chance opening the refrigerator again. He quickly searched the cabinets, but saw nothing they could use.

He suddenly realized the baby was quiet. He hurried back to the bedroom. He let out a breath when he saw the baby squirming in Landeta's arms. Landeta had the milk carton wedged between his knees, its top ripped open. Louis watched as Landeta dipped his finger into the carton and then gently put it up to the baby's mouth. The baby was sucking eagerly.

Landeta looked up. "Don't say it," he said quietly. "Don't even think it."

Louis's anger broke into a low laugh.

Landeta adjusted the baby in his arm. "I heard that," he said. "I heard you laugh. So I guess this means you're not pissed at me anymore?"

Louis was quiet. He *had* been pissed. At Landeta's need to come here, to somehow prove he was still the cop he used to be? At his clumsiness, his neediness, shit . . . his blindness?

No. He was mad at himself. For getting sucked into this in the first place. For not thinking this through. For not knowing about the tides, babies, and . . .

He turned and walked out of the room. He went to the kitchen, turned on the faucet, and splashed his face. It stung the cuts and bites, but helped him clear his head. He saw a towel, grabbed it, and soaked it with water.

He went back to the bedroom and held the wet towel out to Landeta. "I'm not pissed at you," he said. "I'm pissed at myself."

"You made a decision when you got in that boat tonight," Landeta said. "Just like Rafael did when he turned out that lantern."

"You know you winged him," Louis said.

Landeta took the towel and wiped his face. "But he's alive?"

"Yeah, I just saw him. He was with the others."

"How many men do you think there are?"

"There are seven cabins. I'm guessing only the seven men I saw."

"Any ideas?" Landeta asked.

"I don't know. There is no phone in here and I'm not taking any chances on getting caught inside that house."

Landeta threw up a hand, silencing him. He pointed to the doorway. Louis drew his gun and slid up behind the door.

The floorboards creaked. A small figure stopped in the doorway.

Louis lowered the gun to his side. "How long have you been there, Roberto?"

The boy looked back at Louis. "I was asleep," he said softly. He was looking at Louis's gun.

"I remember you," Roberto said. "You came here for lunch yesterday."

Roberto looked at Landeta and the baby. He went slowly over to them and peered down. "Is that a baby?" he asked.

"Yes," Louis said.

The boy was quiet, staring at the baby.

"Louis," Landeta said softly.

"What?"

"I'm sorry. For getting us into this mess."

"Forget it. Just think of a way to get us out of it."

"Our chances of getting anywhere on our own are slim, you know."

"Yeah, I know." Louis dropped down onto the bed, closing his eyes.

Landeta pulled the blanket off the bed and wrapped the baby in it. He was looking at Roberto, who was still staring down at the baby.

"Louis?" When Louis looked up, Landeta nodded toward the boy. "Hostage?" he asked quietly.

Louis ran a sleeve over his sweaty face and let out a tired breath.

"We don't have much choice," Landeta said. "We give him up as soon as we get a boat. And no one gets hurt."

Louis stared at the boy. It was dangerous and illegal. But hell, they had crossed that line hours ago. And Landeta was right: they were out of options.

"All right," Louis said quietly. "Now we just have to get to the restaurant."

"I know how to get there," Roberto said. "There's a path from here to there. But I know a secret way."

Louis glanced at Landeta, then turned to face Roberto. "A secret way?"

"Yeah, I take the secret way when I'm late and don't want my father to see me sneaking in."

"Your father doesn't know your secret way?" Louis asked.

Roberto shook his head, still staring at the baby. "No one knows it but me."

"Roberto, can you show us your secret way?"

He looked up at Louis. "I don't know. If I take you that way you can't tell, okay?"

"Scout's honor," Louis said, crossing his chest.

"Scout's what?" Roberto said.

"Nothing." Louis glanced at Landeta. "Roberto," he said, "do you know how to play hide-and-seek?"

The boy shook his head.

Louis placed his hands on the boy's shoulders. "It's a game and I'm going to teach you."

# CHAPTER 44

The game, Louis told Roberto, was to get to the restaurant without anyone seeing them. They exited through the slit screen in the back of the cabin, and Roberto led them directly into the brush. Louis followed the boy, with Landeta close behind carrying the baby. The moon was gone now and Louis was tempted to use his flashlight, but Roberto was weaving among the low-hanging trees and downed branches like a squirrel, so Louis trusted him to lead the way.

Roberto stopped suddenly.

"What's the matter?" Louis whispered.

"We have to go around," Roberto said.

Louis moved ahead and saw they had come out on the edge of the cemetery. "Let's just go across this way and—"

The boy shook his head vigorously. "I'm not allowed."

"Roberto, we have to—"

"They told me I can't. I can go in the other one, but not this one."

"There's another cemetery?" Louis asked. "Where?"

"Oh, way over on the other side of the island," the boy said, waving a hand. "It's a long ways from here. It's where my mother is buried."

Louis pointed to the coral markers. "Then who is buried here, Roberto?"

He shrugged. "I don't know. I just know I can't go in."

Louis looked back at Landeta, who just shook his head.

"All right, you go around," he told Roberto. "We will meet you over there where the path picks up, okay?"

The boy looked troubled. But finally he nodded and scampered into the brush. Louis and Landeta crossed the graveyard. Roberto was waiting for them on the other side.

He led them back into the brush again. Louis could hear water now, a steady soft gurgle below, on their right. This new path seemed to parallel the one they had come in on, but it was so narrow and overgrown that Louis could barely stand upright.

But Roberto seemed to know every twist and turn. He was getting into the game now, hiding behind trees, waiting for them to come up, jumping out silently but with a big smile. It was clear the boy was at home in the woods, unafraid of anything. He felt as safe under the night sky of stars as a boy in a bunk bed under a glow-in-the-dark cosmos on his ceiling.

Louis glanced back. Landeta was falling behind. Louis grabbed Roberto and gestured for him to stop. They waited until Landeta caught up. He was breathing heavily, the baby clutched to his chest. The blanket had come undone and the baby's legs were dangling free.

"Mel, let me take it," Louis said.

"No, no . . . I'm okay, I'm okay." Landeta wiped a hand over his face. "I just gotta rest for a minute."

Before Louis could say anything, Landeta eased himself down to the dirt.

Louis turned to Roberto, who was staring at Landeta and the baby. "Roberto, how far is the restaurant?" he asked.

"Oh, it's a long ways yet."

Louis looked around at the brush, then turned back to

Roberto. "Okay, it's time to hide now," Louis said. "Do you know where we could go?"

"Sure, I know a good place. Nobody ever goes there but me."

Louis looked back at Landeta, but he was just sitting there, his eyes closed. The baby was starting to fuss again. Louis knew he had no choice. He had to trust the boy.

Roberto saw Louis hesitating and tugged at his shirt. "It's real close. Come on, I'll show you. The only thing that's there is some old bones."

# CHAPTER 45

The baby felt strange in his arms. When Landeta had handed the bundle to him, Louis was surprised at how light it was. He thought of Jay Strickland in that moment, and what the young cop had said about babies. *You're life and death to them, man. You're everything.*

"The mosquitoes," Landeta whispered. "Keep its face covered."

Louis wrapped the blanket over the baby and clutched it to his chest with his left hand. Using his right hand, he pushed his way through the brush, keeping his eyes on Roberto as the boy led them in a new direction back inland.

Louis was gasping by the time they broke free into a new clearing. Landeta followed a few moments later, and they both just stood there, pulling in deep breaths while Roberto watched them. Finally, Louis looked around.

The moon was out again and he could see that they were back at the Indian shell mound. But they had emerged out on the inland side of the mound. Louis could see now that there were many mounds, others that had been hidden by the trees and not visible from the first path below.

"This way," Roberto whispered, waving to them to follow.

They walked slowly through the mounds. There were maybe a dozen of them, some just a few feet high, others towering to six feet or more, ten feet across. All were bare, no trees or grass on top, just millions and millions of shells. In the moonlight, the shell mounds had a soft glow, like old ivory.

Roberto led them to the highest mound, nestled back in the trees. Louis waited while Roberto pulled away some brush to reveal an opening. Roberto went in and Louis followed. The mound was unlike the others, U-shaped, like a cave without a top.

"This is my secret place," Roberto said as Landeta followed them in.

"Roberto, do you know what this is?" Louis asked.

"Papa says Indians are buried in here. He says they should be left alone." He hesitated. "You won't tell, will you?"

"No," Louis said quietly.

Landeta sank down to the dirt, head in his hands. Louis could tell he was exhausted. Shit, so was he. Tired, thirsty, hot, bitten up, cut up, filthy, and afraid. Afraid they weren't going to get off this damn island alive.

The baby was quiet. But it was suddenly heavy in his arms. He couldn't stand it any longer. He had to sit. Even if it was just for a few minutes. Just sit, think, and try to find a way out of this. He carefully eased down to the dirt, leaning his head back against the wall of shells, the baby against his chest. There were shards of pottery littering the dirt floor—and bones. Louis saw a jawbone and what looked like a leg bone. He looked up to see Roberto, sitting cross-legged in the dirt, watching him.

"Louis," Landeta whispered, "we have to get a plan. We have to figure out what we'll be up against at the restaurant. Ask the boy."

Louis nodded. "Roberto," he whispered, "how many men live here?"

The boy was quiet for a moment. "Eight. No, wait. That was before Uncle Emilio drowned. So there's seven. But it's eight if you count me."

So he had been right. Seven cottages, seven men. Louis had a sudden thought. "Roberto, your uncle Frank, does he look like your uncle Emilio?"

"They were twins. Twins look exactly the same."

"So that's poor old Uncle Emilio lying in the Fort Myers morgue, wearing his brother's toe tag," Landeta said. "Romulus and Remus. Christ, why don't you ask him about wolves while you're at it?"

"Wolves are beautiful," Roberto said softly. "I saw a picture of one once. Abuela Ana told me a story about two little boys who were left in a river and saved by a mother wolf."

They all fell silent. Louis closed his eyes. But his ears were alert, trying to pick out any odd sound. But he couldn't do it. He wasn't like the boy, who knew every note of his island's night music. He wasn't like Landeta, who had learned to trust more than his eyes. He could only see what was there.

What had he seen exactly? A graveyard without names, a strange table, Angel being marched at gunpoint, an old woman arguing with a young man, and seven men desperately trying to protect something.

But what he *hadn't* seen were other women. Or other children, for that matter.

Louis glanced over at Roberto. He was fiddling with something that looked like an arrowhead.

"Roberto," he whispered, "do you have any aunts?"

"Yes."

"How many?"

Roberto set down the arrowhead to use his fingers to count. "Well, there's Aunt Emma, Aunt Paula, Aunt Cindy, and Aunt Angel. That makes four."

Louis caught Landeta's eye. Then he leaned his head back against the shell wall. They were alive. Thank God for that.

But it still didn't make sense. Emma Fielding had been here for thirty-four years. And the others for twenty or more. So where the hell were they? And who was buried in those five graves back at the cemetery? He looked over at Landeta and knew he was thinking the same thing.

"Roberto, what about Aunt Shelly?" Landeta asked.

"Who?"

"A woman named Shelly," Louis said patiently. "You never heard anyone called that here?"

"No," the boy said. "There was a strange lady living in Uncle Tomas's house for a while. But I don't know her name."

"What did the strange lady look like?" Louis said.

"I only saw her two times. The first time was when Uncle Tomas brought her here. I remember she had really long hair. I thought she was really pretty."

Roberto didn't look up, but his face creased into a small frown. "The next time I saw her all her hair was cut off."

Louis glanced at Landeta. "Do you know where she went?" he asked Roberto.

The boy shook his head. "She never came out of Uncle Tomas's house. And then one day she was gone."

"How do you know she was gone?"

Roberto gave a small shrug. "I didn't hear her anymore. She used to scream a lot at night."

Louis heard Landeta let out a tired breath. When Louis looked back at Roberto, the boy was smiling, holding up a small pointed object.

"This is a shark tooth," he said. "I have a whole bunch of them in here. Want one? Papa says they're good luck charms."

Louis started to shake his head, but the boy was obviously proud of his possessions. Louis took the tooth.

"Thanks," he said.

Roberto smiled.

"Roberto, you said this is your secret place," Louis said. "Do you ever bring any friends here?"

"Friends? What's that?"

"Well, maybe like a brother or sister?"

Roberto shook his head slowly.

"Who do you play with then?" Louis asked.

"The Indians. I mean, they aren't real. I just pretend they are."

Louis wiped his sweaty face. He watched Roberto playing with his small cache of artifacts.

"Well, what now, Rocky?" Landeta said softly.

"I don't know."

Landeta was quiet. "Do you realize what a mess this is?" he said finally.

"Mel, for God's sake," Louis said, putting up a hand. "Yes, I have thought about it."

"No, I don't think you have," Landeta whispered. He scooted closer to Louis. "When we moved Angel, we probably caused her to bleed to death. I shot and wounded an unarmed man. And now we could be charged with kidnapping. Not to mention trespassing."

Louis looked at Roberto, but the boy was busy.

"Cult or no cult, the women are alive," Landeta went on. "They probably came here willingly."

"Shelly didn't," Louis said. "That's what they were talking about in the house. Tomas killed—"

He stopped himself, looking at Roberto, but the boy didn't seem to hear him.

"All right, all right," Landeta said. "If we get out of here alive, the cops can come back and question Tomas. But we don't have any proof that anything else is going on here."

"What about those graves back there?" Louis said, trying to keep his voice low. "What the hell is that all about?"

"I don't know," Landeta said. He leaned his head back against the shell wall. "I don't know."

Louis shifted the baby in his arm, trying to cover it with the blanket. It was awake and quiet, just lying there looking up at him with dark eyes.

"They're hiding something, Mel," Louis whispered. "Something besides Shelly's murder. I know it."

"Forget it," Landeta said. "At least for now."

"I'm not leaving this baby here," Louis whispered. "Or him."

"Louis, the boy is obviously in no danger," Landeta said. "There's no reason to believe the baby is either. Kidnapping carries twenty to life in this state."

Louis knew Landeta was right. They had no real proof of anything, not even that Shelly Umber had been murdered here. Their only option was to try to get off the island, go to Horton, and pray that the chief trusted them enough to listen this time. And they couldn't take the baby or the boy with them.

"All right," he said quietly. He handed the baby back to Landeta and touched Roberto's arm.

"Roberto, can you take us to the restaurant now?"

The boy smiled and nodded, getting to his feet. Louis rose and helped Landeta get up. He realized he was still holding the shark tooth Roberto had given him. He started to toss it down, but then put it in his pocket.

"Let's go," he said.

# CHAPTER 46

"If we get to the restaurant before my uncles, do we win?"

Louis glanced down at Roberto. "Yes," he whispered, his eyes scanning the brush as they walked.

The ground was sloping downward. Louis could feel it as they made their way through the brush. And there was a light ahead, he could see it now, through the trees. But it wasn't a spot of light like the lanterns. This looked more dispersed, like a floodlight.

Louis slowed. Shit, that's exactly what it was. He could see the fence about twenty yards ahead now. The restaurant was behind it and someone had turned on a floodlight in the front.

"What the hell is that light?" Landeta whispered behind him.

"Floodlight. We're at the fence," Louis whispered back. He put a hand on Roberto's shoulder, stopping him. "Roberto, is there a gate?"

"Yes, over there."

Louis looked in the direction the boy was pointing, but he

didn't see anything that looked like a gate. Louis searched the dark brush but didn't see anyone. They had to take the chance.

"Okay, take us to the gate, Roberto."

Roberto led them up to the fence. Louis could see the gate now, but there was no latch, just hinges and a large, rusted keyhole. Louis pushed against it, but the gate didn't give. He looked up at the six-foot fence. No way could he get everyone over it.

"There's a latch on the other side," Roberto said. "If you boost me over, I can open it."

Louis looked down at him. "Make sure you're quiet," he said.

He picked him up and gave him a gentle swing. Roberto caught his leg on the top and grabbed on. Louis let him go and he disappeared over the fence. They heard the soft rattle of metal and the gate swung open. Louis sent Landeta through first, closing the gate quietly.

Louis led them up to the back of the restaurant. It was dark, but Louis could see now that the entire front yard of the restaurant was lit up with floodlights. He could hear water against the dock. And something else, a soft rhythmic thumping. It was someone pacing on the porch.

Louis spotted some crab traps stacked at the corner of the restaurant, and he motioned Landeta and Roberto toward them. They crouched behind the traps.

"Stay here," Louis whispered.

He moved around the side of the restaurant, keeping in the bushes, his gun drawn. In the glare of the floodlights, Louis could see a man on the restaurant porch holding a rifle.

It was Carlos, the same man who had spoken to him near the restaurant garbage bin just yesterday. It hit Louis in that instant: *shit*. Carlos was Roberto's father.

Louis watched him pace. He saw no one else and the inside of the restaurant was dark. Carlos was alone. But there was no way Louis could get the drop on him. Unless he could lure him off the porch somehow.

Louis looked out toward the water. He could see down the slope to the dock. It was only about twenty yards away. The dock stretched far out into the water, and Louis could clearly see that the ferry was afloat. And there was a second boat, a small skiff with an outboard.

Louis looked back at the porch.

Carlos was gone.

Something hard smashed into the back of his head. His body slammed forward to the ground.

A knee dropped hard into his shoulder blades and he was pinned to the ground, arms out, the Glock still clutched in his hand. He couldn't get a breath, couldn't move.

Carlos reached down and wrenched the Glock from his hand.

"Where's Angel?" Carlos demanded.

Louis didn't answer. He could feel the hard press of steel on his cheek.

"Where is she?"

The steel jammed into his face. "She's dead," Louis said.

Carlos eased the barrel and was quiet for a moment.

"The blind man. Where is he?"

Louis was silent.

Carlos swung the rifle, catching Louis's mouth.

"Answer me! Where is the blind man?"

"Right here," Landeta said.

Louis felt Carlos freeze. Then he moved off his back. Louis struggled to his knees and spat out blood. He looked up at Landeta.

*Jesus . . .*

He was holding Roberto against his waist, his .45 pointed at the boy's head.

"Drop the rifle," Landeta said.

Carlos was standing about ten feet away, staring at Landeta, his rifle gripped in his hand, Louis's Glock stuck in his waistband. He took two steps back.

"Drop the fucking rifle, del Bosque, or you'll see this kid's brains in the dirt," Landeta said.

Roberto was shaking. He closed his eyes, but the tears leaked out, streaking his dirty face.

"Papa," he whimpered.

*Oh, God . . . easy, Mel . . . easy.*

Carlos's eyes jumped from Landeta to his son's face. Then he threw the rifle into the sand. Carlos slowly raised his hands. Louis let out the breath he had been holding and got to his feet. He jerked the Glock from Carlos's waistband and stepped back, aiming it at him.

"Let him go," Carlos said.

Landeta waited until Louis had picked up the rifle, then gave Roberto a gentle shove. Roberto ran to his father, throwing his arms around his hips.

"Mel, where's the baby?" Louis asked.

Carlos took a step forward. "Baby?"

Landeta leveled the .45 at Carlos. "Don't move!"

"Mel, where's—"

"Back by the traps. Go, I can hold him."

Louis handed Landeta Carlos's rifle and ran back around the restaurant and behind the traps. He saw the bundle lying on the ground. He slipped his Glock in his waistband and scooped up the baby. He went back to the yard. Landeta still had his .45 pointed at Carlos, who was clutching Roberto to him. Carlos was watching Louis as he came into the light with the baby.

"You can't take the baby," Carlos said.

"Shut up," Louis hissed. "I'll do any fucking thing I want."

Louis looked down at the baby, moving the blanket off its face. In the glare of the floodlights, he could see the baby now, see it clearly for the first time. Dark hair and eyes . . . round black watery pools against shell-pink skin. And hands, tiny little things curled into fists.

"Give me the baby and you can go," Carlos said. "I won't stop you."

"Louis," Landeta said firmly, "give her to him."

"Her?" Carlos said. "Is it a girl?"

"Louis, give him the damn baby!"

Louis pulled out his Glock and held out the baby. Carlos stepped away from Roberto and gathered the baby into his arms.

"All right, let's get out of here," Landeta said.

They started down the slope. Landeta led the way carefully down the dock to the skiff while Louis backed his way down, the Glock still trained on Carlos. But Carlos hadn't moved. The baby was pressed against his chest, the blanket dangling. The baby began to cry.

Louis heard Landeta getting into the skiff. He could hear the baby, too, its cry carrying out to him, like a small, wounded animal.

*Small coral grave markers . . .*

"Louis, get in!" Landeta called.

*A pregnant woman marched at gunpoint to an isolated cabin. A tiny, freshly dug grave. No children on the island.*

*Roberto: Is that a baby?*

*Carlos: Is it a girl?*

*The sign in Latin at the graveyard: Agni Dei. French . . . Latin was like French. He knew French, what the hell would it be in French? Dei . . . God? Agni . . . agneau? Lambs of God?*

"Louis!" Landeta said. "Get in the boat!"

*Jesus, is that why Frank left the island thirty-five years ago, to save his newborn baby?*

"Mel," Louis said, "they're killing the babies."

He started back up the dock, his gun drawn.

# CHAPTER 47

A gunshot splintered the wood on a piling and Louis dropped to the dock. He looked back at Landeta, who had started to get out of the skiff.

"Mel! Go back! Get down!" he yelled.

Louis scanned the yard, squinting against the glare of the floodlights. He could see Carlos and Roberto standing near the porch. Carlos was still holding the baby and did not have a gun. Then Louis saw another man emerge from the trees to right of the restaurant, holding a rifle.

*Christ.* It was Frank. Frank shot at him?

Another shot zinged through the air. Louis buried his head in his arms.

"Tomas!" Frank called.

Louis looked up. Frank was standing there, but his rifle was aimed into the trees across the yard, not at the dock.

"Tomas!" Frank called again. "Come out where I can see you."

Louis saw a figure step out of the brush, across the yard from Frank. He was in the shadows, backdropped by the trees. Louis couldn't see Tomas's face; he was just a silhouette, but Louis could see his rifle, still aimed toward the dock. The rifle had a scope, and Louis knew Tomas could see him clearly in the floodlights.

Another figure came out of the trees, carrying his rifle low, stopping by Tomas. Louis couldn't see who it was.

"Tomas, come into the light," Frank said.

"And let the bastard on the dock shoot me? I'm not stupid, Francisco!"

Louis was flat on his belly. He slowly slid his Glock forward. Tomas was shadowed, too far away to give Louis a good shot. And the handgun was no match for the scoped rifle. Louis knew if he took a shot and missed, Tomas would kill him instantly. He could've done it in any of the first two shots; now he was just toying with them.

Louis heard the lever action of the Savage rifle and another of Tomas's shots popped the water under the dock, making Louis press his face to the wood deck.

"I'm not going to let you kill them, Tomas," Frank yelled out.

Louis snuck a look. Frank had his rifle aimed at Tomas across the yard. And the second man who had come out with Tomas had moved into the light. It was Rafael, and he was moving slowly toward Carlos and Roberto.

"Get away, old man!" Tomas said. Louis could hear Tomas feeding more bullets into the rifle.

"I told you this has to stop," Frank said.

"I'm not going to jail!" Tomas yelled. Another shot splintered the planks near Louis's head.

Frank took a step toward Tomas. "Tomas! Stop! Now."

"What? You gonna shoot me, old man?"

"If I have to."

Tomas laughed. "You no longer have it in you."

A small cry drifted from the restaurant. Louis could see Rafael taking the baby from Carlos.

"What is it, Rafael? Is it a son?" Tomas called.

Rafael was staring down into the blanket. "No," he said. "Oh, God, no. It's a girl, it's another girl."

*Another girl?*

"Then you know what needs to be done," Tomas said. "Go back to the house. Now!"

Louis watched Rafael. He was shaking his head, clutching the baby to his chest. Louis's eyes locked on Roberto. If they were killing the babies, why was the boy still alive? Dear God, did they kill only the girls?

"Tomas, maybe we should listen to Francisco," Rafael said.

There was a long silence. Louis heard Tomas moving through the leaves toward Rafael. A few more feet and he'd be in the light. *A few more feet.*

"Carlos, take the baby from Rafael," Tomas said.

"No!" Rafael shouted, backing up. "We keep this one!"

"Give her back to Carlos or I'll shoot both of you now!"

Louis rose to his knees, aiming into the darkness toward Tomas's voice. Rafael and the baby were backed against the porch. Carlos hadn't moved. He had Roberto clutched to him.

"Carlos! Do what I said!" Tomas yelled.

"No, Tomas," Carlos said, pulling Roberto closer.

Tomas fired and Carlos reeled backward, stumbling into the brush near the porch. Roberto dropped to his knees, covering his head. Rafael spun away, shielding the baby.

Frank fired, his bullet zinging into the brush. Tomas returned fire, his bullet tearing into Frank's shoulder. Frank crumbled to the dirt.

Louis swept the trees with his gun.

Where was he? Where the hell was Tomas?

Louis heard the baby crying, then saw Rafael turning away from Tomas, shielding the baby. Rafael's voice, tight and hoarse, sliced through the air.

"Tomas! No! No!"

*Jesus . . .* Tomas was going to shoot Rafael and the baby.

Louis aimed blindly toward the darkness. He couldn't see Tomas. He couldn't see anything. Then he heard the snap of Tomas's lever-action Savage.

Louis fired at the sound, pumping bullets into the darkness. Seventeen explosions, burnt air, the jerk of the gun in his hand.

Then silence. The magazine was empty.

It was a few seconds before he could hear, and then his other senses came back. There was no sound or movement from the dark brush.

"Stop! Stop shooting! He's dead!" Rafael called out. "Tomas is dead!"

Louis could hear crying. The baby's weak rasp and an intense sobbing that he knew came from Roberto.

"Louis?"

Landeta's voice behind him, anxious.

"Stay there, Mel. Don't move!"

Slowly, Louis stood up, pulling a new magazine from his belt and snapping it into the Glock. He moved cautiously up the dock, swinging his gun from Frank, to Rafael, then to the darkness where he knew Tomas had stood.

As he moved closer, he could see Rafael clearly, standing over Carlos and Roberto. He had the crying baby cradled against his shoulder.

Louis moved toward the patch of darkness where Tomas had been. He saw him, on his back, in the dirt. Louis knelt to feel for a pulse. Nothing. He scanned Tomas's body. Then he saw it, one entry wound just below the right ear. Nothing else, not another mark on him.

He heard footsteps behind him and spun.

"Easy," Landeta said.

Landeta came up to Louis's side and looked down at Tomas. "Where'd you get him?"

"In the neck, one shot."

Louis looked around. Frank was across the yard, alive but struggling to sit up. Rafael was still standing by the porch, holding the baby. Roberto was huddled on the ground by his father's body. Louis could hear him crying.

"Mel, go check on the boy," Louis said.

Louis went to Frank and knelt beside him. Frank was holding his bleeding shoulder, his dark eyes glistening in the lights.

"Go," Frank said softly. "And take the baby."

"I have to bring the police back, Frank."

"I know that. Just go. Now, before the others come."

Louis stood up and went over to Rafael, his gun at his side. Rafael took a step back when he saw him coming. Louis stopped in front of him. Rafael was shaking, his bandaged arm wrapped tightly around the small bundle.

"Where is Angel?" Rafael asked.

"She's dead," Louis said. "She was bleeding and she needed help no one here could give her."

Rafael's face crumbled. "I knew something was wrong," he said softly. "She was bleeding so much, but I couldn't do anything."

Rafael was shaking so hard, Louis was afraid he was going to drop the baby. He looked up at Louis, his hand cupping the baby's head. "Where is she? Where is my wife?"

"On the east side of the island. There's a cloth tied to a tree near her body."

Rafael nodded.

Louis held out his arms.

Rafael's eyes welled. He opened the blanket and looked at the baby, touching a dirty hand to her tiny foot. Then, slowly, he wrapped the blanket back around the baby and held her out to Louis.

Louis gathered the baby into one arm, and turned to Landeta.

"Let's get the hell out of here," he said.

# CHAPTER 48

Louis stood at the bow of the Fort Myers PD patrol boat, the wind in his face. It was still dark and there was a light fog over the sound, but he could see a thin gray glow of dawn in the eastern sky.

He watched the swirl of fog and the black waves roll away in the beam of the boat's spotlight. Maybe they should not have left the island. He had left hoping that Frank could take care of things, that he would not allow any more killing. But he worried Frank did not have the control he thought he had. He wondered if the other men would kill the women, or maybe even destroy the graves of the babies.

The flashing red and blue lights of the other police boats were making his head hurt. He closed his eyes. Exhaustion was seeping in, eating away at the adrenaline that had kept him going for the last couple of hours. His muscles were growing stiff, his skin was starting to burn from the scrapes and bites.

He felt the boat slowing and forced his eyes open. The fog had softened the mangroves into a smudge of dark green. The floodlights were still on, and the fog defused the light, turning the yard into a soft white-gray blur.

The boat turned into the dock and the restaurant emerged from the mist. There were several figures standing in front of it—the del Bosque men waiting in a line, the bodies of Carlos and Tomas laid at their feet. Louis spotted a third body, wrapped in a sheet. He knew it was Angela.

Louis counted five men and a smaller figure he knew was Roberto. There were no rifles raised. They looked defeated, like prisoners ready to be marched away.

Horton came up behind Louis. "They don't look like they're ready to defend anything," he said. "That all of them?"

"Yes," Louis said.

"Well, I ain't taking any chances."

Louis heard Horton giving commands to his men, telling them how he wanted the arrests handled. As the boat throttled down to dock, Louis picked Frank out of the group. His shoulder was wrapped and he was standing slightly in front of the other men.

The boat was secured and Horton's men went up the dock, guns drawn. But none of the del Bosque men moved. Frank put up his hands slowly and then the others did the same. Horton was watching carefully as the officers began handcuffing the men.

Louis followed Horton up to the yard. "I don't want any surprises. You're sure this is all of the men?" Horton asked him.

"Yes."

"Where are the women?" Horton asked.

"I'm guessing they're at the compound in the main house with the old lady," Louis said.

Horton nodded. "I'll send some men inland."

"Al, let me take them in."

"Why?"

"It's hard to find your way around. The fog will make it even harder."

"All right, but I'm going with you."

Louis looked back at the patrol boat. He could just make

out Landeta. He was just sitting there, staring into the darkness.

Horton followed Louis's gaze. "He's not getting off that boat," he said quietly. "He's lucky I let him come back with us. What the hell were you thinking, Kincaid, taking a blind man out here with you?"

"He made the decision, Al."

"It was a damn stupid one," Horton said. "Let's go."

Horton led the way off the boat. The del Bosque men were now seated in the dirt, their hands cuffed behind them.

Louis's gaze fell on Roberto. A uniformed officer had a hand on his shoulder, trying to talk to him, but Roberto's dark eyes were locked on Louis. They glistened with a wild anger.

Louis looked away, meeting Frank's gaze. Frank's eyes were steady and calm.

"Is your mother at the house?" Louis asked him.

Frank nodded. "She's very old," he quietly. "She doesn't understand what is happening."

"We have no choice, Frank," Louis said. "We have to arrest her."

"Let me go with you," Frank said.

"Frank—"

"Just let me talk to her," Frank said. "Please."

Louis hesitated, then went over to Horton. "Frank wants to see his mother before we take her," he told him.

"Fat chance," Horton said.

"Al, I think it might be a good idea to take him with us," Louis said. "It might make things easier."

"You told me they're murdering babies and now you want to make it *easier* for the crazy old bag who let it happen?"

"No," Louis said sharply. He hesitated. "Look, if she has anything to say about this, it isn't going to be to us."

Horton thought for a moment. "All right," he said, and motioned toward one of his men.

Frank was hoisted to his feet by an officer and they went to the fence. Louis went through, with Frank following.

flanked by two officers, and Horton behind. They found the path to the compound and started uphill.

Louis led the way, his step sure, his breathing calm. It was still dark, maybe an hour before dawn, and the fog had settled near the bottom of the trees, making them look as if they were floating in air. Louis felt no fear as he walked now, just a sense of alertness. But he could see the jittery play of the officers' flashlights behind him. The stories, the rumors about the island, had already started to spread.

The lights of the house came into view and they stopped in the middle of the compound. The men were quiet.

"Jesus," Horton said softly, running his flashlight over the cabins. "They got toilets in those?"

"It's not as bad as it looks," Louis said.

Horton shook his head. "Well, let's go get the old lady."

They went in the front door and into a long, dim hallway. There was a staircase and a closed door to the right. The door opposite was open and the light was coming from a room that looked like a small parlor.

Horton motioned one of the officers to search. The other officer kept a firm grip on Frank as Louis led them into the parlor. It opened onto a large room, the one Louis had seen from the window.

Ana del Bosque was sitting in a large wooden chair in front of the stone fireplace. A single lantern sat on the table next to her. She was dressed in black, a lace shawl covering her shoulders, her white hair pulled back from her thin face. She sat straight-backed, her eyes fixed on the door. She didn't blink when Louis came in. Her hands were folded over a large book sitting closed on her knees.

But when she saw Frank come in, her mouth dropped open slightly. "Francisco," she whispered.

"Mama," Frank said.

Louis saw the gleam of tears in the old woman's eyes. Frank saw it, too, and he took a step toward her. The officer held firm and Frank looked at Louis and Horton.

"Let him go," Horton said.

Frank went slowly to the old woman. Her eyes went from the cuffs on his hands up to the bloodied wrap on his shoulder and finally to his face.

"Oh, Francisco, what has happened?" she asked.

"It's over, Mama," Frank said softly. "I have to go. You have to go. We all do."

Ana del Bosque stared up at Frank blankly. "Go where?" she asked.

Louis glanced at Horton. His body was stiff, his face expressionless. He obviously had no sympathy for the old woman. Louis looked back at Ana del Bosque. Neither did he.

Horton stepped forward. "Mrs. del Bosque—"

"One moment, please," Frank said. He knelt by the chair. *"Mama, scio te de hoc secreto totam aetatem tuam tacuisse atque quam ob causam sic egisses."*

The old woman shook her head slowly. "No, no, Francisco . . . *de illo loqui nequam . . ."*

"You have to, Mama," Frank said gently. *"Dic mihi veritatem."*

The old woman closed her eyes. Then she took a deep breath and began to speak again in Latin.

"What the fuck?" Horton whispered to Louis.

Louis didn't answer him. He just stood there, listening to Ana del Bosque.

Finally, Frank stood up and turned to Horton. "She'll go with you now," he said.

"What was all that about? What did she tell you?" Horton demanded.

"Nothing," Frank said. He looked at Louis. Louis was surprised to see tears in Frank's eyes.

Horton leaned into Frank. "What the hell did she say to you?"

But Frank was silent.

"Take him away," Horton said, waving a hand to his man

standing by the door. The officer came forward, took Frank by the arm, and led him out the door.

"I knew you would come someday."

Louis and Horton turned at the sound of the old woman's voice.

"I saw the new bridges, all the houses and people," she said, looking at Horton. "I heard the planes and saw more and more boats every day. I knew it would all overflow and touch us someday. It wasn't Francisco's fault. No one could stop it, really. Times change. *Tempora mutantur.*"

Ana del Bosque's fingers curled around the book on her lap. "We are an ancient family from the land of Asturias," she said, "descended from the great Roman soldiers . . ."

Horton was staring at Ana. "She's nuts," Horton said quietly to Louis.

"Chief?"

Louis turned to see the other officer at the door. "There's no one else in the house," the officer said. "I looked everywhere."

Horton turned to the old woman. "Mrs. del Bosque," he said, "where are the women?"

Her dark eyes glittered in the lantern light, moving from Horton's face to the gun strapped to his side.

*"Tempora mutantur,"* she whispered.

"Mrs. Del Bosque," Horton repeated more firmly, "where are the women?"

Louis stepped forward. Ana del Bosque looked up at him. Maybe it was the fact he was the only man there not wearing a uniform, but her expression softened.

"Where are the women?" Louis asked.

"With their babies," she said, gripping the book tighter.

Louis turned to Horton. "The cemetery," he said.

Horton motioned to the remaining officers. "Take her to the restaurant," he said. Then he turned to Ana del Bosque.

"Ma'am, you have to go with these men now."

She looked up at Horton, then around the room, her eyes finally settling back on Louis. She rose slowly, clutching the book to her chest.

"Please give this to Francisco," she said, holding it out to Louis. *"Ut sciat qui esset."*

Louis took the book. It was an old Bible, its black leather cover rounded at the edges, its gilt letters faded.

"Can you remember that?" she asked. "It's important. *Ut sciat qui esset."*

Louis glanced at Horton. Then he repeated the phrase back to her several times. She nodded and looked at the officers.

"Let's go, ma'am," Horton said.

Ana del Bosque reached over and turned off the lantern. She looked around the room and then went slowly to the door. The officer took her arm and led her out.

Gray light was seeping through the windows, filling the shadowed corners. Louis could see now that it was an ordinary room, with a few pieces of simple but well-crafted furniture, a large braided rug covering the smooth wide boards of the floor. There were several carved animals on the stone mantel and a green glass vase holding a wilting bouquet of wildflowers.

"Show me this cemetery," Horton said.

When they got back outside, the fog was dissipating. A bird had started up its morning song somewhere. The empty windows of the seven cabins looked out toward the big house. In the gathering light, the compound had the benign look of a children's camp, except for the three Fort Myers officers who were standing in a knot. Their guns were drawn and their eyes were traveling over the cabins and the trees.

Louis led them down the path to the cemetery. At the fork, he stopped.

"There's a cabin down there. That's where I found Angel," he said, pointing.

"A cabin? What, like the other ones?" Horton asked.

"No, it's small, one room." Louis paused. "I think it might be where they went to have their babies."

Horton directed one of his men to check it out and they continued on. At the edge of the cemetery, Louis stopped. Everything had changed. The light streamed down through the twisting branches of the giant oak trees, and the morning breeze stirred the hanging Spanish moss like gray veils. A soft blanket of newly fallen leaves covered the ground.

Louis could see the five graves clearly now. And the small, freshly dug open grave with its mound of dirt.

The cemetery was silent, empty.

"So where are they?" Horton asked.

"I don't know," Louis said.

The other two officers were staring at the open grave and the table. Louis was scanning the encircling brush. Horton was looking down at the coral markers.

"How in the hell are we gonna get forensics in here with all these trees?" he said, shaking his head. "Shit, look at this. It's going to be a bitch digging these up."

The rustle of leaves on the far side of the cemetery made Louis look up. A woman came out of the brush and stopped.

She was in her fifties, her long blond hair streaked with gray. Her blue cotton dress hung on her thin body. Her pale gray eyes stared at them with a strange flatness. The same flatness that Louis had seen in the old newspaper photo.

"Emma?" he said. "Emma Fielding?"

"Emma del Bosque," she said. She took a few steps into the cemetery, looked down at the markers, then up at Horton.

"Please don't do this," she said. "Just leave them alone, please."

Horton and the other men were staring at Emma. The two younger officers looked as if they were seeing a ghost.

"Look, ma'am," Horton began. Louis held up a hand. Emma's eyes were on him.

"Please leave our daughters be."

"Is your daughter buried here, ma'am?" Horton asked.

Emma looked down at the nearest marker. "Yes."

"How did your daughter die, ma'am?" Horton asked.

"She was taken," she said, not looking up.

"By who?" Horton asked. Then he stopped, shaking his head. "Never mind, don't answer that. Officer, read this woman her rights."

As the officer started reading, Louis heard a sound in the brush. Two more women came out. They were in their forties, and wearing the same shapeless dresses as Emma. The taller of the two had her stringy blond hair twisted into a braid that hung over her shoulder. The other woman was heavier, with wild black hair framing a full face that resembled Tomas's.

*Jesus. Cindy Shattuck and Paula Berkowitz.*

They waited until the officer was done before speaking.

"Why did you have to come here?" Paula asked.

"We were looking for you," Louis said. "All of you."

Paula looked at the other women. "Why?" she asked.

Louis stared at the three women. They were acting like Angel had, treating them not as rescuers but as intruders. He glanced at their left hands. All were wearing the coral rings.

"Okay, let's get this over with," Horton said. He motioned to the other officers. They came forward but then just stopped, looking from the women to Horton, unsure what to do.

"Take them to the restaurant," Horton said.

The officer hesitated, then pulled out his handcuffs. Emma held her hands out in front of her, nodding to the others to do the same. The officer gently pulled her arms behind her, and cuffed her.

Emma's gaze moved to Louis. "This is our home," she said.

"You have to go," Louis said.

"Where are our husbands?" she asked.

"At the restaurant," Horton said. "And that's where we're taking you . . . now."

Emma looked back at Cindy and Paula. Then she started slowly toward the path. The other women followed her. The two officers glanced at Horton in confusion.

"Go on," Horton said, waving a hand.

When they were gone, Horton turned back and scanned the cemetery, shaking his head. He shot Louis a look of disgust, then turned on his heel and was gone back up the path.

Louis looked up at the sky. The sun was up over the trees now and the last of the fog had burned off. The Bible Ana del Bosque had given him was heavy in his arms and he hoisted it up, looking at its worn cover.

He opened the cover to the first page. On the frontispiece was an elaborate family tree, illustrated with biblical scenes. In flowing script, someone had written across the top *La Familia del Bosque*. The tree was filled in, but the ink was so faded and the handwriting so tiny Louis couldn't make it out without his reading glasses.

Closing the Bible, he tucked it under his arm. His eyes traveled over the coral markers. Something over near the mangroves caught his eye and he went to it. It was another marker, half buried in the mud and roots. It was crusted with mold, its edges rounded by time, the coral tinted tea-brown from the mangroves.

Why was this one grave so far from the others? But then he understood. It was probably one of the oldest graves and over time, the tides had washed the soil away from beneath it.

He looked back at the other markers. Had there been others like it, other graves that had washed away over time? How long had this been going on out here?

Louis reached down and started to pull the little marker out of the mud, then stopped. He knew he shouldn't move it; it was part of a crime scene now. But if left, it might tumble into the water.

Setting the Bible in the leaves, he picked up the marker and moved it only a few feet toward the others, kneeling to secure it in the dirt. Wiping his hands on his jeans, he rose. He picked up the Bible and started back toward the restaurant.

# CHAPTER 49

Louis could feel the sun on his face, and it stirred him awake. He rolled over on his back and kicked off the sheets, hoping a small breeze would wash over him. But the humid air was still.

The phone rang. He ignored it, lying perfectly still until it stopped. He briefly wondered what time it was, but then decided he didn't care. He stared at the ceiling, his brain numb, unable to kick into a new day.

The phone started ringing again.

*Shit.*

He pulled himself up slowly, planting both feet on the floor. When he put his face in his hands he could feel bumps and ragged skin against his palms. He tried to stand. His back muscles were knotted, and his thighs burned.

How long had he slept? What time was it?

The phone finally stopped. He limped to the kitchen and started searching the cabinets for coffee. Issy curled against his legs.

"I guess you're hungry, too," he said. He shook some Tender Vittles into her bowl, then went back to looking for coffee. He found a bag in the fridge and shook it. It was empty.

He stood there, leaning on the refrigerator door and staring into the shelves. Orange juice. That would work. He opened the carton and took a long swig. It burned like acid on his split lip.

"Jesus Christ!"

He wiped his mouth, wincing. Man, he needed to go see what he looked like. He walked back through the living room, feeling a hundred years old. His eyes caught the book shelf, and then the small skull sitting there.

He stopped in the bedroom doorway, his brain trying to work out of the morning fog.

The sixth coral marker on the island, the broken one stuck in the mangrove mud. He went and picked up the skull, turning it over in his hands. Was it possible this skull had washed away from the del Bosque cemetery?

He glanced around his living room. The Bible that Ana del Bosque had asked him to give to Frank was on the sofa. He set the skull in the chair and picked up the Bible. Taking it to the table, he put on his reading glasses and sat down, opening the Bible to the family tree on the frontispiece.

The tree went back to the 1800s, twisting with branches of double Spanish surnames. Louis recognized the name Marcelo Leon del Bosque as the man Bessie Levy had told him was the original emigrant from Spain. Next to him was his wife, Bianca Quinones Marquez y del Bosque. But the other old names meant nothing to him so he decided to start with the present and work backward.

He found Roberto's name at the bottom and traced it up until he found his great-grandmother, Ana del Bosque-Padilla.

Under Ana's name were her children: the oldest son, Edmundo, and Francisco and his twin brother, Emilio. Ana had another child, a daughter named Taresa. She had been born in 1931 and died in 1932.

Taresa was the only girl baby on the tree who had a name.

The other entries said only BABY GIRL with the dates of their deaths. There were five such entries on the del Bosque tree.

Five entries, five graves. So who had been buried in the old grave that had been washed away? Ana's daughter, Taresa?

Louis closed the Bible. He knew he could never prove it. No one would be able to tell when the sixth grave had been disturbed, any more than they could pinpoint the exact age of the skull on his shelf.

He looked back at the baby skull on the chair.

"What do I call you now?" he said.

The phone started ringing again. Louis rose and went to the bedroom to grab it.

"Kincaid," he said.

"You should've been here an hour ago," Horton said.

"Yeah, I know, Al."

"We're waiting on you. Come to the interrogation rooms." Horton hung up.

Louis dressed and drove to the station. Outside he saw two TV vans, and Heather Fox standing on the grass doing a remote. He drove around back and parked among the cruisers to avoid her. Inside, he made his way down the hall, and was buzzed into the holding area. An officer waved him to a window.

Behind the double-sided glass, seated in a wooden chair, he saw Ana del Bosque. Her gray hair had come loose from her bun, falling down the sides of her thin face. She wore paper shoes on her feet and a shapeless orange smock.

Horton was standing over her. He looked frustrated, with the slow boil of anger reddening his neck.

Louis looked at the officer. "She got a lawyer?"

"Refused one."

Louis looked back. Horton walked a circle around Ana, hands on his hips. "So, you're telling me all those babies died naturally?"

Ana sat stiffly, her knotted hands in her lap. "I told you no such thing. You make assumptions."

"Then what happened to them?" Horton asked.

Ana did not reply.

"Well, old woman," Horton said, "let me tell you something. Emma Fielding told us the babies were killed as part of some ritual you people perform."

"It's Emma del Bosque, and you are lying."

Horton leaned into her. "You're all going down for this. Every last one of you. It won't matter who actually murdered those babies—you're all guilty. And we'll prove it when we dig them all up."

"You're digging up the graves?" she asked.

"Yeah, all of them."

Ana's eyes closed briefly.

"And then we'll start on the other graveyard," Horton said. "I wonder how many murdered people we'll find there."

"You'll find—" Ana stopped.

Horton waited. Louis knew Horton had poked a hole in Ana's facade and now he was just waiting to see if it opened further.

Ana looked up at him slowly. "If I tell you the truth, will you leave my family in peace?"

"The live ones or the dead ones?" Horton asked.

*Jesus, Al . . .*

"Both."

Horton shook his head. "I can't promise that."

Ana took a breath, her small chest rising and falling under the orange material.

"I killed Mateo."

"Who's he?"

"My husband. I killed him in January of 1932. He is buried in the other cemetery, along with the rest of my family."

Horton stared at her. "How'd you kill him?"

"I shot him."

Horton walked in front of her. "What about the babies?"

Ana was speaking so softly, Louis had to lean closer to the intercom to hear her.

"I killed them, too," she said. "All of them."

"How?"

"I smothered them," she said. "No one else was involved."

Horton was speechless.

Ana looked at him. "Is that enough?"

"Why?" Horton asked. "Why just the girls?"

She looked away. *"De illo loqui nequam—"*

"Don't start that shit, lady."

But Ana was finished talking. Louis knew it. She closed her eyes, crossed herself, and folded her hands.

Horton let out a breath. "Stand up, Mrs. del Bosque."

When Ana stood, she barely reached Horton's shoulder. "You know by telling me this, you've confessed to the murder of six people?"

Ana gave him a small nod.

"And you'll be going to prison? You know that, right?"

Her eyes moved to Horton's face. "Not for long," she said softly. "Not for very long at all."

A few minutes later, Horton came out of the room. He stopped when he saw Louis.

"My office," he said. He went briskly down the hall and Louis followed. When they walked in, Louis was surprised to see Landeta sitting by the window, his elbow propped on the sill. There was a small television on the credenza behind Horton's desk, filled with Heather Fox's face. The sound was muted and under her chin, in red letters were the words AWAY SO FAR CULT?

"Did you hear that crock of bullshit?" Horton asked Louis. Then he looked at Landeta. "The old bag confessed to killing every one of them and her husband."

Landeta looked at him slowly. "Isn't that what you wanted?"

"Oh, yeah," Horton said. "I got a whole family full of murdering sonofabitches and the only one I can put in jail is an old woman who will probably die before the ink's dry on her confession."

Louis and Landeta were quiet.

"And if that's not enough," Horton went on, "I got a gun-toting daddy who wants to know why he can't see his new-born daughter, and the rest of them are talking to me in Spanish."

Louis looked away. He didn't need this. Not from Horton. Not today.

Horton took a breath. "Add in the three very strange women who keep asking me when can they go home, some guy who only *looks* like Frank Wood lying in the morgue, a graveyard full of baby bones that will take forensics a fuck-ing year to excavate, and two dead Mexicans, one of them shot by you, Kincaid, and we got a real mess here."

"Spanish," Louis said.

"What?"

"They're Spanish, not Mexican."

"You think I give a shit *what* they are?" Horton asked.

Louis was silent, his chest starting to tighten.

"And you know what's even worse?" Horton continued. "The old lady's confession will probably stand up. Not one of those other loonies is telling us a damn thing we can use. And no ME is going to be able to tell how those babies died. Not after all these years."

"You got Frank Woods," Louis said. "Maybe he'll tell you the truth."

Horton shook his head. "Oh, yeah, the original suspect. He's been away from that island for thirty-five years, Kincaid. How much do you think he *really* knows? Or can prove?"

"He knows more than you think," Louis said.

"We questioned the man for three hours, Kincaid. He ain't talking and I have nothing I can hold him on."

Louis thought about Frank and Emilio, wondering not for the first time if Emilio's death really had been an accident. A month ago, he would have said Frank didn't have it in him to murder someone. That had been his instinct from the start, the reason he had pursued this case. He had always felt that Frank didn't kill those women. But had he killed Emilio? Had he been so desperate, so driven to survive, that he had murdered his brother to take his place? Louis wasn't so sure of what was inside any man anymore.

He looked over at Landeta. He was cleaning his glasses with a tissue.

"But we do have one thing," Horton said, his voice tinged with sarcasm. He waved a piece of paper. "The bullet that killed Shelly Umber came from that Tomas guy's rifle. Nice piece of work, gentlemen . . . killing the only real suspect we had."

The office fell silent. Horton raked his brush cut with his thick fingers, and sunk into his chair.

"Al," Louis said, "where's the boy?"

"With DCF. He'll go into foster care for a while."

Louis looked at the television. Heather Fox was interviewing some guy with glasses. The name underneath him said he was a child psychologist and cult deprogrammer. Louis knew they were probably talking about Roberto.

"You know what this whole mess amounts to?" Horton asked. He looked up at Louis, then over at Landeta, waiting for an answer. "I think your whole fucking Rambo act is going to end up being for nothing."

Landeta stood up suddenly. "Tell that to Louisa in a couple of years." He walked out.

Horton watched him leave. "Who the hell is Louisa?" he asked Louis.

Louis didn't answer. He just stared at the television. They had switched to a shot of the island now. Louis could see the yellow crime scene tape stretched between the trees, and the cops standing the dock, patrolling against gawkers.

Horton sank down in his chair. He glanced at the television, then looked at Louis.

"Don't you have anything to say for yourself?" he asked.

Louis looked at him. "Yeah," he said. "You asked me to work this because I could play it different than a cop could. I could get it done in a way your guys couldn't."

Louis rose. "And that's exactly what we did, Al."

Louis left, closing the door behind him before Horton could say anything. He hurried out of the station and through the crowd of reporters. He saw Landeta standing at the corner, waiting to cross the street.

Landeta heard him coming and turned. "Horton's right. They probably will never face charges, you know."

"Fuck it," Louis said.

The WALK sign started blinking and Louis took a step. Landeta followed. They walked on in silence for a moment.

"Louisa?" Louis said.

"I couldn't name her Melford," Landeta said. "And if you laugh, I will shoot you, right here on the street."

They turned down Hendry Street.

"You gonna walk me all the way home?" Landeta asked.

"Shit, no," Louis said. They stopped, facing each other.

They both just stood there for a moment. Louis knew what Landeta was thinking, what he was feeling. Whenever a case was over, no matter how it turned out, there was always that letdown that came after the adrenaline had stopped pumping. That feeling of being spent yet still itchy to get back to the high. He knew how much Landeta was going to miss it.

"Hey," Landeta said. "How about coming back to my place for a sandwich or something? I think I got a Heineken left."

Louis met Landeta's gaze and could see it in the man's eyes that he wanted to talk. Hell, *needed* to talk.

Louis pulled out his sunglasses and slipped them on. "Nah, I can't. I got some things I need to do."

"Okay. No problem," Landeta said.

Louis heard the disappointment in his voice. "I'll take a rain check, okay?"

"Yeah. Fine." Landeta turned and walked away.

Louis watched him for a few minutes. When Landeta got to the door of O'Sullivan's, he hesitated only a second, then walked on.

# CHAPTER 50

Louis pulled up in front of Frank's house. His Civic wasn't in the drive and there were a bunch of plastic-rolled newspapers lying in the tall grass. Picking up the del Bosque Bible, Louis got out of the car. At the front door, he rang the bell. He could hear it echoing in the house.

He jumped off the porch and peered in the front window. The drapes were open enough to let him see that the living room looked untouched, like no one had been home in a long time.

Louis went back to the door and reached into the planter for the key. It was still there. He unlocked the door and went in. The house had a closed-up smell, with the sting of old cigarette smoke still lingering in the air. But someone had taken the trouble to straighten things up some. Louis went into the bedroom. The bed had been made, the ashtray emptied. Louis opened the closet. Frank's library uniforms—his slacks, shirts, and ties—were still there. He went to the dresser and opened the top dresser. It was empty except for a couple of pairs of brown dress socks.

Louis turned to look at the room. The bookcase. Its shelves were empty. Every book in the room was gone.

Louis went back to the living room. The shelves in here were bare, too. He turned toward the mantel. The picture of Diane was gone.

Louis let himself out, locked the door, and got back in his car. He sat there for a moment, hands on the wheel, staring at Frank's house.

Where the hell could he have gone?

He started the Mustang and pulled out. On Cleveland Avenue, he turned left and headed over the Caloosahatchee Bridge. When he pulled into the lot of Diane's apartment building, he spotted her Honda but not Frank's Civic. He went up and rang the bell, the Bible under his arm.

He heard a sound behind the door and knew she was standing there, looking at him through the peephole. He also knew she wasn't going to let him in.

"Diane, is your father there?" he called out.

She didn't answer.

"I have something to give him," Louis said. "Have you seen him?"

The door jerked open. Diane squinted out into the sunlight. Her hair was combed, her makeup perfect, too perfect. He could tell she had been drinking. Not today, but last night, and the bags had still not gone down under her eyes.

"Leave me alone," she said. Her eyes darted past him out to the parking lot. He knew she was looking for TV vans.

"I just need to give this to your father."

Diane's eyes went to his hands. "What is it?"

"His family Bible."

"Family?" she said. "Those animals out there on that island?"

Louis was tempted to open the Bible and show her the names of all her cousins and nephews. "It's your family, too," he said.

She threw up her hands. "Oh, no," she said hoarsely. "I have no connection to them. They're freaks, monsters. I have no family."

"What about your father?" Louis asked.

"My father . . . I . . ." she whispered. Her hand shook as she ran it over her hair.

"Diane, have you talked to him?" Louis asked. "Have you heard his side of this or just what's on TV?"

"I haven't talked to him since . . ." Diane's voice trailed off. She was leaning against the doorjamb, like it was hard for her to even stand up.

"Do you know what happened thirty-five years ago?" Louis asked. "Do you know what he did? Why he left that island?"

She shook her head slowly, closing her eyes. Louis knew she had seen the television reports, read the stories in the papers. But Horton hadn't released all the details yet, so whatever was getting out was vague enough to allow for conjecture and titillation. The public's imagination filled in the rest. Diane probably didn't even know that if her father had not left his home thirty-five years ago, she would be buried in that island cemetery with the other babies.

Louis started to tell her, but then he stopped. It wasn't his place. He had no right. It would have to be Frank's decision to tell Diane the truth.

"He turned his back on his family for you," Louis said.

"I can't," she said. "I can't deal with this right now."

"Diane, he's your father. He's all you have, for God's sake. Talk to him."

"I thought I buried my father," she said bitterly. "Do you know what that feels like? I buried a stranger who only *looks* like him? I buried a man I don't even *know.*"

She was struggling not to cry. But for the life of him Louis couldn't figure out for whom.

"Leave me alone," Diane said. "I just want to be alone."

It was the way she said it, forcing out each word like it hurt, that gave him the briefest feeling of pity. How did a human being become so detached, so unconnected?

He knew he shouldn't do what he was about to do, but he couldn't help it.

"You have a grandfather, you know," Louis said. "Your mother's father. He's still alive."

Diane's eyes widened. "My mother's . . . ?"

Louis nodded. "Yeah, he lives over on Pine Island, St. James City. His name is James Reardon."

"Does he . . . ?" She stopped.

"Know about you?" Louis nodded. "He's old and he's not well. You should go see him, before it's too late."

Tears fell silently down her face. "I have to go," she said. She started to shut the door but Louis put up a hand to stop it.

"Diane," he said, "just tell me where your father is."

The tears had left streaks on her powdered face. "He went back," she said.

He let go of the door and she shut it.

The Deadhead took off his red ball cap, smoothed back his stringy hair, and put the cap back on. He throttled the boat's motor up and turned his face into the breeze. Louis was sitting in the front, watching the gulls float and dip on the currents. The sky was pearly gray with coming rain and the water was choppy.

"Hey, man," the Deadhead called out, "what you wanna go out to that creepo place for?"

Louis ignored him.

"I heard there was a cult out there," the Deadhead yelled over the outboard. "I heard they was eating dogs and cutting off babies' heads and all sorts of weird shit, man." He shook his head. "Probably fried the dogs up and served 'em in that friggin' restaurant."

"Shut up and drive," Louis said. He had already paid him the hundred bucks he owed him and now twenty more. He didn't need to listen to his shit.

The Deadhead was silent the rest of the way, pulling the boat up to the dock about thirty minutes later. There were two police boats there, and several officers were standing in the yard of the restaurant.

The officer nearest the dock saw the Deadhead coming in and started to wave him off. Louis recognized Jay Strickland, the cop on Sanibel with the Vespa. Louis signaled him, and Strickland motioned the boat in.

Louis could see the yellow crime scene tape up at the restaurant. It was cut and flapping in the wind so he knew the restaurant had already been cleared.

Louis picked up the del Bosque Bible and got out, telling the Deadhead to wait for him. Strickland met him in the middle of the dock and walked with him toward the restaurant.

"This is some case," Strickland said.

"Yeah."

"They aren't telling us much, you know," Strickland went on. "Is it true, about the babies and everything?"

Louis stopped. He could see the confusion in Strickland's eyes, and all the questions any normal person, any father, might have about this whole sick thing. But he could also see there was no way in hell it could be explained.

"I can't talk about it," Louis said. "Sorry."

Strickland nodded.

Louis shifted the Bible to his other arm. "You seen Frank Woods around?"

"He's inside," Strickland said. "Chief called and said let him in the restaurant since the techs were finished with it. I thought it was strange but the chief says technically the island belongs to him now so we can't keep him out."

"Thanks." Louis went inside.

It was dim and cool inside the restaurant. The chairs were all upended on the tables and there were some cardboard boxes stacked on the floor near the entrance. They were filled with books. Louis looked up at the bar. The Poussin painting was still there.

"I should take that down."

Louis turned to see Frank standing by the kitchen door. He was wearing old khaki shorts and a faded green T-shirt. His right shoulder was wrapped in gauze. He came farther into the room, looking up at the painting.

"I was about Roberto's age when I started working in here," Frank said. "I remember when my uncle Alfonso came home with it. It was right after he came back with his wife. He said he found it in an old store over on Pine Island. No one ever told me what was going on in the painting. I always thought they were just having a party."

Frank looked at Louis. "It's by Poussin. It's called *The Rape of the Sabines.*"

"I know," Louis said. "I also know what it means."

Frank looked back at the painting. "Do you see the woman in the middle, the one who is listening to her abductor? She isn't fighting him at all. She's going peacefully."

"That didn't make it right," Louis said.

Frank let out a breath. "No, of course not. The Romans had a way of idealizing their crimes."

Louis watched as Frank went over to a table and took off one of the chairs. He set it upright and sat down. His eyes were traveling slowly over the restaurant.

"The women weren't abducted, not like most people might think," he said.

Louis came in and set the Bible down on one of the tables. "How was it done?" he asked.

"When a del Bosque man came of age, around eighteen, he was told to go off the island and find his wife. That's how I met Sophie at the drugstore."

Louis thought about the paragraph in Frank's book about the Asturian rite of passage, how the young men would ride through the village symbolically beating the women.

"Emilio and I used to take turns going over to Pine Island to get the things we needed, and he was the one who saw her first," Frank went on. "But I was the one she wanted."

Frank was staring at the painting. "He never forgave me

when we got married. But Mama told him he had to find his own wife. So he brought Emma back."

Frank looked over at Louis. "I know you think it was wrong, that the women were too young, that they didn't know what they really wanted. But they were happy here. They were loved and taken care of. They didn't want to leave."

"Shelly did," Louis said.

Frank shook his head. "Tomas was mean. And he didn't have the patience to find a woman who wanted to come."

"So he abducted Shelly?" Louis asked.

Frank nodded. "And he raped her."

"And then he shot her when she tried to escape," Louis said.

Frank nodded again, more slowly. "That's when I knew things were changing out here. That's why I came back. I thought I could . . ." His voice trailed off and he ran a hand over his face. "I don't know what I thought."

Louis came forward to stand in front of Frank. "How in the hell could the women be content when you were killing their children?"

It had started to rain, drumming softly on the roof and sending a briny breeze through the restaurant. Frank didn't answer or look at Louis. He was staring out at the open door. Louis knew he wasn't going to talk. Frank Woods knew the "why" behind all of it, but he would never tell it. He hadn't told Horton. He wasn't going to tell now. He would go to his grave protecting his sick, twisted family. Suddenly, Louis just wanted to get out of there.

"I have something for you," Louis said. He put the Bible down on the table in front of Frank.

Frank looked at it. "Where did you get this?"

"Your mother told me to give it to you."

Frank ran his fingers over the worn cover.

"She told me to tell you something," Louis said. "It sounded like *'ut sciat qui esset.'* " Louis waited, but Frank didn't look up. "Does that mean anything to you?"

Frank didn't move.

"Fuck this," Louis muttered and started for the door.

"So he knows what he is," Frank said. He looked up at Louis. *"Ut sciat qui esset.* It means 'so he knows what he is.'"

Louis shook his head. "So what the hell are you, Frank?"

Frank opened the Bible to the frontispiece. He pressed his palm gently down on the family tree.

"I had a sister," Frank said. "I was very small when she was born but I remember her. I remember when she was born she had all this beautiful dark curly hair." Frank didn't look up. "But there was something wrong with her, her back was twisted. I remember hearing them talk about it, Mama and my two uncles. I stood outside the door one night and listened but I didn't understand. Then the next day, Taresa was gone. When I asked Mama what happened to her, she told me that Taresa was God's mistake and He had taken her back."

Frank was silent, looking down at the Bible.

"Ana killed her," Louis said. "That's how this all started?"

Frank looked over at him and nodded. "Later, long after I left here, I figured out that Taresa probably just had a condition called spinal muscular atrophy."

"But why the others?" Louis asked tightly.

Frank stared out at the open door. "She was afraid they would be the same, their bones twisted. She was convinced our blood had become tainted somehow."

"Why just the girls then?"

Frank covered his eyes with his hand.

"Why?"

Frank pushed the open Bible across the table. Louis came forward and looked down at the del Bosque family tree. His eyes traveled over the names and the lines that linked them. Each del Bosque man was connected to his wife. Each child was connected to his parents.

He was seeing exactly what was there. Then suddenly he saw what wasn't there.

Four lines connected Ana del Bosque's children to her. The same four lines connected to Mateo del Bosque. There was no line between Ana and Mateo. Mateo wasn't Ana's husband, as she had told Horton. He was her brother.

"Incest?" Louis said. "That's what this is all about?"

Frank looked up, wiping his face. "I didn't know any of this for sure until yesterday."

"When you were talking to your mother in Latin," Louis said. "That's when she told you?"

Frank nodded. "I always suspected it. I mean, I didn't have a father. Mama told us his name was Eli and that he had died and was buried with the rest of the family in the cemetery, but I never saw a marker with that name on it."

Louis looked back down at the Bible. "So Mateo was your father, too?"

Frank nodded woodenly. "My grandparents had died, so it was just the three of them living here by then—Mama, Mateo, and Alfonso. Mateo started raping Mama when she was just fifteen. She gave birth to my brother Edmundo. It didn't stop, and she had me and Emilio. Mama was twenty-two when Taresa was born. She shot Mateo right after that."

Louis looked down at the Bible. "And Alfonso?"

"Mama told him he had to go off the island and bring back a wife. He was the first. She told him the blood had to be purified."

Louis was silent, thinking, putting the pieces together. "And the baby girls? They were killed to prevent more incest?"

Frank hesitated, then nodded. "To keep it from happening again."

Louis turned away, shaking his head. After a moment, he turned back to Frank. "Did you know about the babies?"

"No, we were not told until it was necessary. I didn't find out until Sophie got pregnant," Frank said. "A few weeks before she was due, Mama came to me and told me she would take care of birthing the baby."

Louis didn't say anything.

"But I couldn't stay away," Frank said, his voice soft. "I snuck out to the birthing house and waited. It took forever. Then I heard a baby cry and Mama came out carrying my daughter. I asked her where she was going and Mama told me the baby had to be given back to God."

Frank looked up at Louis. "I couldn't let it happen. I told Mama we would leave, that I would take my wife and baby to the mainland and live."

"She just let you go?"

Frank nodded. "But I was never to come back. That was our agreement."

Louis went slowly to the open door, drawing in a full breath. He remembered the cabin where he had found Angel. It was isolated, away from the family compound, away from the eyes and ears of the other women. Maybe so they could deny it was happening? Ana del Bosque had told Horton that she had smothered the babies. But then Louis remembered how Rafael had looked as he led Angel to that cabin. Had it become the man's responsibility to kill the newborn if it was a girl?

Louis closed his eyes. *Responsibility.* Jesus, was that ever the right word?

The rain had stopped and it was quiet for a moment. Louis could hear the cops outside in their yellow slickers, see them standing under a tree, laughing as they lit up cigarettes.

"Why didn't you tell the police any of this?"

Frank looked at him. "I wanted only to stop it. Besides, you have an old woman to put on trial. What more do you want?"

Louis started to turn away.

"Diane doesn't know any of this," Frank said quickly.

Louis looked back at Frank. He had left his home and family before he would sacrifice his own daughter. But the guilt was there, decades of it, there in his shattered face.

"You need to tell her," Louis said.

Frank shook his head.

"She has a right to know, Frank."

When Frank looked up at him there was a spark of anger in his eyes. "About what? About the incest? About what I carry in my blood, what I have passed on to her? She told me once she never wants to have children. Can you imagine hearing that from your own child, can you imagine how that makes you feel?"

His eyes welled. "Relieved. I feel relieved."

Frank looked away quickly. Louis didn't know what to say. He started for the door.

"You won't tell her, will you?" Frank said quietly.

Louis turned back. "No."

Frank nodded slowly. "Good. I just want her to be happy and have a normal life. If I stay away from her, she still has a chance."

"Where will you go?" Louis asked.

"My place is here," Frank said, closing the Bible. *"Vulpes pilum mutat, non mores.* The wolf changes his skin, not his habits."

# CHAPTER 51

When Louis came out of the restaurant, he noticed a man coming around the side of the building. He was carrying a large plastic evidence bag, but it was the way that the man was holding it that told Louis what was in it.

The man was cradling it gently, respectfully.

Louis watched the man take the bag down to a waiting patrol boat and carefully hand it over to another man. It had begun to rain again, just a light drizzle, and in the flat light the green of the trees and the yellow of the cops' rain slickers seemed to jump with color.

Louis stood there, watching the men in the patrol boat for a moment. Then he came down off the porch and stepped out into the rain. He paused, then turned right and headed to the fence.

He went through the open gate and walked slowly up the path. There was no one in the compound when he got there, but the yellow tape was still draped around the house and cabins. He continued on, crossing the compound and heading down the path on the far side. He followed it as it sloped gently downward toward the mangroves.

Ahead of him, he could hear the thud of shovels against dirt, and a murmur of voices.

He came to the clearing and stopped behind the yellow tape. It looked like a small camp. A canvas canopy had been erected over most of the cemetery, with a second smaller one off to one side. There was a portable aluminum table under the small canopy, and a man in a blue windbreaker was bent over some equipment, looking at something with a magnifier. There were two men working on the graves. One was digging with a small shovel and pouring small amounts of the dirt onto a screen held by the second man, who then sifted through it. They worked slowly, carefully, their eyes searching every clot of dirt for small bones.

A flash drew Louis's attention upward. Another man in a raincoat was photographing the process and the site.

Louis's eyes wandered over the graveyard. He heard one of the men say something about a blanket. He looked back to see the man with the small shovel carefully extracting a piece of cloth from the dirt. When he held it in his latex-gloved hand, Louis could see it—brown with mold but with its satin edging still intact.

Louis watched as the man put the cloth in an evidence bag. Then he carefully reached into the hole and lifted out a tan object, like a tiny bowl. Louis felt a small kick in his heart. It was a piece of skull. He watched while the man put it in an evidence bag.

The technician working behind the table stepped away, ducking under the tape. He stopped under an oak tree and lit a cigarette, cupping his hand over the match against the drizzle.

Louis went over to the aluminum table, stopping outside the tape. He looked down. There were two plastic evidence bags, both about twelve by fifteen inches, both sealed and signed. Both the bags seemed to be filled with what looked to be just old rags.

Louis bent closer. Inside one bag, a few bones had fallen away from the cloth, and he could see them pressed against the clear plastic. They were clean, smooth, and stained brown from the tannin that had seeped in from the mangroves.

Louis reached out and touched one with the tip of his finger through the plastic.

Tiny. They were so tiny.

*I'm pregnant, Louis. It's yours.*

*I'll just get rid of it.*

His throat tightened, and for several seconds, he stood perfectly still, the sound of the sifting dirt and the rain on the canopy in his ears.

"Hey, get away from there."

Louis drew his hand back and looked up. The man who had stepped out to smoke was staring at him. He tossed down his butt, crushed it out in the mud, and came over.

"You got any authority to be here?" he asked.

Louis shook his head.

"Well, get moving. We've got work to do here and you're in the way."

Louis stepped out from under the canopy. He stood there for a moment in the rain. Then he wiped his face with the heel of his hand and went back up the path.

# CHAPTER 52

Someone was out on the porch, banging on the screen door. Louis dropped his armload of dirty laundry on the bed and started out to the living room. When he saw Pierre standing behind the screen, he tried to duck back in the bedroom before he was seen.

"Louis!" Pierre called out. "I know you are in there! Let me in!"

Louis let out a sigh and went and unlocked the screen door.

"Why did you lock it?" Pierre asked, coming in. "You never lock your door."

"What do you want, Pierre?" Louis asked, going to the kitchen. He jerked open the refrigerator.

"The pool needs skimming," Pierre said.

Louis popped the top on a Dr Pepper and took a swig. "I told you I'd get to it."

"When? For a month you do nothing around here," Pierre said. "If you don't start pushing your weight around here, I will have to charge you rent and—"

The phone rang and Louis went to the bedroom, picking it up.

"Louis, it's Mel."

"Hey," Louis said. "Where you been hiding for the la
two days? Thought maybe you went back to Miami or som
thing without saying good-bye."

"Nah, not yet." Landeta paused. "I had a few things
pick up at the station. Listen, how about meeting me for lunc
at O'Sullivan's? I got some news on the case you might wa
to know about."

Louis glanced back at Pierre standing at the bedroo
door. "Sure, give me a half hour."

He hung up and started out the door.

Pierre hurried after him. "Louis! Where are you going'

"Sorry, *flic* business. Close the front door when you leav
Pierre."

A tirade of French followed Louis out to the Mustar
parked under the gumbo limbo.

On the drive across the causeway, Louis thought abo
Landeta, wondering again what he was going to do now th
the Away So Far case was over—or at least their part of
Shit, he wondered what he himself was going to do.

*Probably skim the friggin' leaves out of the pool for tl
rest of my life.*

At O'Sullivan's, Louis paused just inside the door to tal
off his sunglasses. It was a little after eleven A.M. and tl
place was near empty. He saw a couple of guys at the end
the bar sipping on Bloody Marys, and way in the back, h
bald head silhouetted by the jukebox lights, he saw Landet

Louis stopped at the bar, got two Diet Cokes and son
lemon wedges, and headed back.

"Morning," Landeta said, looking up.

Louis sat down. "So what's up?"

Landeta was just finishing a cup of coffee. "The wome
are being released this afternoon."

Louis sat forward. "How do you know?"

"I got a friend at the prosecutor's office. Since the o

ady confessed, Sandusky can't make a case against the oth-
rs. The old lady, yeah, but not the other women."

"What about the men?"

"Charges are still pending, but it doesn't look good there,
ither."

"How can they believe the old lady did all of this? How
an they not prosecute the whole family?"

"You'd need a Bugliosi for that."

"Who?"

"The Manson prosecutor." Landeta pushed his empty cof-
ee cup away and drew the Diet Coke near. He squeezed the
emon wedge into the Coke. "People said Bugliosi would never
e able to convince a jury that Manson was guilty without a
motive, that he would never be able to explain *why* Manson
would send those girls off to kill somebody and why they
beyed him. That's when he came up with the Helter Skelter
heory. And suddenly a jury could understand the crimes."

"I don't see the parallel," Louis said.

"Well, not one of the del Bosques is talking. We have no
physical evidence. And what did you and I really see on that
sland? A man holding a rifle and walking with a pregnant
woman away so she could have her baby in private. A family
rgument. And five little graves, with no way anyone can tell
ow they died."

Landeta took a drink of his Diet Coke before he went
n. "Unless Sandusky can tie all that together with a well-
onstructed and intelligent theory about families, Roman
oldiers, incest, and tradition, and make it *believable,* he will
ever get a conviction. It was hard enough in the Manson
ase, and Sandusky doesn't have half the brains of Bugliosi."

"Those women let their children die, Mel," Louis said.

Landeta nodded. "Yeah, they did. But did they really have
choice? Emma, Cindy, Paula—they all had nothing before
hey got to that island. Then suddenly, they have a man who
oves them. And a nice, big family. Such as it was."

"You're making excuses for them," Louis said.

"Not excuses. Reasons."

Louis was shaking his head.

"It's over for them, Louis," Landeta said. "DCF has the
hands in it now. Little Louisa's mother's dead and her aunt
even if they don't go to trial, are certainly weird enough
call unfit. She won't have a problem finding someone
adopt her."

"What about Roberto?"

"DCF will probably charge the family with truancy an
other crap like neglect and living in an unsafe environmen
Sandusky will make sure he at least saves the souls of th
two surviving children. Makes a nice sound bite, don't yo
think?"

Louis was quiet.

"I know people over at family services. I can arrange fo
you to see him, if you want," Landeta said.

"Roberto?"

Landeta nodded. "Someone needs to let him know thing
will be all right eventually."

"I'm the last person who should be telling him anythin
like that," Louis said.

Landeta was working on his lemon peel. "We did th
right thing, Louis," he said.

Louis didn't reply. His fingers picked at the cocktail na
kin under his soda.

"They let Woods go," Landeta said.

Louis nodded. "I know. I saw him out at the restauran
We had a long talk."

"Oh, yeah? You get anything out of him?"

"Yeah . . . the 'why.' "

Landeta cocked his head. "He told you why they did it?

Louis nodded. A part of him didn't even really want to g
over it again. A part of him just wanted to forget the whol
damn thing. But he knew now that Landeta wanted to kno
the why as much as he himself ever had.

"Ana del Bosque was raped by her own brother when she was a teenager," Louis said. "Her daughter was born with spinal atrophy, something babies get from inbreeding. So Ana del Bosque killed her."

Landeta shook his head. "What about the others?"

"An attempt to keep the blood pure, Frank said. Jesus, you'd think this was the Middle Ages or something."

Landeta heard the disgust in Louis's voice and didn't ask any more questions. He just took a drink of his Diet Coke.

"Well, if the old lady ever comes to trial, she'll have motive for one of the murders at least," Landeta said. "But I doubt she will see the inside of a courtroom. For any of this."

"They need to pay for what they did," Louis said.

"They will, in one way or another," Landeta said. "That family will never be the same. They'll always be the weird family from the Island of Bones. People will tell stories of how they slaughtered babies and forced their wives into slavery. They'll be freaks, with TV cameras in their faces and reporters following them wherever they go."

"The county closed down the restaurant," Louis said.

Landeta pushed on the lemon peel with his thumbs, exposing the pulp. "Well, maybe Frank can sell his story to the *National Enquirer* or someone will pay to make a movie of the week."

Louis was quiet, staring down into his glass.

"What's the matter?" Landeta asked.

"They deserve to be in prison," Louis said.

"Oh, they will be," Landeta said. "Everyone knows who they are and everyone thinks they're guilty."

He bit into the lemon. "The world is going to be one big prison for them for the rest of their lives."

# CHAPTER 53

Louis made his way through the clutter of cameras an
reporters and slipped inside the entrance of the Fort Myer
Police Station. He had called first and had been told th
women had been released.

Rather than force the women into the media pack outside
Horton had allowed them to wait in a conference room o
the second floor. Frank Woods was on his way, Horton ha
told him, to take them back to the island.

Louis reached the top of the steps, stopping to catch hi
breath. He wasn't even sure why he was here. What was it h
wanted to know? He already knew why the killing had starte
Did he really expect any of them to tell him why they allowe
it to happen?

But still, he knew he had to ask. There had been some
thing about this case right from the beginning that gnawed a
him unlike any other he had worked. Maybe it had been find
ing the baby skull just days before Shelly Umber floated up
But he couldn't seem to let it go. Not yet.

He walked down the hall, pausing at the open door o
Landeta's office. It had been cleaned out. All that was le
was the desk, the chair, and the empty bookcases.

Louis continued down the hall to the conference room and opened the door slowly.

The women were seated at the large, polished wood table, backlit by the sun streaming through a window. Louis closed the door and stepped to the side so he could see their faces.

Paula Berkowitz was closest to him, dressed in the shapeless cotton dress, her hands folded in her lap. Next to her was Cindy Shattuck, her blond braid now half undone around her face. Emma Fielding sat nearest the window and her wary gray eyes followed Louis as he stepped around the table.

"We don't have to talk to you," Emma said.

"I know that," Louis said. "But there's some things I need to ask you. Off the record."

The women looked at the floor. They sat as stiff as stone statues, specks of dust floating in the air above their heads.

Louis slipped into a chair across from Emma. She looked up at him slowly, her expression a mixture of anger and sadness.

"How could you let them kill your babies?" Louis asked softly.

Emma shook her head. "Francisco said Abuela Ana admitted to everything. He told us not to talk to anyone else. He says they still might put us in jail."

"We don't want to go to jail," Cindy said.

"Someone has to take care of Roberto," Paula added.

"Roberto isn't going home," Louis said. "The state will keep him until all this is over, if not forever."

"What about the baby?" Cindy asked.

Louis looked at her. "You ask about a baby you were going to let die?"

"It's her grandchild," Emma said. "Rafael is Cindy's son."

Louis looked back at Emma, trying to keep his voice even. "What you let happen was wrong," he said.

Emma's gray eyes hardened. "You sit in judgment of a situation and people you don't even know. You came to our *home*, you shot my nephew, and now your people are desecrating the babies' graveyard. You just want to punish us for being what we are, for being different."

"You murdered children," Louis said.

"We *survived*," Emma said.

"That's not surviving."

Emma shook her head. "What do you want from us?"

"I want to know why you let it happen. Just tell me why," Louis said.

Paula started to speak but Emma hushed her with a raised hand. "I was twelve when my stepfather first climbed into my bed," Emma said.

Louis felt this chest tighten. "You don't need to tell me—"

"You need to hear it," Emma said. "I was fourteen when my mother dragged me off to a doctor and he put me on a table and stuck something up inside me and killed my step father's baby." She paused. "My mother let it happen. She knew about it, but she just let it happen."

Louis couldn't move. Emma's face was stiff but her eyes jumped with emotion.

"After my brother Neil left, I was alone," she said. "I used to lock myself in my closet at night, praying I would die." Emma straightened her shoulders. "Do you know what it's like to be twelve years old and want to die?"

Louis was quiet.

"I met Emilio del Bosque at the grocery store one day when my mother sent me to get her cigarettes. I was only fifteen. He offered me a candy bar. I was afraid to take it because I figured he wanted sex in return."

"Mrs. del Bosque—" Louis started.

"Let me finish. We met every week for six weeks. He would buy me sandwiches and sodas, things I couldn't afford. He never asked a thing of me . . . not once." Emma took a breath, looking at the other two.

Paula was staring at the table, and Cindy had her eyes closed.

Emma looked back at Louis. "Then one day he took me to the island for lunch. His brother Edmundo, his uncle Alfonso, even Ana, they were all kind to me. They had something . . . something I never knew existed. They had family, love . . . traditions. They were *normal.*"

Emma paused again, glancing back at Paula. "Then Emilio said it was time to go home," she said, more slowly now. "I begged him to let me stay. I told him I would do anything he wanted. I was sixteen when we were married."

Louis put a hand to his brow.

"Later I found out about Sophie, that she had been the one he really loved. I was his second choice, but I didn't care. Emilio was kind and loving, and made a good home for us."

Louis let his eyes drift to the window.

"A year or so later, I gave birth to Carlos. Emilio was so proud . . . God, how he loved that child. Edmundo and Pedro both had sons and for a few years we were really happy. They opened the restaurant and we had money coming in. We had everything we needed there on the island and life was good."

Emma paused, but Louis didn't look at her.

"Then I became pregnant again," she said. "When the time came, Abuela Ana took me to the birthing house and I had a little girl," Emma said. "I heard her cry but Ana told me later she just stopped breathing. For months, I cried. Then one day Emilio told me he couldn't stand my tears anymore and he told me that our baby had been smothered." Emma paused again.

This time Louis looked at her. Her face was empty, her eyes still dry.

"I was only told that was the way it was done. To this day, I don't know why."

Louis briefly thought about telling her, but changed his mind. "When you get back to the island, ask Frank," he said. "He knows."

Emma blinked in surprise and glanced at the other women. "He knows? Is that why he took Sophie away?"

"Like I said, ask him," Louis said.

The scrape of a chair made Louis look at Cindy. She rose and went to the window, turning her back to them. Emma watched her, her expression suddenly tender, almost maternal. Then she turned back to Louis.

"You probably want to know why we didn't leave," Emma said. "I thought about it. We all did at one point. But there was nowhere to go. I had a son and a husband. Where was I going to go?"

Louis heard Cindy crying softly.

"When you finally have something good," Emma said, "when you finally feel connected to something or someone, you'll do anything to keep from being alone again."

Louis shook his head.

"I know you want us to somehow pay," Emma said. "My husband and son are dead. Paula's son, Tomas, is dead. The only thing I have left is my grandson, Roberto, and he isn't coming back." She paused. "How much more do you want to punish us?"

Louis felt a pull in his chest, and it bothered him because it felt like a pang of sympathy and they didn't deserve his sympathy.

"So let me ask you a question," Emma said. "What would you have done?"

Suddenly, he wanted out of here. He didn't want to deal with the women, their pathetic stories or their dead children. He rose and went to the door.

"I gave you an answer," Emma said. "I think you owe us one."

Louis faced her.

"What would you have done?" Emma repeated, standing.

Louis looked at the other two women. Cindy was staring

ut the window. Paula's head was down, her cheeks streaked with tears.

"I can't put myself in your place," Louis said. "I'm sorry." He left, closing the door behind him.

# CHAPTER 54

Louis leaned back against the closed door and let out a long, slow breath.

They had all been so young when it started, just teenagers. Desperate girls who made selfish decisions to keep what was left of their lives intact. Maybe some part of him did understand. Maybe he had some sympathy for the twelve-year-old girl who had her childhood ripped away by her stepfather. Or the teenage girl who had been bounced from one foster home to another. Or Angela, who just wanted something better than slaving away in a tomato field all her life.

Louis pushed off the door and started down the hall. He stopped at the top of the stairs.

Coming up the steps was a heavyset woman dressed in a dark blue suit, carrying a briefcase. She had Roberto by the hand. His head was down as he trudged up the stairs, a half step behind her.

"Come on, Robert," she said impatiently, "we don't have all day."

The boy's eyes shot to her face. "It's Roberto."

The woman paused to catch her breath on the landing. Roberto looked up at Louis. Someone had found him some clean clothes. He was wearing jeans, clean new Nikes, and a Teenage Mutant Ninja Turtles T-shirt. He looked stunned, like someone wandering alone in a foreign country where he couldn't understand the language.

For a moment, Louis didn't move or speak. Roberto's dark eyes were locked on Louis and in them Louis could read all the questions: *Why am I here? Why is my father dead? What's going to happen to me? Why did you do this to me?*

Roberto's eyes stayed steady on Louis's face until the woman started tugging at his hand again, pulling him up the remaining steps.

Louis stepped aside to let them pass, and Roberto shuffled by him silently. Louis watched them.

"Roberto," Louis said.

The woman turned. Roberto did not.

"Do I know you?" she asked.

"I know him," Louis said. "What is he doing here?"

The social worker sighed. "He wanted to see his aunts before we left. He's here to say good-bye."

"I'd like to speak with him. Please."

"I don't think—"

"I work with the police department," Louis said.

The woman looked down at Roberto. "Do you want to talk to him, Robert?"

Roberto shrugged. Louis came forward.

"Can we be alone, please?" Louis asked.

"I don't think that's a good idea," the woman said. "The boy is very upset and he might—"

"I'm not going to take him anywhere," Louis said.

The woman hesitated, then let go of Roberto's hand. She walked about twenty feet down the hall, sinking into a chair near the conference room door. She watched as Louis took Roberto by the shoulders and eased him down to the first step, then sat down next to him.

Roberto kept his eyes on his feet.

"Roberto, I want you to know how sorry I am," Louis said.

Roberto didn't reply.

"And that I know what you're going through," Louis said. "It's not easy, I know that."

"You don't know anything," Roberto mumbled. He pulled his knees to his chest. His eyes were on the two cops in the lobby below.

"When I was your age, I had to leave my home, too," Louis said. "I didn't want to go, but I had to."

Roberto's eyes welled. "I want to go home."

Louis wanted to touch him, but he didn't dare with the social worker watching.

"I know," Louis said. "I felt like that, too. But I had to go live with somebody else for a while. Until things could be straightened out."

Roberto didn't look at him. "How long?" he asked.

*A lifetime . . .*

Louis took a deep breath. "Well, there are some things that have to be sorted out first about your family, and if the judge decides . . ."

He stopped. He would only make things worse by lying. He knew what was ahead. "I don't know when you can go home," he said.

"Do I have to stay with her?" he asked.

Louis looked back at the social worker, who was still watching them closely.

"No," Louis said.

Robert's chin quivered. "Then who's going to take care of me?"

*Someone good and kind? Someone who will make you believe that you might, someday, be able to trust people again, like Phillip Lawrence did for me?*

"They'll find a place for you with a family and—"

"I already have a family. I want to go home." He was crying now and he buried his head in his knees. "I miss Papa and I want to go home. Why did you have to come? It's all your fault."

"Roberto . . ."

Louis reached out and touched Roberto's hair. The boy jerked away.

Louis heard the social worker's heavy footsteps coming toward them. He rose slowly. Roberto was still huddled on the stairs, crying.

"I think you should go," the woman said.

Louis hesitated, looking down at Roberto. He went slowly down the stairs. At the bottom, he stopped and looked up. Roberto and the social worker were gone.

He pushed open the door and wedged his way through the reporters. When he reached the other side of the street, he looked back at the second-story window of the police station.

Horton's words came back to him. *Your whole fucking Rambo act is going to end up being for nothing.*

No, he couldn't let himself believe that. Not even if he thought about what was ahead for Roberto. If he believed it was all for nothing, he would go crazy.

It wasn't all for nothing. It was for one baby's life. You didn't just turn away and let someone take an innocent life.

Louis stared up at the window.

*Jesus . . .*

He felt a trickle of sweat make its way slowly down his back and the air was suddenly too thick to breathe in. He was standing completely alone, but he felt as if he'd been punched in the gut. He took a shallow breath and blew it out, looking across the street at the blur of faces and color in the media pack.

Wiping a hand over his brow, he turned, unsure where to go. He felt the urge to move, to run. But there was nowhere to go—except back to an empty cottage. He started toward his car, reaching for his sunglasses.

*Forget it, Kincaid. It's just this case. Just those pitiful women, those small graves, and that damn baby skull. Nothing a six-pack and a nice sunset won't cure.*

He pulled out his car keys and reached for the door of the Mustang. A pay phone on the corner caught his eye, and he hesitated.

*Admit it. You want to talk to someone. You need to talk to someone.*

He walked to the phone, fishing for change. He dropped a quarter in the slot and dialed the number.

# CHAPTER 55

"You make a mean hot dog," Landeta said.

They were sitting out on the screened-in porch of Louis's cottage. Landeta was sprawled in an old wicker chair, his feet propped up on a table, a paper plate in his lap. Louis sat hunched, elbows on knees, an empty Heineken dangling from his hands. It had been too hot to eat inside. A wisp of a breeze was coming across the low dunes, barely strong enough to stir the sea oats. The water out in the gulf was as flat as a mirror. Pierre's fan whirred away in the doorway and Issy was stretched out on the cement floor, trying to get her belly cooled.

"Fuck, it's hot," Landeta said, setting the paper plate aside.

"It's August," Louis said. "You want another dog?"

Landeta shook his head. "Got any dessert?" he asked.

"Stale Ho-hos."

"I'll pass."

They were quiet. Louis was looking out at the gulf. The sky was starting to turn pink. He got up and went to the refrigerator, returning with a Heineken for himself and another Diet Coke for Landeta.

"C'mon," Louis said. "Let's take a walk."

Landeta followed Louis out the screen door, and across the sandy yard.

"We going to the beach?" Landeta asked.

"Yeah. It'll be cooler down there."

They headed up over a small dune. Landeta stopped in the sea oats, his face turned toward the water to catch the small breeze.

"Damn, that feels good."

Louis took a drink of his beer. "Mel, I need to ask you a question."

"Sure. Go ahead."

"Who the hell is Rocky King?"

Landeta laughed. "He was an NYPD detective on television in the fifties."

"Supercop kinda kind of guy?"

"On the contrary. Rocky had no brilliant ideas or special powers and wasn't even particularly smart."

"So?"

"He was a stubborn sonofabitch who just tracked down clues, followed leads, and stayed on the case until he figured it out."

They walked a little farther, and then Landeta stopped and sat down on the sand. Louis dropped down next to him, kicking off his flip-flops.

Louis gazed out at the water. There were no islands to be seen on this side of Captiva. No clumps of green. Just the pure, flat, blue-green expanse of the gulf, fading away to the horizon.

"I saw Roberto today," Louis said.

"How was he?" Landeta asked.

"Not good. He was with a DCF woman. He said he wanted to go home. And that it was all my fault he couldn't."

"Look, they'll find him a good home. A year from now, he'll have a foster family, a puppy, and they'll all be eating Happy Meals together. The kid will be playing Nintendo with his friends instead of sitting in a bone pile talking to ghosts."

Louis picked at the label on the Heineken. It wasn't going to be that easy, but he knew there was no way Landeta could understand that.

"Mel, you got any kids?" Louis asked.

"Couldn't get a woman to hang around long enough." Landeta was looking out at the water and sky. "You?"

Louis took a drink, resting the bottle on his knee. "I almost had one. Knew a girl in college. I got her pregnant."

Landeta popped the top on his can of Diet Coke. When he didn't say anything, Louis went on.

"I told her all kinds of crap. Like it wasn't mine, I wanted to finish school, I couldn't deal with it."

"In other words, you were a shit-head."

"Yeah."

"What happened to her?"

"She left school and got an abortion."

Landeta took a long drink of his Diet Coke. "You sure?"

Louis kept his eyes on the gulf. *Sure?* Hell, he had never thought about it before. There was no reason to think she *hadn't* done what she told him she was going to do.

"Shit," he said under his breath.

"What?"

"Like I really needed to be thinking about that possibility right now."

Landeta didn't answer. He set the can of Diet Coke in the sand and took off his glasses. His eyes were closed and he was leaning back on his elbows, his face upturned to catch the faint breeze.

"Is this why you called me?" he asked without looking at Louis.

"I called you to invite you to dinner, that's all."

Landeta let out a low chuckle.

"What's so funny?" Louis asked.

"Man, you love living on your little island, don't you?"

Louis didn't answer. He looked back out at the water.

"What was her name?" Landeta asked.

"Kyla." Louis took a drink of beer. "I fucked it up," he said softly, shaking his head.

Landeta was quiet. Louis finished off his beer quickly and looked out at the pink and orange sky. The silence grew, and so did Louis's need to fill it.

"Do you think Horton was right?" he asked finally.

"About what?"

"About what he said, you know, that this was all for nothing?"

Landeta let out a long breath. "You can go crazy thinking of things like that."

Louis was quiet again. "What are you going to now?" he asked finally.

"Enjoy the sunset," Landeta said. He had not moved and his eyes were still closed.

"I mean about work and shit."

"I don't know. I haven't quite figured the rest of my life out yet."

Louis cleared his throat. "Look, Mel . . . you know, if you wanted to—"

"Shut up. You're fucking up my sunset."

Louis looked back out at the water.

"You know, memory is a strange thing," Landeta said after a moment.

"How so?" Louis asked.

"I mean you can't always rely on it," Landeta said. His eyes were still closed. "I have a whole library of images in my memory, things I use to remember what something looked like, things I use to make me feel like I'm not groping around in the dark when it gets bad."

Louis was quiet, looking out at the gulf.

"I guess what I am trying to say," Landeta went on, "is that you might not be remembering that thing in college all that clearly. Memories can be . . . unreliable."

Louis looked at Landeta. His eyes were still closed.

"You did the best you could at the time," Landeta said. "I think that's all any of us do. When you know better, you do better."

The waves were a gentle hiss on the sand. A flock of pelicans were flying up the beach toward them, and Louis watched them as they went by in a perfect V, gliding silently over the water. The birds were beautiful, no sound, no effort, moving through their world with not a single wasted motion. Louis watched them until they were gone.

"The boy will be all right," Landeta said.

Louis looked at him.

"And the baby is alive. You did the best you could."

Louis leaned back on his elbows on the sand. The sun was hovering just above the horizon and the water and the sky were a blaze of orange, yellow, and red.

"So when you going back to Miami?" he asked.

Landeta didn't answer.

"Mel? When—"

"I'm not. I'm staying here."

"Here? Why?"

"I don't know. I just decided this minute. Maybe it's because you can't see the sunset in Miami. Maybe it's the people here. They leave you alone, let you be."

A small breeze was starting to come up. Louis closed his eyes and drew in a deep breath of the tangy salt air. He listened to the breaking waves.

"Tell me what it looks like," Landeta said.

Louis opened his eyes. "What?"

"The sunset."

"I'm not falling for that again. I know you can see it, some of it anyway."

"All I can see is a big blur of color."

"Well, that's all it is."

Now Landeta laughed as he shook his head. "Christ, you're hopeless. Tell me what it looks like."

Louis looked back at the sky and shrugged. "I told you it's colorful."

"Try again," Landeta said.

Louis took a deep breath. "Okay, it's red at the bottom and kind of yellow at the top."

Landeta shook his head. "You can do better than that, Rocky."

Louis stared at the sunset. "It's really red and really yellow. Fuck, Mel, you tell me."

Landeta lifted his face to the sky, his eyes closed. "The clouds are wispy, and it's like someone tossed a bunch of yellow and pink feathers against a freshly painted red wall. And the sun is laying itself down on the water, giving in, like you would if you were going to sleep and knew you had nothing but good dreams ahead."

Louis looked at Landeta, then back out at the sky.

"I can't do better than that, man," he said.

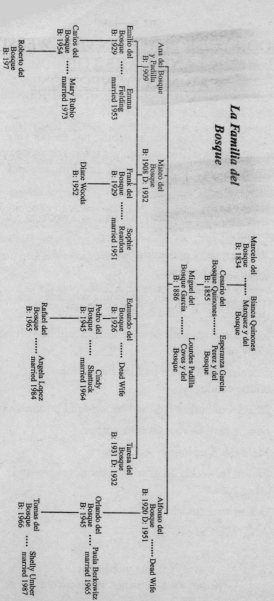

*La Familia del Bosque*

# <u>BOOK YOUR PLACE ON OUR W</u>
# <u>AND MAKE THE</u>
# <u>READING CONNECTION!</u>

We've created a customized website just for our very special readers, where you can get the inside scoop on everything that's going on with Zebra, Pinnacle and Kensington books.

When you come online, you'll have the exciting opportunity to:

- View covers of upcoming books
- Read sample chapters
- Learn about our future publishing schedule (listed by publication month *and author*)
- Find out when your favorite authors will be visiting a city near you
- Search for and order backlist books from our online catalog
- Check out author bios and background information
- Send e-mail to your favorite authors
- Meet the Kensington staff online
- Join us in weekly chats with authors, readers and other guests
- Get writing guidelines
- AND MUCH MORE!

**Visit our website at**
**http://www.kensingtonbooks.com**